"International intrigue and adventure paired with a simmering romance and a marriage of convenience equals one fast-moving story you won't be able to put down! Grab Susan May Warren's *Sunburst* today!"

Lisa Harris, bestselling author of the Nikki Boyd Files series

Praise for *Sunrise*

"In the romance novel *Sunrise*, a once-couple reconciles in the rugged landscape of Alaska's beautiful frontier."

Foreword Reviews

Praise for *The Way of the Brave*

"*The Way of the Brave* grabbed me at the first chapter and never let go. Susan May Warren is a master storyteller, creating strong, confident, and compassionate characters. This book is no different."

Rachel Hauck, *New York Times* bestselling author of *The Wedding Dress* and *The Memory House*

"The first in Warren's Global Search and Rescue series combines high-adrenaline thrills and a sweet romance. Perfect for fans of Dee Henderson and Irene Hannon."

Booklist

"Warren lays the foundation of a promising faith-influenced series with this exciting outing."

Publishers Weekly

Praise for *The Heart of a Hero*

"Susan May Warren whips up a maelstrom of action that slams Jake and Aria together and keeps the pages turning. Twists, turns, and constant danger keep you wondering whether this superb cast of characters can ride out the storm."

James R. Hannibal, multi–award-winning author of *Chasing the White Lion*

"Warren keeps readers in suspense throughout a Category 5 hurricane and its perilous aftermath with harrowing details. Amid the chaos of this natural disaster, the characters' understanding of heroism is underscored by Christian messages of self-forgiveness, grace, and sacrifice."

Booklist

"*The Heart of a Hero* by Susan May Warren was perfectly woven in a way that had me never wanting to leave the book."

Urban Lit Magazine

SUNBURST

ALSO BY SUSAN MAY WARREN

Montana Rescue

Wild Montana Skies

Rescue Me

A Matter of Trust

Troubled Waters

Storm Front

Wait for Me

Global Search and Rescue

The Way of the Brave

The Heart of a Hero

The Price of Valor

Sky King Ranch

Sunrise

Sunburst

SUNBURST

SUSAN MAY WARREN

a division of Baker Publishing Group
Grand Rapids, Michigan

Published by Revell
a division of Baker Publishing Group
PO Box 6287, Grand Rapids, MI 49516-6287
www.revellbooks.com

Printed in the United States of America

Library of Congress Cataloging-in-Publication Data
Names: Warren, Susan May, 1966– author.
Title: Sunburst / Susan May Warren.
Description: Grand Rapids, MI : Revell, a division of Baker Publishing Group, [2022] | Series: Sky King Ranch ; 2
Identifiers: LCCN 2021041201 | ISBN 9780800739836 (paperback) | ISBN 9780800741563 (casebound) | ISBN 9781493436323 (ebook)
Subjects: LCGFT: Novels.
Classification: LCC PS3623.A865 S84 2022 | DDC 813/.6—dc23
LC record available at https://lccn.loc.gov/2021041201

This book is a work of fiction. Names, characters, places, and incidents are the product of the author's imagination or are used fictitiously. Any resemblance to actual events, locales, or persons, living or dead, is coincidental.

Baker Publishing Group publications use paper produced from sustainable forestry practices and post-consumer waste whenever possible.

22 23 24 25 26 27 28 7 6 5 4 3 2 1

Soli Deo Gloria

DEAR READER,

I always dedicate my books the same way: Soli Deo Gloria. *Because this is my heart—for God to be glorified in every story he gives me. But if I could add a second dedication, it would be to my beautiful daughter-in-law, Ovoke Precious Izu Warren of the Delta Tribe in Nigeria. She and my son Peter met in Italy, where he served as a Navy Corpsman. I fell in love with her the moment I met her—her beautiful smile, her sweet personality—and I couldn't wait for her to join our family. Because of the pandemic, we weren't able to attend their wedding in Italy—nor was she able to have a traditional wedding in Nigeria.*

This story is my way of giving her the wedding she always dreamed of and to honor the culture we are so blessed to be invited into via her family.

I'm deeply grateful for her insights into Nigerian life and culture. When she came to America (when they got engaged), she made goat soup for us (so I had to put it in the book!). Then, we met on Zoom for hours, and she explained to me the traditions and helped me brainstorm how to make them work for my story (and my story to work for them!). She read my manuscript, helped me with the pidgin, and even sent me Nigerian wedding vlogs, pictures, and Nigerian movies to watch. Most of all, she let me into her heart to experience her culture and her background.

We are so blessed to have Precious in our lives. I couldn't have picked a better wife for my Peter. (Good thing God already had them chosen for each other!)

I hope you enjoy reading this journey in Nigeria as much I enjoyed writing it. Thank you, Presh!

Blessings!

Susie May

PROLOGUE

FOUR YEARS AGO . . .

Ranger wasn't here to get into trouble, but wow, she was pretty.

And clearly his brother Colt noticed too.

"She's cute."

Ranger looked back at Colt, who sat across from him on a high-top stool on the deck of the Bahama Mama, a beachside resort in Key West. He was nursing a mojito, the minty smell mixing with the jalapeno-and-onion spice of the ceviche dip on the table.

"I don't have time for romance," Ranger said, but yes, he'd been watching the woman armed with a camera take shots of the sunset as its rays cast over the frothy ocean and the cobblestones of the long pier at Mallory Square. The fire hovered above the horizon, the clouds a deep purple, with a deep amber rim over a golden spill of light and a darkening orange simmer.

The perfect place for Ranger to unwind. Sorta.

"Stop taking life so seriously. I mean, who wears khakis and a dress shirt to dinner?" Colt lifted his mojito but shot his smile at a girl in a bikini and a white cover-up headed toward the pool. "Meeting a hot girl just might be good for you."

Colt had *vacation* written all over him, in his half-open

Hawaiian shirt, his past-reg long dark hair, his sunglasses. Not to mention the wicked tan he'd gotten while Ranger spent the better part of the day in the fifty-foot free-ascent dive tower on the Army Spec Forces Underwater Operations school over on Fleming Key.

A mix of music—from the mariachi band at the hotel to a guitar player in the square playing "Peaceful, Easy Feeling"—added to the festive air of the nightly sunset festival. Black-winged seagulls dive-bombed tourists' treats—fish tacos, coconut shrimp, and French fries dropped on the cobblestone surface—while jugglers and a magician performed for tips as hundreds of tourists set up chairs or pressed against the deck railing hoping to catch the last rays of the sun in the southernmost tip of America.

"What's wrong with my clothes?" Ranger asked. "You said we were going out for dinner."

"At a *tiki* bar. Catch up, dude. Sheesh. Do you ever go out with your team?"

"Yes." No. Sometimes. Most of the time to make sure his buddies got home safe. Okay, so he was a little boring.

Ranger Kingston was the guy who got the job done.

His gaze drifted over to the woman again. Beautiful and petite, she wore her full and curly dark hair pulled back in a pink handkerchief, and she had on a white sundress, a patchwork satchel over her shoulder. As he watched, she crouched and took a picture of a seagull perched on one of the pier posts.

He looked back at Colt, who grinned at him.

Ranger reached for a chip. "Nope. Sorry. Women are trouble. Something you should probably remember."

He raised an eyebrow, but Colt lifted a shoulder, looked out at the sunset. "Old news."

It probably wasn't old news to their brother Dodge, who still hadn't returned home after the epic fight between him and Colt six years ago over, yes, a girl.

A girl Colt probably didn't even like—not in the way Dodge did. As in, give your heart and soul for life to one person.

Worse, Colt had kissed her. Ranger had seen it happening, inserted himself into the drama that followed, and since then, watched his family disintegrate. He talked to Dodge. He talked to Colt. And all three of them occasionally talked to their sister, Larke, as well as their father, who was still back at Sky King Ranch in Alaska.

But Dodge and Colt didn't speak to each other.

Maybe never would again.

Still, Ranger couldn't help the desire to keep the family together, somehow, so of course he invited Colt down to the Keys during his training. After all, Colt had re-upped too, and this time had secured a position in the elite Delta Force.

"I'm here for my free-diving cert, nothing more," Ranger said, finishing off his lemonade. The woman had moved into his periphery now, taking a picture of another woman who painted the sunset, her easel set up in the square.

"How's it going?" Colt's gaze hung over Ranger's shoulder, on the dance floor. Probably on some cute girl dancing with her girlfriends.

"I have a fifty-foot test dive in two weeks that I don't want to fail. Right now, I'm hunting forty feet, so I'm making progress."

"Isn't this just an add-on cert? Something to fill the gap before sniper school? You could do this in your sleep."

"Hardly. It's all about relaxing, about learning not to take a breath when your body is calling for it, mind over matter, and yes, technique. But my breath hold time is improving."

"Relaxing is the key? Oh bro, this is why you need me."

Ranger laughed. Yes, he needed Colt, but not quite how his brother wanted to help. He needed, most of all, to know that Colt was okay.

That inside the happy exterior, his anger had died to a

simmer, maybe long enough to see that he was forgiven. Or could be, if he wanted it.

Colt picked up a chip, the tags around his neck glinting in the sun. His smile dimmed. "Had a buddy who nearly died during the ascent test. Panicked. Experienced a shallow water blackout." He dipped the chip into the seafood mix. "So . . ."

"I got this, Colt."

The girl now stood in the middle of the square, taking a shot of a knife juggler, tattoos covering his bare upper body. She put the camera down, watching the man. Yes, she was pretty. Cute, pixie nose, a wide mouth, eyes that shone—or that might just be the sunlight.

Still, something about her caught him.

She lifted her camera and took another shot.

Then, she turned the camera lens, her back to the sunset, and circled the pier.

Stopped the viewfinder on him.

He averted his eyes, back to Colt. "So, where to next, after your leave?"

"Back to North Carolina and then . . ." He lifted a shoulder. Which was correct—as a member of Delta, he might end up anywhere, anytime.

"Good thing you could sneak—oh no." His gaze had, of course, returned to the woman, and she still had the camera on him.

As if taking his picture.

He slid off the high top. "Be right back."

The sun hovered just above the horizon, backdropping her, silhouetting her in white as he walked toward her. She lowered the camera. He stood maybe a foot taller than her, but she didn't move as he closed the gap between them. Instead, she lifted her face, cocked her head, and said, "What can I do for you, sailor?"

"What?"

"I just saw you, the way you scanned the plaza, the way you sat in your chair . . . You're an operator, aren't you?"

He blinked at her.

"Don't worry. I didn't take your picture. But you're not doing a great job of being on vacation, if that's why you're here."

He stood, taken aback. How—

"Your shirt, for one. It's an Oxford. At least roll up your sleeves. And maybe wear flip-flops instead of dress shoes. I dunno, but just an idea. Otherwise, how're you going to feel the sand between your toes?"

"I don't like sand between my toes," he said before he could stop himself.

"A BUD/S reaction? Not so fond of sand after inhaling it for six weeks?"

Who *was* this girl?

She stepped over to him, showed him the digital viewfinder. "See, no pictures of you, or your buddy. Now that's a sailor who knows how to be on vacation."

"He's not in the Navy," Ranger said and took off his sunglasses to see the pictures better. Nope, not a one of him and Colt, although she'd captured a couple holding hands, a beautiful shot of a seagull dive-bombing a fish with the backdrop of the sunset, and one of the juggler, a knife glinting rose gold. "Pretty good shots."

"Thanks." She let the camera drop around her neck and gestured toward the Bahama Mama. "You're staying at the same hotel I am. I saw you walk by the pool earlier today in your BDUs, so . . ."

Right. The Navy had put him up at a hotel near the base because of the overflow in military housing. "I'm doing some training."

She crossed her arms. "Of course you are."

He frowned, but she suddenly put her hand on his arm. "We're missing the sunset. C'mon!" She practically pulled him over to the railing, shoving into a space between an elderly couple and a woman with a stroller. She stood up on the railing and pulled her camera to her eye. "Isn't it glorious?"

Only a wink of sunlight remained, but indeed it *was* glorious. Liquid fire spilled out across the jagged horizon, a trail of golden luminescence across the waves. Overhead, orange seeped into the deep indigo sky, painted in shades of lavender and magenta.

He'd seen plenty of sunsets, all over the world, but agreed this was an especially pretty one. Especially when she rested her camera on the railing and looked back at him, grinning. "I got it."

The sun slipped away, and the crowd clapped as if it might be something spectacular. It was, really.

Each day, a gift.

He held out his hand as she jumped down.

"Now, we celebrate. Have you ever eaten a conch fritter?"

He opened his mouth, not sure if he should abandon his brother, but she grinned. "Your buddy is gone."

He turned, and sure enough, Colt had vanished. A waitress was cleaning their table.

Huh. He turned back to her. "Conch fritter sounds dangerous."

She grinned. "So there *is* a fun guy inside there."

Maybe. She took his hand, pulling him toward the Mallory market. Inside, all manner of vendors served everything from French fries to ice cream to, yes, conch fritters. He ordered a basket and sauce, and she met him with two cups of lemonade. They walked out to a table in the square. The stars began to arrive, and a slight wind carried a hint of something fresh. Maybe rain.

She sat and he set the fritters down. "I hope that's Caribbean dipping sauce. It's the best." She reached for a fritter, dipped it, and handed it to him. "Tell me this isn't the best thing you've ever tasted."

He took the conch. "Not until you tell me your name."

She took a piece, dipped it. "Noemi. And you are?"

"Ranger." He put the fritter in his mouth. "This is good."

Shoot, he liked her. And for the first time in hours, he wasn't thinking about breath holds and rates of ascent.

"Told you." She wore a smirk.

He could play this game. "Have you ever eaten octopus?"

"Of course." She shook her head as if saying, *Silly man*. "How about coconut tree grubs?"

"Do mopane worms count?"

She leaned back, folded her hands in her lap. "A delicacy in Zimbabwe. Interesting. No. It's on my list." She leaned forward. "How about crickets?"

"Salted and deep fried are the best." He took another fritter. "But have you had horse sausage?"

She made a face. "That's like eating a dog."

"Also good—"

"Please. I like you. Don't wreck it."

He laughed. "Okay, fine, how about giraffe weevils?"

"They taste like shrimp." She took a drink of her lemonade.

"So, what, you travel the world tasting crazy cuisine?"

"No. I just travel the world. Peru, Egypt, Thailand, Korea, New Zealand. I teach English as a second language. Short-term gigs that allow me to dig my feet into the soil of a new country."

"And now you're in Key West taking pictures."

"It's a stopover while my father fixes our sailboat. We had a bit of damage when our autopilot went out." She pointed to herself. "I'm in the brig for falling asleep on watch."

He gestured to the nearly empty basket. "Then the last one is yours."

She took it.

"So," Ranger said, "you're staying at the hotel while—"

"Dad works in the yard. I probably should be helping him,

but he gets a little crabby when he's fiberglassing, so . . ." She shrugged. "No. He's great. Just a little bossy sometimes."

Or protective, and Ranger could guess why. Pretty girl, seeing the world—it seemed like a recipe for danger if she wasn't careful.

She drew her straw to her lips. "I saw that nice ride you came in on too."

Oh, the motorcycle he'd rented? Seemed like a fun and easy way to get down to the Keys after his flight into Miami.

She kept looking at him, smiling.

"You want a ride?"

"I thought you'd never ask." She put her cup down.

"Now?"

She stood up. "The night is young, sailor. And the best stars are on the south side of the island."

He stood too. "Um. But . . . you just met me. I could be a murderer."

She walked over to the trash can. "Are you a murderer?" She turned, met his eyes. In the glow of the lights that soaked Mallory Square, her eyes turned a deep golden brown, her dress almost ethereal, caught in the wind. It felt a little like an angel peering into his soul.

"No."

"I didn't think so." She grabbed his hand again. "Besides, if you hurt me, my father will dismantle you."

Oh. Well, he got that too.

She practically led him to his bike, parked in front of the hotel. He had his keys in his pocket. He got on and held the bike for her, and she climbed on behind him.

For some reason he expected her to put her hands around his waist, but she held on behind her, her legs against his, leaning with him as he drove them through town to the south beach.

The moon was rising, the stars so bright, they shed silvery light upon the beach. They parked and she climbed off the bike.

"You're going to have to take those fancy shoes off."

They weren't fancy, but he *was* a little buttoned-up. Maybe Colt was right.

He needed to relax.

He slipped out of his shoes and socks and while he was at it, rolled up his khakis. She stepped up to him and unbuttoned his shirt cuffs. "These too." Then she headed out to the beach.

He followed her, pushing up his sleeves, his feet sinking into the silky, cold sand. The surf rolled onto the beach in the distance as if in thunderous applause. Noemi dropped her bag some ten feet from the surf and raised her camera.

She stood a long time, and he caught up to her before she was done with the shot. "Narrow aperture gives you the best picture of the moon," she said. "Widest shot, nice and crisp. Shutter speed around 125. I wish I had a longer lens, but I think it turned out." She showed him the picture on the viewfinder.

The moon was caught just hovering over a silver surf, a hint of luminance on the indigo plane. "It's beautiful. You're a real talent."

"It's a hobby. I once sat for sixteen hours in Peru stalking a harpy eagle." She capped the lens of her camera. "My father says he should train me to be a sniper."

He wanted to laugh, but it felt a little too close. "What did you say?"

"A sniper. You know, a guy who—"

"I know what a sniper is. Why did your dad say he should train you?"

She lifted a shoulder. "Because he thinks I should know how to take care of myself. He put me through a SERE school scenario when I was a teenager."

He'd gone a little cold. "Is your dad an operator?"

"Sometimes." She put her camera into her satchel. "Okay, ready for a swim?" She reached for the hem of her dress.

"Hey—wait—um—" His heart had suddenly slammed into his chest. "Stop."

But her dress was in a puddle on the sand, and she stood there, in a one-piece swimsuit, also white. "What?"

He stood, nonplussed.

"Did you think I was stripping down?"

He swallowed, his pulse calming. "I . . . I don't know what to expect."

"Take a breath there, sailor. Nothing's going to happen here. I'm harmless. I just wanted to swim under the moonlight. No big deal."

She headed into the ocean.

Oh brother.

And now he stood in the sand like an idiot, not sure if he should shuck off his shirt and . . . this just felt so terribly unhinged.

Had Colt put her up to this? He nearly looked around for his brother, half expected to find him doubled over, laughing. *"Who says trouble? Fun, bro. Stop taking life so seriously."*

But no brother, just an empty beach, a few boats tied up at a nearby dock, the smell of fish and brine and sand and a pretty girl standing at the edge of the surf, her hands up, as if in praise.

He walked toward the waves.

Her scream rent the air.

She danced back, picking up her feet, turning.

Right behind her, coming out of the brackish tangle of mangroves, charged a massive animal.

No. Not an animal. A *crocodile.*

What—?

He sprinted toward her and before he could think through his actions, kicked the reptile with everything inside him on its soft—or not so soft—belly.

It was big. Heavy. And his feeble kick did nothing more than knock the creature off course, just a little. It rounded on Ranger.

But he was already up the beach. He caught Noemi on the way and flung her up into his arms, running fast until he hit the pavement.

When he reached it, he put her down, but she climbed up onto a short retaining wall.

He stopped, turned.

The reptile stood on shore, some thirty yards away, its pursuit abandoned, the moonlight glistening on its dark hide. Then, just like that, it retreated and slipped back into the water.

Noemi put her hands on his shoulders, standing just about eye level. "So maybe I won't go swimming."

And something inside him just sort of snapped. He laughed and laughed, and she pulled him toward her in a hug until he lowered the top of his head on her shoulder.

"There you are," she said, pushing him away. "Finally."

He looked up at her, still laughing. "Who?"

"The guy who watched me tour the square."

"I didn't—"

"You *did*. I saw you." She held his face in her hands, meeting his eyes with hers, something magical in them. "And I knew that guy, *this* guy, had a big heart just waiting to be awakened."

He narrowed his eyes. "Are you flirting with me?"

"Oh boy, you're in worse shape than I thought." She smiled then, her golden-brown eyes alight in the moonlight, and the smell of her, maybe coconut oil she'd used by the pool, and a hint of the salty air, conspired to stir something deep inside him.

Something he'd successfully ignored for the six years of training and deployment.

Maybe, yeah, his heart—because there was no room for excess emotion in his job. And he was *always* on the job.

"But like I said, nothing's happening here." She let go of him and jumped off the retaining wall. "Yet." She bent to brush the sand off her legs. "Tomorrow, when you pick me up for dinner, then we'll see."

She waited near the bike as he ran down to retrieve her satchel and dress. By the time he returned, the sky had started to rumble. She put on the dress, then her satchel, as he put his shoes back on.

He climbed on the bike, and she got on behind him. Slipped her arms around his waist. And shoot if he didn't take the long way around the island. It may have been a bad idea, because the skies opened up, and by the time they reached the Bahama Mama, they were both drenched, his white Oxford plastered to his torso. The rain spilled off the tiki roof into the parking lot and lightning cracked the sky.

They both got off and made a dash for the lobby. He stood, shivering, sopping wet, not quite wanting to leave her, the way she smiled at him. Her dress clung to her body, her hair dark and curly, and maybe she was right . . .

She *had* awakened something inside of him.

He just hoped it didn't get him killed.

ONE

Forty-two seconds to freedom.

Noemi had done the math. Freedom lay just two hundred yards out of camp, buried in the thin shimmer of fading orange light caught between the thick-trunked Kuka trees and past the brown and yellow grasses, ramshackle houses, battered motorbikes, and the smoking campfire simmering rice in a pot.

Forty-two seconds away.

She'd have to run past the two guards who stood barefoot, smoking cigarettes, AK-47s hung on old belt straps over their bony shoulders. Clearly not devout adherents to the Islamic Haram, these terrorists who had kidnapped them three weeks ago. Not devout, but still dangerous.

"Is tonight the night?" The whisper came from behind her, from Blessing, the fifteen-year-old girl also hidden in the hijab and abaya their kidnappers had forced the women to wear.

Noemi didn't care—the abaya kept her warm when the night closed in, protected her from the ants and moths that burrowed into the ground beneath her.

The costume also hid the assortment of weaponry she'd acquired. Like a dull-edged dinner knife she'd discovered near the firepit and had quietly honed to a fine point. And a shattered mirror, now wrapped in a piece of cotton and secured to the waistband of her filthy underwear.

But most importantly, it hid Freddie's cell phone.

Either he hadn't a clue that he'd dropped it last night or . . . or the twelve-year-old boy soldier who'd been assigned to guard them under the massive tamarind tree had finally become her friend.

She prayed so. No, more accurately, Selah prayed. Because her friend was under the illusion that God actually cared. Might even show up to rescue them. Nope—Noemi did the actual work of planning their escape and dearly hoped that she didn't get found out.

She couldn't bear another person getting hurt—or killed—because of her. Even if he might be a terrorist.

Now, she glanced at Blessing, her dark brown eyes the only thing she could see of her beautiful face. "I don't know," Noemi said to her question. Escape, tonight? "Maybe. Stay alert. If they—"

"Stop talking!" one of the guards shouted. She thought his name might be Jala. He was older, gray woven into his dark knotted hair. He wore a pair of tattered slippers and his ribs stuck out from his black threadbare T-shirt. She guessed him maybe a buck forty, sopping wet.

Sometimes Noemi pictured herself walking out of camp, daring Jala to follow her. She wasn't a wisp of a girl, and her father had taught her skills. If not for Jala's gun . . .

Noemi turned back to the rice she stirred. In it, she'd added wild onion and Kuka leaves, which she hoped might help Colt heal from his recent go-round with the real tough guys.

The ones who threatened, randomly, to execute him. It was a sort of evil game they played.

Smoke stirred up around the fire, filtering into the fading sunlight. Every night, the same war raged inside her.

Survive. Evade. Resist. Escape.

Master Chief Pete Sutton would never have been imprisoned this long—three excruciating weeks. She imagined her father looking down from heaven and shaking his head. *"You're not here to survive this. You're here to take charge of it."*

Fifty feet away, in another section, a couple men walked to

the edge of the dusty camp and fired off their weapons. Beside her, Blessing jumped, but Noemi took her hand.

"They must have seen a wild dog." Selah came over from where she had been gathering firewood from the outskirts of camp. The men liked her better—probably because of her blond hair and the way she never snapped back at them. Selah was calm in the chaos, and at night when the darkness settled, she sang hymns. But it wasn't enough to drown out the cacophony of the savannah at night—the high-pitched squeak of the gray hornbill, or the chipped whine of guinea fowl, or worse, the incessant cackle of a francolin.

But the real danger were the wild dogs that roamed the outskirts of the camp. Feral and bold, sometimes they ran right in toward the fire and she had to ward them away with glowing sticks.

She imagined the dogs retreating into the darkness where they waited to gobble her up.

Coward.

If she didn't run, they'd never be rescued.

Just forty-two seconds. She'd use the dusk to hide herself behind the massive tree, then scuttle through the brush and grasses, parallel with the dirt tracks that wound through the wild savannah plains of northeastern Nigeria, away from the lush and beautiful montane forests to the east.

Away from the city of Jalingo, toward rescue.

Except, after the raid of the school there, she probably wouldn't find anything but fear in the community. No, rescue had to be somewhere else.

Maybe her uncle's home in southern Nigeria. If she could get there.

Selah added a gnarled stick to the fire, one of the many fallen from the massive tree that imprisoned them at night. "Did you talk to Moses?" She gestured to one of the four men across the compound. They hadn't bothered handcuffing Dr. Aaron

Hanson—not with his gunshot wound slowly turning septic. The sixty-year-old American had stopped moaning a few days ago. He mostly lay in the shade where Noemi and Selah had moved him, not even bothering to swat at flies.

He emitted a terrible odor, and the sight of him could make her weep. *I'm sorry.*

Moses, their translator, tried to bargain for medicine for him, early on, and had lost two teeth in the terrible wound one of their captors had delivered with the butt of his machine gun. His mouth had finally started to heal. But he sat, legs drawn up, head on his knees, humming, most of the time.

Moses didn't deserve to die out here, not after everything he'd done for them.

The other two men, however, were bound hand and foot. Maybe because they'd been armed. Or because they'd fought back.

Because they were American soldiers who would, despite their injuries, grab the first chance to escape.

Noemi had a feeling that at least one of the two had been a SEAL. *"Calm is contagious."* She'd heard the blond—a man named Fraser—say that as the truck had jostled them into the night. He hadn't groaned, not even once, despite the terrible set of his arm, his broken wrist.

Reminded her way too much of another SEAL, the one who lived deep in her memory. Tough, his emotions carefully tamed, the kind of guy who could look pain in the face and not blink.

Ranger Kingston probably hadn't a clue what he'd done to her heart, either, but it had been the right thing, letting him go, walking out of his life.

Her broken heart was her own stupid fault.

It was the darker one, the tougher one—ironically, Ranger's brother Colt—who the rebels most feared. Which was why Abu, the big terrorist with the black eyes and the tribal scars down his face, hauled him out for sport, put a gun to his head, held up a cell phone to record his murder . . . and waited. Waited for him to sweat or swear or just shout at them.

He did nothing, and that made Abu angrier each time.

How Colt stood up to his beatings, she didn't know, but Abu would drag Colt's unconscious body back to the others, and by morning, Colt sat, huddled up with his fellow warrior, watching the camp with those unflinching brown eyes.

She might be a little afraid of him too.

The water in her rice pot boiled up, and she hooked the handle with a stick and took it off the fire, setting it in the dirt.

She just needed a distraction. Something to capture the attention of Freddie and Jala, and forty-two seconds to disappear. Because if she didn't escape, and soon, she had no doubt that one—or all of them—were going to die.

Take charge, Noemi.

She had found and cleaned a couple dented metal bowls and now ladled out the rice into them. Handed one to Selah for Dr. Aaron.

The other she picked up, and with a glance at Freddie and Jala, walked over to Colt. She crouched in front of him. He stared at her out of one eye, the other terribly swollen. His nose had clearly been broken, maybe reset by Moses, but blood caked his nostrils, and a bruise darkened his chin, swelling that too. Blood also edged his ear, but she thought it might be from the nearby head wound.

His entire body bore bruises, and the way he breathed, catching now and again, she guessed he might have a broken rib, or two.

"Hey," he said quietly. "What's on the menu?"

"A nice T-bone," she said and held up a spoonful of rice.

He opened his mouth, let her feed him. "Needs salt."

"I'll tell the chef." She ladled in another mouthful.

He smirked, and under all those wounds was a man who

clearly didn't let darkness control him. He took another spoonful, then, "How are you ladies doing?"

Sweet. She lowered her voice. "I think I can get away."

His eyes widened. "You're barefoot."

"Oh no, really? Shoot. I left my Tevas back at the spa. Whatever shall I do?"

He smiled again, humor in his eyes. "Jala falls asleep right after dinner."

"I know. But Freddie likes to sit with us by the fire. What I really need is a distraction."

Colt swallowed another spoonful of rice. One more, and she'd give the rest to Fraser. A glance at the SEAL said he was listening, but his gaze stayed on the camp. His jaw was drawn in a tight line.

"I can give you that," Colt said softly. He met her eyes.

A fist tightened in her gut. "They'll kill you."

"No, they won't. They want to, but they're too scared. They know I'm an American. I'm worth something. And their higher-ups want to sell me."

"He'd rather die helping you escape," Fraser said quietly next to them.

Colt nodded.

Noemi shook her head. "No."

"Get ready," Colt said. "You'll know when."

She moved over to Fraser. "No." She held out the spoon to him. He was less battered, a handsome man with a Midwestern accent. Both men had thick beards, although they'd been clean-shaven when they'd been taken.

"Don't let his sacrifice go to waste," Fraser whispered.

She practically shoved the next spoonful into his mouth. "I'll figure out another way."

"When?" He said it with his mouth full. Swallowed. "Moses heard them say they were moving us north."

She halted the next spoonful. Glanced at Moses. He was

watching them, too, his wizened fifty-year-old eyes confirming Fraser's words.

"They're watching," Colt said under his breath.

Noemi fed Fraser more. Selah, meanwhile, was trying to get Dr. Aaron to eat, urging him awake. She put her hand on his forehead, her mouth pinched tight.

"They can't move us. Dr. Aaron will die," Noemi said.

"He won't be going with us," Fraser said and took the last spoonful.

Oh. Because he'd already be dead.

If she wanted to save the man who'd given so much to Hope School, the one who had trusted her when she said the trip to the village of Lakawa would be safe, she needed to leave, now.

She cleaned out the bowl and stood up, met Colt's eyes. "Don't die."

He grinned. He still had all his teeth despite a bloody mouth. "You're so bossy, Master Chief Sutton."

She shook her head, but yes, maybe her father *had* rubbed off on her.

Yeah, well, she'd gotten them into this mess.

She could get them out.

When she returned to the firepit, Blessing was stirring the rice. Noemi ladled out more and gave it to her to eat. Noemi had probably lost fifteen pounds in the last few weeks. Frankly, despite her love for jollof rice, this was a far cry from the flavorful Nigerian dish cooked in tomatoes and pepper puree.

"Dr. Aaron isn't moving. He won't even wake up." Selah had given her bowl to Moses, who ate it heartily in the fading light.

Noemi glanced at Jala, who had thrown down his cigarette into the dust, and Freddie, now wandering toward their campfire. He'd sit with her and eat the rice. She guessed he felt safer with them than with his fellow boy soldiers at the other camp.

Then she met Colt's eyes.

He drew in a breath. Gave a nod.

Please don't die.

"Hey, you, skinny guy. I need to—"

"Shut up," Jala said and walked toward him. Noemi winced as he kicked Colt, who pulled up his knees to protect himself.

But the scuffle had turned Freddie and, in that time, she'd stepped back, toward their tree.

Their tree. A massive, ancient tamarind with a canopy of gnarled, arching arms that both imprisoned and hid them.

And around the back, where no one noticed, she'd broken off a few limbs to create an escape.

Colt kicked back at Jala, grabbed his ankles with his feet, and managed to topple the man over. Freddie headed toward the ruckus.

Noemi took off.

She slipped under the hanging branches of the tree, then around it to the back and broke free from its twisted arms into the grassland.

She pulled the long abaya up past her knees, freeing her legs.

Forty-two seconds.

The sun had fallen behind the horizon, long dark shadows cutting through the twilight.

Her foot crunched on something prickly and she bit back a cry. *"The only easy day was yesterday."*

The massive Kuka tree loomed ahead.

Safety, her heart in her throat, her breaths fast.

Twenty-three seconds.

Her foot caught a branch.

She hit the dirt, rolled, and gasped, staring at the sky, her heart wild.

Get up. *Get—*

A shot echoed into the air, and she rolled to her knees, stayed down.

"Woman!" Abu's voice.

She didn't move.

"I will kill him if you don't come back."

She closed her eyes. *"Don't let his sacrifice go to waste."*

She turned, started crawling.

"Kari!"

She stilled at the new voice. *No!* The pidgin word for *daughter*.

"Kari, run!"

Moses. She spotted him in the fading light, a frail outline as Abu held a gun to his head.

And then, Abu pulled the trigger.

The memory of Moses's body jerking violently, the way he crumpled into the dirt, would live with her forever. That, and the scream that emitted from her before she could slap a hand over her mouth.

"Take charge of your fear."

She buried her face into her hands. Breathe.

Then, *Run*.

"Woman," Abu shouted. "Come back."

She couldn't look. Couldn't turn around, couldn't move.

Run! The voice came from inside her, but it still galvanized her, sent her running. *I'm sorry— I'm sorry—*

Another gunshot, and she refused to look.

"The next one kills her. *You* kill her!"

She slowed, turned.

Abu held Blessing by the nape of her neck, the gun to her head.

No—she was a child.

Just a *child*.

She held up her hands. "Stop! *Stop!*" Her eyes filled as she ran toward him. "Stop, please— No!"

Abu laughed and shook Blessing, forcing her to her knees, pressing the gun to her head.

Noemi burst through the brush, right up to him, then threw her arms around Blessing, her body a covering. "What is wrong with you? She's a child!"

He laughed again. "She is old enough to be my bride."

Noemi went cold.

"And so are you."

She pulled Blessing up, put her behind her. Stared at Abu. "I would rather be dead than marry you."

He moved close, his rancid breath near her ear. "Be careful what you wish for."

A ripple went through her.

He gestured with his head back to camp and she didn't look at Moses's body as she stumbled back to the tamarind tree.

Nor did she look at Colt as he lay in the darkness.

She'd probably killed them all.

Once upon a time, Ranger would have taken the shot. Could have taken the shot.

Should have taken the shot.

But he wasn't in charge, not anymore. Wasn't even on the team.

Which meant he had to lie here in the dirt and wait like a dog in the bush until Hamilton Jones said *execute*.

Which had better be soon.

"They're taking the girls back into their camp." The words, softly spoken, came from the man hunkered down next to Ranger. Fellow former SEAL Jake Silver hadn't even breathed hard when the ruckus went down in camp some five hundred yards from their position—a pocket tucked under a smooth-barked tree. The forest was alive around them with grunts and chirps, the buzz of crickets, and all manner of insects.

Ranger could practically feel the bugs on his body, but then again, he'd been prone, dressed in a ghillie suit, a Leupold 10x power scope to his eye, sweaty, grimy, and hungry for the better part of two days.

All the time watching his brother Colt get beaten. So that was fun.

"Your brother is a tough nutter," Jake said.

"Tougher than smart," Ranger replied—and he wondered if, from his position, their brother Dodge, the oldest of the triplets, was thinking it too.

Frankly, Ranger thought Colt might end up at the other end of the muzzle of a gun held by Big T—as in Terrorist Thug.

Ham had identified Big T as one Abu Mussaf, head of a splinter Boko Haram group out terrorizing local villages for profit.

They'd hit the jackpot with Colt's travel party. What Colt and his Jones, Inc. cohort Fraser Marshall were doing out in the middle of the bush with their client, Dr. Aaron Hanson, Ham didn't know. Just that they'd called in the field trip, along with two women and a local girl, just before they'd gone radio quiet.

Ham's team—Jake, Skeet, and North—had flown in two weeks ago to hunt them down. A call to Ranger a week ago had put him on a plane home to fetch his chopper-pilot brother, Dodge, for a snatch-and-grab deep in the bowels of northeastern Nigeria.

Now, two very long days later, Ranger was hungry, tired, thirsty, and barely able to resist sending Abu into the dirt when he put a gun to the girl's head. He assumed it was a girl—after all, she was dressed in traditional Muslim clothing.

"Not sure what your brother said to Mr. Skinny to earn his last whipping, but my guess is that it had something to do with Storm and her escape attempt," Jake said.

"Storm?"

Jake looked over at him, his eyes white against the grime on his face. "X-Men? Excellent hand-to-hand combat skills? Force of nature?"

Ranger nodded.

Jake had that right. Storm seemed a little fearless, if not

tough, standing up to Abu a few times, trying to take care of Dr. Hanson. Intel from Ham said she was an aid worker from the refugee school.

"They're dragging Colt back to the others. Looks like he's still breathing, at the very least."

The fist in Ranger's chest released. *I'll get you, bro. Hang on.*

The camp was settling down. Storm and the other two women had been forced back under the massive tree that hid them.

Abu was messing with the kid who'd been on watch, pushing him around while a number of others stood in a circle around him, the fire flickering on their faces.

Oh, this wouldn't go well for him.

But it might be exactly what the rescue team needed.

"Ranger, I need you and North on the extraction of Selah and the other women." Ham's voice came through the coms, into his ear, echoing Ranger's thoughts. Jones, Inc. possessed some high-tech gear when it came to security and search and rescue. The entire team had been watching the activity in camp on a screen like it might be hostage reality television.

Waiting. Counting. Analyzing.

"Through that tree, then?" Ranger asked. The woman's escape through the back of the colossal tamarind tree had opened the door.

"While Skeet and Jake cause trouble in the big camp, you grab the ladies and meet us at the exfil point," Ham said. Dodge had stashed their chopper in a remote area two klicks south.

"Dodge and I will extract Colt, Fraser, and Dr. Hanson."

"Colt is still out," Jake said.

"No, I see movement." This from Dodge, the first indication he'd been watching. But of course he'd been watching.

Dodge, more than anyone, had reason to save Colt's backside. A sort of redemption op.

Whatever. Ranger just knew they couldn't let their brother be executed by terrorists. As a former Delta operator, he deserved better.

Despite his mysterious discharge.

"Go get 'em," Jake said to Ranger as he shed his ghillie suit. He left it in the bush and, with the darkness settling around them, crept out to a massive, thick-trunked Kuka tree two hundred yards from the camp.

Ham and his team also moved in the darkness, positioning themselves behind a large burned-out hut a hundred yards or less south of Colt's position.

"Jake, hold until we're made. No need to attract attention."

"They're busy with the kid."

"Ranger?" North's voice as he watched from the perimeter.

"Nearly in position." Ranger had found the break in the tree, hit the dirt, and was creeping through the elephant grass toward the opening. "You got me, North?"

"Yep," North whispered.

"Try not to scare the ladies," Dodge said. "You look like a terrorist."

And he probably smelled like one. He halted under a large whistling thorn, nearly pressed his hand into one of the long spires, and made a mental note not to run into it on their exfil.

"Ready."

The odor of smoke, creosote, and burning rubber filtered from the camp, with laughter in the distance, and crying, loudly, from a boy soldier they'd brought to their side of the camp. Ranger closed his ears to it—he couldn't save the kid.

"Execute. Execute. Execute."

Ham's voice lit a fire in Ranger and he stood, hunched over, and arrowed toward the opening in the tree.

It took a few seconds for his eyes to adjust, but he spotted the women. They all wore the hijab and abaya, and he took a guess that the one with her back to the tree, holding the smaller girl in her arms, was Storm. The other woman sat with her knees up, humming.

They hadn't seen him.

"Don't scream," he said, holding up his hand. He crouched, maybe five feet away. "I'm here to help." Then he ripped open a Velcro patch on his vest and revealed a US flag patch.

Storm lifted her head, and her eyes widened. Then she clamped her hand over the younger girl's mouth. "Shh."

Attagirl.

"Come with me."

She climbed to her feet, took the younger girl's hand. The third woman followed. Across the camp, and outside the dark shaggy tree, laughter and shouts raked the air. But nothing amiss.

Hopefully Ham had already reached Colt.

"What about the guys?" Storm said, her voice low. "We can't—"

"It's handled." He crouched near the entrance and glanced out into the darkness, where the terrain scrubbed the sky in variegated shadows. No moon tonight, thanks to Ham's timing, but the stars still shone, vast and bright against the deep velvet of the sky. Out here, they seemed close enough to pick, hold on to, wish upon.

He wished for success.

"Run!" he whispered and pushed Storm out of the hole, then the smaller girl, and finally the third woman.

They dissolved into the darkness. He followed them out, hearing more than seeing them run through the bramble. They were slow, their abayas limiting their strides, and Storm kept turning around, reaching for the girl.

He finally pushed up to the front. "Put your hand on my vest. Hold on to each other."

Storm grabbed the back of his vest, clenched the girl's hand in hers.

"Stay low." He crouched, his eyes on the massive Kuka tree.

A shout, the ricochet of bullets against the air, and then Ham's voice. "Jake, we have company."

"I got ya."

More shots from camp as Jake cleared their tail.

"Keep moving," Ranger said to the women. He slowed his pace, not wanting to run them into the thornbush, and for a moment, he was Jake. Keeping his heart rate down, stock pocketed tight into his shoulder, cheek set behind the scope while his eye centered on the crosshairs. Target in the center. The half breath, hold, then steady squeeze of the trigger.

The recoil of the .300 Winchester Magnum—target down.

He missed it. The calm, the control of his emotions, the satisfaction of protecting his brothers. But that life was over. Now he was the one dodging bullets, hoping Jake had his back.

A shot scurried the air near him and he grabbed Storm. "Down! Hold!"

He knelt, scoping their six, and spotted a small group of men now edging out into the night.

Crosshairs. Breath. Hold. Target down.

The recoil hit him, and he easily absorbed it before he turned to the next target. Shots fired around him but he held.

Another man down.

Machine-gun fire and one of the women was screaming.

"Get to the tree!" He grabbed Storm's abaya, tugged her up. "Run!"

She scrambled to her feet and obeyed, lighting past him. The girl got up behind her.

"Go!" She took off, followed by the third woman.

The soldiers stepped over their casualties, shooting, shouting. Ranger ducked, an eye toward the tree.

The women had vanished into the night.

The shooting stopped and he popped up. Found another target.

Crosshairs. Breath. Squeeze.

Another man down and this time one of the men shouted. Turned, waved his arm toward the brush. He might have seen the muzzle flash in the darkness.

Ranger took him out.

The other two men stopped, their buddy down, and turned, fleeing back to camp.

Buh-bye.

Ranger whirled around and beelined for the tree.

No more shooting his direction, but gunshots continued to pepper the air from the far side of the camp.

"Passing Bravo," Ham said, indicating they'd extracted Colt, Fraser, and Dr. Aaron.

"Alpha acquired," Ranger said, reaching the Kuka tree.

The women were shapeless under their abayas, nearly melting into the darkness. "You ladies okay?"

Storm pulled off her hijab. "Where's Blessing?"

He could barely make out her features in the night, but her voice nudged something inside him. "Who?"

The other woman also pulled off her head covering, revealing blond hair. "The younger girl. She was between us." She began to work off the abaya.

Storm had pulled hers off already. "Did you see her?"

He turned and scanned the darkness. In her abaya and hijab, he hadn't a hope of seeing her. "I thought she was behind you."

"We all sort of scattered," the blond said. Selah, he supposed.

"She has to be out there," Storm said and made to leave the cover of the tree.

He put his hand on her arm. "Nope. You stay here. I'll find her."

She stiffened under his touch but obeyed. He radioed Ham. "We have a problem. One of ours is missing."

He crouched as he stepped out from the tree. Anyone with

a night vision scope could see him, pick him off. "Jake, do you see her?"

A moment, then, "Maybe. She's about thirty yards southwest from you, between the tree and camp, to the south. Her clothes are caught in a bush."

Ranger held back a word and scanned the area. Nothing. "Let me know if I'm getting close."

He headed to the south, working his way toward camp, the grasses thickening, the smell of mud and smoke deepening. He slid under a lonely jackalberry tree. "Closer?"

"Hold up. There's a search party headed your way."

Shouts. Strident voices. A few curse words, he guessed, by their tones. He brought his scope up and found them, a group of three men, one cutting away the forest grasses with a rough-edged machete. The other two behind him, carrying AK-47s.

One of them was Skinny.

Ranger put him in the crosshairs.

A scream, and suddenly Machete had pulled up the girl, her abaya ripping as he yanked her free from the acacia tree. He flung her at Skinny.

Right in the field of Ranger's scope.

She screamed again.

Ranger winced. "Tell me you have a shot, Jake."

"Negative. She's in the sights."

He watched, his body tight, breath half held as Skinny grabbed the screaming girl, pulled her against him, and started to drag her back to camp.

Machete walked behind him.

"If I take the guy with the machete, can you get the other?" Ranger asked.

"Yes."

Ranger's heart thundered in his chest, loud in his ears, as he let out his breath, held it. Darkness edged into his periphery, but he narrowed his eye. Kept Machete in the crosshairs.

If he missed, the girl would be lost, headed to slavery in the Boko Haram.

"Now, Jake."

Ranger squeezed the trigger in tandem with Jake's shot.

His target ducked, and in the recoil, Ranger thought he went down.

Nope. The shot might have winged him, but Machete grabbed the girl's legs and took off with her and Skinny, running past their pal's body. Jake, at least, had made his shot.

"Negative shot," Ranger said tightly. He put the scope again to his eye. "No shot." Not with the trio running in and out of the elephant grasses, dodging acacia bushes.

"Do you have the Americans?" Ham's voice now.

"Affirmative."

"Proceed to exfil."

The words punched him, a hit to the sternum. They couldn't leave her behind.

But she was not the mission either.

He headed back to the tree.

North had arrived, and Ranger spotted him holding tight to Selah. She, too, clung to him, her arms around his neck, weeping.

Ah. And now it made sense—so, not just a mission for North.

Sure, he got it—he'd be dismantled if someone he loved was in trouble, kidnapped, their life threatened. Hence why he'd deleted true love from his game plan. Love was a liability.

It had nearly happened—derailing his life, his goals hanging in the balance all over a woman. It was four years ago, but was fresh enough for him to remember the woman he'd given up, and why.

Noemi Sutton.

The Master Chief's only daughter.

A woman who had nearly cost him everything.

He ignored the spectacle of emotions and ducked behind the tree.

"Did you find her?" Storm's voice came from somewhere in the shadows of the tree. She practically melded into the darkness, just the whites of her eyes visible, but again, the voice sounded . . . wait . . .

It couldn't be— He blamed North and the sliver of old memories.

"They found her. She's back in the camp." He turned to North. "We gotta go."

"No." Storm materialized from the darkness, toward the wan starlight that illuminated her form, her face, her tight jaw, those eyes, now hot with fury.

Oh no—

She stood her ground. "I'm not going anywhere without Blessing."

Not Storm. But yes, the moniker might be accurate because this woman, with her fierce golden-brown eyes, had the blood of her father, a SEAL, in her. And in the space of two weeks, once upon a time, she'd upended Ranger's world in every way possible.

And now she was at it again.

He forced his voice steady. "She's not the mission. Let's go." He reached out for her hand.

Big mistake. She jerked away from him. "You clearly don't know me if you think I'm leaving without her—"

"Noemi." Her name just slid out. Soft, quiet, not a hint of betrayal at the sudden surge of emotion.

She stilled. Stared at him.

"I do know you. And that's why we need to run."

TWO

Well, hello, hello. Ranger Kingston, right here in the shadow of a Kuka tree, deep in the heart of Nigeria.

It took a precious second for Noemi's brain to confirm his presence—all six foot two of him, dressed in black tactical gear, smelling like the earth and a couple days of manly odor. Those aqua-blue eyes the only thing recognizable—mostly because she'd more easily believe that her father had risen from the dead and joined this rescue op in the heart of Northern Africa than that she was staring into the gaze of the man who'd once told her that she "wasn't worth his career."

Apparently, however, she was worth his life.

No. The *mission* was worth his life. She needed to get that straight, right now. He hadn't shown up to save her, despite what her heart wanted to believe.

More, one look at him told her he'd turned into exactly the man he'd wanted to be.

Which meant she wouldn't throw her arms around him and hold on. Still, "Ranger?"

He took a breath and nodded.

Noemi had to be dreaming. Or this could be a nightmare, because it was quite possible that Ranger Kingston didn't have a heart inside that Kevlar vest.

Not one that gave off a noticeable pulse, at least. Which meant Blessing was doomed to her fate with the Boko Haram rebels.

His words rounded back to her. *"She's not the mission. Let's go."*

She expected that, really. She knew him. But clearly, he'd forgotten her. "You'll have to throw me over your shoulder or drag me out by my hair if you think I'm leaving without her."

Silence thundered between them as he stared at her. Then he looked at the other man. North, from what Noemi could guess, the former SEAL who Selah couldn't stop talking about. No wonder she rushed into his arms.

And just like that, Noemi was back in Key West—

Nope, nope, *not* going to revive the past now. Ever. "I'm serious, Range."

"I have no doubt," Ranger snapped, "but we can't stay. It won't take them long to regroup and hunt us down. Colt and Fraser are valuable targets—"

"I get it. But so is Blessing. She was the daughter of a tribal king and—"

"And the problem of the Nigerian government."

She stared at him, her jaw tight. "Unbelievable."

"I don't make the rules."

"Yeah well, she might not be your mission, but she's mine. You don't have to tag along."

"Stop." His jaw tightened and he took a breath. "Fine." He turned to North. "Take the women to Charlie. I'll get the girl and meet you—"

"You're not hearing me," Noemi interrupted him. "I'm going to get her—"

"You're going to get us both killed!"

She took a step away from him. "She's my responsibility. I got her into this mess."

His mouth twitched.

Please, Range. "I'm a sharpshooter, and you know it. I can help."

"You're barefoot."

"What is it with—"

"We have to go, Range." North already had Selah by the hand.

Ranger looked between her and North. Finally, darkly, he turned to her. "Obey everything I say. *Everything*."

She nodded.

He faced North. "Thirty minutes. If we're not there, leave. I'll find you."

North was a big man, not as tall as Ranger, but wider shoulders. His voice bore a Midwestern accent. "I don't like it."

"Me either. But she'll get heavy."

Was that a joke?

"Don't be late," North said, and he and Selah disappeared into the night.

Ranger rounded on her again. "*Everything* I say."

"Aye, Master Chief."

"Senior Chief," he said as he pulled his Sig Sauer 9mm from his right hip holster. Handed it to her. Then he pulled out a couple clips from his vest pocket. "You remember how to reload?"

"In my sleep."

He slapped them into her hand. "Don't shoot me."

She wasn't sure he was kidding.

Lifting his H&K, he peered through the scope. "Okay. She's sitting under the same tree Colt was. It doesn't look like she's secured. There's one guard watching her. Abu is back in the other camp, shouting. It seems like he's rounding up a posse." He lowered the gun and held out his hand. "Let's go."

She slipped her hand into his. No romance there, it was simply a way to control her. Still, she stopped shaking as they stepped out of the relative safety of the Kuka tree and back into the elephant grasses.

When he crouched, she crouched. When he stopped, she stopped. He finally moved her hand to the back of his vest, and she held on to the mesh belt there, letting him guide them through the darkness, creeping around acadia trees, through the thick grasses, and behind a burned hut until finally he held up his fist.

Hold.

The whole thing felt a little like one of the rare vacations to Montana with her father. They'd stay at a friend's cabin where he'd take her hunting and teach her survival skills.

Ranger pointed to Blessing who sat huddled in her abaya, her head down, her shoulders shaking.

Yeah, well, she'd be terrified too. Had been terrified since the moment she'd practically run back into captivity and thrown herself on the mercy of Abu.

The fact that he hadn't dragged her away to be gang-raped seemed nothing short of a miracle. But no more miraculous than Ranger appearing in the darkness no less than an hour later, like a grimy answer to Selah's prayers, to help them escape.

Another reason why Noemi should stay with Ranger to rescue Blessing. In Blessing's terrified state of mind, she might just fight him.

"Be careful," she whispered. "She's scared."

He glanced back at Noemi. Nodded. "Don't shoot unless someone is on my six. We need to keep this quiet. They won't expect us to have stuck around."

He was probably right about that. Anyone with good sense would be miles away by now.

She'd put Ranger's life in danger, twice now. *Please, God, don't let us get caught. Or killed.* Maybe Selah was rubbing off on her, but it couldn't hurt.

Jala sat a few feet away from Blessing, his cigarette ember an eye in the darkness. The fire provided an eerie glow.

On the other side of the camp, a few men got into an old Subaru and lit off on the two-laned rutted dirt road that led southwest from camp through the shrubland.

Abu paced around the fire, still shouting, the flames hot as they spit sparks into the sky.

Now. The thought pulsed inside her even as Ranger dissolved into the night, lethally silent. She watched, her breath held as he moved behind Jala in one move and a second later, let him drop into the dust.

The starlight caught his knife a moment before he wiped it then sheathed it.

Two more steps and he crouched in front of Blessing. She looked up.

And screamed.

No!

Ranger slammed his hand over her mouth, then pulled her up, against him, and dragged her out of the camp. She kicked at him, and from across the darkness, Abu turned, searching.

A couple soldiers picked up their weapons, heading across camp, and Noemi centered the gun on them. Oh, she didn't want to shoot anyone.

Ranger appeared and crouched next to her, breathing hard, fighting a struggling Blessing. "Calm her down."

She turned to Blessing, her hand behind her neck, her face close. "Stop. It's me, Noemi. You're safe."

Hardly, with the shouts now rising from the two soldiers—yep, that was a dead body.

Ranger grabbed the gun from her hand and lay down cover fire. Then he lifted her up by the arm. "We go, now."

She had hold of Blessing, who had stopped screaming, and practically pushed her in front of her, behind Ranger.

And then they ran.

Shots peeled off behind them, the night smelling of gunpowder, gasoline, smoke, and death. She kept her eyes on Blessing, and ahead of her, Ranger, who kept turning then finally pushed them ahead of him. "Head toward the forest!"

The forest, aka the tangle of brush and tall locust bean trees and fat shea butter trees, of spiny whistling thorn and jackalberry and all manner of baboons, monkeys, and wolves—not to mention jaguars and the lethal black mamba.

She might take her chances with the rebels.

But . . . obey everything, right? So she grabbed Blessing's hand and took off for the rise of forest in the distance, some half mile away.

Behind her, Ranger let off a couple shots.

She kept running.

He caught up and grabbed her hand, passing her, pulling her along. Spiky acadia tore at her legs, and her feet were cut and bleeding, but the shouting behind them had died.

Ranger led them at angles, changing routes, but always toward the woodland. The trees rose around them—tall, flat canopies darkening their steps.

She was out of breath, Blessing weeping beside her.

"Range—stop. We need to—"

He glanced back, his steps slowing. "We won't make the exfil."

She leaned over, catching her breath. "Where. Is . . . it?"

"Another mile, southwest." He pointed toward a valley, cut out between darker shadows. "The chopper is there."

In the quiet, she could hear the occasional, distant shot. Still, the forest sounds rose like a cacophony around them. Birds shrieking, crickets and frogs singsonging, the random, terrifying roar.

Yes, roar. As in an animal that could eat them.

He looked at her, and for the first time, smiled. "You're safe with me."

He *meant* it. Wow, he really meant it. Did he completely forget how he'd dismantled her? Okay, yes, maybe she was safe in the physical sense, but really, she'd *never* been safe around Ranger Kingston.

Once upon a time, the man could steal her heart with a smile. It had taken her four painful years to get over him.

No, he was far from safe. She wouldn't be a fool again.

The shot came out of the darkness like a slap, and at first, she didn't think he was hit. Ranger just stood there, his breath a hard gasp.

Then he gritted his teeth and bent over. "Get down."

She obeyed. But even in the darkness she could see the blood dripping down his arm. "You're hit."

"Mm-hmm." He pulled up his gun, sighted through the scope.

Time seemed to stop as his breathing slowed, as he stayed silent, searching. And then, "Gotcha." The word was so quiet it was downright terrifying.

He squeezed off the shot, and the gun recoiled. He groaned, something deep in his chest.

"Ranger."

"Let's go."

But he was slow to his feet and losing a lot of blood. He wobbled, and she grabbed his arm. "Stop. We need to slow the bleeding."

He nodded then, miraculously, and hit a knee. "In my pack, upper back pocket—there's some wound seal." He turned, and she opened the pack, found the tube of blood-clotting agent.

"Where are you shot?"

"Shoulder, I think." He closed his eyes.

"Don't pass out."

"I have a shot of morphine and some adrenaline in there too."

"Can you take off your vest?"

"Nope. Just stick it in there and shoot. Hurry."

The bullet had ripped his shirt, so she found the hole with her fingers. She knew, when he grunted, that she'd hit the wound.

"This might hurt."

"No duh, doc."

She shot the blood-clotting agent into the wound. He closed his eyes, his breath drawn in.

Blessing sat, unmoving, a few feet away from them, her eyes wide, as if milliseconds away from losing it.

Okay, yes, maybe it was good Ranger wasn't the kind of guy who let his feelings get the better of him, because right now they needed someone coolheaded.

"Now the morphine." He spoke through clenched teeth. "It's an auto-injector. Just hand it to me."

She obeyed, although she was perfectly capable of—

He shot himself in the thigh. "Okay, let's go."

"What about the adrenaline?"

"Not yet." He reached for her hand. "We have a bit of a hike."

Right. He'd use it when the morphine wore off.

They took off through the forest, letting the night protect them, the forest sounds masking their movements. An occasional growl lifted the skin on her neck, and the insects buzzed in her ears. He was practically running, but not so fast that she couldn't keep up. Blessing ran behind them, wordless, but better now.

The canopy opened now and again to starlight.

"How far?"

"Not much," he said. But he'd slowed a little.

A hum had started deep in the background, and at first, she thought it might be a vehicle. He kept moving, the woodlands loosening even as they hiked uphill. The air had changed, no longer the clogged, brutal odor of fire, but something fresh, as if—

Water.

The hum was a waterfall, or a river . . .

Oh no . . . crocodiles.

"Ranger—"

"I hear it." He had turned, as if to confirm the sound wasn't a vehicle, then rounded and headed forward. The ground had turned from grassy to rocky as they climbed, and clearly they were headed toward a gorge of some sort. "We'll find a way around it."

He gave her hand a squeeze.

So he hadn't completely forgotten.

They topped the hill and came out to a clearing littered with rocks and grass and overhanging locust trees and—

"That's very so down, o," Blessing said in pidgin as she came to the edge.

Yes. Very far down.

Ranger pulled out his radio. "Ham, this is Ranger. Come back."

The radio hissed, then, "What's your ETA?"

"Got a little roadblock. We're farther than I thought."

"We're at Charlie, but the doc is fading, and we have company."

Ranger winced, put the radio to his forehead, then nodded. "Go. I'll meet you in Lagos."

Silence.

"Negative. Get here."

Behind them, voices sounded, and Noemi turned. They stood uncovered, in the starlight, like bright targets. "Range—"

"Ham, we have company too. Go. I'll find you."

A beat, then, "Stay alive. See you soon."

Ranger pocketed the radio. "C'mon." But his move toward the nearest locust tree was cut off by a shot. The bullet whizzed past her so close she could smell it.

"Down, get down!" He grabbed them both, dragged them over to the locust tree, but already three men had appeared.

He was bleeding again as he hunkered down, set up the H&K, and set out a barrage of fire into the night.

She grabbed his Sig Sauer from his hip holster and squeezed off a shot. But in the darkness, it went wide and maybe her hand shook a little because more bullets chipped bark off and Blessing was screaming—

"Jump!"

He'd flung his H&K, on its strap, over his shoulder, and now grabbed her hand. Then Blessing's. Noemi tried to yank hers away, but he shook his head. "Everything."

Oh— He must have seen her face because he added, "Trust me."

And then he pulled them, running, to the edge of the cliff and over.

THREE

Oh no, now she'd really done it.

Gone and actually killed a Navy SEAL. No, killed *Ranger Kingston*, one of the toughest men she knew.

"Ranger, wake *up*." Noemi pressed her fingers to his neck, and confirmed, yes, a pulse still pumped, so why did he lay in the grass unmoving?

Not far away, huddled in her abaya, Blessing shivered, her crying soft, just watching with wide eyes.

All was silent in the darkness, their pursuers clearly hesitant to make the crazy jump.

She didn't blame them. She'd nearly lost her mind when Ranger had yanked her over the edge into the abyss—

He groaned.

"Range?"

They'd floated—if you could call their floundering, the near drowning that had occurred as floating—downriver maybe a mile before she managed to pull them out.

Mud embedded her pores, and the smell of the water—a sort of moldy, putrid odor—made her wonder what diseases lingered in the river. They weren't so far from shore that a crocodile wouldn't decide they'd make a lovely meal.

Ranger groaned again and she leaned him up, slapping his face. "Wake up, wake—"

He grabbed her wrist. "I'm awake."

But as he let her go, he winced, and then tried to push himself up. After a bit, he simply gave up and lay back. "I need a second."

Right. "I think we lost them."

He eyed her. "What happened?"

She stared at him. "Don't you remember?"

"It's hazy."

"Seriously, how much blood have you lost?"

"My guess is quite a bit. I might need that adrenaline now."

He'd pulled the pack and his gun off him when he landed on shore the first time, and now she went over to retrieve the pack. "You forced us off the cliff."

"I remember that."

"Do you also remember the twenty-foot fall into crocodile-infested waters?"

He said nothing and she abandoned her search through his pack. "Range?" She rushed back to him.

His eyes were closed, but he was smiling.

"You think this is funny? We could have broken our necks. You had no idea what was down there."

"Take a breath, Noe. I knew there was a river. We'd looked at it on the map." His smile had vanished, and for the first time, he really looked at her. "You think I'd do something I thought would hurt you?"

She just blinked at him. Clearly, he had forgotten their last full conversation. "*This was a huge mistake.*"

No duh, pal. And she wasn't going to make it again.

"Blessing can't swim. Which I get is something you might not know, but you let go of us, Ranger. Let go!"

His mouth twitched. "Sorry."

Only then did she guess his letting go might have had something to do with his wounded shoulder.

"Yeah, well, she panicked," she went on. "And of course, I tried to help, but she crawled on top of me and I nearly drowned—and would have if you hadn't ripped her off."

He was staring at her now, just listening. Maybe he *didn't* remember.

"You don't remember swimming with her to shore?"

He shook his head.

"Or dumping your gun and pack before coming back to get me?"

He made a face.

Huh. Because as she'd tumbled through the water, the river faster than she could have imagined, as she'd tried to cling to rocks or overhanging trees, suddenly he appeared, right there, his arms around her, pulling himself tight to her. "Hold on to me," he said, as if she needed a reminder. And then he turned, and she gripped his vest and he'd started swimming. Against the current, to the opposite side.

What happened next, she couldn't explain. Maybe the current caught them, but suddenly, he was spun around and holding her, his back to the shore as the current dragged them down the inky river.

Overhead, the stars had given little help, the river cold and fast and lethal until it finally slammed Ranger against a rock. He huffed out a deep grunt but held on to her. Then, "Swim to shore."

She nodded, and he pushed her toward the shore, some ten feet away. The river ran less rapid here, and she fought the current, finally grabbing a boulder, and pulling herself from the shallow depths. She crawled on shore and turned around.

Ranger was gone.

"Range!" She stood up, searching but didn't see him. "Ranger!" She ran down the shoreline, tripping over rocks and boulders in the darkness, splashing into the water. *There.*

He seemed to be hung up on a twisted, naked branch of a downed locust tree, and he was thrashing, trying to break free.

Then, he took a breath, and disappeared beneath the surface.

She climbed up on a rock that extended into the water, just a few feet below him and waited. And waited.

Please.

She was already in the water, slipping down to brace herself against the rock, when she realized he'd broken free. His body floated to the surface.

The current grabbed him.

No—no! She waded out, braced her foot against the rock, and grabbed his vest just before he floated out of reach.

Then, somehow, she dragged him to shore. Blessing had caught up with her, running down the shoreline, grabbed the other side of his vest, and helped pull him into the clear.

"Breathe, Ranger. Breathe!" She had leaned close, ready to give him mouth-to-mouth resuscitation when she realized he was, indeed, breathing.

He'd just blacked out.

Now, she just kept staring at him. "You don't remember me saving your life?"

He looked at her. "You saved my life?"

"Yes. Pulled you from the waters of death. Saved you from the choir invisible." She got up and returned to the pack. "I think that makes us even."

She dug around for the adrenaline and found an EpiPen. "Is this it?"

"Not even close."

She turned and he'd somehow sat up, his smile gone. "This isn't the adrenaline?"

He held out his hand. "I mean, I hardly think you pulling me like a buoy out of the water—"

"You weren't a buoy. You were a freaking boulder. It took both Blessing and me to get you to safety, and then you scared me to death by almost not breathing."

He took the adrenaline from her and shot himself in the leg. "*Almost* not breathing."

"It's a thing."

He looked up at her, his face sharp edged, those aqua-blue eyes shiny under the starry sky, still impressive despite his shoulder wound. For a moment the craziness of it all simply took her breath away again.

Ranger Kingston was here, in the middle-of-nowhere Nigeria.

It was just like God to send her the one man she hoped to never see again. She sank down on the sand. "You scared me."

His lips tightened. "I don't know what happened. I must have had a shallow water blackout." He reached for his pack and she handed it over to him. He deposited the empty tube inside. "Thanks. You did save my life."

A shallow water blackout. Oh. My. But there it was, their past right in front of her again. And she didn't know what it cost him to say that, but maybe not as much as she thought because he looked up and smiled at her. Unexpected. Sweet. Devestating.

Oh no. She couldn't do this again. Let a man into her heart who was only destined to destroy it.

"We need to get out of here," she said and found her feet.

"I need to check in." He lifted his radio and tried it. Not a hint of static.

She met his eyes. "It went swimming. Along with the phone I stole from one of the guards—I tried to turn it on, but it's dead. Maybe it will dry out."

He nodded, probably too exhausted to take it all in. "Okay. So, the chopper is . . ." He pulled out a map from the top of his pack, looked up at the stars, at the river, and then spread the map out between his legs. "Here." He pointed at a place southwest of them—more west than south though.

"How far is that?"

"Ten klicks maybe. The river brought us way out of range."

"And we'd have to cross it again."

He looked over at Blessing. She'd gotten up and now was pulling off her soaking hijab and abaya.

"The team is gone anyway," he finally said. "But coming in, we spotted a village." He turned back to the map. "Here." He pointed to a place downriver, maybe five miles. "Think you two can make it?"

"Please. The only easy day was yesterday. I was raised by a SEAL, if you forgot."

He folded up the map and shoved it into his pack. "That, I will never forget, Noemi."

He didn't look at her, but she heard his words anyway.

"Why didn't you tell me your father was a SEAL?"

She hadn't lied. She was just bound by the same rules he was.

It didn't matter anymore, anyway.

"Let's go."

But Blessing had sat down again in the dirt, her legs pulled up to herself, not budging.

"Blessing?" Noemi crouched in front of her. "We need to go."

She shook her head.

"Honey, we can't stay here. The men . . ."

The girl looked up at Ranger then, her eyes on the man who still looked very much like a terrorist, if not better armored and well fed.

"Ranger. Tell her something . . . I don't know. Tell her she's safe." When he didn't move, she got up. "She's scared. And she's a Christian, like you. Maybe . . . tell her God loves her or something. You know, like the stuff you used to say to me, about God having a good plan for us, and how he won't forsake us."

He drew in a breath. Met her eyes. Then shook his head. "Sorry, Noemi. I'm not . . . I've got nothing."

And neither did she. If Ranger had anything, he had faith. It was the one thing that she counted on. Sure, he was brave and strong and solid, but he also believed that God was with him.

It kept her from wondering, from fearing that something terrible had happened to him.

"I don't understand—"

He walked past her and crouched in front of Blessing. "Listen. I know you're scared. But if you don't come with me, then those bad men are going to find you and do terrible things to you. I'm your only chance at staying alive. So either get up and come with me now, or I'm walking away." He stood up.

Oh. Wow.

Noemi felt freshly punched, her throat raw.

But yes, now *there* was the Ranger she remembered. The one she walked away from—practically fled—with her heart in pieces.

"Good job, Ranger," she said. "Now we all feel better." She held out her hand to the girl. "Get up, honey. I'm not going to let anything happen to you." Blessing took her hand.

His jaw tightened. "Keep up." Then he whirled around and headed out into the night.

And she sighed, pulling Blessing along. Because she was terribly, painfully right.

She had somehow killed Ranger Kingston.

Just get to the village.

Get to the village, secure a vehicle and a cell phone, contact Ham, and get out of Nigeria.

And most of all, stay upright.

Because Ranger hurt everywhere, but nowhere more than in his chest, because just being around Noemi had a way of ripping open old wounds. Old desires.

And of course, his biggest regrets.

The sounds of the night rose around them as they walked along the river. The rush of the water, the chirrup of birds, the washboard warble of crickets, the occasional roar and moan of a bigger animal. He held his H&K in both hands, not because he feared their pursuers—their leap into the river and chaotic downstream journey had done its job—but because the weight of the strap on his shoulder could cut him in half.

He'd broken something—his collarbone, his shoulder, *something*—because he could barely move his left arm. The gunshot had gone through, so sure, his muscle was shredded there, but it was worse than that. The clotting agent, which had slowed his blood loss during their run from the camp, had loosened during his little swim and now blood warmed his sleeve. He was probably leaving a trail as wide as the Alaskan Highway.

Not only that, but he must have bruised his ribs when he'd slammed into the rock, despite his tactical vest, which accounted for why every breath, every step sent a spear of heat through him.

"Pain is just weakness leaving the body." Or so said his SEAL instructors.

If he were alone, he might find a place to hole up and just rest. But he wasn't alone. And Blessing, at least, was a liability. The girl was terrified, and that only led to bad impulses that could get them all killed.

There wasn't room for emotion on a battlefield.

"Tell her God loves her or something. You know, like the stuff you used to say to me, about God having a good plan for us, and how he won't forsake us."

He'd been a fool back then. Or maybe now—he wasn't sure. All he knew is that they had about six hours until daylight, and by then he wanted to be on a plane back to American shores, and then, probably, Alaska.

After all, he had nowhere else to go, did he?

A snap behind him and a tiny scream made him turn.

Noemi had slapped her hand over Blessing's mouth, but now she pointed to a snake disappearing into the rushes. "Sorry."

"You okay?" He shouldn't have barked at the girl, probably.

Blessing nodded, but Noemi looked at him. "You're walking too fast. She's barefoot."

Never mind that Noemi was barefoot too.

"I'll slow down." He slowed to walk beside them, the air

muggy and heavy on him. The adrenaline had started to wane from his body.

"What are we going to do when we get to the village? You can't walk in there, all kitted up. You'll scare everyone."

He'd thought about that. "I'll sneak in, get a car—"

"Steal a car, you mean."

He pursed his lips. "You have a better idea?"

She fell silent.

"Listen. I'm just trying to figure out our next step without alerting the entire country to our presence. We're not exactly legal here."

"I know. I just . . ." She shook her head. "Most of these people live in poverty. A vehicle is a big deal. I don't like the idea of stealing it." She sighed. "I still can't believe that you're here. How did you even find us?"

He didn't want to let on to the truth—that he hadn't known she was among the group. Not that it would have changed anything.

In truth, if he'd known, Ranger would have stood up shouting, "Pick me, pick me," because, well, regrets. "Colt works for a security company run by an old SEAL teammate, Hamilton Jones. And Fraser Marshall used to be on the teams too. So, Ham called me when he discovered his guys had been taken. Lit a fire under us when he heard they might be executing Colt."

She shivered. "They played at it. Set him up in front of a camera, stood with a machete over him. I think they were hoping he might break. He just stared at the camera . . . no emotion. Ready to die."

Huh. Well, he supposed that's what he'd do too.

"What happened back in camp? Colt started a ruckus."

"You saw that?"

"We've been surveilling you for a while, developing a plan. When you staged that little getaway, it showed us a way in." He glanced at her. "Your dad would have been proud."

She met his eyes, briefly, smiled. "I think he would prefer if we'd never been taken."

"How did you get taken?"

"It's my fault, really," she said. "One of my jobs is to find living relatives of the refugee orphans, and then reunite them. We discovered that Blessing has family living in Lakawa, and when we didn't hear from them—we tried to call a few times—we thought we'd just take a day trip. Dr. Aaron was visiting the school—he and his wife are major benefactors—and I thought he'd enjoy seeing a local village. Selah came with us, of course, because she speaks fluent pidgin, but really, the entire trip was my idea."

They'd come to a bend in the river, the water slowing here as a tributary cut west. The wind rustled through the trees, the air carrying something feral. He slowed.

"When we got there, the village was deserted. Or so we thought—"

He put a hand on her arm. "Stop." Then he motioned them down.

Under the glistening light of the moon, an elephant splashed in the river. High-pitched squeaks came from another, smaller elephant on the opposite shore.

"Dey be a parade of elephants over there." The words came from Blessing, who pointed out the dark shapes. "We be quiet, we no scare."

He got up. "Vest."

Noemi grabbed hold of his webbing.

Just her hand on the vest, tugging it slightly, made him want to gasp. Okay, so he was more injured than he thought, and frankly, starting to feel nauseous. As if he might have blood pooling in his gut.

That or some kind of bacteria from the river.

Yeah, he would be crocodile fodder by now if she hadn't pulled him out.

"The village wasn't deserted?" he asked as he began walking. The sun had started to dent the far horizon, just faintly. They had two hours until full daylight, but they were moving at the pace of a box turtle.

"No." Noemi had moved up beside him, Blessing falling behind. He glanced over to see if she was keeping up. So far, so good.

"We found the entire village—some one hundred people—in the village church. All dead."

He stopped. Stared at her. "What did you say?"

She, too, stopped. "They were dead."

"What do you mean, dead?"

"Um. As in—"

"I know what you mean, but I'm asking how. Boko Haram attack?" It would give a reason for their sudden kidnapping.

"No. They were on pallets on the floor, or hammocks. They died of a disease. And a fast one."

"Ebola?" And now he could feel those tiny bacteria filling his veins, eating cellular tissue . . .

"I don't think so. They had a rash and pustules."

"Smallpox."

"That's what Dr. Aaron said. But although smallpox has an incubation of up to fourteen days, it's only really contagious once it has started showing pustules. And even then, it takes four to seven days for the illness to run its course. It seems unlikely that word wouldn't have gotten out to the other villages. I took pictures and he took samples, but we were still in the church when these guys showed up on a truck. There were just a handful of them, but they shot Dr. Aaron and jumped Fraser. Then they grabbed Selah and . . . Colt could do nothing but surrender."

No wonder his brother was willing to get beaten—or die—to help them escape.

"They dragged us to this camp, and we sat there for three weeks, wondering what they were going to do to us."

"Sell you all," he said crisply. "Colt and Fraser would net a nice sum, once they figured out they were former operators. And . . . well, I don't want to think of what they'd do to you." He glanced at her. "They didn't—"

"No."

Her simple answer released a sudden, wrenched fist in his chest.

"But only because of Moses, I think."

"Moses?"

"Our interpreter. He kept bargaining with them, telling them we were valuable and not to hurt us. They killed him when I . . ." Noemi swallowed.

"It wasn't your fault," he said quietly. "They were probably always going to kill him. They were just waiting for the right time."

She ran a hand across her cheek. "I know that's what my dad would have said, but"—she lifted her shoulder—"I was just trying to get help."

"You *did* get help."

She looked up at him.

He offered a smile, and for a second was back in Key West. *"Take a breath there, sailor. Nothing's going to happen here. I'm harmless."*

Not even a little true.

"You were very brave, Noemi." He looked away. "The big question is . . . what did you see in that village that made them want to take you—"

A roar stopped him. It echoed out over the river, carried in the wind, something of hunger, of power, maybe of warning.

"Lion," Blessing said.

Perfect.

He slowed, put his scope to his eye and scanned the area. He'd lost his helmet in the river, and his naked eye saw nothing, despite the loosening of the darkness.

"Let's pick it up," he said.

He got no argument from the ladies as they veered away from the river, following a footpath etched into the grassland. It led them through a thick woodland, the forest awakening with the sounds of doves and geese, a hornbill, and a strange whooping in the distance.

"Baboons," Blessing said, now keeping up with him. "Sunrise soon."

She was dressed in a short-sleeve blouse and a patterned skirt, her hair pulled back. Pretty girl, young, but she'd survived, so he had to give her props for that.

The root came out of nowhere. Just like that, he hit the dirt. The crash was so abrupt—so stupid—he just lay there a second, seeing gray, his shoulder pain crumpling him.

"Range!" Noemi crouched beside him. "Are you okay?"

The dawn had dented the gray, and he saw now that she wore a pair of grimy khaki shorts and a long-sleeve, cotton-gauze shirt. Her hair had dried into tight curls, clearly the result of their dunk in the river. But shoot—still beautiful.

"Yeah. Sorry. A little light-headed." He pushed himself up, but he emitted a groan, and the world spun. So maybe he'd also lost a little too much blood.

"Oh my gosh! Ranger, your clothes are saturated." She pulled back her hand from where she touched him, then tried to help him as he sat up. "You're still bleeding."

"Yeah. But I'm out of med supplies, so—"

"So nothing." She reached for his vest and unclipped it.

"What are you doing?"

"Checking out your wound. We need to stop the bleeding."

He gritted his teeth as she took off the vest. They really didn't have time for this, but even as she lifted the protection off, as the weight released, he found his body giving way.

It felt a little like BUD/S all over again, holding himself together by sheer will. One breath at a time. One step at a time.

"Let's get you against this tree," Noemi said, looking at Blessing.

"I can—"

But Noemi stepped right over him, grabbed him around the waist, and hiked him in one big move against a nearby tree.

He nearly stopped breathing and not just because of her presence. When she set him down, his entire skeleton seemed to shatter inside him, pieces jabbing into soft parts, and he gasped.

"Sorry."

He leaned his head against the tree, just trying to take small breaths. *Don't pass out. Don't—*

"I'm going to be sick," he said and then rolled over and, yeah, let out the meager contents of his stomach. Nothing but bile, but he felt a little better.

Except when a trail of blood emerged from his spittle. He wiped his mouth. Grimaced.

"Now I'm scared," Noemi said. She stepped back from him. "You're in bad shape."

"I just need a second—"

"You need an entire emergency room!" She stood over him now, stalking away, standing with her back to him.

Blessing just stared at him.

He felt like an idiot. Get *up*.

He put his hand to the tree. "The village isn't too far."

Noemi whirled around, came back to him. "Sit. Stay. I'll go to the village and get help."

"That's a bad idea."

"That's the *only* idea." She knelt next to him. "I won't give up if you won't."

His mouth tightened. "There's a thousand euros in my vest. Front pocket."

"There's the Ranger I know. Principled despite the moment." She grabbed the money roll from his vest.

"No. I'm just not sure you know how to hot-wire a car."

"Please." She held up the cash. "But I'll try this first."

He grabbed her arm, the movement sending waves of pain through his body. "Be careful."

She wove her fingers into his hand. "It's my turn to save you, sailor. I got you into this mess." Then, she leaned forward and kissed his grimy, sweaty forehead.

"Auntie Noemi." Blessing stepped up to her. "I will stay here and pray."

He wished that made him feel any better. Especially since, as Noemi ran into the dusky sunrise, another deep-throated roar lifted over the grassy savannah.

If she just kept her mouth shut, no one would get killed.

At least this was Tae's working theory as she sat in her room at the Alaska Regional Hospital in Anchorage.

And so far, so good. It did require her to stifle her gut-level response to the nurse's questions, to effect a thousand-yard stare, and to generally put her life into the hands of others—Nurses. Doctors. And now a stranger named Barry Kingston.

Apparently, Barry was her current last resort.

But he came with a hideaway in the Alaskan wilderness, a generous offer to house her until her memory returned, and no questions asked. Like, how she'd ended up in a snowbank near a remote ranger cabin, nearly frostbitten and severely hypothermic.

The doctors had their own questions—like why she hadn't regained her speech or her memory after emerging from the induced coma. Two CT scans, an MRI, meetings with a psychologist and a speech therapist, an EEG biofeedback test, and even an EMDR treatment and still . . . nothing.

She just couldn't risk it.

Nurse Oolanie came into the room. She'd been the one who cared for Tae during her wanderings in the shadows, when her brain warred with waking up at all.

The nurse was pretty—round face, dark hair, sunny disposition. She could nearly convince Tae that everything would be okay.

Nearly.

Tae turned from where she sat in a wheelchair facing the massive picture window. The sun arched high over the Alaskan range to the north, Denali still snow-capped and formidible, but over the past few weeks since she'd been rescued, spring had swept across the Alaskan bush, greening the world.

Turning Alaska from treacherous to breathtaking.

If only.

Admittedly, she'd mostly been staring at her reflection, despite the beauty beyond. She hardly recognized the woman who stared back. Her blond hair had turned limp, scraggly, long and brittle, her eyes a pale blue, still a little disbelieving. And her bones seemed to rub together with the weight she'd lost.

Pitiful.

But maybe anyone who came looking for her would simply keep right on looking.

"Ready to go, Jane?"

She nodded at the nurse.

"Perfect." Nurse Oolanie opened the door and motioned someone inside.

The man seemed kind enough. Probably late sixties, he wore a hat imprinted with the words Sky King Ranch over his nearly white, almost-shaven hair and sported a thick mustache, a leather jacket, and jeans. "Hey there, Jane," he said as he came toward her, his hand out.

She shook it, no words offered.

"This is Echo, my, um, future daughter-in-law." He gestured to a woman with green eyes and golden-brown hair in braids, who was wearing a fleece jacket. She gave Barry a smile at his stumble over her introduction.

"Hey there," she said. "Actually, my fiancé and I were the ones who found you."

Oh. She knew a man had found her—had a foggy recollection of being carried by him out of the snow—or maybe she simply dreamed it after Nurse Oolanie had told her the story. It seemed, however, his voice might be buried deep inside.

She also knew this woman's voice, deep in her bones.

She nearly opened her mouth to offer a thank-you.

Nope. The best thing she could do for them was stay silent. Unknown.

She nodded and offered a smile.

"Okay, so, she's ready to go, Mr. Kingston," said the nurse. "Thanks for being willing to take her. Dodge put his name on her intake paperwork, so we didn't know who else to call."

"Glad to help, Sissy," Barry said and glanced down at Tae. "You can stay as long as you need."

Again, the kindness. She didn't know what to do with the rush of emotion that filled her chest.

Please, let her not hurt anyone.

The nurse held out a bag to Echo. "Just a few things from the hospital bin—clothing and her toiletries from her stay."

"Still no luck tracking down her family?" Echo said as the nurse got behind the wheelchair.

"No. We ran her fingerprints and DNA through the system, but she's not listed."

Of course she wasn't. At least not in the ones accessible by the national health database.

"Poor thing. Having no one, no memory, no speech." They exited the room out into the hallway, Echo walking behind her, speaking to the nurse.

"And the doctors can't figure out why. Maybe she just needs time. And there's no better place to rest in Copper Mountain than Sky King Ranch."

"We've just reroofed one of the cabins, and we're working on the others," Echo said. "And the field is full of wildflowers—it's gorgeous down by the lake."

"There's a rumor that Ranger came home," said the nurse. "Moose saw him at the Midnight Sun Saloon with Dodge." They reached the elevator and Barry Kingston called it up.

He turned. "Yeah. Came home about a week ago and said Colt might be in some kind of trouble." He glanced at Echo, and Tae didn't have to be a psychologist to see that he was hiding something.

More than trouble was her guess.

"Dodge and Ranger went to see if they could help out." He turned his back to them as the elevator dinged.

"Really. So . . . you think Colt might be coming home too?"

Funny, the sound of her voice. Casual, but oh so interested. Made her wonder who this Colt was.

They entered the elevator, and the nurse turned the chair around.

"Maybe," Barry said, but he took a breath. "We hope they all come home."

So, this trouble was something dangerous.

Silence ballooned inside the box.

They landed on the first floor, and the doors opened into the lobby. Nurse Oolanie wheeled Tae out to the front.

"I'll get the truck," Echo said and pushed through the doors.

Barry Kingston stood, shifting weight, glancing down at her then back to Nurse Oolanie.

"Let us know if her memory starts to return," she said.

"Will do. Don't worry. We'll take good care of her."

A truck pulled up into the circle. Barry headed for the door even as Echo got out and walked around to the front.

"Can she walk?" Echo said as Nurse Oolanie pushed her to the sidewalk.

Tae nodded her own answer, but the nurse spoke up. "Yes. She is weak, though, so watch her."

"She can't be that weak," Barry said, opening the door as the nurse locked the wheels. "She survived an Alaskan blizzard out in the elements."

Yeah. What he said.

Still, Tae wobbled a little as she pressed out of the chair.

"Got her?" Nurse Oolanie asked as Barry reached out for her hand.

Tae took it and let him help her into the back seat.

He closed the door behind her, turned and said something to the nurse.

It felt weird for them to speak about her as if she wasn't there.

But maybe she wasn't. She wasn't anywhere.

Taylor Price was gone from this world. Echo got into the driver's side, Barry in the passenger seat. And as they pulled away from the curb toward someplace north of the hospital, deep in the Alaskan wilderness, she knew she intended on keeping it that way.

FOUR

Just keep moving. Don't look back.

Forward is your only option.

With the sun denting the darkness to the east, Noemi could just barely make out the thatched and rusty tin roofs of the village, carved out of the wooded hillside.

The grasses had thinned, replaced by tiny garden plots cordoned off by stick fences. Inside grew tall cornstalks, cocoa, and coffee plants. A wind whipped from hills surrounding the village, carrying with it the scent of life, of the mango trees growing near the houses, a hint of dust. It raked the layer of grimy sweat from her body.

She stopped behind a massive Kuka tree and surveyed the community.

Maybe twenty houses, all clumped together around a central packed-dirt courtyard. A goat ran from behind a house, its bell clanging. Brightly colored laundry—royal blue, yellow, pink, and orange dresses—hung on lines between the houses. A building that seemed like the community center sat in the middle of the village, a wooden porch encircling it. A thin, wire-haired gray dog lifted its head, sniffed the air.

She probably smelled like the local wildlife. Looked like it too.

Elsewhere, more dogs barked, and a rooster crowed out the morning. A battered motorcycle was propped against a cement building, a red hen pecked the ground around it. Beside the door, a wisp of smoke lifted from a metal drum—its fire maybe dying, maybe stirring to life.

Her gaze went again to the motorcycle.

That could work.

She eased out from behind the tree.

A shout lifted in the air and she stilled, turned to see a woman, a jug on her head, dressed in a long pink-and-green-patterned gown, a deep-orange headscarf. She carried a machete in one hand and lifted it. "Who are you?"

Noemi held up her hands as the woman came toward her.

"Who are you?" Her voice carried into the morning.

"I'm . . . I need help."

The woman stood in front of her. Middle-aged, she wore her years in her hips, her eyes. "What is this bikpela?"

The woman gestured to the blood on her shirt, her hands. Ranger's blood. Noemi wiped her hands on her shorts. "It's not mine. But my friend is hurt. I need help."

The woman was shaking her head, gesturing with her machete. "Comot. No wahala! No wahala!" She stepped closer to Noemi, met her eyes, and shouted. "Comot!"

Noemi eyed the machete, then took a step back. "Listen, I just need a car . . . or that motorcycle." She pointed toward the house. "I need to help my friend. He's hurt."

The woman lowered the machete. "American?"

Noemi didn't know if the woman was referring to her or her friend, but she took a chance and nodded.

The woman pursed her lips. Then, "Follow me." She stalked past Noemi into the village, shouting at a dog that darted near her. She set the jug near the smoking bin, then headed toward the community building.

Noemi eyed the bike as she walked by. A Suzuki GS450. With a kick start. Her gaze found the ignition wires that ran from the engine to the faring. She'd just have to pull the wires from the bottom of the instrument cluster until they broke, then find the yellow and green wires from the magneto and cross them. At least then she'd have spark. She'd bet, by the condition of the bike, the lock was broken.

She'd just have to kick start it, and she'd be gone.

Oh, for Pete's sake. She was as bad as Ranger.

A small child had appeared at the door of the house, a little girl wearing a green dress, her hair in tiny tufts around her head. The woman looked at her and gestured her inside. "Make you no vex me!"

Noemi glanced at the child, who headed to the building.

"Now, *now*!" The woman stood on the steps of the building, gesturing. Noemi climbed the steps to the porch and stood at the entrance, wordless.

Inside was a small church, a few plastic chairs pushed against the once-whitewashed walls, a wooden cross on the wall at the front.

"You sit." The woman pointed inside.

She entered. The peaked roof had gathered the heat of the building, leaving it cooler in the shadows of the early morning. A candle at the altar sat half burned, misshapen.

"Sister?" A middle-aged man had entered behind her. Tall and rail thin, he wore a blue button-up shirt and a pair of worn dress pants, fraying sandals. He smiled at her, his eyes gentle. "I am Ibrahim Yusuf, and you are safe here."

Strangely, her throat tightened, her eyes filling. He walked over to her, gestured to a nearby chair. "You need help."

She found herself nodding, and a tear escaped. "I thought . . . I thought maybe you were Fulani."

"We are a Christian village, sister," he said. "Are you hungry?"

Famished, but that didn't matter. Still, she found herself nodding.

He turned to the woman who stood at the door. He said something to her in a local dialect, and as she left, sent a quick glance at Noemi she couldn't read.

"Please forgive Sister Gimbiya. She lost her husband to the Fulani and is still grieving." His gaze swept over her. "You are hurt?"

She scanned her body, the blood on her blouse, the scratches on her legs, some of them open. And her feet, yes, they bore significant damage, despite the toughening of the last three weeks. "I'm not hurt. But my friend is."

"Your friend. Is he American too?"

She stilled. "I just need transportation." Her gaze went to the window. A small group of onlookers had gathered outside. Elderly men, a few women, children. Some of the younger men carried machetes.

"Don't be afraid." Ibrahim lowered his voice. "We know about you, the Americans taken hostage."

She should leave. And for the first time wished she'd carried Ranger's Sig Sauer into the village. Or a knife, at least.

"I don't want trouble," she said, her voice soft. "I just need transportation. I . . . I have money—"

Gimbiya walked through the door holding a wooden bowl, a massive green leaf on the top. "Wusai do dey go?" She walked up to Noemi. "Come chop."

Noemi looked at the bowl. Gimbiya lifted the leaf. Rice with tomatoes, seasoned with black-eyed pea leaves.

"Come chop," Gimbiya said again.

Noemi took the bowl. "Thank you."

Gimbiya bowed her head as she backed away. Then she turned to Ibrahim. "Wetin dey happen?"

"I no no," he said. But he lowered his voice and spoke something softly to her.

Gimbiya looked at Noemi. "Na so?"

Ibrahim turned to Noemi. "She wants to know if you are serious about having money."

She glanced outside. Heard her father's voice. *"Take some risks."*

"Yes," she said.

"How much?"

"A thousand euros."

Gimbiya drew in a breath, then turned back to Ibrahim. "Abeg! No waste my time."

"God don butta your bread," he said quietly.

She considered him, then turned to Noemi. "Gi mi." And held out her hand.

"Sold," Ibrahim said and smiled.

Sold? She looked between Gimbiya and Ibrahim. Okay, um. They'd just have to figure out how to fit on the bike.

It was better than nothing.

She reached into her front pocket and pulled out the wad of bills. Please let her not be handing over her life too.

Gimbiya practically snatched the money from her hand, unrolled it, and counted it. Then she looked at Noemi and gestured with her head.

Noemi followed her out of the church, down the steps. The small crowd parted. Ibrahim walked behind her.

"It belonged to her husband, but she can't drive it, so it sits. But her daughter needs surgery, so this will get what she needs. You're a miracle. An answer to prayer."

They walked toward the house. Noemi expected Gimbiya to stop at the motorcycle, but she continued, past the house, opening a gate that led to a tiny garden. Tomatoes, onions, and potatoes grew in the small plot, chickens roamed the yard, and a goat, heavy with milk, was tied to a post.

Beyond the plot a thin trail led to a ramshackle hut, mostly covered with an overgrowth of trees and vines. She opened a broken gate and stood back.

Inside sat a very old, dented, formerly white Peugeot station wagon. A crack ran diagonally across the windshield, and the front fender had been tied on with chicken wire.

What?

Noemi stepped into the tiny garage and peered inside the car. Orange interior, although covered in dust and mice droppings. Four speed, on the dash.

"Does it run?"

Ibrahim nodded. "Her son uses it, sometimes, for hauling coffee or cocoa beans. The tires are thin, so you might need to replace them, but there is a spare in the back. And a half tank of gas, so you can take the extra diesel."

He pointed to the canister on the floor.

"Are you sure? I can't take—"

"Yes, you can. She needs the money. You need the car." He turned to two boys who had followed them to the makeshift garage. "Azi, you and Emenike push it out."

Noemi watched as the two boys, early teens, scooted around the car to the back. One opened the rear hatch window and climbed through to the driver's seat. He sat in it and grinned at her.

The other pushed and slowly the wagon rolled out of the garage. A narrow path led out of the village and down the road. If she followed it west, she'd meet up with Ranger and Blessing.

The driver braked and got out. She turned and spotted the villagers who crowded into Gimbiya's garden.

Gimbiya also spotted them. "Comot!" She shooed them away with her hands.

Noemi got into the car. It smelled thickly of rodents, dust, and age but, hooyah, wheels.

She could almost believe Ibrahim's words. A miracle. Huh.

Or, just happy circumstance. She set the rice on the seat, then turned the key. The engine coughed, then died. At least the battery worked.

The car turned over on the second try, a cloud of diesel exhaust fogging the air. She put it in gear, then pressed the brakes. They seemed tight.

She popped the hood, got out and opened it. Located and pulled out the oil stick. Grabbing a leaf, she wiped off the oil, then dipped the stick back in to check the level. Blessing must be out there praying her little heart out because, although the oil was sticky, the tank was almost full.

Noemi opened the radiator. Water, check.

When she closed the hood, Gimbiya stood next to Ibrahim, tears cutting down her cheeks. Noemi walked over to her. "Thank you."

Gimbiya nodded, then turned away.

"Be safe, sister," Ibrahim said.

Noemi got in the car. The dash was ripped, but the steering worked as she put the car into first and eased down the rutted road. She'd traveled through the woodland east, so she followed the road west, then north when it turned. The smell of the river beckoned through the open window. The sun had risen, turning the morning golden.

Yes, she stank and felt as if she might be harboring a frenzy of bacteria in her hair. Her clothes were nearly brown with grime and the smell of the rice made her want to stop and shove her face into it. But they had a car.

A *car*.

Now all they needed was cell phone service.

She found where they'd turned off, into the bush following the footpath, and directed her car into the rutted grass. It wasn't so thick that she couldn't simply follow—

Blessing stood in the middle of the path, holding a stick, her face as stiff as a Maasai warrior. In the sunlight, she looked brutal, her hair matted, her clothing soiled. No wonder Gimbiya had panicked when she'd seen Noemi.

And why Ibrahim had offered her food.

She braked and got out. "It's me!"

It took a moment, but Blessing lowered her stick, then let out a cry. "Oh, auntie! Come quick! I think he is dead!"

He didn't want to say goodbye.

See, this is why Ranger didn't do dating, or even casual friendships with women, because eventually it would lead to this—

A beautiful sun-soaked day on the ocean, his face to the wind, and a woman's laughter in the air as they sailed across the Boca Grande Channel back to Key West.

A beautiful day with a beautiful woman who had somehow gotten inside his heart. Two weeks, and he'd started to wake up with Noemi being the first thing on his mind . . . When could he sneak in a moment to see her? He'd started hungering for her smile, her laughter. And when she touched him—let her hand linger on his arm, or brushed against him, shoulder to shoulder—it ignited a desire that felt downright dangerous. She was easy to talk to, easy to be around.

Easy to love.

Shoot. He just might be falling for her, hard.

And tomorrow, it would end.

Unless, somehow, he figured out how to . . . oh he had no idea. It wasn't like she could follow him to sniper school.

And then he'd be back with Team Five.

The teams had always been his life. But for the first time, maybe he wanted more.

"I told you sailing was the bomb." Noemi's voice raised from behind where he stood at the wheel of the thirty-foot sailboat he'd rented for the day. He'd gotten a swim in early this morning and one final practice before meeting her at the Key West boatyard where her father was still patching up their sailboat.

He'd seen their sloop from afar as they pulled out on the pretty little Catalina. It was still up on stilts in the yard, her father standing under the blue hull, sanding a hole near the waterline under the keel. A solid man, maybe six foot, blond hair, his skin bearing a hint of red, as Norwegian as they came. He lifted a hand to Noemi as she blew the horn.

She'd taken the helm off the dock and barked out orders to him as Ranger learned how to reel out the jib sheet and the mainsheet, how to steer so the wind guides were horizontal, and the different angles of reach.

"See how the wind is coming at us?" Noemi explained as she stood at the wheel. She wore a pair of black shorts and a red swim top, her hair back in a red headband. "This is close haul. Our sails act like the wing of a plane, pulling the boat forward."

They were heeled over, and he sat on the lower side, trailing his hand in the water. A pod of dolphins had followed them once they got into open water, diving and racing the boat for a good mile. The sea was gentle today, the wind less than ten knots, and the boat skimmed along at a nice five-knot speed. The sun glistened into the blue, and he couldn't wait to get in the water, do some snorkeling.

He was better in the water than out.

"I love sailing." Noemi capped her lemonade. Set the container in the beach bag of snacks. "My dad picked it up after my mother died. I think she always wanted to sail, and it was his way of connecting with her."

He wore board shorts and a sleeveless Key West–branded shirt she'd picked up for him but had ditched his baseball hat when the wind tried to grab it. "When did your mom die?"

"When I was fourteen. She had brain cancer, which is super ironic since she was a brain surgeon." She looked down at him, her smile wry. "That's when my dad stopped traveling so much."

He hadn't gotten the entire story about her father, but the man was military of some sort—he knew it, from the things she didn't tell him and the way she didn't ask too many questions about Ranger's life. Like where he was going next.

Or maybe she simply didn't want to wreck the magic either.

"I'm sorry. That's rough when you're an only child."

"It was. I'd been at boarding school most of my life, so we weren't close. But I loved her."

He lifted his face to the sun. "I have two brothers and a sister, and it was still tough when my mom died. She also had cancer. I was six."

"Oh, that's young."

"Yeah. I was pretty close with my grandfather, so that helped, but my brothers didn't handle it well. My oldest brother kept to himself. Didn't talk about his grief. Sort of dove into helping my dad, learning to fly. And Colt—"

"He's younger than you?"

"Middle. I'm the youngest. By five minutes."

"You don't look alike."

"The three of us are fraternal."

She glanced at him, grinning. "I'm not complaining, sailor." She turned back to the wheel. "We'll need to tack soon."

He got up and stood behind her. "Colt was with our mom when she died, and he just sorta fell apart. Got into trouble, started fighting. My sister, Larke, seems to think he was trying to keep from feeling it."

"Yeah. I think my dad did that for a while. Buried himself in his work. He never does anything halfway, but I think it's just a way for him to forget what he lost. My parents were crazy about each other. Let's tack."

He held a line in each hand. She gave the signal, and he released the line in his left hand and pulled with his right. The mainsail switched positions across the boat.

The boat heeled over the other way.

"Good job," she said. "Your turn to steer."

He stepped up to the helm. "So how did they meet each other?"

She sat on the bench, her legs up, her eyes to the sky. "Italy. My dad was wounded on an op—" Her mouth closed as she looked at him, her eyes wide.

He laughed. "I know he was an operator. It's okay."

She considered him a moment, then, "My mother worked at a medical base in Italy. She specialized in head trauma, and he'd had a percussion injury. Thankfully it wasn't serious, and after he was sent stateside, they kept in touch. He eventually came back to Italy, married her, and they moved to San Diego. She was a few years older than him, but no one made him laugh like my mother."

"Was she Italian?"

She shook her head. "Nigerian. She moved to Italy for school."

"Have you ever been to Nigeria to visit her family?"

"No. But someday. It's on the bucket list."

"It feels like that's a fairly large list."

"It is. And it includes seeing a shark." She nudged their snorkel equipment. "Don't let me down, sailor."

He couldn't stop himself. Not with the question just aching inside him. "So, what happens after this?"

He'd meant sort of cosmically, but she lifted a shoulder. "I'm heading to Uganda. I have an opportunity to help in a refugee camp. My freshman college roommate, Selah, is a missionary of sorts, and she asked if I'd help teach English."

"Dangerous country."

"I'll be okay. My dad taught me skills."

Maybe he shouldn't ask, but, "Skills?"

"I'm an expert marksman, I know how to make a fire with a mirror, and I can tie ten different knots, blindfolded and underwater."

He looked at her. "Really?"

"Not underwater." She smiled. "Just making sure you were listening."

Oh, he was listening. Especially the part about Uganda. Where terrorists ravaged small villages and last year two aid workers went missing. Too close to South Sudan for his liking. In fact, so much of Africa was overrun with militant groups.

"Have you thought about Madagascar? I hear that's a nice place to visit."

She splashed him. "Not hardly. It's in the middle of a drought."

"How about Miami?"

"You sound like my father. Listen. I'm smart. And careful. And . . . okay, if I ever get into trouble, I'll call you. How about that?"

He turned to her and knew he wore too much earnestness in his eyes. "Promise."

She blinked at him, and then grinned. "Well, well."

He hadn't a clue what she meant by that. But as she got up and slipped under his arms, pressed her back to him, his entire body alerted to her tucked up against him. She smelled like the sea and a hint of mint, maybe something in her hair.

Ahead of them, the Dry Tortugas and Fort Jefferson rose on the horizon. Already the ferry had pulled up to the dock, and a few sailboats anchored offshore, near the south coaling dock ruins. The spray of the ocean dappled the heat of his skin, and he couldn't wait to get into the water.

"So, was becoming a SEAL your way of coping?"

He stilled, not sure—

"With your mother's death." She put her hands on his wrists, holding on as the boat skimmed through the waves.

Right. "I guess so. I poured everything I was, since I was a kid, into becoming an operator. It's all I am."

"No, it's not." She turned in his arms, put her hands around his waist, looked up at him.

Oh, she was pretty, smiling up at him like that. "Noemi." He swallowed, met her eyes. "Wow, I want to kiss you."

"Keep your hands on that wheel, sailor. I just like holding on. Because I know tomorrow you're leaving me."

He blinked, his throat tight.

"Unless, of course, you don't pass your exam and have to repeat this evolution." She laid her head on his chest. "Just, please don't die."

He had nothing for that. "Noemi. I'm not going to die."

She looked up. "It's fifty feet without air. I know how they do the test. You have to make it down, and back up and—"

"You know about the test? How?"

She leaned back. Ducked under his arm. "I know that it's dangerous. And that I would be very, very sad if anything happened to you." She pointed to a place in the anchoring area. "Let's go there."

"I'll be fine."

Her lips thinned to a line. "Says every operator before they go into battle."

He turned the boat so the sails luffed, then looked at her. Her eyes glistened. He touched her face, cupping her cheek with his hand. "I'm not unprepared. I train and train so I'll be ready. The more I sweat in training—"

"The less you'll bleed in battle. I get it." She wiped a hand under her eyes. "Sorry. I'm not sure what's wrong with me. Let's anchor."

But he didn't move, the sight of her crying finding its own anchor inside him. "Noemi. I don't . . . what if . . ." But he hadn't a clue what to say. Just . . . not goodbye.

She looked at him, those golden-brown eyes in his. "Promise me you won't die."

"I can't make that promise. You know that. But I can tell you that I'm trained. I'm strong, and God has my back. I believe he has a good plan for me, and he won't forsake me. And I *do* promise that I'll do everything I can to stay alive."

She touched his chest, hooked a finger into the neck of his shirt. "That'll do. Now, kiss me, sailor."

It took everything inside him not to devour her. As it was, it took only a second, the words, the look in her eyes like a tug around his heart, breaking him free of all the rules he'd been trying so very hard to keep.

Suddenly, he didn't have a clue why.

He leaned forward and kissed her, his mouth hungry for hers, the desire for her washing over him, like the sunshine and the ocean breeze. She tasted of lemonade—sweet, spicy—and smelled like hope, and when she put her arms around him and pulled him in, his mind simply stopped working.

His heart took over.

He pulled her to himself, his hands in her hair, so much surrender, so much acceptance in her touch, it unleashed something inside him.

Fear.

Something cold and dark and it lanced his chest and wrapped a fist around his lungs and—

What was he *doing*?

He stopped, backed up, looked at her, breathing hard. Oh . . . no. No—

"Ranger?" She looked up at him, her arms moving around to his chest, where his thundering heart might give him away. "You okay?"

Not even a little.

"Yeah," he said, and started to move away, but she grabbed his shirt, pulled him back down.

Then she cupped her hands on his face. "It'll be okay. Breathe. You're okay. Really. This is what happy feels like."

Was it? Because it felt a lot like drowning. Complete with the loss of breath, and panic.

They'd taught him how to fight the sense of drowning, way back in BUD/S. How to not let it take him out, even when he was over his head. Suddenly, he seemed to have forgotten all his training.

She pushed him away. "Now, don't let us drift into that other boat."

She pointed over his shoulder, and sure enough, they were heading with the current, right into the speedboat's broadside.

"Whoa!" He grabbed the wheel.

They scooted past the boat.

She laughed. "One close call after another."

She had no idea. Not with the taste of her still on his lips, water glistening on her perfect skin. He picked up his water bottle of lemonade.

"Let's heave to and anchor. We'll dive over to the reef," she said. "Lock off the jib."

She took over at the wheel while he secured the jib. "Helms alee," she said as she released the mainsheet and tacked. The mainsheet luffed as she headed the boat into the wind. It slowed as the wind blew the jib downwind and the main upwind, counteracting each other. She put the helm to lee position.

"That's a cool trick," Ranger said.

"I have more where that came from." She turned, her hands on her hips.

"Okay, Wonder Woman. Let's get in the water."

She let out the anchor. He leaned over, watched it hit the bottom, maybe ten feet below. When he turned back, she was already pulling on her fins.

They spent the afternoon exploring the ruins off the fort, then swam into shore and toured the national park.

The sun darkened the water with a trail of amber light as he pulled up the anchor and braced it on the cathead.

"Take me home, sailor," she said, huddled in a towel and eating out of a snack bag of Doritos. She handed him a chip.

"Thanks."

"Don't want you to go hungry."

Yeah, this little chip wasn't going to tame the raging beast inside.

But as he turned, the sun at his back, racing the line in the sea home, he realized she was right.

Happy. He was happy.

And he'd still never been more stinkin' afraid in his entire life.

Now, the night started to descend around them, the wind whipping up, spraying water into his face at the helm.

"Do you want me to drive?" She had changed into a pair of

leggings and a long-sleeve shirt, and admittedly, he was cold. In fact, he was shivering.

"Ranger?" She came up to him, put her hands on his arms. "You can let go of the helm. I have this."

He couldn't let go, his hands tight on the wheel. Around him, the night had darkened, the ocean hitting their bow, hard, dropping them into the troughs of deep swells, jarring his body.

Everything suddenly hurt. And the wind . . . the wind had changed, turned into a dark, persistent drone, settling deep into his bones.

Something wasn't right—wasn't . . . right . . . something . . .

"Ranger? It's okay, let go. Let—"

He wasn't in the sailboat, or even in the ocean, but in a vehicle and—

With a hard breath, Ranger opened his eyes.

The world had turned dark, but moonlight glowed dimly through the window of . . . wait, was he in a *car*? No, a station wagon, wedged into the back, his entire body on fire from the ruts and jerks as it—where *was* he?

Rain pelleted the hood, the sound almost deafening.

And that's when he saw a form over him. Petite, the dim light on her face betraying a woman with her hair tied back in a scarf.

He had his hand around her neck, hers holding his wrist. "Let go," she said tightly, calmly.

Oh! He released her. "Noemi. I—"

"Shh. It's fine. You're safe, for now. But you need to let me help you. You've lost a lot of blood, and we're headed into a checkpoint. If they see you in here, we're dead."

"If who—what's going on?"

He rolled over, despite the sudden whoosh of pain.

Another woman sat in the driver's seat, her hair tied back in a scarf as well. The dim green light from the front dash lit up her face enough for him to blink into recognition. Blessing?

He looked back at Noemi. "What happened?"

"You passed out. Hold still."

His vest was off, and a bandage of sorts tied his arm to his body. Now, Noemi packed into his wound a wadded-up bandage. The car smelled of mice, or maybe bats, and age and—"You found a car?"

"More than that. I found another secret stash of cash in your vest. What, were you planning on buying our way out of Nigeria?"

"If I had to—what are you doing?"

"We stopped in another village, and I got ahold of some clothes and medical supplies. And surprise, surprise, you have more morphine. Holding out on me, Jack?"

"No, I just . . . it's for an emergency."

"Emergency shot comin' right up. Buckle up."

"Wait—no—I need to stay awake."

Too late. She delivered the last of his morphine into his thigh. He was too tired to hold in a groan.

"Just sit tight. We're approaching the Benue River and there's a bridge. But it's guarded."

"Guarded?"

"Nigerian police."

He started to rise, but she put her hand on his chest. "Calm down. We have a plan. But not if you go all Rambo on us and start making grunting noises. I need you small and quiet. Okay, sailor?"

"I don't understand."

"I know." She was drawing a blanket over him. Headlights, or maybe a distant light, splashed into the car.

Only then did he see her eyes, the fear in them. They looked bloodshot, as if she'd been crying. He caught her wrist with his free hand. "What happened?"

She met his gaze. Swallowed. "Blessing thought you'd died. Scared me to death. Thankfully you'd just passed out, but . . ."

She closed her mouth, looked away, then back at him. "Don't die on me, Ranger. You made me promises."

Had he?

Only then did he notice that she'd changed clothes. She wore a dress. And something like a backpack around her middle. It made her look pregnant.

She packed up the morphine pen. "Listen. We're going to be okay. We have twelve more hours to my uncle's village."

"Your uncle's village?"

"My mother's brother. He lives in Delta State. He'll help us get out of the country, if we can get there."

He leaned back, feeling the morphine seep into him, the panic releasing its hard fist. No—he had to stay alert. "Where are my weapons? My vest—"

Suddenly, she leaned forward and kissed him, something hard and focused and deliberate.

It silenced him, drove the thoughts from his head, all but the sudden, crazy, completely inappropriate desire to reach out and pull her hard against him.

Maybe never let her go.

Yeah, he was clearly drugged. More, sleep pulled at him. No—shoot. *Noemi!*

She leaned back and finished pulling up the blanket to his shoulders. Leaning forward, she put her mouth against his ear. "Trust me. And whatever happens, don't move."

Then she covered him with the blanket, and he slid softly into the shadows.

FIVE

"Is he asleep?" Blessing looked over from the driver's seat, and again, Noemi couldn't believe she was letting the fifteen-year-old drive. But apparently she'd been driving since she was ten, and weirdly, had suddenly developed nerves of steel.

Maybe it was something Ranger said.

"Yes. Maybe. I don't know. I shot him with morphine, so probably. But I told him to be quiet."

Please let Ranger sleep. Because she could hear his voice in her head. *Are you crazy?*

Or maybe that was her father's voice—she couldn't be sure. Frankly, it might even be her own.

Because this was most definitely the crazier of her ideas.

To her credit, it wasn't just her idea. Blessing had helped concoct it.

"How's his bleeding?"

"I think I stopped it." And in the meantime, he'd scared her out of her skin. He hadn't meant to strangle her, Noemi knew that.

Really.

His hand around her throat was just a reflex of her hurting him as she tried to bandage his wound.

He was an operator—of course he'd strangle anyone hurting him.

It had nothing to do with it being *her*. Of course not.

Still, it sat in her heart like a rock.

He really meant it when he said he didn't want her in his life.

Well, no worry. As soon as they got to her uncle's village of Okwagbe, Ranger could be rid of her.

She swallowed back the stone in her throat.

He'd barely roused when she and Blessing dragged his thousand-ton body to the wagon, put the back seat down to make room, then hoisted him across the whole back end. Then, needing a GPS, she tried, again, to turn on the phone she'd stolen from Freddie. No joy. So they'd followed cattle roads southwest until they'd hooked up with the A3, and then headed south.

The road led them to the outskirts of Lafia, a city where Blessing could dicker for fresh clothing, fruit, medicine, and gasoline.

They had enough fuel, maybe, to get them over the massive Benue River, through Makurdi, and down to Delta State.

Or they could get stopped by the police patrol at the bridge, found out, detained, and then who knew what would happen to Ranger. It depended greatly on the payroll of the security force. He might be imprisoned, if he had no visa, but if the wrong group got their hands on him . . .

"Get out the kobo." Blessing held out her hand for the naira bills.

They'd exchanged fifty euros when they'd purchased clothing in Lafia.

Noemi handed her the money. *Please, let this work.*

Maybe God was watching over them, because there was no other reason for the sudden deluge that opened up from the heavens five kilometers from the Benue River crossing at Makurdi.

Darkness hovered over the entrance of the bridge, just a few lights shining across the cement in the distance. A log blocked the road, and a track where cars had moved around it glistened under the headlights.

"I don't see anyone," Noemi said, hunkering down in her seat, her hands over the bag of clothing under her dress. She'd ripped up pieces of her bloody shirt and wadded them in between the seats.

"They're here," Blessing said as she slowed. "Just wait."

It took only a moment, then a light shone out from a hut near the river. A man emerged wearing blue pants and a blue rain slicker, an AK-47 hanging from the strap over his shoulder. The rain pinged down on him as he stalked over to her window.

Blessing rolled it down a crack.

"How far, sista?" he said, the rain dripping off his hood. "Wusai do dey go?"

"My auntie. She's pregnant. I'm taking her to the hospital."

Noemi put her head back and closed her eyes, groaned a little.

"Wetin dey?" The light shone over her.

"Can't you see? Her water's broke!" Blessing picked up the red rags.

His light burned on Noemi's face again.

And then it flickered to the back seat.

Noemi swallowed back the stone in her throat.

"Na so."

"It's just her bag," Blessing said, adding exasperation to her tone. "Some food. Abeg—why you dey give me wahala? She's in pain."

Noemi groaned again, and then let out a cry.

"Abeg, let us go—"

"Do you have something for the boys, sista?"

Blessing must have slapped the naira into his hand because he stepped back.

And then, just like that, they were around the roadblock and onto the massive bridge that spanned the Benue River.

Blessing looked over at her and grinned.

Grinned.

And Noemi suddenly felt brilliant. Maybe it wasn't a crazy idea to drive halfway across Nigeria to a family she'd never met. Maybe Ranger wasn't going to bleed out and die in the back of this ancient, smelly car.

Maybe she wouldn't leave Nigeria with a broken heart.

And now she was just living in a fairy tale. But the drive had raked up way too many memories, not in the least the feeling of his hands in her hair, the taste of him on a sunny, salted-air day.

What was the pidgin word for "trouble"? *Wahala.* Yes, Ranger was wahala to her heart.

The sooner she got him back to his team and out of her life, the better, for everyone.

They crossed the bridge, the sprawling city of Makurdi spread out before them. Lights glowed in pockets closer to the center against the dark pane of night. They'd been driving all day, her entire body hurt, and she reeked, she knew it.

She climbed into the back and lifted the blanket off Ranger's head.

"He needs a hospital," Blessing said.

"He's shot. If we bring him to a hospital, they'll start asking questions." She hadn't exactly solved that piece of the puzzle yet.

"We can find a healer in your uncle's village. An herbalist. They'll know what to do."

What she needed was a cell phone. But she didn't have the faintest clue how to get ahold of Ranger's contact, Ham.

What she really needed was Ranger, awake and healthy.

She returned to the front seat, then reached under her dress and pulled out the bag wadded with their soiled clothing. They passed homes, some two stories, others smaller, most of them situated inside compounds or behind metal gates. Even at this time of night, the road was clogged with Land Rovers, motorcycles, pickups, sedans, and vans, all honking, drivers shouting out their windows.

Blessing drove, stone-faced, into it all. They passed a roundabout with a massive stone basket sculpture filled with fruits.

Noemi reached back and grabbed the bag of plantains.

"Let's stop at a Tito Gate," Blessing said. "I'm starved."

"We can't risk anyone seeing him," said Noemi. She picked out the blackest plantain she could find. "Here."

Blessing took the fruit and peeled it, one hand on the wheel as she merged behind a group of motorcycles.

"You're a good driver."

"My brother was better. And he was a year younger than me."

"I didn't know you had a brother."

Blessing kept her gaze on the road. "They killed him."

Right. Noemi looked out the window, the city fading as they headed for the tropical forests to the south. "I'm sorry."

"You know Ranger from before, don't you?" Blessing glanced at her. "And he knows you."

"We met a few years ago."

"He say your name while he be sleeping."

"Worry, probably."

Blessing made a sound. "We should switch drivers. I'm not allowed to drive until I'm eighteen." She pulled over then glanced toward the back. "It sounded like something else. Like sadness." She got out.

Huh. Noemi walked around the front of the car and slid in. She hadn't a clue what to do with Blessing's words.

They'd left civilization behind, mostly, just small villages between them and their next big city, Onitsha. The smell of the tropical forest hung in the air, and Noemi rolled down the window. The rain had stopped. She pulled out onto the dark highway.

"Were you two lovers?"

She glanced at Blessing. "No. Just friends." Although the word sat inside her like a burr.

No, they'd never been *just friends*. Even from the beginning, something sparked between them. Fact was, she'd never behaved with anyone the way she'd been with Ranger. He'd been intriguing and so knotted up that she'd let herself flirt with him.

Okay, her flirting might have been over the top. But then they'd settled into a friendship—dinners out, riding around the island, visiting museums, snorkeling. Sailing.

"We had a sort of fast-and-furious vacation relationship," she said. "But it never got serious."

Oh, she was full of all sorts of lies today. Because it had turned serious about two days into the vacation. Terribly, heart-wrenchingly serious. Like he might suddenly be the home she never thought she needed.

"I saw you kiss him," Blessing said.

"He was freaking out. I was trying to shut him down." At least that was the story she was telling herself. It had nothing to do with an impulse from the past.

"You loved him though."

She stared at the road, the headlights breaking through the darkness. "Yes. Yes, I did. But I never told him that." She looked at Blessing. "And you aren't going to either, okay? Promise?"

Blessing nodded, her eyes big. "Did he love you?"

She sighed. "It doesn't matter. He has an important job that doesn't have room for love."

"Are you trying to cost me my career? This was a huge mistake."

Shoot. Even now the memory could burn tears into her eyes. She blinked them away.

"He be very brave," Blessing said.

"Yes, he is. He's a Navy SEAL. There are few braver."

"Do you think he'll live?"

She drew in a breath. "I know he'll do everything he can to stay alive."

And so would she. Whatever it took.

"Go to sleep. I'll wake you when we get to Okwagbe."

The night settled around them, the landscape turning lush with the tropical forest of south central Nigeria. She let her elbow hang out the window, the wind in her hair. And, for a bit, allowed her memory to settle her back onto the boat. That last ride under the stars.

Before the sadness.

She sat with her feet propped up on the bench. Ranger stood at the helm, his legs slightly apart, his hands easy on the wheel.

Wow, he was a handsome man. Tall, wide shoulders, strong legs and muscles—she'd gotten a good look at all those back muscles today while they snorkeled. He was a porpoise in the water, easily free-diving to the bottom of the reef at Fort Jefferson and gliding along longer—much longer—than she thought possible. More than once he rolled over in the water and lay on his back, kicking, staring up at her, grinning.

Show-off.

Such a beautiful, glorious day, and she longed for it never to end. Because tomorrow Ranger would nail his exam, and then . . . *then* he'd leave. No, not just leave—*vanish*. Just like her father had over and over. Maybe her mother had simply died of worry. She knew it wasn't science, but she couldn't get it out of her head that the worry had seeped into her mom's brain, taken over, and turned to cancer.

Maybe it was better—merciful, even—that they'd sent Noemi away to boarding school. Better not to know . . .

But her imagination made everything worse.

The wind had kicked up and sprayed chilly water into the cockpit as they splashed into wells, or a wave rocked them over.

"You're a natural," she said. "You should get a boat."

He looked over at her. Oh, those eyes could simply pin her in place. She had a little trouble keeping her words straight around him. And she found herself doing crazy things. Like daring him to swim with her that first night. What if he hadn't been the honorable man he was?

Except he *was* a man of honor, and she'd known it that first moment he'd walked up to her, his face solemn, his identity as a SEAL at stake. She didn't know whether she was in trouble until she'd roped him into seeing the sunset with her.

When he'd stood behind her, making sure she didn't fall off the railing as she took the picture, she knew.

She needed that quiet, calm, solid presence in her life.

But she also wanted the man of passion she'd glimpsed, and tasted, today on the boat. And now that she'd experienced it, it had turned her hungry for it.

No way was she letting him vanish into the night.

"I always thought I'd get a plane," Ranger said. He sat down next to her, one hand on the wheel. "My family runs a bush pilot service in Alaska."

"Alaska. Never been there."

"It's a beautiful place to take pictures."

If that was an invitation, the answer was yes.

"Not sure when I'll get back there. My sister just separated from the Army—she was a medic in Afghanistan—and she's flying with my dad. She keeps bugging me to go home, but . . ." The sails luffed and he steered the boat back into the wind.

"But?"

He sighed. "My brothers had a massive fight years ago. Colt kissed my other brother's girlfriend—"

"Wow."

"Yeah. Dodge dismantled him. I've never seen him so angry. I got in the middle and managed to calm him down, but . . . it's a deep wound. Dodge joined the Air Force while Colt was still in the hospital. They haven't talked since."

"But you just spent a week with Colt."

"He had a week of leave from his unit."

"Army?"

"Delta Force."

"Another underachiever, I see."

He laughed, and she could live in it forever.

"We used to have a lot of fun. The three of us shared a room—at least until my mother died—and we'd wrestle at night until my dad yelled at us to go to bed. Living in Alaska is its own adventure. I grew up riding horses and four-wheelers, skiing, and learning to fly, although Dodge and Larke are the only ones who got their pilot's licenses."

"It sounds perfect." She leaned into him, and he put his arm around her. Not quite the embrace of before, but maybe she was panicking for nothing.

He hadn't exactly reached out to kiss her since before their swim, since his weird reaction.

The one that told her he was about to push her away.

But he was still here, still sitting with his arm around her. *So, stop panicking.* "I'm an only child, and I grew up at a boarding school, so my best family memories are the end-of-the-year pickups where my parents would take me away for a weekend of fun to make up for all those months away. We'd go to Disneyland, or the beach. I'd have three days with them before I went to summer camp."

"Three." He frowned. "I'm sorry."

"What? They were busy. And I made friends. Learned how to rock climb and ride horses and paint and play chess—I won the spelling bee for the state of California when I was fourteen."

The words raked up a terrible heat in her chest. She turned away. Blew out a breath.

Funny how grief could knock you over at the oddest moments.

"Noemi?"

"It's nothing."

He made this humming noise, deep inside.

She'd learned to recognize it as thunderous disagreement.

Fine. "When I won the state bee, I expected my parents to be there. But they weren't, you know? I got worried, so I lied to my teacher and took a bus back to our house in San Diego. But they weren't there either." She wove her fingers through his, over her shoulder. "I sat on our front step for hours until a neighbor came over and asked who I was. She didn't even know my parents had a daughter." She swallowed, hating the rasp of her voice. "Anyway, she told me an ambulance had taken my mother to the hospital a few days prior, and she drove me to the Naval Medical Center. I asked for my father at the desk and of course they tracked him down. He was sitting outside the critical care unit where my mother was dying."

Ranger said nothing, the stars watching them against the dark vault of sky.

"He was shocked to see me, but he didn't even yell at me for ditching school—I think he was so afraid to leave her, worried she might die while he was gone, so he was secretly relieved I'd shown up. She died about six hours later."

She wiped her wet cheek, salty with the spray. "At least I got to say goodbye."

"Yes," he said quietly.

"I hate goodbyes," she added softly.

"Me too."

Please. Oh, right then she wanted to turn to him, to hold on to him. *Please, Ranger . . .* what? Don't leave? He was a SEAL. Of course he had to leave. And then what—she'd follow him from base to base, training op to mission, clutching his BDUs?

She knew better, thanks.

She was a distraction at best. At worst, an annoyance.

Probably better to be the one who left first.

If only her heart would agree.

The boat jerked in the water, the sails taken by a gust, and he got back up.

"I got this," she said and took the helm. Ahead, the harbor lights of Key West glittered against the horizon.

"I can take us in, Noemi," he said.

She shook her head. "I'm used to sailing alone."

But he made that deep rumble in his chest again and didn't step away, just curled his hands over her shoulders, warm and present, and it made everything inside her ache.

She guided them into harbor, then luffed the sails and coasted up to the pier. Ranger jumped out and tied the boat off. Music from the nearby beach bar drifted out across the harbor. "Sundown" by Gordon Lightfoot.

Yep, when she felt like she was winning, she was just losing again.

She wound up the jib, and Ranger helped her take down the mainsail. Then they closed up all the hatches, pulled the motor out of the water, and grabbed their gear.

He took her bag in one hand, her hand in the other, and walked up the pier toward their hotel.

The tiki bar area was still hopping when they arrived. And along the outskirts, she spotted her father sitting in a beach chair, looking out over the dark ocean, a lemonade in his grip.

He raised a hand to her and then got up. Walked over to them. She dropped Ranger's hand. Her dad studied him with his cool blue eyes.

"Dad, this is Ranger. Ranger . . . Pete Sutton."

"Mr. Sutton," Ranger said and shook his hand.

"Choppy water out there," her father replied.

"Nothing I couldn't handle," she said, but her father was looking at Ranger.

"The kind of night where a sailor can get lost."

"Made it back to shore, Dad. We're good."

His gaze remained steady. "Don't lose your bearings, son."

Ranger nodded. "Yes, sir."

Oh brother. She turned to Ranger. "Dinner?"

"Starved." He hadn't broken his eye lock with her father.

"Let me drop my stuff off."

"I'm not going anywhere."

For Pete's sake. But as she headed to her room, his words had settled inside her. *"I'm not going anywhere."*

Behind her, a grunt stirred Noemi out of the memory—too soon, because she would have liked to replay the rest of that night.

That beautiful, glorious, perfect night.

"Ranger?"

He made another sound. She reached back in the darkness of the car, stretching, found his shoulder, and then his hand took hers. Warm. Solid. Tight.

"I'm not going anywhere."

No, he never had.

He was still very much present in her heart.

His grip loosened after a bit, hopefully a good sign, but just in case, she found his mouth and loosely cupped her hand over it until it warmed.

Still alive.

She drove in quiet then, watching as the moon fell to the lee side of the night, the forests thick and tangled. When she dropped into the valley some eight hours later, toward Onitsha, with the sparkling, wide Niger River spread out below, she grabbed the bag and shoved it under her dress.

Just in case.

But no one came out to stop her as she motored over the bridge into the city. Early morning cooking fires, exhaust, and the scent of city garbage layered the air as she drove by stone-gated neighborhoods of tin-roofed houses. A handful of motorcycles joined her on the darkened road.

Blessing stirred but didn't waken.

And then they were free, headed south, safely in the state of Delta.

She really hadn't a clue how she might find her uncle's town of Okwagbe, but before that, Ranger needed a doctor.

On the dash, Freddie's phone blinked to life.

She picked it up. Huh. An older, clunkier phone, but maybe that had kept it from getting too saturated. Unfortunately, it wouldn't connect to any cell towers.

Blessing stirred again as Noemi hit the road. "Wetin dey happen?"

"Trying to figure out how to get to Okwagbe. I think we're about four hours away."

"And den what?"

"We find a doctor. Any bright ideas?"

"Auntie, don't you see it? We go to da church."

"Church?"

"My father say that God be with us. Always. No doubt. Go to church."

"God has my back."

Fine. She was fresh out of brilliant ideas.

The sun hung high on the horizon as they drove on the rutted highway, through a handful of villages. About an hour from Okwagbe, while passing through the city of Ughelli, Ranger woke up and asked for water.

Blessing climbed into the back and gave him a drink. "His bleeding has stopped," she said as she returned to the front. They'd slowed, the road clogged with early morning motorcycles, buses, and pedestrians. "But he's very warm."

"It's not far." Maybe. Please.

The low gas light pinged.

"Oh, dey be wahala."

They had at least thirty kilometers left.

And suddenly, this entire trip felt crazy. What, she was going to pull into Okwagbe and suddenly be welcomed with open arms by an uncle she didn't know . . . and then he'd, what, take them in and doctor Ranger, no questions asked?

She should turn around, head to the nearest hospital, and stop being so paranoid.

Smaller houses and dirt roads led off the two-laned road. Goats, cattle, and the occasional vegetable or fruit stand bordered the road, while massive oil trucks passed her, edging her over to the side.

The wagon coughed, thirsty. "C'mon, honey, don't give up on me." She patted the dashboard and drove another three kilometers before the wagon coughed again.

"There," Blessing said and pointed to a sign off the road. The words THE LORD'S FAVOR CHRISTIAN ASSEMBLY CHURCH were scrawled across a plywood sign with an arrow pointing down a thin dirt road.

"We need to find a petrol station and then we can make it to Okwagbe."

"Auntie, go!"

The wagon coughed again, and she pulled off, drove down the road toward a small building tucked into a tropical enclave bordered by tall iroko trees.

She pulled up to the small yellow building, a cross at the apex of the roof.

Dust drifted up around the car as it knocked, sputtered, . . . and died.

And there went the last of their gas.

A man had come out and now stood on the front steps. He wore a clean, red pinstriped shirt, a pair of dress pants and shoes, and watched as Blessing got out of the wagon.

She ran up to him while Noemi leaned over in her seat and made sure the blanket covered Ranger's vest and weapons. But really, there was no disguising he was a warrior. A broken bloody warrior, but still a man who didn't go down easily. They'd wedged him into the back end, his legs bent and at an angle, and sweat dripped off his brow, not just from his fever. But, he still breathed.

"Sista, can I help you?" The pastor was at her door, Blessing standing behind him, nodding.

Here went nothing.

She got out, brushed herself off. "Yes. We need a doctor."

The man looked into the back of the wagon, frowned. "That is a white man."

"Yes."

He stepped back. "What trouble do you bring me?" His gaze went to Blessing, then back to Noemi.

"Abeg," Blessing started.

Noemi echoed her. "Please. He has a fever."

The pastor walked around to the back, then opened the tailgate. Peered inside. Lifted the blanket. Ranger's weapon lay next to the pack. He dropped the blanket and backed up, held up his hands.

"No wahala. No, no wahala."

Aw, she *knew* it. Because despite Blessing's words, and even Ranger's so long ago, she'd never met a God who wanted to help.

Frankly, she felt a little like she might be an annoyance to him too.

Which meant she was on her own. Her mess, her responsibility.

She stepped up to the pastor. "Listen, pastor—"

"Samuel."

"I'm Noemi—" And yes, she took a chance, because her tribal name just might buy her clout, if not belonging, so, "Ofejiro. And this man is under my care. I need a healer, a doctor, but not a hospital, hear me? Please, can you help me?"

Samuel's gaze had gone back toward Ranger's gun. "I'm so sorry, but—"

"For God's sake, help this man!" She didn't mean for her voice to shrill, but frankly, she had nothing else.

She put her hands over her face, her eyes burning.

The crying wasn't an act, but maybe Blessing thought it was and decided to capitalize on it, because beside her, her voice lifted in desperation. "Abeg, Pastor. You must help him. This man is her husband."

Oh.

No.

She looked at Blessing, who also wore tears.

No!

But the pastor suddenly frowned, and for the first time, took a step toward Ranger. "Is dis true?"

And maybe it was her fatigue, or her hunger, even simply the terrible, deep longing she'd buried inside, one that she no longer bore the strength to hide . . .

Just like that, she was nodding. Yes, yes.

In a different life, yes.

He's my husband.

Besides, it was just a small lie. What harm could it do?

SIX

He wanted to live. More than anything, ever, in his life, Ranger wanted to live.

No, he wanted to *breathe*. His entire body ached for it, his diaphragm convulsing, his lungs burning.

Mind over matter. The rules for free diving.

But something wasn't right. He wasn't ascending, the light at the top was still dim, his body weighted. It wasn't supposed to be this way.

Noemi.

Her face flashed in his head and something warm and sweet swept through him. Noemi would be waiting.

No, that wasn't right. He'd left her. Long ago. Except, she still felt right here. Her laughter, the feel of her—

His chest burned.

To the top, kick harder. But still, his body wouldn't move.

And the world began to wink out at the edges.

No. He would not die here.

He'd made promises.

He kicked again, hard, and then—

"Ranger!"

He lay on the deck, gasping, his chest on fire as he blinked his eyes open. Except, no, this wasn't right either. His instructor, Master Chief Gray, and another man. Oh, he knew this man. Blond, wide shoulders, his face hard—

"Ranger, wake up!"

The voice ripped him free, and he opened his eyes.

Not the tower deck at the Army's Key West base, his life flashing before his eyes.

He lay in a small room, about as big as the bachelor housing back in San Diego, blue curtains blowing from open windows. The early morning sounds of birds filled the room, along with the scent of something herbal. A fan stirred the air, and with a start, he realized his boots were off. His shirt, also gone.

As were his pants.

Sheesh, he was practically naked.

"Ranger, wake up."

The voice he didn't immediately recognize, but the face was familiar. Blessing. A scarf wrapped her head, and she looked freshly washed, wore a pink skirt, a white blouse. "You get up now. Time to hide."

Huh?

He looked around. Pictures of children, hung near the ceiling, tilted down to face the room, and a cross hung on the far wall, painted a light blue.

"Get up, get up." Blessing tugged on his arm. "You hide."

Hide?

The door opened, and a large woman in a yellow dress careened in. She turned to Blessing, shouting in pidgin. He hadn't a clue what she was saying.

In the meantime, he sat up. Managed not to groan as his bones shifted inside.

He prodded them gently, wincing. Then he crawled his fingers up his left arm and found his wound tightly bandaged. A sling bound his arm to his chest.

Someone had bathed him. Gone was the blood, the smell of sweat, although a light sheen still layered his forehead, and the room did a quick swish.

He might throw up, nausea rising inside.

The woman was still shouting, and now turned to him.

"She say it too late. De men here for you."

The men?

And then he heard it. Shouting outside, and yes that was Noemi's voice. What—?

He pushed himself to his feet, grabbing on to a nearby table when he wobbled.

"I don't think you should stand."

"Where's Noemi?" He took a step, and aw, shoot, he was falling. He reached out and suddenly Blessing was there, her hand around his waist to steady him.

"She's outside. I think you lay back down."

The other woman had left, casting him a look.

Yeah, he wasn't thrilled about standing around in his skivvies either. He pulled the sheet from the bed and wrapped it around him. "I need to get outside."

Blessing sighed and tucked herself under his right arm. "I no get you."

Yeah, well sometimes he didn't get himself either.

Especially when it came to Noemi. She had sort of this dangerous magnetism. "When did we get here?"

"Yesterday. It's morning. You sleeping long time."

She walked him through the house, a simple front room, plywood flooring over stone, a meager kitchen, two more rooms, the doorways covered with curtains. Patterned overstuffed furniture was shoved against the walls.

The shouting came from outside.

"Wait. Where is my vest? My gun?"

She looked up at him. Shook her head. "Mama Esther say no vex her with gun in the house."

Perfect.

He made less than a menacing force standing in a sheet. Still, through the window he saw Noemi outside, standing with a short man, silent as a group of other men shouted at them. She parked herself in front of the stoop, her arms out.

As if, what, barring them entrance?

"He's not here to hurt you!" she shouted. "He's wounded."

The larger woman—Mama Esther?—stood at the door, her arms folded under her massive bosom. She shook her head. "Yawa don gas."

"You be in trouble, uncle," Blessing said.

Yeah, he got that part. Although he didn't exactly know why.

He pushed through the door.

The crowd exploded like he might be Elvis back from the dead. Shouting, and suddenly Noemi jumped up on the stoop, stood in front of him. "No wahala! No wahala!"

"What's going on?"

She glanced up at him as the shorter man took a step forward, started to plead with the crowd. Ranger counted seven men. Three of them carried machetes, and they could do real damage. The other four were older, gray-haired, but built—farmers, maybe. They kept gesturing to him, then back to themselves.

"The pastor took us to a local herbalist's house, and she bandaged you up," Noemi told him, her eyes still on the men. "But when her husband came home, he found our car and your guns, and it all sort of exploded from there."

"I don't understand."

"Only terrorists or cops have guns," she said. "And, of course, you're white, and they're all wondering why you're here. The pastor is trying to explain that you're here to help me."

Ranger blew out a breath. "Did he mention the real terrorists, the ones who kidnapped you?"

"Yes. And that's what has these men worried. They think they'll follow us. Pastor Samuel's speaking a local dialect, but he is on our side. I think."

The pastor was gesturing fast, using his hands.

From the looks of their surroundings, they were in a snug neighborhood, small cement homes with tin roofs all situated on plots of land surrounded by massive thick-leafed trees. Many of the houses were behind walls and gates, with gardens inside.

A dirt path ran from the house Ranger exited to the dirt road, a few cars parked in the tall grasses.

Hens meandered the street.

So, not in the savannah anymore. "Where are we?" he asked Noemi.

"I don't know. I was headed toward Okwagbe, but the car died."

Right. He had a recollection of a car somewhere in the back of his head.

One of the men advanced and Ranger stiffened. "Did you tell them that we're just passing through? Just get me a phone, and we're out of here."

"Yeah, well, our car is out of gas, and I'm not exactly sure if we're going to get it back. I think the pastor might have traded it for your medical help."

Perfect. "And my vest and pack?"

"In the room, hidden under the bed. Mama Esther didn't want the guns inside."

Another man started shouting, his machete raised, and that was just *enough*.

Ranger was too tired to control the edge in his voice. "We're not here to hurt you. For Pete's sake, look at her. Look at me. Do we look in any shape to bring trouble?" He was shouting, and it cost him more energy than he thought. The world swayed.

The pastor turned to him. "Go back inside. Go! Go!"

The shouts dimmed as a black Land Rover pulled up outside the house, followed by a van. A handful of police officers piled out of the van, all armed.

Uh-oh.

A man exited the back seat of the Land Rover. He wore a black kaftan, matching pants, and a machete at his belt.

He walked up to the now quiet group.

One of them ducked his head, in a bow.

He walked past them, right up to the pastor. "How una dey?"

The pastor ducked his head as well. "Mister Dafe."

The man spoke to him and the pastor turned to Ranger to translate. "The king wishes to see you. This is his head of security."

What? There was a king in the land? Aw, and he probably came with a dungeon. Except, if it meant Noemi and Blessing got out of this in one piece . . . yes, okay.

"It's my fault," Ranger said over their conversation. "The guns belong to me."

Noemi turned. Put her hand over his mouth. "Stop talking. The last thing we want is—"

"Silent." Mister Dafe wore his hair close cropped to his head and had dark eyes. Ranger decided to obey. For now.

The pastor stepped up and began to speak in the local dialect, but Dafe never took his eyes off Ranger.

Ranger stared back.

The man looked down at Noemi. Frowned, then turned to the pastor. Asked a question.

The pastor gestured to Noemi, then Ranger.

The head of security set his gaze on Noemi, but his eyes softened. "You be Ofejiro?"

She nodded, and Ranger couldn't help but put his hand on Noemi's shoulder. Just in case he had to yank her away.

"Your mother be Mercy Rukevwe Ofejiro?"

She nodded again, slowly.

Abruptly, Dafe turned, also nodded.

The front door of the car opened, and a man stepped out. A big man, dressed in a deep-blue ornamented kaftan and matching pants, a thick gold necklace around his neck. He wore a thin, salt-and-peppered beard and he smelled expensive. Like money. And power.

"This is the Ovie," Dafe said, his voice a baritone. "He is our king."

And Ranger stood here in a sheet. Was he supposed to bow?

The Ovie walked up to them. Scanned a look over Noemi. His eyes glistened, and he reached out and touched her face. A gentle touch, as if in wonder. "I dey miss your mother."

Noemi's breath caught.

"I be your uncle. Onanefe Godstime Ofejiro. To you, Uncle Efe."

Seriously, Ranger had clearly missed a couple chapters while he'd been out. "Your *uncle*?"

"And dis be your husband."

He stilled. What—?

And then Noemi nodded.

Nodded.

Wait—was that a *yes*? As in affirmative?

Uncle Efe looked at him as if in confirmation, and Ranger just froze.

But he'd been trained to adapt and improvise and, if it meant the guys with machetes calmed down— "Yeah," he said. Even nodded.

Sure, they were married. Why not? What harm—

"Aw, this is no good," Uncle Efe said suddenly. He shook his head. "No good at all."

Noemi also froze.

The man turned toward Ranger. "You marry my niece without asking for bride price?"

Without what?

"Uncle—" Noemi started, but the man put up his hand.

"I'm her uncle. Her father is dead, you come to me before you marry. Ask permission. Pay bride price. Then have wedding—not before."

He took a step closer, and Ranger moved Noemi with a press to her shoulder and stepped into the gap. He might be in just his underwear, but the big man needed to step back. "Just take a breath, Your Highness. Obviously, we didn't know—"

The king's band of merry men clearly didn't love Ranger's

movement and suddenly, the no-weapons rule became clear. Only the ruling class got AK-47s.

A couple of them unslung the weapons from their shoulders.

Ranger raised his hands. "Keep the safeties on, boys. No one needs to die here." He looked at Uncle Efe. "Fine. How much for the bride?"

"Ranger!"

"I got this, Noemi." He didn't look at her. "I'll pay your price. How much for Noemi?"

A beat.

Then, suddenly, Uncle Efe burst into laughter, something loud and bold and bracing, and Ranger just stood there, blinking, his gaze going from the now laughing brute squad back to Uncle Efe.

Yeah, yeah, laugh at the American.

"So, um, no bride price?"

"Oh," Uncle Efe said, his massive hand coming down on Ranger's good shoulder. "There be a price. Big price. For big man." He pointed at Ranger. Then at Noemi. "For pretty niece. But not here. Not now. We negotiate at introductions."

Introductions?

Uncle Efe turned to the crowd, said something in the local dialect, and they began to disperse.

The pastor turned to them. "The Ovie says he'll take you to his house. You'll be safe there."

Huh. Could they negotiate this?

Clearly not, because Uncle Efe gestured to the house, and one of the minions pushed past Ranger.

What was happening here?

"Come, come. My family will meet you." All smiles, laughter still in his eyes. He leaned toward Ranger. "I got you good. You dey be scared."

Um.

The minion emerged carrying Ranger's vest, his backpack.

Another retrieved the guns from a nearby station wagon. So that's what Noemi had shoved him into. Felt like an old Humvee.

"Come, come." Uncle Efe walked toward the Land Rover.

"I don't have pants," Ranger said, more to himself, or maybe Noemi.

"I will give you pants!" Uncle Efe said. He opened his door, and his eyes shone. "My niece has come home. We will kill a goat!"

Noemi looked at him, her eyes wide, but Blessing laughed. "I love goat pepper soup." She climbed into the back seat of the Land Rover.

"Goat pepper soup?" Ranger asked.

"It's actually very good," Noemi said. She made a face. "Sorry about this."

"I'm not sure what's happening," he whispered to her, "or how we suddenly got married. But . . . if I have to buy you to get us out of this mess . . ."

"Funny. And it's a long story. I'll tell you later."

She got in next to Blessing.

Oh boy. Talk about drowning . . . He was right back in Key West, trying to come up for air.

Thunder rolled overhead. Or maybe just beside her. Because Ranger sat smashed next to her and Noemi could practically feel the confusion pulsing off him.

Okay, everybody just calm down. It wasn't like he was really going to have to marry her.

Probably.

And maybe someone should be thanking her for finding a doctor to bandage his wound, wash him, and take down his fever.

So she'd brought the village ire down on them—they were safe, right?

If Blessing's reaction to the appearance of Noemi's uncle, his goon squad, and their current ride was any indication, they really had been rescued by a king of Nigeria. Blessing had grabbed Noemi's hand when they got into the car and now glanced over at her, grinning, her eyes shining.

Please, please let this not be a massive mistake.

"Tell me, daughter"—Uncle Efe turned to Noemi—"how did you come to be here, in Delta State, without my knowing?" He had put on sunglasses but smiled.

She glanced at Ranger. Probably the word *honeymoon* wouldn't cut it. So, "I was working at a refugee camp in northeastern Nigeria, and I was kidnapped."

He gasped.

"Yes. And my, um, husband, came to rescue me."

"Why you let her come here alone?" He directed the question at Ranger. "Don't you know it's dangerous?"

"That's a good question," Ranger said, his gaze on her. "Why did you go alone?"

Oh brother. "He had to work, uncle. And I can take care of myself."

Funny, both her uncle and Ranger made the same grim noise in their throats.

"This is how he got wounded?" Her uncle gestured to Ranger. "Shot?"

"Yes," Ranger said. "But I'm fine. I need to contact my friends and tell them we're okay."

"Yes, yes, no problem," Uncle Efe said. "But first, Noemi must meet her family, and we must have introductions!"

"And goat pepper soup," Blessing added.

Both Ranger and Noemi looked at her. But yes, the jollof rice Noemi had eaten earlier at Mama Esther's house had barely stuck to her ribs. She'd been so worried about Ranger, watching Mama Esther stop the bleeding and infection with a poultice of onions, salt, turmeric, garlic, and eucalyptus. The woman had sat for hours by his bedside applying the poultice and a cold cloth to his head, drawing the fever from him.

Noemi sat on the floor in a corner, trying not to nod off.

She should have taken him to the hospital.

"It is too late for stitches," Mama Esther had said when they arrived, Pastor Samuel leading the way. When he'd offered their car in trade, Noemi was too tired to disagree.

She should have hid the guns better.

Mama Esther had offered them a bath, but Noemi had simply wrapped her hair up, given herself a sponge bath, and changed clothes. Blessing, however, took Mama Esther up on the offer and came out smelling like oranges and mint.

Not a hint of guilt on her face for the lie. Then again, the lie just might have saved them all.

And at the time, it didn't seem like a big deal.

Oops.

"When the village elder called with the news of an American and an Ofejiro woman, I had to investigate. Your auntie Precious will be over her head to see you," Uncle Efe said as they headed south on the highway. The landscape had turned from savannah to jungle on their way, and now tall plantain, orange, and palm trees thickened the forests on either side of the road. A few massive fronds had fallen, turned brown under the blistering sun.

Inside the Land Rover, the AC whisked off the fine layer of perspiration that had embedded in her pores since arriving in Nigeria five months ago.

It felt like an eternity.

"I heard about your father's death, Noemi, from my nephew in America. He says it was in the paper."

She nodded.

"Terrible accident, to drown at sea. Especially for a sailor."

She didn't look at Ranger, but she felt him tense. "It was."

"You should have come back to us then," he said. "We would

have given you a grand wedding." He turned back and said something to his driver in what sounded like Urhobo.

"We wanted . . . something quiet," she said.

Ranger looked away, out the window.

"Quiet? What is quiet? You are Ofejiro! We will give you such a party."

"I love parties!" Blessing said, and Noemi looked at her, her eyes wide.

Ixnay on the artypay!

Did the girl not see what she'd gotten them into?

They slowed as they entered the village—no, scratch that—the *city* of Okwagbe. They passed office buildings and two-story houses set back from the road behind gated compounds, a number of churches, their steeples high above the red-roofed houses, all manner of storefronts, vegetable stands, gas stations, and restaurants. Pedestrians, motorbikes, and buses piled high with goods jockeyed for space in the road. It felt like a smaller version of Warri.

"How big is Okwagbe?" Noemi asked.

"Two hundred thousand. We have the biggest market in lower Ughelli."

"It's big enough for us to score a cell phone," Ranger said under his breath.

"You can use Uncle Efe's phone," Noemi said quietly.

"Not until I can trust him. I need a burner phone."

The driver honked as a truck overloaded with chicken pens cut in front of them.

"You are lucky, daughter," Uncle Efe said, "that I am at my country house this week. I am often at my home in Warri. There, word of your arrival would not have traveled so fast."

They slowed at a roundabout, and a couple children ran out, banging on the car, holding a bag of fruit. Uncle Efe laughed and rolled down his window, spoke to them, and handed over a couple coins. He retrieved the fruit.

"Fresh mango. My wife Angel loves them."

They cut off the main road, and in the distance, the sun glinted off a wide, dirty brown river. The Forcados, if Noemi remembered correctly. The side road brought them through neighborhoods, with children playing fútbol, boys running beside the car, little girls in brightly colored dresses. A few women looked up from where they stood, chatting, bags on their heads, their bodies wrapped in patterned skirts.

A world of color against a backdrop of dirt roads and humble living.

And yet, not all of Nigeria lived humbly. Two-story homes with satellite dishes attached to the roofs, gated compounds, and sleek European cars in the cobblestone courtyards sat amid tiny one-story stone houses with minuscule garden plots. And between them, two- and three-story apartment buildings with balconies that hosted bicycles and hanging plants and children staring at them through the cement balustrades.

They left the town, and the road stretched along the river, where men threw in nets from fishing boats, and small ferries laden with fish, fruit, and vegetables chugged down the water.

"The Forcados meets the Niger to the south, and we can take our oil right to the Gulf of Guinea."

"Is that what you do, uncle? My mother said once you owned an oil company."

He turned back to her, grinning. "Daughter. I own *all* the oil companies. After all, I am the king of Okwagbe."

Was he kidding? Before she could get a read on him, they turned onto a paved drive.

Ahead of them sprawled a huge compound. Whitewashed cement walls, over twelve feet tall, ran a hundred yards both directions with an impressive solid black gate barring both the entrance and a look-see inside.

They stopped and the driver rolled down his window, shouted out of it.

In a moment, a man in a white-and-blue uniform, a small cap, and carrying a gun came out and unlocked the entrance.

They drove inside.

Blessing gasped.

Maybe Uncle Efe wasn't kidding about being a king, because certainly they'd arrived at a palace of sorts.

The driver pulled into the white cobbled courtyard and around a fat-girthed, spiky-trunked date palm tree. It pulled up in front of a grand three-story whitewashed building, complete with a wraparound second-story balcony. At the front of the house, an expansive garden filled with pink calla lilies, gorgeous purple bird-of-paradise flowers, and tall white amaryllis bordered a stone veranda, heavily seeded with potted palm trees. The house easily spanned a hundred feet, with rounded floor-to-ceiling windows and a turret on one end of the structure that had a Juliet balcony off the second story. Towering palm trees arched from beyond the end of the house.

Flanking the house, on either side, were smaller buildings. One looked like a garage, with a number of arched doors facing the courtyard. The other was a two-story building with just a veranda across the front, also heavily flowered.

From the oversized double mahogany doors, a uniformed man came out and descended the stone veranda, standing next to a beautiful spray of pink camellias. He opened the door for Noemi's uncle.

"First we will meet the family. And then we will eat!" Uncle Efe said as he exited the car.

"When do I get those promised pants?" Ranger asked.

"It's so beautiful!" Blessing said as she got out the other side.

Noemi debated, then followed Ranger out. She still wasn't sure if he wouldn't fall over on her.

The flowers sweetened the air, birds chirruped, and the scent of something cooking swept over her.

She'd died and gone to paradise.

Maybe Ranger felt the same way because he simply stood there, his fist holding his sheet tight around his body. "And I need my boots too."

Or maybe not.

"I have them," Noemi said. "They're in your pack, along with another wad of cash. You're like the Cayman Islands—secret cash everywhere! Who brings three thousand euros into a country?" She cut her voice to a whisper as they followed Uncle Efe into the house.

"Apparently a guy who needs to buy a bride."

"You're not buying me."

"Talk to the man." He gestured to Uncle Efe with his chin.

And then she stopped. Because if she thought the outside of the estate was opulent, the inside—

"Wow," Blessing said. "Wow, o!"

Indeed. The flooring was pure white travertine. A curved staircase wound up to a second floor that overlooked an expansive living area, cordoned off by two thick stone columns. Past the overstuffed white leather furniture, the gold-toned lamps, and an oversized goldfish sculpture in the middle of a glass coffee table, a dramatic floor-to-ceiling arched window overlooked a patio, and beyond that, it looked like . . . a pool?

"It's so beautiful!" Blessing slid off her shoes and walked into the great room. "I've never seen a fireplace so big!"

Uncle Efe had taken off his shoes and now turned and extended his arms. "Welcome home, Noemi! Everything I have is yours now." He walked over and put his hands on her shoulders, met her eyes.

In them, for the first time, she saw something familiar.

Her throat thickened.

"You were lost, and now you're found. Come meet your family."

"I think Ranger—"

"Ah, yes. Your husband. He needs clothing, yes?"

She nodded.

"Go with them, husband." He directed the two men who'd come in behind them up the stairs, and Noemi looked up to see they carried Ranger's belongings.

Without his guns, of course.

"I'll stay with my, um, wife. Thanks," Ranger said, and Uncle Efe smiled again.

"Ah, he doesn't trust his uncle yet. I understand." He pointed at his head. "I was a soldier too, once."

He gestured to Noemi. "Come, come." Then he headed down the hall that flanked the living room.

"Come, come," Noemi said to Ranger.

He gave her a look.

She smirked.

"I don't see what's so funny. Did you see those walls out there? We're gated in here."

"You're just mad because you don't have pants."

"Oh, honey, don't get me started— Is that a pool?"

They'd headed down the hallway into a long mahogany dining room set with a table that could host twenty-four. And along one wall was a wine rack, filled with bottles. Solid-gold brocade drapes also flanked these windows, and the view looked out again on the patio, the expansive pool, and a lush garden of sego palms, thick fronds, and more calla lilies.

"Holy cow," Ranger said.

Blessing was in front of them and now turned, grinning. "It's like heaven."

"Only if it has a phone."

"And a tub with hot water," Noemi added.

A smile nudged Ranger's face. Despite his grumpy demeanor, the wear and tear on his body, his three-day-old beard, and even the way he held his toga, he was still terribly, brutally handsome.

And those blue eyes missed nothing. He was probably judging the distance to the far whitewashed walls, maybe even devising a plan over them.

Uncle Efe led them into another room, and the moment the door opened, the smells rushed out to grab her.

The kitchen.

Voices rose from inside, all in Urhobo, and Noemi slowed.

Ranger caught up with her. "You okay?"

"I . . . I don't know. I've spent my entire life wondering what world my mother left behind when she married my dad. She tried to tell me—taught me how to make jollof rice and we had the occasional Owho soup, but . . ."

He touched her shoulder. "Take a breath. It's been something you've wanted for a long time. For what it's worth, I know your dad would be happy for you."

She looked at him. "Really?"

He gestured with his chin. "Go in there and meet your family. I'm not going anywhere."

His eyes fixed to hers a long moment, and then she took his hand. He held on and she walked into the kitchen.

Apparently, Uncle Efe and Blessing had briefed their audience, because the room went silent.

A big room, with a large, worn-wood-topped center island and two stoves, with pots bubbling on both of them, the steam leaching up by two silver vents. Wooden cabinets lined the walls, and two women in aprons and white chef's hats stood with their hands folded, grinning at Noemi.

But the audience that mattered most had risen from another long table, this one cluttered with fruit, burlap bags of rice, and a bowl of boiled eggs. Two women stood, one of them with a baby on her hip, both dressed in multicolored skirts. The older woman wore her hair tied up in an orange headwrap. Big-bosomed and heavily made up, she held Uncle Efe's hand. He stood beside her, grinning.

"I told you," he said to her.

"I can't believe it." Her English was crisp and British. "I just can't believe it."

"Noemi, this is Auntie Lydia, my first wife."

His, um, first wife?

The woman stepped forward, giggling. "You are Mercy's daughter?"

Noemi nodded and Auntie Lydia raised her hands as if in praise. "Heaven almighty, God don butta my bread!" Then she threw her arms around Noemi, pulling her tight to her sweaty chest.

Ho-kay.

But Auntie Lydia wouldn't let go, rocking with her, humming, crying.

"Okay, okay." Uncle Efe unwrapped her arms from around Noemi.

Auntie Lydia continued to cry, stepping back, humming louder.

"This is your auntie Angel, my country wife."

The younger woman, with the baby on her hip now sucking its fist, stepped up and curtsied. "Cousin Noemi. I'm so honored to meet you." Her words sounded thought out, as if not easily formed.

Noemi curtsied back.

Suddenly, a boy slammed into the room from the open door, breathing hard. "I found her! She was in the garden."

Found who—

And then a woman appeared at the door and Noemi froze.

Petite and beautiful, despite the white in her hair, which was braided and piled up on the back of her head and held with a bright pink scarf, she wore a matching pink-and-yellow-patterned dress, which she'd hiked up as she ran.

Now, she stood in the doorway, just staring at Noemi. "Oh. You look just like her."

Noemi's thoughts exactly, because for a moment, she was twelve, watching her beautiful mother greet her at the door of her dorm room on her last day of school. Petite. Her hair in long braids, wearing a headband and a bright-yellow shirt, jeans. *"It's time to come home."*

She stupidly broke into tears.

"Oh, there, there, daughter," the woman said. "I'm your auntie Precious. You're safe now. You're home." She walked in and pulled Noemi to herself.

And shoot, didn't she smell like her mother too, something on her skin—a lotion or maybe just the scent of the garden. Maybe that's why Noemi let herself sink into the embrace. Let herself hold on until she could reel herself back in.

Auntie Precious finally eased her away, her beautiful brown eyes holding hers. "You are brave, just like my big sister." Her gaze then went to Ranger. "And who is this?"

Oh, she didn't want to lie. Not to this woman, this replica of her mother who could probably see inside her soul and read her heart just like her mother could. She took a breath, and the truth filled her chest—

"It's her *husband*," Uncle Efe said.

"What?" Her mouth opened. "We have heard nothing of this. The marriage of my sister's only daughter. How can—"

"Stay calm, sista. He has come to Nigeria to request the bride price. They will be remarried, here, as tradition says."

Oh no.

"Yes, yes." Auntie Precious turned back to her. "That is right. Your mother will be so happy as she looks down on you both from heaven."

Oh boy.

She looked again at Ranger. "This man is wounded. Why is he not in bed?" She barked at the cooks, gesturing, then turned to Noemi. "And where are your shoes?"

"It's a long story, sista," Uncle Efe said.

"Get them upstairs to their room." She patted Noemi on the cheek. "We will get you sorted. Take your husband upstairs. My housekeeper will bring up clothing for you both."

By now, more children had arrived, sneaking into the room to line up along the walls. Little girls with tufted hair and dresses, boys in white shirts and long pants, sandals. All of them well-groomed and eyeing her—no, Ranger—with open curiosity.

Probably she did need to get him upstairs and at least clothed, if not cleaned up. And in bed where he could sleep.

"They should eat," Uncle Efe said.

"We will bring them food." Auntie Precious caught Noemi's face with both her hands. "They will sleep, right?"

Noemi nodded. In fact, fatigue had started, suddenly, to pull at her.

Auntie Precious let her go. "And then, tonight, we will have a celebration, with introductions."

Perfect. She'd meet everyone then.

Auntie Precious clapped and spoke to one of the boys. Then to Noemi, "Follow Jaife. He will show you your room."

It wasn't until Noemi got to the top of the stairs that she caught the singular tense of the word. Behind her, Ranger said nothing as they followed the ten-or-so-year-old down a hallway, passing bedrooms and suites and finally walking up a small stairway to a round landing. Narrow, tall windows looked out on both the courtyard and the back garden.

The turret.

Jaife opened the door and she moved inside.

Ranger followed.

"You have the best room in the house, auntie!" Jaife said.

"Thank you, Jaife," she said.

He grinned at her, then closed the door.

"This floor doesn't look too comfortable," Ranger said.

Indeed. Gorgeous white travertine, with an elegant chandelier that dripped from the ceiling. A bathroom off the back held a soaking tub, a shower, and two enormous mirrors under equally grand stone-topped vanities.

And one four-poster bed.

It was beautiful, with tall mahogany posts that rose ten feet in the air, a white sheer gauze that wound around the top, and gold silk bedding, but still.

One bed.

"I'll take the sofa," she said and pointed to a gold brocade settee near the window.

"That's not a sofa. It's a bench. I get you're small, but you won't fit your right leg on that."

"You let me decide what I can fit on that sofa. You're taking the bed."

He sighed. "Fine." Then he walked over and eased himself onto it, face up.

She noticed his gear sat near a tall mahogany wardrobe. She walked into the bathroom and stared at herself in the mirror.

Oh. My.

She might have put her hair up and given herself a sponge bath, but it did nothing to dent the snarls of her hair, nearly dreadlocks. Her arms and legs were covered with scratches, not to mention her poor feet—torn, bruised, and now desperately painful.

She needed about a week in a real bath.

A knock came at the bedroom door and she opened it. The housekeeper stood there with a pile of clothing, a headwrap, pants, a kaftan for Ranger.

Slippers for both of them.

"Thank you," she said, and the woman bowed. "Hey, Ranger—"

He'd already dropped off to sleep.

She set the clothing on a bench at the end of the bed and walked over to him. Put her hand over his mouth.

Still breathing.

"What are you doing?"

Oh. So not sleeping. "Checking to see if you're alive."

"Don't worry, you're my beneficiary."

"That's not funny."

But he smiled again. Then he opened his eyes.

She sat on the bed next to him. "What have I gotten us into?"

"Yes. I would dearly love to know how we got into this mess." He closed his eyes. "But later. After food. And sleep. And a phone."

"And introductions."

"Right. Those." He scooted up on the bed, tugging his sheet with him.

"Do you think we'll really have to get married?"

He shook his head, his eyes still closed. "We'll get out of here before then. Don't worry, wife. I'm harmless. Nothing's going to happen . . ."

She watched as his eyes softly closed and noted those dark whiskers against his chin. Those lips that had, once upon a time, made her feel like he'd never let her go.

And her only thought was . . . *Shoot.*

SEVEN

He'd slept like the dead, and still Ranger ached everywhere. His muscles, his bones, his cells, even his mitochondria hurt as he opened his eyes.

Sunset.

It cascaded through the gold drapes and into the room, across the ceiling, turning everything an eerie orange.

He'd slept half the day away.

But Noemi was safe, he knew it, and for the first time since recognizing her voice in the chaos of their rescue op, he let the knot in his gut unravel.

How she'd gotten them from that terrible moment on the riverbed when he'd let her walk away to right now—him in a massive bed, the smell of grilled meat finding its way through the window, the scent of a tropical storm in the air, and the sounds of laughter somewhere in the house—he didn't know.

But he respected it.

Ranger rolled over, worked himself up, and pushed off the bed, reaching out to grab the mahogany spire at the end of it. The world finished churning and he headed into the bathroom.

Stopped at the massive mirror and took a good look at himself.

Not a pretty sight. Mud had worked into his beard, and his hair felt like it might be a home for fleas—dirty, tousled, and knotted. He should have gotten a haircut before leaving for Nigeria, but he'd been pretty deep in darkness and had only popped his head out when Ham called.

He'd likely go back under when this op was over.

Which it wasn't. Not yet.

He turned on the shower and returned to the sink, waiting for the water to warm. Someone had patched him up using some kind of mud mixture and he picked at it. The pain kept him from taking it off. It would wash away in the shower. His collarbone was red, swollen, and tender—that must be what he'd broken in the fall.

He unwound his sling but kept his arm close to him as he got in the shower and sank into the heat. Days rolled off him and pooled in the grime at his feet. Along with it, the mud on his wound also released, but he kept the shoulder out of the spray, not wanting to loosen any more scabs. The shot had gone right through his arm, but he had no doubt he had an infection, at least of the wound. Hopefully it hadn't gotten into his blood.

He turned the heat down after a bit because he'd started to feel a sweat break out, then he sudsed up his hair. Rinsed it. Then washed it again.

He'd feel human if he could shave. But barring that, he was at least upright and ready for . . . well, whatever Uncle Efe had in the way of family introductions.

What he wanted to do was find a phone. Hopefully Noemi had scored one. Sure, he could use Uncle Efe's, but the last thing he needed was a trace to Ham's location. It wasn't personal. It came with his training.

Most of all he needed to end this op, asap.

But he'd seen Noemi's face when she spotted her auntie Precious. Her sobs had torn something deep inside him.

Probably that same something that had made him nearly stride up to her at her father's funeral and pull her into his arms. Torture had to be seeing the woman he'd loved sitting alone in the front pew or standing solo as her father's empty casket was lowered to the earth. Oh sure, she'd been surrounded by SEALs, but they carried their own grief.

And really, they couldn't exactly comfort her when it was their fault he'd died. His body washed away in the currents of the Pacific. A dangerous nighttime training HALO jump. He'd pulled his cord . . . and then vanished. They hadn't even recovered his chute.

Ranger couldn't get past the fact that they'd let a decorated Navy SEAL die during a training exercise.

So, no, even if Ranger found a phone, he'd check in and then . . . he couldn't leave. Not yet, anyway. Not until he knew Noemi was safe. Really safe. As in no-more-terrorists-trying-to-find-her-and-kill-her safe.

He'd wrapped a towel around his waist and was examining his wound when he heard the bedroom door open.

Ranger pulled on the pants to the outfit Uncle Efe had delivered. Lightweight, jade green, they fit like hospital scrubs. Then, he opened the bathroom door.

Noemi stood in the room, her back to him, staring down at the lawn, wearing a white dress, her hair back in a white head-wrap.

"Hey," he said. "You okay?"

She turned, and he was caught up in time, to that day at the pier when she'd looked almost angelic.

Wow, he was probably just hungry.

But she *was* pretty. No makeup, but those golden-brown eyes, that sweet, full smile, that beautiful hair he loved to weave his fingers into—

Stop. *Get ahold of yourself, sailor.*

"Yes. What a crazy day. I spent it with my, um, family." She folded her arms and leaned back against the windowsill alcove. "So, a few interesting facts—my uncle really *is* a king. Of his tribe. So, there's that. And he's probably a billionaire."

"Hence the house."

"One of three, apparently. He also has a home in Lagos. And, by the way, another wife there. Which makes that a grand total of three."

"Busy guy."

"He has thirteen children. Seven of them are here. Three are grown and away at college. The rest are in Lagos."

"Wow."

"Contrast that to my auntie Precious who is a widow. Her husband was in the military and was killed fighting the Boko Haram a few years ago. She's about ten years younger than my mother and went to Oxford to get her law degree. She came back to Nigeria to work for my uncle's company and met her husband. They never had children."

She walked over to him. "Are you sure you're okay? You're sweating."

"It's Nigeria. It's about ten thousand degrees." They had no AC on, and only a slight breeze came through the open window.

"Right," she said. "I went swimming. It was glorious. It's so weird—two days ago I was running from terrorists, today I'm eating pineapple and lying in the sun."

"Yeah. I often feel the same way after a quick mission. We drop out of the sky, sneak through the desert to find and eliminate a target, then sneak out and I'm back in Coronado eating burgers the next night."

"How are you with goat meat?"

He laughed.

"My uncle is setting up for the introductions tonight."

"Wait. What do you mean *setting up* the introductions? Didn't we already meet?"

"Marriage is a formal event here—this is the ceremony where you ask the king and the tribal elders to marry me." She gave him a soft smile. "I'm so sorry. We need to put a stop to this."

"Not until I can figure out how to get us home. Right now, we're safe inside these walls." He rubbed a hand through his beard. "I'm going to need a razor."

"I got you pants. What more do you need?" She grinned at him.

And just like that, he fell into it, sweet, familiar. "Maybe help getting this shirt on?" He held up the kaftan. It fell to his knees.

"Sure. C'mere." She climbed up on the bed and stood over him. "Turn around."

He obeyed, and she gasped. "Range. You have a bruise on your back that looks . . . it's really bad. It's purple and . . ." She touched it.

His groan emerged before he could stop it. "Really?"

"Seriously. For a SEAL you sure are a wimp. I barely touched you."

"You did *not* barely touch me. Good thing you're not a doctor." And, by the way, that was *former* SEAL. He hadn't exactly corrected her, not once, over the past few days, and he didn't know how to do it now.

"I stopped your bleeding, didn't I?" She hopped down and circled around to the front of him. Made a face. "That shoulder is pretty inflamed."

"What do you want? You took me to a herbalist. Who knows what was in that concoction."

"You should thank me because she's one of the best." But she leaned up on her tiptoes, her hand on his chest as she examined the wound.

She smelled good. Like roses or lilies or something sweet, her face so close he could probably lean down and . . . *stop*.

That was the last thing he needed. Especially when he still had no future to offer her.

She stepped back. "You slept all day, completely missed the ah-mazing Akara—it's cooked black-eyed peas, deep fried, and it sounds gross, but it would blow your mind. And the cooks made chin chin, which, by the way, I saved you some." She gestured to a basket she'd brought up and put on the bench. "They're sorta like donuts."

She climbed back on the bed. "Okay, kiddo, hands up."

He put one in the air.

"Hmm. This isn't going to work. You're too, um . . ."

"Muscular?"

"I was going to say decrepit, but whatever. Here." She bunched up the shirt and carefully pulled his injured arm into the sleeve. Then she moved the neck over his head and helped guide his good arm in. Then she tugged the shirt over his body.

"Not a terrible look, I guess." She stepped back and folded her arms. "I guess I'll marry you."

"About that. What—how did we end up married, again? We didn't stop by Elvis's Parlor of Love while I was sleeping, did we? I mean, I know I was out of it, but I feel like I'd remember walking down the aisle to 'Love Me Tender.'"

"Silly man." She turned to the basket and unwrapped a bowl of puffy brown donut-like rolls. "They don't have Elvis here. It was called Forever Love and Instant Marriages Chapel."

"Right."

"I'm so hurt." She shook her head and handed him a donut.

He put it in his mouth. Yeah, it had donut written all over it. And with it, his stomach roared to life.

"Oh my," she said. "Well, good for you, there's a party going down after you lay out the cash for your bride."

"I hope a thousand euros is enough." He sat down on the bed, his entire body feeling a little tight, almost nauseous with the donut.

Weird.

"A grand? That's all you're willing to pay for all this?" She stood up and did a showy sweep over her body.

"How about my life? I did give you that."

Her smile fell, and shoot, he didn't know why he said it. The words had just sort of fallen out of his mouth.

"Yes," she said quietly. "You did give me that. Or almost." She looked away. "I'm sorry about all this. I should just tell them the truth." She made to move away, but he grabbed her wrist.

"Stop," he said. "What are you doing?"

"I'm doing the right thing. What I should have done the moment Blessing said we were married."

"Blessing said that? Why?" he asked.

She looked at him, a hint of misery in her eyes.

"Why, Noe?" He tugged her closer. Her skin was so soft under his grip.

"I asked her about that—she said she panicked. She was trying to save your life, but she justified it because she thinks . . . I'm still in love with you."

Still? Wait—what? His chest tightened. And then, because clearly something was wrong with him, and he'd lost control of his faculties, he asked, "Are you?"

Her eyes widened. "What? In love with you? Please. Are you?"

"Am I what?"

"In love with me?" She shook her wrist from his grip.

Great. Now he'd made her mad. "Why would you say that?"

"Because Blessing said that when you were delirious, you were calling out for me."

"I was never delirious."

"You tried to strangle me. Please tell me that was delirium."

He stared at her, a rock falling through him. "I tried to do *what*?"

"I was bandaging you in the car and you sort of came to and freaked out and grabbed me around the throat"

"Oh, wow, Noemi— I'm so sorry. I would never, *never* hurt you. Please know that."

"At least not willingly. Only if you had to, right? For your career?" Her eyes sparked a little, bright with hurt.

And it hit him, right in the center of the chest, the memory of his words. *"This was a huge mistake."*

Okay, yes, of course she'd been hurt—he'd been a jerk. Maybe still was. But he'd nearly died because instead of training, he'd given in to his desires. His emotions.

Her.

And right then, he'd had to make a choice. Now, he had to live with that choice. "Right."

She looked away, then ran her hand across her cheek. Her voice softened. "It's okay, Range. I'm not . . ." She sighed and looked at him. "I'm not sure where that came from, but listen, I am deeply grateful that you risked your life for me. And enough of these games. Yes. Blessing said we were married, for whatever crazy reason, and I wasn't exactly sure that the pastor would help us unless you were my husband—"

"Because I was hurt—"

"More that you're a white man, dressed like a soldier. So, yeah. I lied. And I thought it would just be that once, to get you help, and then my uncle showed up, and . . . it just happened again—"

"I was there."

She met his eyes. "Yes. You were. And thank you for playing along. I'm not sure what he would have thought if . . . well, I think Urhobo rules are a little strict about men and women spending time together alone—"

"I hardly think running from terrorists constitutes spending time together alone . . ."

She cocked her head. "I wasn't only referring to now."

Oh. "Right. Okay. But that was then, this is now, and . . . okay, I get it—"

"But you don't have to. I'll just go down there and tell them the truth."

"No, you won't."

She creased her brow. "What?"

"No, you won't go tell them the truth." His voice gentled, and he reached for her hand again. This time, she let him take it. "Listen. Like I said, right now we're safe. And I need time to figure out what is going on, and frankly, I'd feel a lot better if you were where I could see you. So we'll sort out the sleeping part, and I'll go be introduced to your uncle and whoever and cough up my thousand euros and maybe buy myself the right to be your husband. At least for a few days until we get out of here, safe and sound. Okay?"

He hadn't noticed that he was rubbing his thumb over her hand until she tightened hers in his. "Yes. Okay," she said. "And in the meantime, I should probably tell you that I have a cell phone."

"What?"

"Yeah. I stole it, which I'm not super proud of, but I used it to get us here—or most of the way here, because it died. But I asked if I could borrow a charger—"

He leaned down and kissed her. Just a quick kiss, something more out of reflex than desire, but the moment he did it, something ignited inside him.

He pulled away fast.

She raised an eyebrow. "Well, you're welcome."

"Sorry. That was—"

"Don't worry, I get it. I kissed you in the car. Which was probably why Blessing thinks I love you."

Huh.

She lifted a shoulder. "So, maybe there is something left over of those two weeks."

He drew in a breath, trying not to let whatever was happening inside him, this crazy churn of emotions, make him say something stupid.

"Friends?" She held out her hand.

He shook it, feeling a little silly, but . . . okay. "Friends."

"Good. Now, before you go ask my uncle for my hand in marriage, you're going to need this." She pulled out a bottle of Schnapps from the basket.

"I don't need a drink to face your uncle."

She laughed. "It's not for you, silly. It's a gift. For him. Apparently, I can be bought for a thousand euros and a bottle of Schnapps."

He took the bottle. "Don't be so hard on yourself. If I had a goat, I'd definitely offer that too."

She grinned again. Friends. Sure, whatever.

"So how is this supposed to work?" he asked. "Will you tell me what to say?"

She headed toward the door. He followed her. "Hardly. I'm not even allowed to be in the room."

He stopped. "Wait—I'm doing this alone?"

She opened the door and held it for him. "What, you need a team to get the job done?"

"Usually, but . . . what if I say something wrong?"

"Just do whatever he says. We'll live through this."

He followed her down the hallway, then down the stairs and into the great room.

Her uncle stood in front of the window, watching his children play in the pool. He wore an elegant white kaftan and a massive coral necklace, a white cap, ornamented with beads. He turned when they came down and then nodded to Ranger. "Are you ready?"

"Let's get this negotiation started." He'd sort of meant it as a way to break the tension, but Uncle Efe didn't smile, so Ranger added, "Your Highness."

Uncle Efe raised an eyebrow.

"I think you call him Ovie," Noemi whispered. She said it like o-vee-ay. "I'll be in the next room."

Perfect. Abandoned.

Ovie Efe gestured down the other hallway, and Ranger followed him into a well-appointed office. An expansive mahogany desk sat against one wall, banked by floor-to-ceiling bookshelves. Along the opposite wall hung oversized pictures of former chieftains, or maybe just ancestors all ornately attired in native wear.

And under them sat a row of seven robed, ornamented men, all watching him with a solemn look.

At the head of the row sat a large gold-plated, padded chair.

Ah, the throne.

The Ovie sat in it, then offered Ranger the only remaining seat, a lonely straight back chair that faced the group.

He lowered himself into it, biting back the ache in his bones.

Ovie Efe started speaking in his native language, explaining something to the men, then turned to Ranger. "Welcome. These are my village eldermen. They will determine if you deserve to be married to our daughter."

Huh. Pretty sure that was a big N-O, so good thing this wasn't for real. Still, he felt like a fraud when the Ovie asked, "Why are you here, son?"

It was just part of the mission. Adapt. Improvise. "I'm here to ask permission to, um, marry Noemi Sutton."

"Noemi Ofejiro." The Ovie picked up an oversized white ostrich feather and fanned himself.

"Yes."

"And where is your family?"

Um. "Alaska."

"Do they approve of this match?"

His mother would most definitely approve of Noemi. Creative, vivacious, smart— "Yes." And Colt had liked her, too, from the very start. "Most definitely."

The Ovie nodded, no smile. "And you will provide for her?"

Oh. "Yes."

"How?"

"My family has a ranch in Alaska." Not exactly an answer, but the Ovie nodded, then turned to the men and translated. He received nods from the elders.

The Ovie considered him. "Tell me why you want her."

Why he wanted her. The memory of her helping him with his shirt or feeding him donuts easily came to him.

But the answer was really found in the past. In the way, for two weeks, she'd loosed the tight coil in his chest, helped him breathe, see the world as brighter, wider, more colorful.

He was all black-and-white, focus and duty, a life without blurred lines.

Maybe thinking through all that took too long because the Ovie cleared his throat.

The elders, too, cleared their throats.

He stared at the chief and said the only thing that made sense. "Because I love her. Because she's the one woman—the only woman—I want to be with."

The Ovie raised an eyebrow. Shook his head. "Americans. Always so emotional."

What—? And sure, he might have overspoken, but if he were the one asking questions, it felt like the right answer.

Maybe the man could see through him to his lies.

Only right now, when everything hurt, when exhaustion loosened the hard clamp he had on his heart, it didn't feel so much like a lie.

The Ovie translated, and the other men made the sound again, like they were clearing their throats. As if they'd made a decision, in unison. Then one of them stood and began a long speech in Urhobo.

Ranger sat, his insides churning—feeling, still, not quite right.

The man sat down, and the chief turned to him. "He has given you the blessing of the elders."

"Great." Ranger shifted, and the room swam. His entire body felt a little numb.

"Now we agree to terms," the Ovie said.

Terms. Right. "I don't have a lot of money."

One of the elders rose and handed over a piece of paper. At least it wasn't a number on a napkin. The list was written in English and Ranger scanned it. Somehow, his vision wouldn't tighten, the words moving in and out of focus.

No, not now—

"Can you procure these items?"

He took a breath and forced away the nausea. Scanned the list.

A bottle of something to drink for the Ovie. A bottle of

champagne for the wedding. A plate of kola nuts. A hat for the Ovie. A head tie for Noemi's aunt Precious, three bags of salt, a bag of rice, and, of course, 1.5 million for her chastity.

He blinked at the number for a long moment. One. Point five. *Million*.

For her *chastity*?

"It's in naira," the Ovie said quietly, somehow reading his thoughts.

Ranger was too tired to do the math, but he thought that might be about three thousand euros.

Still steep, for a guy whose boot was empty.

"Agreed?"

He nodded. As soon as they charged Noemi's cell phone, he'd put an end to this. In the meantime, this list would buy him some time, maybe. "Yes, sir."

"Good. Now the nuts." The Ovie snapped his fingers and the door opened. Ranger glanced over and Noemi walked in with a tray holding a bowl of round, brown nuts. She curtsied in front of her uncle, kneeled, then extended the tray to the elders, then the Ovie, and finally Ranger.

"Were you listening the entire time?" he whispered as he took a nut.

"Shh. You're doing great."

She got up and stepped away and he bit into the nut. Bitter.

She leaned down to his ear. "It gets sweeter as you chew."

It did, but it didn't settle any better in his gut when he swallowed.

"What did you bring for us?" the Ovie asked.

What did he bring . . . *wait*. He handed over the Schnapps.

The Ovie took it, nodding. "Now we drink."

No, oh *no*, because the nut wanted to come back up. He blamed it on his empty stomach, and probably the way his entire body ached, but now he was also lightheaded and . . .

He was going to lose it.

"Excuse me." He got up, but he wasn't going to make it to the nearest bathroom, wherever that was.

He headed toward a basket on the floor near the desk.

Except now the room spun, darkness winking in and out of his vision.

"Ranger?"

The voice sounded far away. But he needed that basket.

His outstretched hand missed the basket, and then his knees buckled—

He hit the floor.

"Ranger!"

He looked up at Noemi just as the world closed in. "Nailed it, baby."

Her eyes widened.

And then he was out.

Ranger had nearly died asking if he could marry her.

She didn't believe in signs, but if she did . . . well, that one seemed a bit *neon*. Not that Noemi ever planned on really marrying him, but maybe his fear that she'd someday cost him his career—not to mention his life—wasn't so crazy after all.

"How's he doing?"

The question came from her auntie Precious, who'd knocked before she entered and now stood at Ranger's bedside.

For the past two days, after his stay at the hospital, the man had slept like the dead, and that had scared Noemi more than she wanted to admit. Of course, it was to be expected after surgery, but still . . .

"I can't believe he went through that entire introduction with two broken ribs and internal bleeding. He's a tough man, your husband."

Auntie Precious wore a blue dress, her long hair pulled back in tiny braids. She carried a tray and now set it down on the table in the corner. "I brought you some soup and bread. You need to sleep, Noemi. You look tired."

She was. Because the moment Noemi tried to drop off to sleep on the mat she'd made for herself on the tile floor after Ranger had gotten back from the hospital, was exactly the moment she feared he'd stop breathing.

And with the fear came the memory of him collapsing in her uncle Efe's office three days ago, the blood that he vomited, the way she couldn't rouse him . . .

She'd nearly lost him.

Again.

"You can't heal him by sitting next to his bed day and night. Come eat with us. The children are wanting you."

She did enjoy her cousins—had learned to play Ayo, a game played on a board with seeds and six holes on each side. And after being beaten soundly over a dozen times, she finally figured out a strategy. She'd also played Ludo, which was a lot like Aggravation, an old game she'd played with her mother.

Being in her uncle's compound felt very much like walking back in time, with the smells of onions, peppers, and curry seasoning the kitchen, as well as the recipes the cooks served—boiled plantain and Onunu, a yam and plantain dough that went with soup.

And every time Auntie Precious laughed, she heard her mother.

She'd forgotten how much she missed her.

"Dr. Chibundu says that he'll be here tomorrow, but that Mr. Ranger is doing well for his injuries. Has he woken?" Auntie Precious pressed her hand to his forehead. "He is still warm."

They were all warm. The daily rainstorms swept the heat from the day but added to the general mugginess that weighted the air. The house fans kept them cool, as did the tall ceilings and stone walls, but for the life of her, Noemi couldn't understand why a palace like this didn't come equipped with central AC.

Still, she didn't hate hearing the constant chatter of the forests surrounding the compound, the grebes, pigeons, and hornbills that sang from outside the walls.

"He ate this morning, and he stirred a bit ago."

"Good. I'll have the cooks make broth." She stopped near Noemi. "It was very romantic, what he said to Efe. Don't worry, he'll pull through."

"She's the one woman—the only woman—I want to be with."

Yes, she'd heard that, and it was romantic . . . But he didn't mean it, and they both knew it. She gave Auntie Precious a smile. "I hope so."

"Keep praying. God is with him."

Noemi frowned. "Is he? Because if you haven't noticed, he's been shot. And spent three days with internal bleeding. That doesn't feel like God is protecting him."

Auntie Precious sat down on the bench beside the bed, next to Noemi. "Or God brought him exactly where he needed to be. He might have ended up in a hospital in a village instead of under the Ovie's care with his private physician." She patted her leg. "No, Emuvoke, God is with him."

Her aunt had started to call her by her tribal name, and for the first time, Noemi had begun to feel herself part of this world.

She'd even taught her how to make goat pepper soup with Blessing, who had barely left Auntie Precious's side since they arrived.

"Efe told me what happened. That you were kidnapped. Why was your husband not with you at the refugee school?"

"He was . . . working. He's not just a sailor, auntie. He's . . . he's a special kind of sailor."

"Ah. Like the Seventy-Second Paratrooper Battalion." She folded her arms. "My Jayamma served with the Seventy-Second." She stared at Ranger, and her hand pressed her cheek.

"Such dangerous work. Such good men." She turned to Noemi. "It must have hurt him terribly to know you were taken. But also, to know he had to do his job. A heart torn between two duties."

Oh, her auntie had no idea. "Yes."

"Is he the same as your father? A SEAL?"

She looked at her. What did it hurt? She nodded.

"Your mama, she loved your father fiercely. But she feared for his life often. He was a brave man too."

"He was." So brave it had cost him his life.

"It is the love that brings him home, right?" She smiled and winked.

Oh. "I . . ."

"I see you haven't slept in the bed yet." She nudged her with her shoulder. "The floor is no place for a wife. And the Nigerian nights get cold. You don't want him to suffer." Her eyes shone.

"Auntie!"

She laughed and got up. "The Ovie asked for 1.5 million naira. And he agreed. He must love you very much."

Or he just planned on skipping town before he had to pay it. "Yes. He does," she said, but the lie settled inside like a burr.

"Oh, Oyinbo mhe." Auntie Precious put her hand to her niece's cheek. "I am glad you are not alone. I have worried so for you after your father died. You should have come home sooner."

Her eyes filled at the endearment her mother had also used, and she blinked hard.

Auntie Precious smiled, her eyes also glistening. "Let me know when he wakes and we'll bring broth."

Oh, he'd be thrilled. Her last attempt at broth for Ranger had been met with a crisp "If that's not a hamburger, take it away."

"Thank you."

Auntie Precious left, closing the door behind her.

Outside, amid the sounds of the birds calling, thunder rolled and a light mist of rain trickled down. The afternoon storm wafted a freshness into the room.

Still, a light layer of sweat dotted Ranger's brow. Noemi went to the bathroom, got a washcloth, and returned, setting it on his forehead.

He hummed, as if sighing deep inside.

He looked so peaceful, the warrior fallen, his dark lashes against his face, his almost black hair tousled. A stubble had returned on his chin after a nurse at the hospital had shaved him. His chest rose and fell under the sheet, his shoulder wound cleaned, bandaged, and healing well, finally.

She should have taken him to the hospital right off. But maybe Auntie Precious was right—who knows what would have happened.

He hadn't gone down easily.

"A heart torn."

Almost literally. The broken rib had frayed his spleen, the blood filling his gut. A slow leak, but enough that if he hadn't collapsed, if they'd been anywhere else—even on a plane—he might not have survived.

She sat down on the bench, listening to him breathe. Wow, she was tired. And with the soft patter of the rain, the gentle breeze, yes, everything inside her longed for slumber.

"The floor is no place for a wife."

Maybe, but she wasn't his wife. Still, what if he stopped breathing?

She walked around the bed to the other side. He took up less than half, and she wasn't *that* big. If she gently just eased herself onto one side . . .

She lay on her side and tiptoed her fingers over to his chest. Set her hand softly on it.

Waited until she felt the gentle rhythm of his breathing, then closed her eyes.

The bright corners of the day softened, a soothing darkness drifting over her.

She could smell him, too, a particular scent that belonged only to Ranger. She breathed it in.

"You're still here."

She let the memory take her, sweeten her dreams. Ranger, standing in his T-shirt and shorts waiting for her in the tiki bar area of the resort. A fire flickered in the pit outside the hut area, casting sparks into the night.

Thunder rolled, but she suspected it was outside her dream because the night seemed clear, the clouds parted to reveal the stars.

"I told you I wasn't going anywhere." He smiled at her, although something sad still lingered in his eyes.

He didn't want to leave her. Despite his brain telling him that it was over, his heart had made him stay—she was sure of it.

They ordered dinner by the fire, ate peeled shrimp and fresh papaya, and she told him a story about her last trip to Peru and climbing Machu Picchu, the Inca citadel ruins. He told her about the time his brother Colt tracked down and killed a bear in Alaska.

Neither of them talked about the future.

He didn't leave after dinner either. Instead, he found them an empty cabana chair on the beach, not far from the blazing fire, and they climbed into it. She lay her head on his chest.

Listened to his heartbeat.

A countdown to the end.

"Have you ever been to Alaska?" His voice was soft, his arm around her shoulder. "It's beautiful. Our family owns land that sits in the shadow of Denali. As a kid I didn't appreciate the beauty, but having been in . . . well, less-than-beautiful places, it's probably the one place on earth that still takes my breath away, that gets me out of my head." He kissed the top of her head. "Well, the second place, maybe."

She closed her eyes. "I'd like to visit."

He said nothing for a long time, then, "I used to imagine, after I got out of the military, that I might move back. Maybe help my father turn the FBO into a sort of resort where people could escape. We have horses and cabins and . . . it's a great place to raise a family."

A family. She lifted her head. "You want a family?"

The fire flickered in his aqua-blue eyes. "I . . . I don't know. It doesn't matter. I'm a lifer in the Navy, so . . ." His gaze, however, didn't meet hers. "Do you?"

Her mouth opened. "I've never thought that far. I just sort of follow where my heart tells me to go next. My parents loved me, but I sort of got in the way of their lives . . ." She looked away. "I'm never getting married, so it doesn't really matter. There's a world out there that needs help, and I want to do my part. And I don't think that includes settling down. Kids need a home. Two parents. I'm not going to do to my kids what my parents did to me."

She'd never said that out loud before, but with Ranger, she felt safe.

He looked out into the darkness, the stars playing on the water. "I get that. And I agree. I'm not getting married either."

"It's a nice dream," she said.

"Maybe. But I don't have dreams. I have duty."

He fell silent then, his breaths evening out, and after a bit, she lifted her head.

Asleep. Well, he *had* gotten up at four a.m.

She lay back down, the breeze soft as the night closed in and the fire died. Shut her eyes.

No, she'd never been to Alaska. But she might like it.

"Noemi, wake up—oh!" He sucked in a breath. "Wake up!"

She stirred as Ranger sat up, easing her away from him, and opened her eyes. She must have dozed off—

Except, sunlight spanned the eastern horizon, the stars gone, the sky a pale lavender.

"I'm late." He got up, then reached out to help her up.

She practically fell off the cabana chair. "What?"

"It's after four. My exam starts in an hour." He took her hand. "I have to go."

She scrambled after him. Caught his hand. "Ranger. Will I see you . . . after?" Oh, she hated the fear in her voice. She had promised herself she wouldn't cling.

Would let him go without a backward glance.

But she'd never meant for this to go so far either.

He turned then, however, and caught her arms, met her eyes. "Yes. I'll find you, I promise."

He bent, as if to kiss her forehead, but she lifted her face.

He paused, met her eyes. Then he curled his hand around her neck and pulled her to himself, his mouth to hers.

It was thorough, if not quick, and in that blink of time, she still had him.

Then he touched his forehead to hers, let her go, and headed across the tiki deck to his room. Took the stairs two at a time.

She hadn't even wished him well on his exam. The loss of his presence set a boulder in her heart.

Inside their suite, her father was up, waiting for his coffee to brew in the tiny kitchen. He wore his BDUs.

So, back to work already. She should have guessed that he would have been tapped for duty, despite his leave. The life of a SEAL instructor.

He glanced at her, then frowned. "Where—"

"It's not what you think." She closed the door. "We fell asleep in one of the cabanas."

His jaw tightened.

"Nothing happened, Dad." She could still feel Ranger's body against her, the warmth of it.

"I'll find you."

"I'm going to bed." She shuffled to her room and fell onto the queen mattress, sleep finding her.

She didn't even hear her father leave. Or return.

But she did feel his hand on her shoulder, shaking her awake. "Honey, wake up."

She wore lines in her cheek from the pillow, the ceiling fan stirring the conditioned air. "What?" She opened her eyes.

Her father bore a hard, almost anguished expression. She sat up. "What happened?"

He ran his hand across his mouth, then took a breath. "There was an accident today on the Army base."

Oh, please—

"I didn't know the man you were with was a SEAL or I might have stepped in."

"Dad!" She grabbed a pillow. "Is he dead?" She pulled it to herself.

"No. But he's in ICU."

ICU.

"What happened?"

"We're not sure. He was doing fine. The test had him going down to the bottom, unlatching a hatch, then closing it and rising to the surface, but he never made it. We're not sure if he got hypoxic and confused, or if he just didn't prepare well enough, but . . ."

"He drowned."

"Blacked out. And yes, took in water. We were able to revive him on the deck, but he took in so much water—his lungs were full and he began to dry drown. They have him sedated while they pump out his lungs."

She slid off the bed. "I need to go—"

Her dad blocked her. "No. He's in ICU, and the military won't let you in."

"You can get me in."

He took a breath, his mouth tight. Shook his head.

"Why not?"

"Because this is a bad idea. He is a SEAL, and you know—

honey, you *know* the sacrifices your mother made for me. I don't want that for you."

She stared at him and something inside simply broke. "It doesn't matter what you want. You abdicated the right to dictate anything of my life when you left me on the steps of Massanutten Academy a week after my mother died. Are you kidding me? A week!"

"I had a job to do!"

"Exactly. I've been on my own for nearly *six* years." She walked over to her dresser and grabbed out a hair tie. "I can make my own decisions."

"It's exactly because of that—and of this moment—that you need to calm down and listen." He stepped into her path. "SEALs get hurt. And if they're not hurt, they're gone." He shook his head, his voice pitching low. "Worry killed your mother, and I'm not going to let it kill you. I won't." He took a breath. "And Ranger knows that."

She just stared at him, her chest rising and falling. "Dad. What did you do? What did you say to him?"

"What someone should have said to your mother."

"Oh, Dad—" She shoved past him and into the bathroom, slamming the door behind her. Leaned against it, breathing hard.

"Honey—"

"Just get me into the ICU," she said through the door.

Now, next to her, under the African heat, Ranger stirred, shuddered as if waking from a nightmare. Noemi opened her eyes.

Sat up.

The rain had let up, but twilight filtered into the room.

She shouldn't have gone. Should have listened to her father.

Should have let that kiss—that perfect, hungry, heart-wrenching kiss—be her last memory.

"I know better, Noemi. I know better but I didn't listen to myself."

His words had thundered to her, as fresh as when she stood by his bed hours later, after he came out of sedation. A thousand miles from the man who left her that morning. His eyes reddened, a sort of horror in them.

She knew, deep inside, that he was trying not to unravel. And it wasn't just that he hadn't passed his test, or even that he nearly drowned.

"Why didn't you tell me your father was a SEAL?"

Oh. "I didn't know it mattered. Besides, you couldn't have figured it out?"

His mouth tightened. "Yes. Maybe. But really, Noemi? You're Master Chief Sutton's daughter? Are you trying to cost me my career? This was a huge mistake . . ."

He looked away from her then, out the window, where the sun shone on a glorious, blue-skied day. "I'm sorry, but this can't work. Ever. I just . . ." And then he looked at her and said exactly what she knew, deep in her heart, her father had said. "The only thing I've ever wanted was to be a SEAL. I can't jeopardize that. I'm sorry."

She supposed it was better than him blaming her.

Still, he meant it because he hadn't looked away but held her gaze, his mouth a tight, unwavering line.

She knew that look. Her father wore it also, most often when she'd pleaded with him not to send her back to Massanutten.

Of course she didn't argue. Wouldn't.

She wasn't going to beg Ranger to want her. So she just stood and lifted a shoulder. Kept her voice easy. "Calm down, sailor. I told you. It's no big deal." She picked up her bag and touched his leg, her only hint at a real goodbye. Took a breath. "See you 'round."

His mouth opened, but she turned and walked out the door.

Thinking back to that moment, it had probably taken more courage to walk away from Ranger than to escape from a terrorist camp.

Now, she stared down at him in the fading sunlight, coming back from the edge of her worst fears.

But he wasn't back, not really. Because when he opened his eyes, he'd still be a SEAL. *"She's the one woman—the only woman—I want to be with."*

Maybe. But only in the place between sleeping and awake. Because in real life, his world didn't have any room for her.

And in truth, she wasn't sure his heart did either.

What she needed to do was stop playing marriage and find them a way home.

To let him go.

Before her heart broke all over again.

They wouldn't find her here.

Tae stood at the stove in the Sky King Ranch lodge kitchen, frying up a concoction of venison, onions, and garlic, the smell rooting in her bones.

Nearly a week at the ranch and she never wanted to leave. And not just because she could wrap herself up in a wool blanket and sit in front of the massive floor-to-ceiling stone fireplace, reading one of the Louis L'amour novels from the bookcase that flanked it. And not because the place radiated strength and safety, from the thick-beamed vaulted ceilings to the massive picture window that overlooked the mountains to the north. And not just because Nurse Oolanie had been right—the beauty soaked into her bones, the fresh air healed her frostbitten lungs, the bold expanse of the Denali massif stirred courage back into her soul.

But because here, at night, no one could hear her scream.

No one rushed into the room of her private cabin at the sound of her voice, rising from a nightmare—the ones with Sergei's hands around her throat, the rasp of her own breathing in her lungs, regret burrowing into her chest, thanks to the words of a man named Roy. *"It's up to you or we all die."*

No. Not yet. She needed more time.

She could still hear Barry's voice, sometimes—*"She can't be that weak. She survived an Alaskan blizzard out in the elements."*

Yes. Yes, she had. That, and so much more.

She couldn't ask about the accident, but even her sketchy sleuthing on the computer that Barry had loaned her revealed nothing of the wreckage of a plane lost somewhere south of Denali's shadow.

So, maybe she could stay lost.

Remake herself as Jane of the North who knew how to make venison chili.

"That smells delicious, Jane," Barry said from where he sat at the long granite island. "Which one is it?"

She held up a recipe card that she'd found in a bin of cards on the counter. Scrawled in a woman's handwriting, the paper was heavily stained with oil and tomato sauce.

He nodded. "Aw. One of my wife's favorites. Ranger improved on it—he added the cinnamon." He took a sip of coffee and set down his Kindle. She couldn't help but notice the size of the type—bright and bold.

She'd noticed, that first day, when he'd brought food down to her at the cabin by the lake, that he'd felt his way around the room—not exactly fumbling, but checking twice before he set something down or slowing before he grabbed a door handle or a pot, as if not quite seeing it.

He'd held the railing of the steps, taking his time as he walked down, and right then she'd determined to take him up on his offer to eat at the lodge.

So, not blind, but maybe losing his sight. Which was why he'd overpeppered the goulash he made two nights ago.

He didn't seem to mind when she found the recipe cards

yesterday and slid one for venison stroganoff across the table to him for approval.

"Maybe you're a chef," he said now as he reached for a corn muffin, hot from the oven.

Not even close, but she did like to cook on her days off, once upon a time. She nodded and smiled.

"Still nothing in the old noggin' comin' back?"

She shook her head. Frankly, with everything inside her, she wished that she could forget. Erase Sergei and every lie he'd told her.

But then what? More people would die.

She just needed time—not just to heal, but to sort it out. Put the puzzle together.

Until then—she opened a can of tomatoes and dumped them in, then stirred in the cumin, chili powder, and red peppers.

"That smells amazing." He got up and walked over, leaning near the stove. "Reminds me of my daughter, Larke. She loved to go through Cee's recipes and pull out one that her mother would make. She'd serve it up and we'd sit around with our memories. The boys had a harder time remembering their mother—she died when they were six. Larke was only eight, but she has a better memory. But mostly, they relied on me."

He took out a spoon and now dipped into the chili, tasted it. Made a noise of approval. "You have the touch, Jane. There's something else here . . ."

She held up the cumin. But what she really wanted was to ask how he managed to go on and raise three sons and a daughter, to run a bush pilot service—she'd done some internet searching—and not lose himself in his grief.

Or give in to the urge to disappear into the woods.

He set the spoon in the sink. "I don't know how you bear it. Not knowing who you are, where you've been, the people you left behind. I might be losing my eyesight, but my memories are as vivid as the day I made them. The birth of the triplets, watching Larke take her first solo flight. Standing at the end of the aisle in the little Copper Mountain Chapel, waiting for Cee to marry me." He leaned against the counter, folded his arms over his chest. "I wonder who is looking for you."

She swallowed and looked away.

He sighed. "Sorry. Are you sure you don't want us to post a picture, maybe put it in the paper, or on the internet? I'll bet—"

She shook her head, the words bundling in her throat. *No. Please—*

"Right. I suppose there's a reason you were alone, in a blizzard, miles away from anywhere."

Her mouth pinched, and she turned back to the chili.

"I might be scared to find out too."

She nodded like, yeah, that was it.

From the office off the kitchen a phone rang, and Barry headed for it, finding the doorframe first, then entering the office. She heard a "Hello."

She couldn't stay here forever, she knew that.

Really.

But no one else was left. And if they found her . . .

"Thanks for letting me know, Echo."

Barry's future daughter-in-law had come over every day since Tae had been here, maybe to check on her, but Tae had a feeling it was just as much to check on Barry.

And his daughter, Larke, had also called. He hadn't mentioned the mysterious mission his sons were on.

Handsome sons they were, although they were far from identical. He had a picture of the family on the mantel, and the boys clearly had their own personalities. They were young in the picture, maybe fourteen. Barry stood flanked by two of his sons. One stood with his hands clasped behind him, smiling into the camera. Larke, the daughter, stood beside him, and next to her was yet another brother, dark hair, wearing a smirk of a smile.

The other boy, standing beside his father, wore a hat backward on his head, his dark hair long and curling out the back. He gave the camera a double thumbs-up, his grin a little cockeyed, clearly not taking the shot as seriously as his brothers.

Trouble, if you asked her. She'd met those kinds of boys, the kind who could charm her out of her math homework. Or cajole her into giving away lethal secrets.

Like her name.

Barry came back into the room. "Good news. The guys found Colt. He's on his way home."

Super.

She just hoped he didn't bring trouble home with him.

EIGHT

Something wasn't right.

Ranger opened his eyes, stared at the plastered ceiling of his bedroom, listening to the whir of the fan. He couldn't wrap his head around it but . . .

Wait.

Where was Noemi?

Every time he'd waken over the past few days, she'd been here, right here, sitting on the bench by his bed. He knew he didn't deserve it, but something about her smile and her urging him to drink some wretched fish broth—or even her need to check on his stitches—had made him feel like everything was going to be okay.

Despite the fact that this op had gone so terribly south.

Except she wasn't here, and sure, she was probably fine, but it didn't stop him from pushing up from the bed and shaking his head to clear it.

He had some vague recollections—him doing a Humpty-Dumpty after meeting with the king and all his men, waking up in a hospital, then just Noemi, sitting by his bed.

Or sleeping on the floor.

Some hero he was.

He also, however, remembered her voice, her touch on his chest—or maybe he'd dreamed that.

He'd dreamed quite a lot over the last few—how many?—days. Things he hadn't let himself remember.

Like saying goodbye to her at the Key West military hospital so many years ago. And of course, the excruciating few hours he'd watched her at her father's funeral, regret like a vise in his chest.

He didn't know how long he'd been down—the days sort of blurred together—but as he sat, trying to get a fix on his surroundings, a beast roared in his gullet. Thankfully, he no longer felt as if he'd been run over by a Humvee.

In fact, when he got out of bed, his legs didn't want to give out on him, his shoulder didn't fight back, and he even looked in the mirror and didn't wince.

Which meant it was time to find his feet and figure a way out of never-never land, and pronto.

The first thing he needed was his hands on Noemi's cell phone.

He showered and pulled on a pair of clean cotton pants and a kaftan, managing it on his own, and then found sandals and headed down the hall.

The smell of curry, onions, and stewing meat led him to the kitchen. He knocked on the doorframe as he entered. A female chef stood stirring a pot of what looked like porridge.

"Hello," he said, and she nearly dropped her spoon. She turned.

"How far?"

Huh. "I don't know?"

She smiled and shook her head. Then pointed to a room behind him. "Down the hall."

He turned, his stomach in rebellion, and headed down the hall, now following voices to another room.

The double doors were half closed but not entirely, and when he heard Noemi's laugh—he could identify it anywhere—he knocked on the doors, then pushed them open.

Oh no.

Noemi stood on a dais, wearing a long green skirt in a sort of rich brocade. Emerald green, it hugged her waist, skimmed her body, then flared out at the knees, with golden stars embroidered into the hem.

She wore a gold bodice with cap shoulders and a low back, and the look of her—elegant, beautiful—simply stilled him.

Oh. Wow. His mouth moved without a thought. "That's gorgeous."

"Ranger!" She turned, as did her aunt Precious and Uncle Efe's wife—the first one?—Auntie Lydia. Everyone started shouting.

He held up his hands. "What?"

"You're not supposed to see the bride's dress before the wedding day," Precious said coming up to him, pressing on his chest, and shoving him out into the hall.

Oops.

Except . . . uh-oh.

This thing was really *on*.

Oh boy.

He stood there, listening to his heart beat in his head, not sure—

Noemi came out of the room. "The dead has risen."

She'd taken off the dress, wore a simple yellow maxi skirt and a white blouse, her hair pulled back into a tight bun at the back of her head. No makeup, and she looked so . . .

Breathtaking. As if she'd reached inside herself and discovered someone new. Or maybe just new to him.

He liked it. Shoot. He cut his voice low. "What's going on? They're planning a *wedding* in there."

She made a face and grabbed his arm, toting him down the hall to a massive bathroom. Pushed him inside and shut the door behind them. "Keep your voice down. Everything echoes around here, but yes—they are full-throttle wedding planning."

"But—"

"Listen. What was I supposed to do? You were down for the count. Besides, you agreed to the bride price."

"I agreed to hand over a thousand euros and a bottle of Schnapps, not . . . wait. Are they going to dress me up too?"

She seemed to be hiding a smile. "Probably."

"Noemi—"

"Listen. I was there. I fed you a kola nut."

"I was delirious."

Her smile fell.

"I mean, not that I won't pay the bride price—and I think, by the way, they're playing the American guy, because they asked for 1.5 mil for you, sweetheart."

"A bargain, if you ask me." She folded her arms.

"No doubt. But they also asked for—I can't exactly remember the list, but maybe some rice and a bag of nuts? And a hat for your uncle? Where, exactly, am I going to get my hands on these things?"

"Amazon?"

"Funny." He leaned against the sink.

"Listen, I know it's gotten way out of hand. But you told me not to tell them the truth and made me promise to obey everything you said."

He rolled his eyes. "*Now* you listen to me."

"Okay, truth is, I can't break Auntie Precious's heart. She's absolutely thrilled that we're getting married." She looked distressed. "I don't know how to stop it."

"I get it."

She rubbed her arms. "I'm probably never getting married, so this is . . . this is their one shot to give me—really, my mother—the Nigerian wedding that she never had."

Never getting married? Right. She'd told him that. "Your parents didn't get married in Nigeria?"

"No. They eloped in Italy. My auntie Precious told me it broke her father's heart. And I just . . . I thought . . ."

"It's fine." He touched her arm without realizing it. Her skin was soft, and a memory rose. He dropped his hand. "I'll pay the money, give them their gifts, and maybe it'll help salve the wound of us leaving before the big day."

"It's three days away."

A beat. "Seriously?"

She shrugged.

Oh boy. Which meant he needed an exfil, on the jiffy. "Did you charge that cell phone?"

"Yes. It lit up, and then died again. I think the battery is shot. As long as it's plugged in, it works, but—"

"Where is it?"

"In our room, but there's no service there—or, really, anywhere in the house. The walls are too thick."

"Perfect." He ran a hand through his hair. "How long have I been out?"

"It's been over a week since you showed up at the terrorist camp."

"A week. Wow. Ham is going to murder me. I have to get ahold of a working cell phone."

"What if we went shopping for all the things on the bride price list? And while we're at it, you can pick up a phone."

He looked at her. "Brilliant."

"Yeah, well, it's called adapting and improvising." She smiled at him, and something warm went right to his bones. "I'll talk to Auntie Precious, see if we can go tomorrow, if you're up for it." She turned toward the door, but he reached out to stop her.

"What?"

"I should have talked to you at your father's funeral."

Her smile fell and she just blinked at him. "I was pretty—"

"Alone. You were alone. And it killed me to see you that way, but I thought that talking to you might make it worse. And that was—I was a jerk. I shouldn't have decided for you how you'd feel."

Her mouth opened, then closed. She looked away. "It was a bad day. You didn't make it any worse, Ranger."

Right. He let out his breath. "He was a good man. And he loved you, a lot."

She nodded, swallowed, and maybe he should stop talking, but—

"After we . . . after I left Key West, he tracked me down in Coronado, before sniper school, and he told me you'd left for Uganda. But he gave me your address. I think he was sorry for . . . well, what he said to me."

"About dating his daughter?"

"About risking my life and my team by my emotional choices. And my guess is that he meant you."

She just blinked at him. And he felt like a fool because, according to her words, he hadn't been a big deal.

He didn't know why those words still sat in his heart. Stung.

Whatever. She was right to walk away because he *hadn't* chosen her. Not really. It wasn't like his heartfelt letters to her had somehow gotten lost in some remote post office in dusty Uganda.

"Thanks for telling me."

"I just thought you should know that he did care. He loved you."

The words fell between them.

I *loved you*.

The thought pulsed, and suddenly his mind was back in Key West, Noemi standing by his hospital bed, wordless, as he told her he didn't have room for her in his world.

Funny, she hadn't even acted upset. Just gave a sort of shrug, then walked away.

Which only made him feel like a fool, so of course he hadn't written to her.

Clearly, he'd put too much into their relationship. Which meant he was totally overreacting about the wedding.

Even if he did find himself at the end of the aisle with her, it wouldn't mean anything.

His real job was to keep her safe. And that meant hanging around the palace until he could track down Ham.

But first—"Can you help me find some chow?"

"Oh, do I have a treat for you." She turned, then paused. "Thank you, by the way. I know my dad loved me, as best he could."

She opened the door and stepped out into the hall.

Shoot. She deserved better than "as best he could."

She led him into the kitchen and spoke to the cooks, something in pidgin. One of the women dipped into the soup they were making—the aroma of tomatoes and curry and peppers rising to fill his gullet—and ladled out a bowl. Noemi tore off a large piece of dough and set that in another bowl.

"Thank you," she said and picked up her bowl and the dough. She carried the bowls outside and set them on a table on an expansive patio that arched out into the sun and around the pool.

A couple children playing in the pool called out to her. "Emuvoke!"

She waved to them. "That's Akin and Tobe, both sons of Auntie Lydia. They live in Warri, but they don't have a pool, so they come here."

"Three wives. I can barely handle one." He sat down at the table.

"Coward." She shook her head. "Actually, I asked Auntie Precious about it, and the other two women are widows from the village. Their husbands were killed, and they both had children, so he married them for economic reasons. It's common, even among Christians." She shrugged. "Auntie Angel is one of them. The other lives in Lagos."

He put his hands up in front of him. "I promise you, I'm a one-wife guy."

"No. You're a *no*-wife guy. But I appreciate what you're doing here." Her voice had dropped, probably for privacy, but she also didn't look at him.

No humor this time. Because she was right.

Mostly.

Unfortunately, the words he'd spoken at the introduction had lingered inside him, filtered through his dreams and latched on. *"She's the one woman—the only woman—I want to be with."*

Shoot, maybe. But he'd made his choice.

And frankly she hadn't really wanted him anyway.

But maybe, right now, inside these walls, he could rewind time. Enjoy her smile. Her laughter. The way that being with her unwound the knots inside him.

At least until he got ahold of Ham and got them out of here.

She joined him at the table and gestured to the bowl. "Dig in."

He looked at her, then the soup. "I don't have a spoon."

"Yeah, you do. Use the fufu."

When he didn't move, she scooted forward and added, "Watch." She worked out a piece of the dough between her fingers and then dipped it into the soup.

Which, for the first time, he got a good look at.

Fish heads, goat meat on the bone, square pieces of what looked like fat, onions and celery . . . or . . . "What is that vegetable?"

"Okra. And this is tripe." She picked up one of the fat slices between her fingers.

"Tripe."

"It's delicious. And there's spinach and some mackerel in here too. A regular potpourri of flavors."

She took the entire dough ball and smeared it through the thick, almost rubbery soup, pulling the meat and juices into the ball. Then she leaned over the bowl and put the entire thing in her mouth.

And swallowed.

"You didn't even chew."

"No. No chewing. The fufu is made of dried cassava and is just a conveyor of the nummy soup. You put it in your mouth, get a good taste of the flavors, then swallow the fufu whole. Don't chew, whatever you do."

"Don't chew."

A cook came out and set down a couple bottles of Coke. Handed them paper napkins.

Ho-kay. Ranger used his fingers to work out a piece of dough, then rolled it into a ball in the palm of his hand.

"Then just dip it into the soup."

He sank his fingers into the soup and swished the fufu around, then leaned over the bowl and popped it into his mouth.

Peppery, and salty, a hint of beef and fish. He swallowed. "It tastes like a beefy shrimp boil."

"It's the ground crayfish," she said and pulled off another dough ball, her fingers still wet with soup.

He dove into the dough for another bite. Their hands bumped and she handed him the fish head. "The eyes are really good."

He raised an eyebrow but took the challenge. "Salty."

She laughed. "I can't believe you just ate a fish head."

"Please. Remember, mopane worms."

She put down a goat bone. "Right. And crickets. Salted and deep fried."

"Good memory."

She lifted a shoulder. "You made an impression, sailor."

Really? "I thought . . . well, it seemed that I wasn't a big deal."

Oh. And he hadn't meant to throw her words back at her, but she just blinked at him, raised her shoulder again.

"Maybe you were a bigger deal than I let on."

What?

She laughed. "At least my dad thought so."

Right.

"So, what do you think of the soup?"

She sat there, her fingers dripping with it, the sun against her skin, her eyes gold and shiny. Maybe this mission hadn't gone so far off the rails, after all.

He had the strangest sense that he'd returned to a place inside himself that he'd tried to forget. Or even run from.

A place that he suddenly very much missed.

"I think it's the only right way to eat soup."

She wiped her hands and sat back in the chair, touching the Coke bottle to her lips. The breeze lifted her fragrance to him.

And all he could hear was, *"Nothing's going to happen here. I'm harmless."*

Not even close.

Nothing might have happened for her, but she had nearly blown his world apart.

Was still at it, actually.

The door opened and Precious came out. She was wrapped in a royal blue skirt, a white blouse, her hair up in a matching blue headwrap.

These outfits—Noemi looked right at home in them.

"I'm glad you've eaten, Ranger. It's time for your fitting."

"Fitting?"

"I think she's talking about your groom's clothes." Noemi grinned at him. "I hope you like green." Her eyes shone.

Oh boy. Clearly, the only thing he was here to protect was his heart.

Noemi had been in plenty of open markets around the world, and they all possessed the same sort of local energy—men shouting prices, bickering, the exhaust of trucks and the bustle of workers unloading potatoes, rice, tomatoes. The odor of fresh fish mixed with the robust scent of grilling meat, the cluck of penned hens, the thump of music from a nearby cafe, and of course the push and shove of the crowd.

"Don't let go," Ranger said and tightened his grip around her hand. "And keep your eyes peeled for a cell phone kiosk."

For a guy who'd gotten out of bed only yesterday, four days after surgery, he was keeping up well.

They were following Auntie Precious—and Noemi kept her

eye pinned to the woman in her red paisley dress and elaborate headwrap—as they wove around vendors under umbrellas or in stalls hawking everything from plantains and chili peppers to cocoa leaves to flip-flops, hats, and kitchenware.

Auntie Precious stopped in a stall, one of a hundred in the massive Okwagbe Market, and gestured to the overflowing burlap bags of rice.

"Ofada rice. Very good," Auntie Precious said. She gestured to the two boys—no more than seventeen—who had accompanied them to the market, along with Dafe.

Noemi didn't miss the presence of the machete on his belt.

The two boys stepped forward as Auntie Precious dickered with the shopkeeper, an older man dressed in a pair of suit pants and a T-shirt. He smiled when she gestured to Noemi and Ranger, nodding.

The happy couple.

But Noemi wasn't under any delusions. Ranger had one purpose in being here—find a cell phone, contact Ham, and get them out of Nigeria. He was as bad as Dafe, his gaze anywhere but on the goods Auntie Precious had picked out.

Maybe because he knew people watched them. No, probably just him, the white man dressed in a blue-and-gold kaftan and a pair of plaid pants with black sandals. Auntie Precious also insisted on a blue kufi hat, as if it might help the poor man blend in.

As if. Ranger walked like a warrior, despite his recent wounds, his body—and maybe his spirit—clearly on the mend. He had just shaved as well, which set him apart from the bearded Nigerian males in the crowd.

But in her mind, the man definitely looked like a prince. Her prince, at least until he got ahold of Ham.

Yes, she was living some kind of Cinderella fairy tale, the orphan turned princess. Especially in the beautiful dress Auntie Precious fitted on her yesterday. Auntie Precious had dug it out of her closet from her own wedding day and refitted it around

Noemi's frame. Noemi tried to ignore the voices inside and focused on the fact that here, now, she could step in and fill the void her mother's leaving had left.

Maybe both she and Auntie Precious were feeling it, because being around the somewhat bossy, opinionated, large-loving woman felt every bit like being with her mother.

"Sit down and eat—you're wasting all this beautiful food!" Auntie Precious's words to her last night around the chaotic family table.

Noemi didn't know if they ate like this every night, but last night they'd feasted on suya—a northern Nigerian beef kebob—jollof rice, and Moi Moi while a golden moon shone down on them. Children jumped into the pool while Auntie Angel and Auntie Lydia yelled at them or wrapped them in towels and pulled them onto their laps, holding the little ones indiscriminately as if they all belonged to them.

All the time, Ranger sat next to her, playing his role perfectly.

After Auntie Precious took him away for a fitting into whatever outfit she had for him, he'd returned strangely quiet.

Strangely demonstrative. Sitting next to her at dinner, catching a soccer ball before it tackled their plates, and even answering a few questions about how they'd met.

"I was on vacation in Key West, and so was Noemi. She was taking pictures of the sunset, and she was so beautiful I couldn't stop watching her."

That had simply delighted not only Auntie Precious but Auntie Angel too, who watched Ranger with an open appreciation.

Yeah, the man had charm in spades when he wanted to.

And it could all conspire to confuse her, especially when she dragged up his words from earlier. *"It seemed that I wasn't a big deal."*

He almost sounded, well, *hurt*. But *he* was the one who called them a mistake. Not worth his career.

And yet, there he sat, all night, his arm around her back.

But she wasn't a fool. The man did duty better than anyone she knew, and that included her father.

At one point in the evening, as Uncle Efe sat with ten-year-old Jaita on his lap, they broke out into singing.

She found herself humming the song as she got ready for bed. "O sifuni mungu . . ."

"That's a Swahili song," Ranger said from where he sat on the stool in their bedroom. He'd pulled off his kaftan and sat in his pants, his feet bare. She resisted the urge to check on his wound.

Now that he was up and around, he could probably take care of himself.

"Swahili?"

"Yeah. It's a popular African praise and worship song. 'All Creatures of Our God and King.'"

She had come out of the bathroom wearing a pair of yoga pants and a long T-shirt that Auntie Angel gave her and headed over to her sleeping mat.

"Not a chance there, princess."

She looked up at him, even as she kneeled on the pad. "What?"

"Not to be too forward but get in the bed. You're not sleeping on the floor."

She knew her mouth had opened, because he just shook his head. "Calm down. Nothing is happening. I just can't sleep if I know you're on that tile floor. I'll sleep on top of the sheets, you sleep under them."

"But—"

"I won't marry you if you won't sleep in the bed with me."

She stood up. "Seriously. If my father could hear you—"

"I'd never walk again, I know. But trust me, he's with me on this. It's either that, or I'm on the floor."

"You're so romantic."

"I've got all the moves, baby." But he got up, smiling at her in victory and shoot, he did. He walked over to his backpack. "By the way, you missed this." He worked out a wad of cash from an interior pocket in the shoulder strap. "Another hundred euros."

"Wow. You've been holding out on me. What else don't I know?"

He'd waggled his eyebrows, and it only stirred to life everything she'd been trying to forget.

His arms around her as he rescued her from a crocodile . . . and from a Nigerian river. The smell of him as they watched a campfire . . . and the Nigerian star-strewn sky.

Those aqua-blue eyes, free of their hooded wariness.

Yes, the sooner they contacted Ham and ended this mess, the better.

She had barely slept with the awareness of him . . . colossally different from the previous nights, when he'd been too wounded to move.

He could move just fine now, especially after a good night's sleep, as they wandered the market. Like pulling her close when she reached out to pick up a piece of fabric for a head tie on a vendor's table.

She noticed him staring at her. "What?"

"There's a couple kids back there eying your purse." It hung over her shoulder and in front of her.

"Calm down, sailor. That's why Dafe is here." She turned to see Dafe shooing away a couple beggar boys, dirty, their shirts torn, barefoot.

She turned to Ranger. "I need some naira."

He peeled off a few bills from the wad he'd gotten when he changed euros. "What are you buying now?"

She whistled to the children. "How far!"

"What does that mean?" Ranger asked her.

"It's a greeting," she said, and sure enough, one of the boys turned. She handed him the bills even while Dafe shouted at them. The boy bowed. "Bless you, auntie." Then took off through the crowd.

She turned back to Ranger. He handed her a wad of money. "You're going to get real busy." But he smiled.

He glanced up at Auntie Precious who held up a beautiful emerald-green length of fabric. "Looks good," he said.

Noemi nodded and picked up a green, gold-embroidered kufi. "For the Ovie?"

"He will wear a top hat, but it's on his list, so yes," Auntie Precious said.

"What isn't on his list?" Ranger muttered as the kufi was added to the bag.

They continued down the row, and sure enough, a few more children found her, little girls in ragged dirty dresses, more boys. She noticed that Ranger slid in close to her as she handed out money.

Even Auntie Precious shooed the children away. "The Ovie has a house for these children. Give your money there."

Yes. But she saw their eyes. Haunted. Empty.

Ranger finally steered her inside a storefront with jewelry. The door closed, a jangle behind it, and she spotted Dafe standing in front of the door.

"Ma'am," said a tall man in a black shirt and suit pants. "What do you need?"

"A necklace," Ranger said. He pointed to three strands of thick coral beads. He looked at her. "Your aunt added it to the list."

Oh.

The man opened the glass and pulled it out. Put it on the counter. Ranger picked the strand up and held it to her neck. But his gaze ranged outside the door. "I think we're being followed."

"Yes, by a thousand children," she said. "It's so pretty." She held it to her neck and turned, looked in the mirror.

He looked over her shoulder, met her eyes. "No. I think I saw the same guy, a few times." His eyes went to the necklace. "Yes, it is pretty, especially on you."

It was. And too expensive. She put it back on the counter. "What, are your Spidey senses tingling?" She pushed the necklace toward the jeweler.

"We'll take it," Ranger said. "And yes."

"You just don't like being in this crowd," she said. "Are you sure?"

"I'm sure," he said, and she thought he meant about the follower, but then he pulled out naira and handed the jeweler the amount. "It's the first thing I've purchased that I've actually picked out."

Oh.

He held her hand as they pushed outside. Auntie Precious was waiting, arms folded, a smile on her face. "Something special for the bride?"

For some reason, heat pressed Noemi's skin.

"We still need salt," Auntie Precious said.

"Of course we do," Ranger said. He lowered his voice as they followed her past a store of dresses. "I think I see a cell phone kiosk just down the row. Can we work our way there?" He nodded toward the end of the row.

Sure enough, a sign rose above the fray advertising electronics.

A boy brushed past, jostling them. Noemi knocked into Ranger. He caught her, wincing.

"Sorry."

"It's okay—hey, you!" He turned to her. "Stay."

What—

But Dafe had already taken off after the kid. "My necklace!" The bag had been cut, her necklace nicked.

Ranger started after him, but she grabbed him back. "Don't. Dafe can handle it."

He gave her a hard look.

"Let's get the cell phone." Her eyes widened as in, *Now, without our guard watching*.

"Brilliant."

They headed down the aisle, his hand vised in hers, until they got to the booth. He pointed to a small Nokia and a sim card, handed over the cash, and in a second, had it in hand. "Now to find a place to call Ham."

She turned, looking for Dafe, and froze. "Ranger."

"Hmm." He had stepped aside, opening up the packaging.

No. That wasn't right. She hadn't seen—

The man appeared again. Three scars across his cheek, his eyes on hers even from thirty feet away.

"Ranger." Her voice had fallen, nearly constricted.

He looked up, the phone in hand. "What?"

The man who looked like Abu had vanished, and maybe she'd been hallucinating. Certainly . . . no, they were four hundred miles from where she'd been taken.

How could Abu find her here?

"Nothing."

Ranger frowned. "You sure?"

"Yeah."

He slipped the cell phone into his pocket. "Let's find a quiet place."

"Ha," she said, her heart pounding. She was just seeing things.

He took her hand. "I saw a table and chairs near the grills. We can go there."

"What about Auntie Precious?"

"She'll find us. The law of crowds."

He started toward the smoke billowing from the edge of the market.

"The law of crowds?" she asked, following close behind.

"Yeah. If you need to find someone in a crowd, just stop worrying about it and you'll bump into them. It's like cosmic fate. Works every time." They edged closer to the grills. "If not, we'll find her after I get through to Ham."

They passed through the fish market, with fresh and dried crawdads, all manner of river fish, and snails.

Beyond that, hens and cocks in pens squawked and cried.

Noemi was near a basket of dried mackerel when the hand closed around her arm and yanked.

She turned, and his vile breath cast over her.

Abu.

He was taller than she remembered—taller than Ranger, and wearing a stained striped shirt, suit pants, and a *machete*.

She screamed, but the clutter of sounds masked it. No one heard.

Except for Ranger. He turned, and almost seemed not to see the man, as if his vision might only be catching up to him.

By then Abu had wrapped his arm around her neck and yanked her away from Ranger—or tried to.

Control the situation.

She turned her head so Abu couldn't cut off her airway. Tucking her chin down, she got her fingers into the space between them.

Then she stepped back into him, her leg around his.

Ranger might have seen her move, because he was right there when she turned, hard, and bent over.

Abu lost his balance just as Ranger's fist landed in his face.

He shouted, and she was free.

Abu knocked over a table as he fell, but she didn't wait for him to hit the earth.

She turned, found Ranger.

He'd picked up a knife from one of the fish vendors.

What? He was going to fight the guy? One-handed? Hardly.

"Run!" she said.

And because he was a tough guy, he seemed to debate, then wisdom kicked in, and he followed her.

They fled down the aisle, turned at a display of nets and then again inside a long, narrow building for goats.

The odor could knock her over, but Ranger grabbed her and pushed her into the darkness near the door, a tiny alcove.

Then he stepped in front of her, still holding the knife. "Shh."

Right. Still the tough guy.

Except he was practically a glowing neon light. She pulled him back. "Get behind me."

"Not on your life."

"Listen, white boy. Get behind me!"

His eyes widened, then he moved in with her to the darkness, ducking his head down against her shoulder. "For the record—"

"Shh."

Sure enough, Abu appeared a moment later, cursing. But the low-lit building gathered the late afternoon shadows and with them pressed in amongst the feed, in the alcove . . .

He kept running.

"C'mon," she said.

Ranger scooted out behind her back into the open, through the fish market and toward the pots and pans.

They nearly ran down Dafe. He stood in front of the jewelry store, holding the necklace in one hand, the kid in the other, murder written on his face and breathing hard.

With him stood Auntie Precious, her face pinched under her elaborate head tie. "Where did you go?"

They'd stopped breathing so hard and now Noemi looked at Ranger.

"Got lost," he said.

She glanced down. He'd dropped the knife. Or maybe hidden it, but suddenly he was all "good job" and "thank you" to Dafe.

But his hand reached down and vised hers. "I think our market day is finished."

"But we don't have the dried mackerel," Auntie Precious said.

"I'll have to risk it." Ranger headed out of the market.

He practically shoved her into the Ovie's SUV and climbed in next to her. She noticed a line of sweat down his face.

He said nothing the entire way back to the compound, his chest rising and falling. Auntie Precious catalogued everything he'd purchased on the list while Dafe eyed them with an almost lethal quietness.

She simply kept seeing Abu.

It happened so fast, all of it. But how could . . . ?

No. It couldn't be Abu . . . maybe she'd imagined it.

At the compound, Ranger pulled her out of the car, his hand again tight in hers, and didn't even stop at the front door when Jaita came running, soccer ball in hand, asking him to play.

Ranger marched her into their bedroom where he let her go, then very quietly turned and shut the door behind her. Pressed his hand to it.

She stepped away from him. "You're scaring me a little."

"How did he find you?" He turned, then ripped the kufi from his head and threw it across the room. "What is going on, Noemi?"

"Is this my fault?"

He stared at her a long moment. "A terrorist tracked you from northern Nigeria. He didn't do it because he missed you, princess. Why is he still after you?"

"Maybe he's after you! You're the one who raided his camp."

He jerked back, blinked.

Silence.

"Okay, probably not," she said after a second. "So just calm down. I have no idea why he'd be after me—or how he found me."

He shook his head. Walked to the window. Outside, children's voices lifted, laughing. And beyond that, over the tall wall, the wide, flowing Forcados River. He hadn't noticed that before. There was a lot he hadn't noticed, apparently.

He sighed. "I missed him."

She stared at him. Ranger stood there in his African outfit, his shoulders rising and falling, and she could almost see the anger balling up inside him. "I missed him. You screamed, and

I turned and . . ." He ran a hand through his hair. "How did you learn to get out of a headlock?"

"Hello. Master Chief Sutton's only daughter. Please."

He exhaled a breath. "If you hadn't been able to . . ." He shook his head. "Sorry. I—"

"Ranger. C'mon. You just had surgery." She walked over to him, put her hand on his back.

He shook his head. "No. I should have seen him. Before he touched you. I should have *seen* him."

"Are we sure it was Abu? Maybe—"

"Noe, c'mon. It was him. I spent two days staring at him. I *know* it was him." He turned and touched her arm. "You did great, by the way." Something filled his eyes, and he swallowed. Then he let his hand drop. "We're not leaving here until Ham figures out a safe exfil. Until that moment, we stay camped inside these walls."

"But—"

"Yes. I know. We're getting married in two days. So unless Ham and Dodge arrive with a chopper and park it in the middle of that soccer field, I guess I'm meeting you at the altar."

"I don't think there's an altar. You have to dance in."

"Perfect."

"And you have to bow in front of the king."

He sighed. "Of course I do. Anything else?"

"Probably." She leaned against the bedpost. "Sorry I got you into this."

He walked up to her. Then, he pressed his hand to her cheek and fixed his gaze on her again. "Listen. It's no big deal. The important thing is that we get out of Nigeria alive."

She knew he meant it as comfort, but she couldn't help it.

A small part inside her wanted to weep.

If she were to marry anyone for real, it would be this man.

Because he was a very big deal, indeed.

NINE

Two days.

Forty-eight hours until he got married.

Ranger lay on his side of the bed, on top of the covers, staring at the chandelier as it glittered with moonlight.

Beside him, Noemi's soft breaths told him that she'd finally dropped off to sleep.

Maybe she'd been reliving today's crazy events too, rolling them over and over in her mind to see how she might have been more alert, less of an idiot.

How she might have kept Abu from creeping up on them and grabbing her.

Good thing Master Chief Sutton had taught her a few tricks because—

Well, he hadn't even *seen* the guy. Even after he grabbed Noemi. Just a blurry shadow on the edges of his vision. He hadn't been quite so aware of his loss—well, not since Somalia, but—

He wasn't getting better. And of course, he knew that, but the proof hit him hard even as they'd run through the market.

It was the one reason why he'd hid himself in the goat barn instead of taking out Abu. Because with darkness and shadows, he could barely see his hand in front of his face.

He was a liability.

Which meant that staying inside this compound until Ham showed up with his team was the only course of action.

"*Where have you been?*" Ham's words the moment after Ranger identified himself on the burner phone. "*We've been looking all over for you. Your brothers are losing their minds.*"

Which brought him first to Colt. "How is Colt?"

"Mending. Dodge sent him back to Alaska, practically against his will, but he wasn't doing us any good here. He and Fraser left with North and Selah almost immediately."

Which meant his brother Dodge was still in the country. And hopefully, still had his hands on that chopper.

Good. "And the doc?"

"Still alive. He's here, in Lagos. We flew his wife in. He's improving, but we got him out just in time. Where are you?"

"At the palace of Ovie Ofejiro. In Delta State."

A beat. "What?"

"I was shot, and Noemi didn't know where to go so she found her uncle, who happens to be a king of this region. So . . ."

"Shot. You okay?"

"Yeah. It's a long story."

"I can't wait to hear it. You safe?"

"Yes. But Abu Mussaf found us at the market in Okwagbe."

Another beat of silence. "How?"

"I don't know. We're inside a fortress, so I don't think he can get to us here, but it's not safe for us to leave."

"Okay. Sit tight. I'll figure out something. Give me a couple days. I'll be in touch."

A couple days. Long enough for him to get married.

And then there was the wedding night, wasn't there?

Nope. Not going there.

They might be getting married, but they weren't getting *married*. The moment they left Nigeria, he wanted her to be able to walk away.

No big deal.

Ranger rolled over onto his good shoulder. Noemi lay under a sheet, on her side, facing him, her eyes closed, the moonlight caressing the form of her body. She wore a hair tie over her dark hair.

He'd put up a small barricade of pillows, just because, but

her hand rested on one of them, as if she might be reaching out to him.

Like she had the night he'd woken to find her hand on his chest. It hadn't been a dream—he remembered the weight of it, the warmth, the sense of her anchoring him.

Maybe that's what it was, this feeling he had around her. Different from the roots the military had given him, she made him feel connected to something bigger.

"You want a family?"

"I . . . I don't know. It doesn't matter. I'm a lifer in the Navy . . ."

His throat tightened.

"It's a nice dream."

She sighed, a low hum emitting from her.

He shouldn't be staring at her, but he couldn't seem to tear his gaze away.

"She's dear to me, sailor. The only daughter I have. She's brave, adventurous, and brilliant." Shoot, and there he was, the Master Chief, still in his head. *"The last thing she needs is a broken heart over a man who might not come home."*

Words spoken by Ranger's hospital bed, of all places. He'd read the Master Chief loud and clear.

Stay away from my daughter.

Aye, aye.

Ranger rolled over and stared again at the ceiling. And sure, he wasn't in the military anymore, but maybe the rules hadn't changed.

He was still a liability in her life.

The hum of the fan in the corner, the sounds of the frogs from the nearby river, the heat of the night settled into him.

Safe. They were safe.

Really.

His eyes closed.

Everything itched inside his ghillie suit. He lay on the top of a six-story building under the cover of night in a backwater town deep in the dark heart of Mogadishu, Somalia, head down, eye to his Leupold 10-x power scope as he scanned the alleyway in front of the shell of a building where their target slept.

A simple body snatch.

General Said Abdi, if he could be called a general of a terrorist group. Only one of the nearly twenty civil war factions in this war-torn country. Also the guy behind a recent attack on a refugee compound.

Taking him out would save countless lives.

Around Ranger, the city was awakening, the smell of cooking fires lit by dried animal dung sending a putrid odor into the air. In this part of town, most of the buildings had been destroyed, the concrete block skeletons all that remained. That, and the refugees, the women and children who struggled to survive.

Ranger wasn't here to save lives. He was here because the Navy had put him on a roof to watch the back of his fellow operators. Because he was the best sniper on the team.

Because he never missed.

The smoke was rising, clouding his vision. Next to him, Ghost, a fellow sniper and his spotter, also scanned the area. Below, insurgents scuttled around like rats, unaware of his overwatch.

"They're in position," Ghost said.

Through his earpiece, his team lead, Master Chief Nez, gave the order. "Execute, execute, execute."

On the ground, the Delta team went in, dropped the two insurgents standing guard near the door.

Ranger listened, scanning the area for any trouble on exfil.

A couple squirters came out holding AK-47s, and he dropped them.

They'd found Abdi, a number of targets eliminated, and the team was exiting.

And that's when the shooting started. One of their own went down right outside the door, and the entire team pulled back.

Ranger hadn't seen him. "Find him, Ghost!" he snapped.

It took only a moment. "On the roof." He gave Ranger the coordinates.

He found him three hundred yards away. An easy shot.

"Are we clear?" Nez's voice.

"Not yet," Ghost said.

Heart rate down. Win Mag sniper rifle stock set in his shoulder, eye focused on the center of the crosshairs . . . a half breath.

Something moved into his vision. A shadow, a darkness. He blinked, it didn't clear.

"Wire's burning, Range. We need to move—" Nez said, his voice tight.

"Take the shot," Ghost said.

He pulled the trigger.

"Miss," Ghost hissed.

His miss answered with a shot that chipped off the stone next to him.

Ghost grunted.

And just like that, chaos erupted. Local insurgents spilled out around buildings, shooting at the force, still trapped in the house.

And Ghost lay bleeding from the head.

Ranger had missed.

No time. No time—

He found the shooter again. Don't panic . . .

No emotion. Center. Breathe.

The shot hit his target in the neck and the man jerked and disappeared.

Ghost's blood seeped into the dirt and cement around Ranger, into his clothing, his pores—

"Ranger, wake up. Wake up—"

A hand pressed on his chest, and his eyes popped open. He

tried to make out the form above him. She had her hand on his wrist, holding it. "It's me, Noemi. You were breathing funny. I think you had a nightmare."

Sweat soaked his body, and his chest rose and fell hard.

"You okay?"

He closed his eyes. "Yeah."

"That was a nightmare, wasn't it?"

He let out a shuddered breath, then nodded and pushed himself up. She had wrapped the sheet around herself, despite wearing shorts and a T-shirt to bed.

He got up—away from the terrible urge to reach out for her and just hold on. Walking to the window, he let the night breeze run over him. In the distance, beyond the compound, the moonlight dipped into the river, turning it into silvery silk.

"No. Not a nightmare. A memory." He sighed. "I got a fellow SEAL killed."

Quietly, "How'd it happen?"

He ran his hand across his mouth. Took a breath. "On an op in Somalia. I didn't see a shooter before he saw us."

"I'm so sorry." She climbed off the bed, dropping the sheet. "But those things happen, Range. It's not your fault."

She crossed the room and stopped when she stood in front of him in the moonlight.

And oh, right then the horror of it all rolled into a terrible ball inside him, and he couldn't— "I'm going blind."

He closed his eyes. There, he'd said it. Out loud, and the truth of it felt like a fresh punch to his sternum. *Blind.*

She said nothing.

He opened his eyes.

She'd closed the gap between them. "Blind?"

So, she had heard him.

"Yes. Macular degeneration. It casts shadows into my eyes, around the edges and in spots and . . . it's why I missed the shot."

"That still doesn't make it your fault."

"It wasn't the first time. It had been happening, again and again, and I had a permanent black spot in my periphery and . . . I was just . . ." He shook his head, looked away.

"Afraid?"

Yes, but he couldn't voice it.

"It's permanent?"

"I medically separated from the Navy six weeks ago."

"Oh, Ranger." She put her hand on his chest.

And this, right here, was exactly what he didn't want. From anyone. From her.

He pushed her hand away. "I'm not decrepit. Or helpless. I'm just blind."

"Agreed." Her expression had changed, her mouth tight. "You're one of the most capable men I've ever known—"

"Don't patronize me. I should have seen Abu in the market today."

"You did—you told me someone was following me."

He gave her a look. "That was . . . a gut feeling. But I didn't see him until he was right there. And frankly, I was no match for him."

"You just had surgery!"

"Because I couldn't see him!"

They were standing a foot apart, her golden-brown eyes fierce in his.

Wow, she was beautiful.

And he'd nearly lost her. Again.

And that, right there, made him take a step toward her. Made him touch his hand to her face, run his thumb down her cheek in a caress.

She didn't move.

And for a second, he just . . . stopped thinking. Let the silky breeze of the night curl around him, the shine in her moonlit eyes pull him in.

He kissed her.

Pure impulse, and relief, and simply the desire he'd been trying to fight for the last week, and he was just . . . tired.

Tired of black-and-white.

Of being in control and of wanting and not having.

Of being alone.

Noemi was color and light and song and laughter and—

And was kissing him back.

She tasted like the night, deep and mysterious and a place to sink into, to hide . . . He pulled her closer and deepened his kiss, her body against his, his pulse racing.

She wound her arms around his waist, lifting her head, careful, it seemed, not to hurt him.

Stop. *Stop*—stop!

He heard the voice, but he didn't care. Shoot, he was right back in Key West, her snuggled against him on the cabana, his common sense nudging him. And him ignoring it with everything inside.

He lifted his arm, wanting it around her and—

Pain sliced through him, the moment severed as he winced and she pulled away.

"Did I hurt you?" Her eyes widened.

Shoot—or maybe he should be grateful because he'd broken free of the terrible tug of emotions, his grip firmly around common sense.

What was he *doing*?

"No, I hurt myself," he said, but the truth settled inside, like a bullet. "Sorry. This was a mistake."

She blinked. "Um—"

His chest burned, even as he forced the words out. "I . . . I don't know what I'm doing. Suddenly, it's Key West all over again, and you're here and you're so beautiful, but . . ." He stepped away from her. "I don't have the first clue what I'll do after we get stateside. I've been living in a rent-by-the-week motel after leaving the base, no job, no prospects."

"Breathe, Range." Her voice was soft. "First . . . calm down. I don't expect you to sweep me into your arms and carry me across some white-picket-fence threshold. Eyes wide open here."

He looked at her. Right.

"Second, you do have a home. Alaska. Your family. Colt and Dodge. The ranch. Maybe it's time to let yourself dream."

A dream had a family in it. Children. A wife.

Noemi.

But she was never getting married—well, not counting their wedding in less than forty-eight hours—and he also had that truth burned into his head. So . . . he met her eyes. "There is no dream."

Her mouth opened a little. Then closed. "Right." She patted his chest. "So, no big deal."

He stared at her, forcing himself to nod. "No big deal."

Then he walked over to the bed and pulled off the pillow. Threw it on the floor where she'd had her sleeping pad.

"What are you doing?"

"Cooling off. The bed is too hot."

She raised an eyebrow. "You can sleep on the bed. Nothin's going to happen."

Not if it was up to him. Because his mouth was saying one thing.

His heart had completely other intentions.

"Just . . . go back to bed, Noemi. We have a big couple of days ahead." He lay down, his back to the cold tile, staring at the ceiling. "I hear there's a big wedding we're supposed to attend."

She stood there a moment, then climbed into the bed. "It's about time you gave me the whole bed."

He smiled.

And had no idea how he'd survive the next forty-eight hours.

Hurry up, Ham.

Auntie Precious was right.

There was no wedding like a Nigerian wedding. An Urhobo wedding.

Her wedding.

Oh, poor Ranger. He hadn't a clue what he'd been in for.

Frankly, neither did she, despite her auntie Precious's warning.

If the past two days had seemed crazy with preparations, they in no way compared to her bridal makeup and trousseau. Her aunties had spent four hours on her makeup—including false eyelashes—and then arranging an elaborate headwrap that looked like a golden fluff of whipped cream. They'd even given her false nails, painted coral.

And then came the dress. Deep, emerald-green skirt that hugged her hips before flaring out in ruffles to the floor, with gold stars embroidered into the hem. The bodice was gold lace, with one shoulder open, florets gathered up the neckline and spilling down one arm. She could barely walk in the gold strap heels.

And then Auntie Precious added Ranger's coral-colored beaded necklace. "These are for fertility," she whispered.

Oh. My.

They finished with a heavy douse of perfume and gave her a gold-handled, white-feathered fan.

Good thing, because by high noon, she was famished, a little lightheaded, and pretty sure she might faint.

Especially when she joined her bridesmaids—Blessing, of course, and her four girl cousins, all wearing gold dresses and green hair ties. Blessing beamed, a sort of joyous glow surrounding her that probably had more to do with her relationship with Auntie Precious and inclusion into Uncle Efe's big family than the big day.

And a big day it was.

Her uncle Efe had constructed a massive tent in the backyard, and from it an African band—complete with djembe drums, a kora, a xylophone, and a number of guitars—played music while guests milled the grounds. Hundreds, maybe a thousand strangers from the village, all dressed in their colorful best, many wearing the deep coral of her necklace, some in green and gold, others in silver and deep blue.

Ranger was going to lose his mind.

She almost didn't recognize him when Auntie Precious led her to her uncle's study where the first ceremony was held. Packed with the tribal elders, and their family, the chatter died when she arrived at the door.

Inside, on his golden throne, sat the Ovie. He wore a gold kaftan and top hat and held a cane.

But Ranger. Oh my, he wore Nigerian green well. His gold-trimmed kaftan fitted his frame perfectly, highlighting his shoulders, his trim waist. Underneath, he wore black pants and dress shoes, very dapper. And he'd cut his dark hair, more of a high and tight cut, although the front was longer, and tousled, an unruly tuft sticking out of the black kufi. Clean-shaven, he wore a solemn expression, like he might be concentrating.

Trying to get it right.

"He's very handsome," Auntie Precious said in her ear as she held her back. "He's doing well. He's already presented his gifts and the Ovie has accepted them. Now he will bow in honor of the Ovie and you may enter."

The music spilled into the house from outside as she watched Ranger take a knee in front of the Ovie. He bowed his head.

Her heart just about exploded. Oh, how she loved this man. Playing the groom to protect her—no, embracing this world with her, as if he knew how much it meant to her to know it.

Her eyes burned with the irony of it all. The one. The *only* man she ever wanted, and it was all for show.

"This was a huge mistake." The words had burrowed down and turned to coal inside her. Alive. Burning, despite her efforts to pretend otherwise.

But today—today was her wedding day. And for the next twelve hours, she'd believe it was real.

"Okay, now, he's ready," Auntie Precious said. "Dance to him."

Dance. Right. Ranger had gone to take his place in a chair near the Ovie. And now he watched her, a smirk on his face as she, yes, danced into the room. Nothing elaborate, just in beat to the music outside that made her move and then as she got closer, shake her shoulders at him.

The men erupted in laughter and Auntie Lydia, also wearing a gold dress and sitting on the other side of Uncle Efe, grinned, nodded.

Noemi bowed to her uncle, and he set his hand on her shoulder and said something in Urhobo.

Auntie Precious came in behind her. "Now you must kneel and bring the drink to the man you choose as your husband."

She worked her way to the floor in the tight dress, put down the feather fan, and then took the drink of something red and probably alcoholic in her hands. She made a show of looking around the room then settling her gaze on Ranger. More laughter.

"Crawl to him," Auntie Precious said.

Seriously?

But he'd bowed for her, so she worked her way to him on her knees while he sat grinning. She narrowed her eyes at him and he waggled his brows and she fought the urge to laugh.

And all she could think about then was the way he'd kissed her two nights ago, under the moonlight, so much emotion in his touch that she'd thought . . .

Well, she'd thought she had him back.

He'd tasted of memories, of safety, of unspoken dreams,

and she'd completely stepped into everything he offered her, ready to give him more.

Probably it was a good thing he pulled away.

But really, he didn't have to remind her it wasn't real. *"I can't marry you, Noemi."*

Yes, she knew that, thank you. Knew none of this was real.

Except, it felt like it, him smiling at her, then taking the cup and drinking the juice, then handing it to her—it *was* juice—for her to finish.

Then, he'd helped her off the floor and she'd stood there, him smiling down at her, his strong hands on her arms, holding her up on those flimsy heels.

Uncle Efe stood, too, and took their hands. Bowed his head.

Oh. Praying.

She closed her eyes. And although she couldn't understand all of the words, something strange rippled through her. As if maybe, this wasn't a game.

Even Ranger's hand tightened in hers.

"Now, sit," Uncle Efe said, and Ranger sat in the chair.

Auntie Precious then turned Noemi around to sit on Ranger's lap, and in the strangest tradition she'd ever seen, her uncle got up holding a wad of cash and began to simply spill it on her. On them. One bill at a time as everyone clapped.

So maybe Ranger might be able to refill his boot. He sat, his arms around her, until Uncle Efe pronounced them married. Then he'd helped her up, and Auntie Precious told them to kiss.

Simple. Short. Sweet. But he'd met her eyes, and she saw desire in them.

It ignited a terrible hope inside her.

Especially since he truly seemed to morph into the man she'd known in Key West. She watched as Uncle Efe and Auntie Lydia, along with Auntie Angel, entered the tent to the applause and bowing of the audience. The band played and a number of women dressed in coral shook beaded balls with rice, singing.

A long aisle ran the center of the tent, bordered by tables and chairs, and at the front sat a gold-rimmed sofa, with three chairs on one side, and one chair on the other.

Uncle Efe sat in one of the three chairs, two of his wives beside him. The third had decided to stay in Lagos.

Auntie Precious came in next, dancing her way down the aisle to the beat of the drums, the shakers, and the singing. The crowd clapped, and she took the chair on the other side of the sofa.

Then she nodded at the couple.

Ranger held a cane as part of this wedding attire but set it aside and turned to Noemi. "This is the weirdest op I've ever been on. But wow, you look beautiful."

And then he began to dance, working his arms gingerly, moving his body.

He looked ridiculous. But he caught her hand. "I am not doing this alone," he said. "Dance, sweetheart."

She laughed and began to dance, moving her hips, her shoulders, her head to the music, the beat. As they danced people moved out into their path and tossed money at them or joined them in dance for a few steps down the aisle. Behind them, her bridesmaids also danced their way in.

The Ovie just beamed at her, a familial look of pride on his face, and it felt so lavish, she had nothing for it except to embrace the crazy joy of it all as she and Ranger danced down the aisle to their sofa throne.

A cake decorated with kola nuts and coral beads—all edible—sat off to the side, and servants emerged with trays of Nigerian salad and grilled goat.

A female emcee rose and for the next few hours, roused the crowd to laughter, whipped up the band, and kept the party going. They cut the cake and the emcee made Noemi get on her knees again to feed Ranger a piece.

She pulled it away, taunting him, and he shook his head, gave a growl. "Already vexing me, wife."

Then he fed her, doing the same, and even the Ovie laughed.

"Kiss!" The chant rippled through the crowd and Ranger leaned forward.

But this time, she hung on to his shirt, lingered, and when she let go, she noticed his smile had dimmed. He swallowed, the desire in his eyes deepening.

The cousins pulled them onto the dance floor, and again, he had no moves, but tried, and she loved him for it.

Painfully, utterly loved him.

She wouldn't think of tomorrow. Just this moment.

Because, in the eyes of Nigeria, and maybe even God, if the Ovie's words were right, they were married.

By evening, the grass was covered in naira, and the crowd had thinned until only the diehard dancers—mostly the cousins—remained.

"I have a surprise for you," Uncle Efe said as the sky turned dark.

The night erupted in fireworks. Green, gold, red, orange. They shot up behind the compound, over the river, and sprayed celebration into the night.

Ranger slipped his hand into hers again.

Auntie Precious stood in front of them. She still looked beautiful, with her coral headwrap, her blue dress. She took their hands. "Here's when you exit to your wedding night. Be blessed. Make many babies."

For his part, Ranger just nodded, his smile fixed.

Auntie Precious laughed and leaned in, kissing her on the cheek. "He is a good man, Oyinbo mhe. Trust him."

The remaining crowd clapped as they left, the women shaking their rice tambourines, the band playing.

Ranger held her hand as she negotiated the stairs.

"My feet feel like they might need to be amputated at the ankles," she said.

"If I didn't have a broken wing, I'd carry you," Ranger said.

"I'll manage."

But when they got to the room, he led her to the bench, then knelt and unbuckled her shoes.

Eased them off her feet.

Then looked up and met her eyes. His smile had vanished. "It's been a wild day. I'll bet you're tired."

Tired?

He got up. Took another breath. "Do you need help, um, getting . . . out of . . ." He raised an eyebrow.

Oh. And suddenly, she had no words, the flirt she so desperately needed, gone.

Silence fell between them. Outside, the fireworks continued to burst as the remaining crowd cheered.

"I sorta feel like that's a little too much enthusiasm."

He said it with such a straight face, she wasn't sure . . .

Then he grinned. "I mean, we really don't need any cheering for what's happening in here."

They didn't? She got up. "What's happening?"

He walked over to the bed, then reached for a pillow. "Sleep."

Oh.

He threw it on the floor, then another one.

She stared at him. He set his kufi on the bench, then turned his back to her as he tugged off his kaftan.

"Seriously."

"What?" He turned back, folding his kaftan and setting it on the bench. His shoulder was healing well, his bruises nearly faded and she just stared at him.

Oh boy.

"Are you okay, Noemi?" He took a step toward her. "We barely ate—"

"I'm fine." She held up her hands. "Just. *Fine*."

Then she headed to the bathroom and shut the door. Stared at her way-too-made-up face in the mirror.

What did she think was going to happen? He'd made it all clear—very clear—what this was about.

"Noemi?" The knock came at the door.

She opened it.

He stood there, his hands braced on either side of the frame, his gaze hard on her.

The desire in his eyes drew in her breath.

He swallowed, his chest rising and falling.

"Range—"

Two steps. Two steps and he was in the bathroom, his arms around her, his mouth on hers. She nearly fell with the power of it, but he had his arm around her, pulling her up against him.

And then she simply held on. His kiss took the breath from her, all thought but the feel of his body against hers, solid, heat radiating off it, his fingers tangled in her hair. He tasted of salt, yet also sweet like the cake. With the brush of his whiskers against her skin, she softened her mouth.

Ranger.

He'd never kissed her like this. Before he was all buttoned up, lines in the sand, kisses at the door, with the barest, occasional hint of what lie beneath.

Clearly a man of deep emotion. Of passion, because now his chest rose and fell, his breaths deepening as he kissed her neck, her cheek, then her mouth again.

The world dropped away. The lies, the past, the hurt, the confusion.

This is what *wanted* felt like.

He caught her face and moved back, meeting her eyes. Said nothing, his aqua-blue eyes in hers.

Yes, Ranger.

She should have just wound her hand around his neck and brought his mouth back to hers. Should have wrapped her arms around him and let him carry her to the bed.

Become his wife.

Instead, "Wow, when you go all in on a mission, you go all in."

Oh no. Because the moment the words fell from her, he blinked.

Then he let her go. Blew out a breath. "Right. Yes. Okay."

"Range— I was just kidding." She reached out for him, but he backed up.

He shook his head. "No. You're right. This is a mistake."

She *wasn't* right.

"Truth is, I want you, Noemi." He blew out a breath, fisted his hands at his sides, as if afraid to touch her. "Right now, I'd like nothing more than to put the pillows back on the bed and throw you on them. To make love to you to the fireworks and cheers. I'd like to say that all this is real, for the next six hours, and when morning shows up, we'll have somehow become different people, able to share our lives together. But"—he swallowed—"you're right. This is a fantasy. A beautiful, perfect fairy tale that tomorrow we're going to wake up from." His voice fell. "And I'm sorry I forgot that."

What—?

"And yes, maybe a week ago I could have not cared. Could have closed my ears to the words in my head and listened to whatever is going on inside." He blew out another breath and took a step back toward her, his hands on her arms. "But that was before your uncle took me aside today and essentially said the same thing to me that your dad did. That you were precious to him. That you were brave and beautiful and bold and that he never wanted to see you hurt." He bent down, pressing his forehead to hers. "Neither do I."

He stayed there a moment, just his forehead against hers, and she couldn't move at the thought of her father—and Uncle Efe—saying those words.

His chest was still rising and falling, as if against a great struggle, his voice almost roughened when it emerged. "You deserve a husband who can give you a future—if you even want a husband, someday. And I don't want to be the guy who steals that moment from you—the real moment, when you pledge your life to someone. I don't want us to wake up with regrets. No matter how beautiful you are, how amazing you smell and . . . well, how much this day felt real. Okay?"

He leaned away. Met her eyes.

Okay? No, *not* okay. Because it *was* real—all of it and she wanted to shout, *Why not? Why not you, why not the dream?*

And then she got it.

"This is a mistake."

Duty first. And she'd nearly made him forget that.

At least this time he'd pushed her away before she really lost herself.

"Okay." The word just emerged, but what else could she do? "Don't worry, sailor. I figured this night would end up with me in the big bed alone."

He sighed. "Right. Good."

She put her hand on his chest, felt his heartbeat there.

He was a good man. And she was no match for his principles.

Sheesh, she was a fool. But she'd been warned, a few times. She scrounged up an easy tone. "So, do you think you can score us some of that cake?"

He smiled then, relief on his face. "Your wish is my command, wife."

"Hurry up, husband. Before the cousins steal it all."

He left, and she took the opportunity to unwind her hair, take off her golden blouse, unwrap her wedding skirt.

Pull off her crazy eyelashes.

Weep, her legs pulled up against her on the floor, the shower running, just in case he came back.

No worries. By the time he returned with a mammoth-sized piece, she was in her bed massaging her feet.

He set the plate down and handed her a fork. Took his own.

Oh, she just wanted this day to end.

"They're still dancing downstairs," he said.

"Of course they are. It'll go all night. Did anyone see you?"

"Please." But he smiled.

Oh, he was going to make her cry again. She forked a piece of cake. "Your dance moves are horrible, sailor."

"At least I'm rich. Your aunties and cousins picked up thousands of naira."

"Pays to be the son of the king."

He looked at her then. "Indeed."

They finished the cake, laughing about the events of the day, but all the time Noemi forced a smile, hoping she wouldn't burst into tears.

He finally wished her good night, like a gentleman, and went to sleep.

On the floor.

She lay in the darkness a long time listening to him breathe.

She finally pushed out of bed as the dawn pressed a blush into their room. She pulled a wrap around her shorts and headed outside.

Maybe to walk. Maybe to figure out why she had to make everything a joke. *"Wow, when you go all in on a mission, you go all in."*

Nice, Noemi.

The party had lasted into the night, but most of the tables had been picked up and the chairs stacked, although the canopy still stood. Noemi walked over to the pool area and sat on the edge, put her feet into the water. Leaned back to let the early rays of sunlight find her face.

Really, she should run and not look back.

"Emuvoke? What are you doing up so early?"

The voice came from Auntie Lydia, who carried a bundle on her head. She came near, her shadow casting over her. "You have left your husband?"

She swallowed. "I . . . he is sleeping."

"Oh. I see that face. There is trouble." She sat next to her, pulling up her red skirt, setting down the mangos that she'd gathered. "He no make you happy?"

Oh, shoot, her eyes were burning. And for some reason, the Ovie's warning to Ranger climbed into her head. "I am happy." And then she was crying.

"Oyee. I see. It is because he is a warrior, right? Because he must choose his duty over love?"

She looked at her aunt. Close enough. She was just a job, a mission, a burden to him.

"Ah, but don't you see. Just because Efe married another didn't mean he loves me less. Or Angel less. He married for duty, yes, but he loves her too."

"Doesn't it make you feel . . . unwanted?"

Auntie Lydia shrugged. "I know I am in his thoughts, even when we're apart. I know he will come back to me."

"And that's enough?"

"I am loved by the king. Chosen to be his. It is enough." She reached out and took Noemi's hand. "And you are enough to have your man come back to you."

She frowned. "I don't think so."

"It seems to me that he found you, even in a terrorist camp. That love would have died for you."

"I will find you." Ranger's voice haunted her.

Oh.

And, he *had* nearly died for her.

"Truth is, I want you, Noemi."

"Love waits for you," Auntie Lydia said, as if reading her mind. "Upstairs."

Noemi looked at her, then past her, through the turret window, to where Ranger lay on the tile, his body warm and solid and, according to Nigerian law, belonging to her.

And maybe, with a little prodding, his heart would too.

She stood up. "Thank you, Auntie Lydia."

Her aunt smiled, her eyes kind.

Boom! Behind her, the world exploded—fire and smoke and earth erupting.

The blast slammed into Noemi, catapulting her into the pool.

The shock of it took her under, but the world turned quiet as the water raged.

She waited a second, then kicked hard and burst to the surface.

Flames engulfed the canvas in an inferno, black smoke billowing into the sky, turning the grounds acrid. Shouts punched through the chaos and behind that, gunfire. A machine gun staccatoed through the smoke and flame.

She treaded water, Auntie Lydia coming up behind her. "The children!" She started for the edge of the pool.

Ranger.

Noemi searched for the turret through the smoke.

No.

Flames billowed through the open windows.

Then, the world exploded again, rocking the palm trees around the grounds. Noemi grabbed Auntie Lydia and pulled her back as a tall palm careened toward the pool.

"Deep breath!"

Then she pulled her aunt under as the world turned bright around her.

She'd just have to stay on her toes. Keep her mouth shut.

And never let him know that she was a liar.

Because if she didn't know better, Tae could swear that Colt Kingston could see right through her.

Right through her attempts to make sure he was comfortable to her hope of checking on the massive bruising that covered his body, looking for deepening purple, or evidence of continued internal bleeding.

The guy was messed up.

Whatever he'd been into overseas—it wasn't good. And she'd only heard a few snippets since he'd walked in the door with a guy named Skeet.

No, not walked, stumbled. The guy should be in a hospital. Instead, he'd somehow materialized from some scary op on the other side of the ocean, looking like he'd done a few rounds with a cement mixer.

Two black eyes, broken ribs—she recognized that by the way he moved—which meant internal bleeding, if not severely damaged organs.

He'd slept for a solid twenty-four hours in the lower-floor guest room before he woke with a moan. She knew because she'd stuck around and made him bone broth. Mostly because the look on Barry's face suggested the guy was in no place to whip up soup for his damaged son.

Instead, he sat by his bed and prayed.

Because evidently, his other two sons were still out there.

Wherever *there* was.

Skeet had stayed the night and left the next morning without much explanation, although Echo had followed him out to the truck and stood in the sunlight, her hands in her pockets, pacing as he talked, her jaw tight.

So, not good.

Tae hadn't known what to do, so she'd sifted through the recipes until she found the bone broth recipe. It turned the house into a potpourri of beefy soup smells.

Barry was asleep on his recliner when she heard the moan from the guest room.

You okay? She nearly spoke the words as she came into the room, biting them back before she obliterated nearly a week of determination.

Colt was struggling to sit up, drawing in a sharp breath, then wincing as she came over. She didn't ask—just wrapped her arms around his shoulders and helped ease him up.

Maybe he didn't need her help—it was mostly a reflex from her intern year. Still, "Thank you," he said, his jaw tight.

She nodded, then glanced at Barry. He'd started to stir.

"Has he been here all night?"

She nodded again.

He raised an eyebrow. "And you are?"

Her mouth tightened, and she shook her head.

"Wow. Already not talking to me." He smiled.

Oh, he was cute. Deep brown eyes that raked over her, a slight, self-deprecating smile, dark hair that fell below his ears, although now frowzy around his head, and a full beard, a result of weeks of captivity—she'd gotten that when Barry woke up.

"How are you doing, son?" He leaned forward in his chair.

Ask him about chest pain. She practically willed it into Barry's brain.

"I like your new chef." Colt looked at her and winked.

Barry laughed. "This is Jane. She's staying with us for a while." He looked at her. "Thanks for the soup."

She shrugged.

"It's the best thing I've ever eaten," Colt said.

She rolled her eyes.

"Seriously. If I ever see another bowl of rice again, it will be too soon." He held the bowl with one hand, forgoing the spoon and sipping it.

"Ranger said you were taken by the Boko Haram," Barry said.

Seriously? Out of Nigeria? She drew in a breath.

Colt looked at her, then back to his father. "Yeah. We think so. It wasn't like they wore name tags, or let us in on their group handshake, but they fit the description. Made the girls wear hijabs and woke us up every morning with a call to prayer."

He took another drink. "Which I politely declined."

Yeah, she bet he did.

No wonder he'd been beaten. She wouldn't have put it past him to try and escape too. And given his build, he'd probably nearly succeeded. The man had muscles—thick arms, a solid torso, and a sinewed leg that stuck out from under his blanket.

But what her gaze fell on was the mess of bruises on his body.

Right then, she nearly blew her cover to ask for a blood pressure cuff. Instead, when Colt handed her the bowl, she sneaked in a press of her hand to his forehead.

He gave her a look and she just smiled at him.

No fever, from what she could tell.

And he kept down the broth, so no vomiting.

"So, Skeet said that Ranger came to get me," he said. "I don't remember much after they grabbed me."

"Ranger *and* Dodge," Barry said. "Both your brothers went after you."

Colt seemed to stiffen then, and she wondered if maybe a rib had slid against his intestines when he drew in a breath.

Where does it hurt?

She hadn't said it out loud—she was sure of it, but he looked at her then, hard, staring at her.

She had reached out to touch him, and now pulled back. Oops.

His gaze settled on her. Stilled. He finally turned to his dad again. "Are they back yet?"

Barry shook his head.

Colt lay back and closed his eyes. "Then I shouldn't be either."

Barry said nothing, and Colt eventually slipped off to sleep.

But his words settled inside her, sharp-edged and raw.

Yeah, she knew what it felt like to be the one who survived.

She didn't know why, but she couldn't bear to leave him then. Barry left and she climbed into the recliner and picked up a book—and read nearly a hundred pages of *Jubal Sackett* before Colt woke again.

This time, the pale shadows of the Alaskan night had fallen through the window, the glow of the bedside light on his face. The shadows softened the bruises, leaving only the high cheekbones, the soft brown lashes closed over warrior eyes.

Yeah, he was devastatingly handsome.

And dangerous. Because she too had fallen asleep, and of course, Sergei had walked into her brain, and she'd woken with the feeling of his grip on the back of her neck. Which had her gasping, and she might have even screamed as she came to.

Not loud enough to wake the house.

But that's when she noticed, in the yellow glow of the light, Colt's brown eyes on her, watching.

Seeing.

Thinking.

"Something you want to share with me, Florence?" he said softly.

She swallowed. Shook her head.

He just stared at her, his chest rising and falling. Finally, "If I can outlast the Boko Haram, honey, I can outlast you."

She closed her book, got up, and walked out of the room.

Bring it on, tough guy.

She hadn't won the CDC's Klimov Award for her tendency to quit.

TEN

It just might have been the worst night of Ranger's life.

And he'd once spent a long and painful night next to a nest of fire ants.

He'd like to blame the tile floor—and sure, that hadn't done anything for his healing wounds—but really, it was the lingering smell of Noemi in the bed, something sweet and floral and painfully intoxicating, the sound of her breath against the night, the sense that yes . . . oh yes . . .

He could have said yes to the look in Noemi's eyes, to the way she smelled, to the taste of her still on his lips, and woken up this morning, um, *married*.

If not for her words—her *reality*—he would have ignored, no silenced, all the warning sirens in his head.

Would have made himself believe there was some kind of happy ending out there for him. For them.

The wedding ceremony had clearly gone right to his head.

No, his heart.

"Wow, when you go all in on a mission, you go all in."

It had ceased to be a mission the moment she danced to him, wearing her wedding dress.

At least for him.

Clearly, Noemi still saw it as a vacation fling. And if he let go, gave in, he'd wake up to Key West all over again. Him, diving in with his entire heart only to realize he was in over his head.

Worse, this time he didn't have a life to run back to after she left him.

And maybe his stupid broken heart wouldn't have even

mattered—not while lying there, wrestling with his resolve to get off the stupid floor and join his wife in the bed. But the Ovie and her father seemed to take up the fight in his head. *"She is precious to me. I don't want to see her hurt."*

Him either. Although it was probably too late because she got up early—nearly before the sun—and slunk out of the room.

Go after her. The thought pulsed inside him, taking up all the room in his brain, and he got up and headed to the bathroom.

Go after her.

No. That was crazy.

But the nearer he got to her, the more he wanted to figure out how to make it work. *"You do have a home. Alaska. Your family. Colt and Dodge. The ranch. Maybe it's time to let yourself dream."*

Ranger cupped his hands under the water and splashed it on his face, stared at his mug, dripping wet in the mirror. More black spots in his vision, in both eyes now, and one large one that cut out his periphery. At this rate, he'd be blind by Christmas.

Beautiful.

He scrubbed his eyes, but no change when he opened them.

Whatever. He turned on the shower and his gaze fell on the coral necklace lying on the sink. He picked it up, ran his thumb over the thick beads. *"I don't have dreams. I have duty."*

The words hit him like a punch to his sternum. Without dreams, the duty was meaningless.

Go after her.

Maybe it *was* time to let himself dream.

He dropped the necklace into his backpack, still on the floor of the room. Okay, so maybe after—

The world exploded. The blast buckled the floor, and Ranger hit his knees and covered his head as plaster rained down on him.

Screams, from inside the house somewhere. Smoke.

Machine-gun fire.

Noemi!

He got up and yanked open the door.

Flames engulfed the curtains at the window, smoke billowing into the room.

It wouldn't take long for the bed to go up, the way the sparks spit into the room.

More screams.

He grabbed up his pack on the way out the door. He was slinging it onto his good shoulder as he emerged to the hallway.

Uncle Efe stood at the top of the stairs, bare chested, dressed in linen pants, barefoot. His eyes widened as Ranger charged down the hall.

"We're under attack!" Uncle Efe said, following Ranger down the stairs.

"Get the kids!" Ranger hit the landing and his heart stopped.

A massive palm tree had fallen lengthwise across the pool, flames blazing down the trunk and from the thick tuft on top. Smoke blackened the backyard.

Precious came out of the bedroom now, shouting in pidgin for the children.

And behind it all, more machine-gun fire.

The Ovie's men had assembled behind the stone patio wall, shooting back.

"Where's Noemi?" Ranger shouted over the chaos.

"I saw her outside with Lydia." This from Angel, who came running from the kitchen.

Then she pointed to the pool, and Ranger went cold. The palm tree's fronds had gone up fast, and now just the trunk burned. But still, they might be trapped at the deeper end.

Uncle Efe had beaten him outside, yelling at his staff in Urhobo. *Yeah, what he said—*

Ranger dropped his pack, took a running start, and dove into the pool. His dive stayed shallow, but he dipped down under the burning tree to the deeper end.

There. Noemi was a ball at the deep end, holding on to Lydia.

He met her eyes, then grabbed her hand.

She followed him, also gripping Lydia, and in a moment, he'd yanked them to the shallow end.

She surfaced hard, gulping in thick breaths. Lydia, too, surfaced and the Ovie jumped into the water.

Gunshots still sounded from beyond the smoke, toward the fence.

"Who's shooting at us?" Noemi ducked her head down.

He had some guesses, but they sounded so far-fetched.

How had Abu found her here?

Ranger pulled her out of the water, scooping up his pack as they ran to the house.

They got inside and found the staff in chaos, the cooks hunkered down in the kitchen, an armed security guard at the front entrance.

Angel stood at the door of the Ovie's office. "The children are inside."

Lydia ran to join her.

Ranger wanted to shove Noemi in there too but, "We have to get out of here," he said to her. Then, to Uncle Efe, "They're after us."

The man looked at him. "I don't understand—"

"Me either, but we saw Noemi's attacker in the market—"

"You are safe here."

"No," Noemi said. "The children could get hurt. We need to leave."

The man's chest rose and fell, turmoil in his eyes. "My men can protect you—"

"No!" Noemi said. "I'm not letting your family get hurt because of me!"

Ranger wanted to hunker down into the Ovie's offer, but Noemi was right. They couldn't risk the family getting overrun. His brain was scrambling over exfil options and coming up empty. "Noemi's right. We need to go."

The Ovie looked from him to Noemi. "Come with me," he said finally.

He ducked, running to his office. He pushed Angel inside, then held the door for them.

All the children, along with Blessing, Lydia, Precious, and Angel were hunkered down in the well between the sofas.

"My windows are bulletproof here. We are safe."

Blessing got up and ran to Noemi, wrapped her arms around her. "I was so scared!"

The Ovie walked over to his desk, pulled out a drawer. "Take the river. My boat."

Ranger hoped he meant the beautiful, red-and-silver hulled vintage speedboat he'd seen tied to the long dock.

"Here." He held out a key on a red flotation chain. "You'll need to unlock the box under the seat. The ignition key is there." He pointed toward the door. "Go out the side entrance. There is a path between the walls to the boathouse."

Ranger saw the plan—get to the boat, take it down the river. Escape out into the sea.

"Right." Ranger turned to Noemi. "Let's go." He opened the office door.

But she just looked at him, shaking her head. "Not without Blessing."

Oh perfect. Here they went again.

"Blessing will stay with me," Precious said. She stepped up to the girl, put her hands on her shoulders. "She will be my daughter. I will care for her."

Super. Yes. That.

But Noemi's eyes filled.

"It's okay, Oyinbo mhe. She will be safe and loved here."

Noemi nodded. Then she caught Blessing's face in her hands. "You are in my heart, sister." She looked at her aunt. A tear hung off her jaw. "How do I thank you for—"

The giant arched picture window in the front room shattered. Gunfire peppered the chairs, the wooden table. Despite their cover in the office, the Ovie and his family ducked. Ranger grabbed Noemi, pushed her down, his body over her.

The Ovie's men answered and for a moment, the attack halted. Uncle Efe picked up a radio and leveled them instructions in Uhrobo. Then, "They'll cover you. Go!"

Ranger found his feet, grabbed Noemi's hand—

"Wait!" She jerked away. Stood there, staring at her aunt and uncle. "Thank you. You gave me—"

Precious pulled her into a hug. "No, daughter. You gave us. So much. Everything."

Uncle Efe stood over her, his eyes wet. "Go with God, daughter." He took her by the shoulders and kissed her on the cheek.

Then he looked at Ranger and nodded, the words unsaid.

Ranger grabbed Noemi's hand again and took off across the house, down the hallway, toward the far end of the palace.

"How—" Noemi gasped.

"I don't know," Ranger said and found the entry door. He banged it open and ran out into the dawn. Smoke fogged the yard—yay—and he ducked close to the house, listening.

"Do you think Abu followed us?" Noemi fell in against him, also breathing hard.

"Wouldn't be hard to figure out where we were. It's not like Dafe and Precious were in stealth mode at the market. Or you, for that matter—let's go." He grabbed her hand again as the gunfire popped from the other side of the yard.

They scampered toward a gate door between the two high stone walls. He unlocked it, then pressed through it to find a worn footpath between an outer wall and an inner wall.

"Or it might not be Abu at all. But I doubt it." Ranger

stopped at the edge of the compound wall and looked out toward the river.

The water seemed clear, despite the black smoke now lifting over the river.

"There," he said and pointed to the silver-and-red closed-bow Sea King speedboat. He guessed it was nearly thirty years old, given the red-and-white vinyl seats, the ancient Mercury motor. It was moored to a dock some thirty feet from the compound walls.

"Ready to run?"

"Call me Usain Bolt," she said.

"Let's move, Bolt."

She outran him to the boat, then jumped into the cockpit. He shouted at her to stay down as a few shots chipped at the boat. He threw himself in, the adrenaline masking the pain he knew he should feel.

But the Ovie's men peppered the attackers, and Ranger used the cover to lift the seat, unlock the box, find the ignition key, and start the engine.

A shot pinged against the windshield. Noemi crawled over from between the seats and unwound the rope from the tie lines.

"Get down!" Ranger snapped.

"Don't get shot!"

He slammed the throttle into reverse and the boat reared away from the dock.

More bullets zipped into the water. One zinged by his head, heating the air.

He rammed the throttle forward and the force knocked her back, against the hull, set him down in the seat.

He nearly overturned the boat as it zagged in the water before he got the steering wheel straightened out.

"Look out!" She sat against the hull, pointed to a fishing boat—

"I see it!" But he hadn't, at least not clearly. He cut hard, missed them and then straightened her out.

Spray kicked up over them, cold on his bare chest.

He glanced at her. "Are you okay?"

"Are you? I thought the bomb had hit the room."

"Was it a bomb?" He cut around another abandoned boat. The fisherman must have fled in the chaos.

"I don't know. Felt like it."

"Grenades, maybe." He glanced behind him. No one seemed to be following them. They passed a village on the south side of the water. "Get my cell phone from my pack. We need to call Ham."

She scooted to the front seat and now opened the pack, digging around inside it before coming out with a phone. Not his.

"What is that?" he asked.

"This is the dead one. I must have put it in here when it didn't charge." She put it back in and found the burner phone he'd picked up at the market.

"Can you take the wheel?"

"Of course." She handed him the phone, then slid onto the seat in front of him.

He sat down on the passenger side. "Fishermen."

"I see them," she said and slowed before she sent them rocking with her wake. Waved, greeting them in pidgin.

"Having fun?" he asked.

"It's much faster than a sailboat." She stood now, one knee on the seat, her hair caught by the wind, the weave they'd added to it now turning it long and tangled.

She looked like some kind of superhero, her white pajamas billowing behind her like a cap. No makeup, her eyes alight.

He was completely undone by this woman. Clearly, nothing fazed her.

He dialed the only number in his contacts.

Ham answered. "Range?"

"We have a problem. Abu just attacked the palace. We had to exfil, and now we're on the river . . ." He looked at Noemi.

"Forcados," she said again, and he relayed it to Ham.

"It looks like it connects with the Niger," Ham said, "then dumps out into the Gulf of Guinea. We can get a chopper there, if you can get out into international waters."

"Range. We're in trouble," Noemi said.

He lowered the phone.

"We're losing fuel."

Perfect. Maybe one of the shots had nicked a fuel line. "No good, Ham. I don't think we have enough juice. Can you pick us up on land?"

Pause. "Not without an incident. But we could get in close. Maybe hang low until dark. And how do you feel about a swim?"

With a bum wing? Not great, but he could probably manage. "We'll figure it out. I'll call you when we're close."

"On our way." Ham clicked off and Ranger blew out a breath. Slid onto the seat, his feet planted as Noemi piloted them through the water.

The sun had risen higher into the day, and with the drama behind them, he started to relax. To their back, the black smoke dissipated into a clear blue sky, the villages along the riverbed quiet, fishermen hauling in their catches, children running along shore, women carrying baskets to their homes.

He let his heart rate slow.

She glanced at him. "Thanks for diving into the pool. I was sorta . . . stuck, I guess. I couldn't figure out a way past that palm tree."

He didn't mention how he'd been terrified, how he'd thought that she'd been hit, lying dead at the bottom of the pool, or worse, crushed by the palm tree.

And that thought turned right into a boulder in the center of his chest.

What had he been thinking pushing her away from him in Key West? He'd thought she'd be a liability.

For the first time in years, he felt his breath in his lungs, the world opening up around him. Blue skies, the sound of the motor in the air. And Noemi, at the helm, glancing over at him, smiling, despite their crazy trauma.

He thought she'd slow him down.

He could barely keep up with her.

"After we get out of here, I think you need to come back to Alaska with me."

He'd had to sort of shout it, and maybe she realized that, so she cut the motor down. Perched on the seat's backrest. "What?"

"I think—"

"I heard you. Why?"

He pointed to a large boulder in the water, and she piloted the boat around it.

"Because, and for the life of me I can't figure out why, Abu is still after you. Do you have any guesses?"

She shook her head. "I don't even know why he took us in the first place. I thought it might simply be for a ransom, but . . ."

"Right. And until we figure it out, I'm not letting you out of my sight."

She stared at him, blinking, her mouth half open.

And shoot, he couldn't help himself. "After all, you are my wife."

His *wife*? It sounded painfully right on Ranger's lips. And with his accompanying smile, the word arrowed right past all Noemi's defenses and spiraled down into her heart.

Took root.

Oh *no*.

And it only grew as they sped down the river, past villages, stopping at a harbor midday to refuel, filling a few extra gas cans, grabbing some boiled corn and fried Akara, cans of orange

Fanta. He took over at the helm until the shadows lengthened, and then he asked her to drive again.

Maybe because he'd gotten on the phone with Ham again, arranging a pickup.

As long as she lived, she'd never forget opening her eyes to see him appear in the water as she crouched in the pool with Auntie Lydia. The look of fear on his face.

"I will find you."

Funny, those were the words that seemed to set in her heart. But in that instant, he'd kept his promise.

But wasn't that who Ranger was? A promise keeper? Calm down—hadn't he promised Uncle Efe that he'd keep her safe? So, his invitation—if she were to call it that—to go to Alaska wasn't about true love.

It was about duty.

Yep, see, that she could understand. She knew the cost, the drive of duty.

Had shouldered the short end of a sailor's duty most of her life.

Darkness followed them down the river, creeping over them as the sky turned from bruised to ashen to black. The smells of algae, fish, wildlife—oh, please let there not be crocodiles—rose up from the river as the night settled. Frogs sang from offshore. They'd pulled into a cloister of reeds and mangroves, waiting for darkness before they edged past the massive cement jetties that jutted out to protect the entrance of the river.

On either side of the jetties, guards sat in stations, their lights burning in the night, the occasional spotlight scraping the water.

Looking for international interlopers.

Ranger sat in the darkness. Watching the night, his jaw hard.

The gulf splashed against the jetties, evidence of the turbulent waters beyond.

She didn't want to leave Nigeria. The thought caught her up, and with it, a swell of pain filled her chest. *"Go with God, daughter."*

Uncle Efe's words, loud in her ears. *"Go with God."*

A little hard to do when God was nowhere to be found.

"She will be my daughter. I will care for her."

Noemi ran her hand across her cheek, found it wet. Silly. She barely knew these people.

Her family. She closed her eyes.

"Princess? You okay?"

She drew in a breath, nodded. "Yes. It just . . ." She gave a harsh laugh. "Twenty-four hours ago, we were dancing under the stars. I can admit, I didn't imagine my honeymoon to be spent on an old speedboat, running for my life."

"Aw, it's not so bad. Look at that sky." He was sitting on the back bench and now reached out and pulled her over to him. She sat at his side. "The only time you see stars like this in Alaska is in the dead of winter. But they're so bright you feel like you're at the top of the world."

The Milky Way spilled glitter across the velvet night, and sitting here with Ranger, tucked against him, sure, it could be romantic. If she were on her honeymoon.

She sighed.

"Not enough?"

"I just . . . it was lovely, wasn't it?"

He paused, then, "The wedding?"

"All of it. Auntie Precious. Auntie Angel, and even Auntie Lydia. She really loved planning the wedding. And Blessing ended up with a whole new family."

"Uncle Efe was a little terrifying."

She laughed. "He likes you."

"He loves you."

Her eyes filled again. "I haven't . . ." She swallowed. Looked away, blinked. *Stop.* The last thing Ranger needed was her falling apart. "It felt strange and weirdly perfect to be there. Like I belonged, instantly."

He lifted his arm and put it around her. Kissed her forehead.

And she was sitting in the cabana, the world right around her.

Ranger's cell phone buzzed. He lifted his arm and leaned away, pulling the phone out of his pocket. "I'm listening."

He went quiet, then, "Roger. See you soon." Then he hung up.

"They're about thirty klicks out. They'll meet us just past the jetties, near international waters."

He climbed up to the driver's seat, turned the engine over.

Seemed to hesitate, then blew out a breath and eased them out of the blind. He kept the light off, traveling by the trace of moonlight, down the river.

Ahead of them, a massive cement jetty loomed, and beyond it, the gulf waters pitched against the wall, the waves creating a loud boom.

"Put on a life jacket, just in case this gets rough," he said. She pulled out a weathered orange jacket and slipped it over her head.

The boat began to rock in the waves as he picked up speed. The guard light scraped against the water, right in their path and he veered away, cut the engine low, waited.

"Hold on!"

The light passed them, and he hit the throttle hard and gunned it into the darkness left in its wake.

The boat took the passage at full speed, and guards came out to the jetty, their lights angled down, shouting.

He kept the engine on high, hitting the chop of the sea. The boat rocked, and more shouts echoed through the darkness behind them.

"Hopefully they won't drag out the gunboats," he said, and she wasn't sure he was kidding.

The sea turned rougher as they flew down the corridor.

And then they were in the open water. The waves threw the

boat sideways, and Ranger fought with the wheel, righting them just as another one crashed over the side and drenched them.

She reached out for his pack and slipped it on.

He was face to the wind, squinting in the darkness.

Behind them, she heard an air raid siren.

So maybe they *were* bringing out the gunboats.

"Ranger—"

"I hear it. We're heading down shore."

He did just that—turned the boat, riding the crest of one wave, falling into the trough, then gunning it as they rode another. He turned south, away from Nigeria.

She could barely make out the shoreline, some three hundred yards away.

He was throttling hard in an attempt to outrun the lights behind them. It seemed they'd begun to wink out, the darkness closing around them even as Ranger fought the swell of the waves.

"We're losing them!"

He glanced over his shoulder. Then back.

She turned around too. "Ranger!"

Her scream came too late. The boat slammed into a massive buoy-slash-pylon set in the sea, its light darkened and useless.

The boat careened off it, flipped, and flew through the air.

The force tore Noemi's grip from her seat and cast her out to sea. She landed hard, the heavy pack jerking her down, the world twisting around her.

She used the gravity of the pack to orient herself and kicked hard, up. Surfaced, barely holding herself above the waves. They crashed over her, drowning her, pulling her down.

Swim.

She'd heard of SEALs having to tread water for over an hour with a ninety-pound pack on their backs. She could probably make it to the villainous buoy.

Kicking hard, she pulled herself through the water, spitting out the sea, her eyes on the shape of the buoy.

When she reached it, she pulled herself against it in an embrace, her arms wrapped in the metal skeleton. Then, "Ranger!"

She hadn't seen him surface. Her eyes had adjusted to the darkness, and she now spotted the boat, upside down in the water, tossed by the waves.

But, no Ranger.

Oh God—please. If you've ever seen me, see me now—

Ranger sputtered up near her, breathing hard. "Noemi!"

"Over here!"

He searched for her, spotted her and swam over, grabbing on to the buoy with one strong hand. "You okay?"

"Yeah. What are we going to do?" She searched the darkness, but even the gunboats' lights had flickered out.

"Can you swim to shore?"

Oh . . . "Not with the pack."

"I'll take the pack."

Sure he would. Never mind that he'd just had surgery. Still, "How's Ham going to find us?"

A wave washed over them, and he came up, shook the water from his eyes. "There's an emergency kit in the boat seat. I'll bet it has flares. I'll get it."

"Ranger—"

"Stay here. Don't move. I'll be back."

And then he was gone.

And gone.

And *gone*.

She clung to the buoy, shivering, trying not to cry.

But in the darkness, he had vanished.

In the distance, a horn moaned over the water.

Please— "Ranger!" She slammed her hand on the water. "Ranger!"

Not like this. After everything, not like—

Ranger surfaced, grabbed on to the buoy with his good hand, drawing in deep breaths. Water slicked off his face, dripped off his chin, his aqua-blue eyes glistening in the moonlight when they met hers.

"I got it." He lifted the emergency box from where he'd clamped it against his chest with his wounded arm.

She held it as he opened the lid and pulled out a flare. "Hopefully Dodge is nearby. And the border control isn't." Then he cracked the flare. It started to spit into the night. He held it out, away from him. But he winced, clearly in pain.

Hooking the pack on the buoy, she hoisted herself out of the water, her feet on the platform.

"What are you doing?"

She ignored him and climbed up on the bars of the buoy, then reached down to him. "Give me the flare."

He handed it to her, and she reached up and wedged it between the upper bars of the buoy, near the dead light. Sparks bit at the night, fell into the sea below.

She climbed back down, shivering hard. Clung to the buoy with both hands.

"Smart."

She said nothing, still trying not to cry.

"Noemi?"

"I was scared. I thought . . ." She drew in a breath. "Nothing."

"You thought I was going to die, like your dad did."

She looked away from him.

"I'm not going anywhere," he said and then moved around behind her. He put his strong arms on each side of her, gripping the bar, his front to her back. "Just hang on."

She let the sense of him seep into her, strength in the middle of the dark, vast waters, just the two of them under the moonlight.

The shivering subsided.

"I'm sorry I got you into this," she said.

His lips whispered against her neck. "First, you did not get me into this. I volunteered. And for the record, nothing could have stopped me coming to look for you if I'd known you'd been taken."

Oh. His low spoken words sent a tremble into her bones.

"And second, there's nowhere else I'd rather be right now than here with you."

Oh, Ranger. With everything inside her, she wanted to turn around, wrap her arms and legs around him, hold on, and kiss him.

Her husband.

I love you, Range. The words pulsed inside her like the waves. "Ranger—"

"Do you hear that?" He pulled away from her, just enough for the water to chill her back, and searched the night. "There!"

She saw it too—the bottom lights of a chopper, the boom now thundering across the water.

Hopefully the search boats were out of range."Can you get on the buoy? I'm not sure they can see us in the water." She nodded and he gave her a little push as she climbed the buoy and waved into the darkness, the waves kicking up with the onslaught of wind from the rotors.

The big bird crossed in front of the moonlight, hovered, and a form dropped into the water. "Someone's coming!"

"I hope it's not the Nigerian special forces," Ranger said.

Please let him be kidding.

In a moment, a light skimmed against the water and a shout issued from the darkness. "Ranger!"

She scampered back into the water, hanging on as a face emerged. He held a flashlight, which shone on them and then on the person holding it.

Blond hair, dark wetsuit, moving through the water like a seal.

"Ham," Ranger said, "you're a sight for sore eyes."

"Tired of hanging around Nigeria?" He reached them, grabbed the buoy with a muscled arm.

No.

"You have no idea," Ranger said.

Right.

Ham was radioing the chopper.

"This is Noemi," Ranger said as the chopper came closer. A line dropped from the open door.

"Glad to meet you." Ham swam over and grabbed the line. A harness attached to the end, and he brought it over. "Let's get you into this."

Both men worked to snap her into the harness. Ranger held her steady as Ham radioed up.

"Almost home," Ranger said. "Ordeal over." He smiled at her.

She wanted to weep as the chopper jerked her into the air.

Ordeal over.

ELEVEN

"Stop pacing and sit down, Ranger. You're making me seasick."

The order came from Ham, who sat in one of the leather chairs facing the back of the luxury airplane owned by one of his contacts. Of course, he had about a thousand contacts—one who also had given him the chopper that Dodge had flown in from Lagos to pluck them out of the Gulf of Guinea. They'd flown from the Gulf back to Lagos where the plane had been waiting.

After the requisite hours of shut-eye, Dodge again took the helm and, with Ham as copilot, was now flying them across the ocean.

Outside, the night had started to wane toward dawn, with a simmer of gold and rose along the eastern horizon. The ocean was almost platinum, and they still had hours to go before they would touch down in Norfolk.

Noemi had bunked down on a set of seats in the very back, curled into a blanket and wearing an oversized shirt Jake had given her. She barely spoke to Ranger after being plucked out of the ocean. Huddled in the back of the chopper, the noise proved it impossible to talk anyway. Jake Silver, one of Ham's men, had sat beside her after buckling her in, and Ranger had taken the seat across, wishing that he could be sitting by her side, putting his arms around her, holding her . . .

He would probably never forget the feeling of holding on to the buoy for dear life, her body pressed against his, warm and safe and exactly where he wanted her.

He didn't want to let her go. That realization hit him as they transferred from the chopper to the plane, and she tucked herself into the back.

"Thirteen hours and we'll be stateside," Ham had told her as she grabbed a pillow from an overhead bin.

"Perfect," she'd said and offered a smile.

Right. What she meant was, "No big deal."

Well, it was a big deal, at least to Ranger, but shoot, he didn't know what to do with those feelings because she was right.

It was over. But he wouldn't call it an ordeal, not by a long shot. Which was why he was pacing the aisle.

"So, you think these guys followed you from their terrorist camp in northern Nigeria all the way down to some prince's palace in Delta State?" Ham asked.

"I don't know who attacked us," Ranger said, "but I'm pretty sure it was Abu Mussaf who found us in the market a few days ago."

"What were you doing in the market?" Jake asked. He sat in a pair of black canvas pants and a black T-shirt. "Sudden urge to buy a souvenir?"

"Something like that," Ranger said.

"I thought you said you were staying put in the compound," Ham said.

"I did. But that was after we saw Abu."

Ham nodded. He had changed clothes, wore a light sweater and a pair of jeans, sat with his arms folded over his thick chest. "What would Abu Mussaf want with an American aid worker?"

"Unless he was after you," Jake said.

"I don't think so," Ranger replied. "He never really got a good look at me, and I think he was after Noemi in the market. He grabbed her, not me." A chill brushed through him. For a moment back there, the heat of being ambushed felt like a fresh jolt in his gut. "No, he was definitely after her."

Ham motioned to a nearby seat. "You really should sit down, Ranger. It's a long flight and pacing won't help."

Ranger just wanted to work out some of the frustration of the attack, of not knowing how or why Abu was after Noemi. Ham had brought Ranger's duffel, and he changed into dry clothes but what he really wanted was to keep an eye on Noemi.

She lay sleeping and for a second, he was back at the wedding, seeing that smile as she danced toward him.

Or as she stood in the bathroom, her eyes round, her mouth open, so close as he'd told her . . . the truth.

He wanted her. In all the ways a man could—in his home, his life, his heart, and yes, in his bed.

He wanted his wife.

Ranger blew out a breath and sat down across from Ham. "I don't know what Abu wants with her. Did she see something? Did she have something of his? Maybe he's using her to get to Dr. Aaron Hanson . . ." He paused. "How is he?"

"Just went stateside, to Wisconsin. Recuperating," Ham said.

"Did you talk to her about when they got attacked?" Jake asked. "What happened?"

"They went to a village where the aunt and uncle of a girl named Blessing lived. When they arrived, she found the entire village, maybe fifty or sixty people, in the church, all dead."

His words dropped like a bomb between them—silence. The men stared at each other.

"Did you say the *entire* village?" Ham asked.

"Were they shot?" Jake added.

"No. Diseased. I asked Noemi if it was Ebola, but she said no, it looked like smallpox."

"An entire village dead from smallpox," Ham said, roughing a hand over his mouth. "Are you sure?"

"No," Ranger said.

"Smallpox is only infectious after the rash has started," Jake said. "They should have been able to stop it the moment patient zero showed symptoms, and before the entire village was infected."

"Unless this virus is like Ebola and is infectious during the prodromal period, between exposure and symptoms. They would have already had it by the time the rash showed up," Ham said.

Ranger leaned back in his seat. "Maybe it's a new virus, something modified from an original strain?"

"If it is, then the World Health Organization should know about it," Ham said.

"Or at least the CDC," Jake added.

Ham glanced at Jake. "But neither one of us got it even after being with Colt and Aaron. And Selah didn't get it, and she nursed him, so it can't be that contagious."

"And I don't have it," Ranger said. "And neither does Noemi, or Blessing, the girl who escaped with us."

"What happened with that?" Ham asked. "One minute you were escaping, another you went back . . ."

"Blessing was captured while trying to escape. Noemi refused to leave without her. I had no choice."

Ham nodded, but one side of Jake's mouth quirked up. "North seemed to think that you and Storm here might have known each other, you know, from before. That you had a connection."

North. Ranger sort of thought that he had been too busy inhaling Selah to notice the sparks between him and Noemi.

He had to smile, though, at Jake's nickname. Storm, indeed.

"Have you met before?" Ham asked, bringing Ranger back from a warm beach in Florida.

"Yeah. When I was in Key West training for my free dive cert, she was there with her father, Master Chief Sutton. Remember him?"

Ham nodded. "That was tragic. I didn't know he had a daughter."

"Yes, and her mother was Nigerian. After we escaped, Noemi contacted her Nigerian uncle, and that's where we were holed up. He's a, well, he's a king."

"You mentioned that. Which brings me back to the *palace*. And an armed guard. Really," Jake said, folding his arms over his head. "And here we were worried about you, thinking you'd gotten in over your head."

Well . . .

"So, what did you do for the last week? Hang by the pool? Eat delicious Nigerian food?" Jake's gaze went past him to Noemi and then back to Ranger. "Rekindle any old friendships?"

Ranger opened his mouth, closed it, and sighed. "Not really," he said and looked out the window.

But his silence betrayed him, and Jake let out a long chuckle.

"I see," Ham said and leaned forward, his elbows on his knees. He, too, was grinning.

Shoot.

"Okay, back to the village," Ham said. "Did Noemi say she thinks it might be a new variant of smallpox? And if so, what if the attack had something to do with the smallpox?"

"And what does it have to do with the Boko Haram?" Jake said. "And why were the hostages never ransomed?"

"Maybe the Boko Haram came in to stop the information from escaping the village," Ranger said. "Maybe they were never supposed to be ransomed. Maybe they were being watched for the virus . . ."

Ham leaned back, those arms again folded over his chest. "Yes, I can see that, except they didn't get it, even after three weeks."

"Maybe Noemi, Dr. Aaron, and the others simply didn't get close enough to them to get the virus," Jake said.

"Or it was no longer infectious by the time they found them?" Ranger reached for a blanket.

"That's possible," Ham said. "But why go after Noemi, days later, a couple hundred miles to the south? What do they want?"

"Me." Noemi stood between the seats, her blanket around her shoulders. "If they had something to do with the virus, they would want the proof gone." She swallowed. "They burned the church as they were leaving the village."

"Now you tell me this?" Ranger looked at her.

"I didn't think it was important!" Her golden-brown eyes sparked. "I might have had other things on my mind, thank you so much." She cocked her head to the side.

Yeah. Like marrying him.

"Okay," Ham said. "What are we going to do when we get to Norfolk?"

"Easy," Ranger said. Maybe he could have cushioned his next words, but he didn't know what to say. "I'm going to Alaska and I'm taking Noemi with me."

Jake raised an eyebrow, glanced at him. "That's only a little Neanderthal. Well done, Range."

Ranger stared at him.

"What are you going to do? Drag her by her hair to your lair in Alaska?"

He opened his mouth, closed it. "Fine." He looked at Noemi, tried to soften the edge in his voice. "I think you should come to Alaska with me." It wasn't really a request, and he knew it. But he didn't actually want to *ask* her, because what if she said no?

So, he just let it sit there.

"Ranger," she said. "It's over. All of it."

He ignored the strange hit to his heart. "Listen, if these guys are after you, I'm not leaving you in Norfolk or wherever you live these days—"

"I don't have a home. I sold the house in San Diego after my father died. I suppose I could go visit my grandparents in Maine, but the last thing I'm going to do is bring trouble to them." She took a breath, and now softened her gaze. "Or to you."

Trouble to him? "Noemi—"

"Listen, I'm really good at just disappearing. I'll do that. Travel, stay on the down low. No one's going to find me, I promise—"

"I will," he said.

She blinked at him.

"I will find you." He didn't know where the words came from. Just that they were lodged inside his chest, and he knew he had to get them out.

I'll find you. Always. "But I'd really like to not have to go looking for you. So, I need you to come to Alaska with me . . ."

She looked at him and gave a half chuckle. "How is Alaska any safer than me lost in middle America?"

He chose to ignore the quiet, dark insinuation that being with him might also be trouble. Instead, "Well, for one, I have my brothers there, and two, I can keep you safe . . ." Or at least mostly, because as the words came out, with them flashed the split-second memory of hitting that buoy with the speedboat. He hadn't even *seen* it. Granted, the light was off and the night was thick, but that was exactly the point. He was clearly starting to bump into things in the night as the darkness closed in and it was only going to get worse. But as long as he had a peep of vision, he would keep her safe.

"I really need you to come to Alaska with me." And now, yes, it sounded like pleading.

He didn't look at Jake or Ham, who had conveniently decided to become very interested in the view out the windows.

She folded her arms over her chest. "Really? Is that an order?"

Now, they looked at him, and eyebrows went up.

He reached for something like an explanation, something easy to give them. "When we were running from the camp, I told her she had to obey everything I said."

She made a harrumphing sound. Jake smiled.

Ranger turned back to her. "No, it's not an order to obey," he said slowly.

"You know that's not what I meant," she said and looked away.

"Great." He was going to have to bring out the big guns. "You need to come because I told your uncle Efe that I would protect you. That I would look after you and that nothing would happen to you on my watch."

"Wow," Jake said. "You act like you two are married."

Ranger looked at him and he could feel Noemi's eyes on him. Aw shoot. Well, whatever. It was going to get out anyway, because in about twenty-four hours he was going to show up at the ranch holding hands with a beautiful woman because, of course, he'd have to be dragging her there, and everyone was going to find out. So, he might as well start getting used to saying it.

He looked at Noemi. Smiled.

"Ranger— Don't you—" she said, warning in her eyes.

"That's because we are," he said.

"*Seriously!*"

"Meet Noemi Kingston, my wife."

Quiet descended in the cabin as Noemi stared at him, no, tried to incinerate him with her gaze. What was the big—

"What did you say, dude?" Dodge stood in the doorway of the cockpit. "Did you get *married*?"

Noemi folded her arms over her chest and cocked her head, waiting.

Well, if it kept her from running off and getting killed . . . He met her eyes. "Till death do us part."

Her new husband had lost his mind. Maybe he'd hit his head during his dunk into the Gulf of Guinea. Or his lack of sleep had turned his brain fuzzy.

Or even, he had a blood clot to his brain.

"*Why did you tell them we were married?*"

She'd nearly shouted the question as she pulled Ranger into the tiny bathroom of the airplane, about twenty-three seconds after he'd outed them to his friends. His *brother*.

Seriously.

He'd barely fit into the room with her, so she shoved him down onto the closed commode. It made him a lot easier to yell at, with him at least closer to eye level.

"Calm down—"

"Listen. I'm not the one who did a one-eighty and decided that we'd ride off into the sunset together. What are you thinking?"

He rested his hands on his knees, met her gaze. "I'm thinking that I don't want to let you out of my sight."

Nope, nope, he didn't mean it the way it sounded, but she took a breath anyway, just to steel her heart. "I can take care of myself."

He blinked at her.

"Oh please. You would have never even gotten into Abu's camp if it hadn't been for my escape attempt."

"Attempt."

"And you would have died if I hadn't gotten us to Uncle Efe's—" But she stopped talking because, of course, he'd been shot because she'd made him go back for Blessing.

His gaze hadn't left hers. And now he smiled. "You were the one who said we were married. And to my recollection, I bought you fair and square—"

"Don't even—"

He laughed. Oh wow, he laughed, and it poured right through her to her bones, shucked the strength right out of them. Shoot, he was handsome in his black BDUs and T-shirt. It outlined all his best features. He hadn't shaved since before the wedding, so he wore a thin layer of dark brown beard, and for a second, she wanted to reach out and run her fingers against it.

Stop!

Who cared that his aqua-blue eyes twinkled as if he might be enjoying this moment where she was the one who stood speechless.

Oh, she could not let her heart be duped into believing this. No, no—

"Noemi," he said and took her hand. "Calm down. It's not forever. It's just until I can figure out what is going on. I need you to come to Alaska with me. My brothers are there, and we'll untangle this. Once I know you're safe, you can leave me again, okay?".

Leave him *again*? That was not how she saw it, ever, but . . . "Fine. Just until we know it's safe. But what about your family?"

"I'll explain it to them when the time comes. Until then, you're my wife, okay?"

Oh boy.

She should have said no.

No, I don't want to play the game anymore.

No, I don't want to lie to your family.

And no, I don't want to pretend we're married. Because the more they pretended, the more she didn't know what was *real*.

Maybe none of it was.

But it felt terribly real twenty-four hours later when she found herself standing in the foyer of the beautiful Kingston family lodge.

When they'd walked through the side door entrance into the main room—she and Ranger and Dodge—a woman with golden-brown hair had gotten up from the long kitchen table where she sat with another woman and a man in a hoodie. The woman practically tackled Dodge, her arms around his shoulders, her legs around his body, as she kissed him.

Oh.

"This is Echo, Dodge's fiancée," Ranger said to her.

Dodge finally let her go, his arms still around her, and finished the introductions. "Echo. This is Ranger's wife, Noemi."

"Ranger's . . . wife?" Echo blinked hard.

Noemi gave her a small smile.

Echo however, grabbed Noemi in a way-too-enthusiastic hug. "Ranger! You sneak, you, getting married without telling anyone!" Echo was pretty and clearly knew Ranger from the way she held Noemi at arm's length and shook her head. "Girl, he must be crazy over you because this guy was a bachelor for life."

Still was, maybe. Noemi glanced at Ranger.

He'd slept on the commercial flight from Virginia to Anchorage, waking for the two-hour layover in Minneapolis long enough to grab a coffee. He'd barely let go of her hand the entire jog through MSP Airport, as if he feared her darting away.

She probably should have run, because extricating herself from this off-the-map ranch—they'd landed in Anchorage and driven straight north toward the rugged mountainscape—might take a little prep. Still, for being so far from civilization, the place didn't lack luxury. A floor-to-ceiling stone fireplace rose two stories in a great room that overlooked a field of wildflowers, and in the distance, the sun still hovered over the snow-covered mountainscape despite the late hour.

The kitchen was no less impressive with a long granite island that held six chairs and a massive range with something simmering on the stove. It emitted a savory, home-cooked welcome.

"I just needed the right girl," Ranger said now to Echo. He reached for Noemi and pulled her to himself. "We met a few years ago in the Keys and I never forgot her. When I saw her in Nigeria, I knew I couldn't let her go again."

"Sweet," Echo said. She turned to Dodge, her voice dropping. "By the way, I need to tell you something. Jane Doe is here."

"Jane—?" Dodge frowned.

"The woman we found in the blizzard. She had nowhere else to go, so the hospital called and asked us to house her."

Dodge was staring at the woman at the table, as if trying to sort through that information when, "Boys?" From an adjoining room an older man emerged, his whitened hair cropped short, his body lean but aged. He was wearing a flannel shirt and a pair of jeans and had the same blue eyes of Dodge and Ranger.

The same smile.

"Dad," Ranger said and let her go to pull his old man into a hug.

"You okay?" Dad Kingston asked. He held Ranger away from him. "Dodge said you'd been shot."

Ranger gave Dodge a look, then turned back to him. "I'm fine. Noemi took good care of me."

Her face heated. Not really, but—

"Noemi?" his dad said, a question in his tone.

"His wife," Dodge answered.

And the lie just kept growing.

The older man turned to her. "Call me Barry." He held out his hand.

"It's not forever." She couldn't place why those words hurt because, um, she knew this. She had walked into this mess with her eyes wide open. Ranger was the one, it seemed, who was blind to the consequences of continuing the farce.

As in, people he cared about could get hurt.

Control the situation.

Okay, fine. They'd untangle the reason why Abu chased her to Okwagbe, then she'd disappear. Like she'd said, she was good at being invisible. She'd done it most of her life.

But she couldn't take the charade any longer. "It's not what you think," she said as she shook Barry's hand. "I know what Ranger said, but we're not *really* married."

Even Ranger stared at her as if confused. She looked at him, hands on her hips, then turned to Echo. "The only reason he got married is because it was part of the mission. It's a long story, but we sort of stumbled into this marriage thing and had to go through with it to stay alive."

And now, silence.

Ranger's chest rose and fell as he met her gaze, something almost hurt in it, as if she'd betrayed him.

She looked away.

"So, you're not married?" Echo asked.

"No—"

"Yes—"

Noemi rolled her eyes. "It's a long story. Sort of. Yes. But not really." Oh boy, that made a lot of sense.

Ranger's jaw tightened. "Whatever." He turned to his father. "It sort of just happened."

"You don't *sort of* get married, son."

"You do when you're Ranger," said a voice from behind them. "Always has to save the day. Even if he ends up married."

She turned. Oh my— "Colt!"

He had pulled his hood down, his dark hair wild and long around his head, his brown eyes warm with tease. The bruises had faded around his eyes, mostly, and he sat at the kitchen table, his hands in the pockets of his sweatshirt. He grinned. "Hey there, troublemaker."

She walked over to him and he pushed back his chair so she could hug him. He lifted one arm around her but didn't hold too tight.

"You okay?"

"Getting there, thanks to Flo and my dad." He glanced at the woman sitting beside him. Blond, blue eyes, pretty, with her hair piled back on her head.

"Hey. I'm Noemi," she said.

Flo nodded, smiled.

"She doesn't talk. Which works out great because it's way too noisy around here with all the page turning." He smiled at their father.

Barry gave his son a look, but she recognized a hint of relief.

Yeah, her too. Because one look at Colt brought up that moment when he'd nearly died trying to help her escape. Her eyes filled and she blinked tears back hard.

"Hey," Colt said putting his hand on her arm. "We lived. Survive. Evade. Resist. Escape. Done, baby." He looked over at Ranger. "Marriage is a new twist, but can I be the first to say I saw this coming, back on Mallory Square? So, not for a second do I think this was part of some mission." He threw in one-handed air quotes. "But you kids tell yourselves what you want to believe."

He paused, then his gaze went to Dodge. "And, by the way, Dodge, thanks. I was pretty out of it, but I appreciate what you did."

Dodge gave him a nod, drew in a breath.

Silence fell between them.

Colt offered a smile. "And congratulations. Echo filled me in on all the fun. You two belong together—we've always known that."

More silence.

Then Dodge drew in a breath, and finally nodded. "Thanks, bro. And of course I'd come after you. I'm just sorry it took so long."

"Naw." Colt winked. "I had them right where I wanted them."

On the stove, whatever was cooking started to boil over and Flo leaped up and ran to the pot.

"How long until dinner, Jane?" Barry asked.

Jane?

The woman turned, flashed them five fingers.

"We'll wait until after dinner to get you settled," Barry said. "Colt's in the guest room, and Dodge can stay upstairs in his old room, so I guess you'll have Larke's room, Ranger." His gaze traveled from Ranger to Noemi.

As did Ranger's.

And the look he gave her traveled down her spine and ignited every cell in her body. Suddenly she saw him, shirt off, standing in the bathroom, her mouth still tasting of his kiss. *"Truth is I want you, Noemi."*

"I'll sleep on the first available sofa, thanks," she said.

Ranger's mouth tightened, but he offered a nod.

Barry must have seen the exchange because, "If it's okay with Jane, you can stay in the guest cabin with her. There are two bedrooms."

Jane/Flo nodded from the kitchen.

"Perfect," Echo said. She turned to Barry. "Mind if I set her up with some of Larke's leftover clothing?"

"Good idea, Echo."

Ranger was still looking at Noemi, his eyes enigmatic. Yeah, well, they couldn't keep sharing a room. Not if . . . well, not if she wanted to get an annulment down the road.

If she even needed that. It wasn't like Uncle Efe would track Ranger down and make good on his word.

No, they'd trekked miles away from their vows made under a sunburst African sky.

This was just another mission, another op.

And as soon as it was over, she'd keep moving.

No big deal.

TWELVE

It felt surreal for Ranger to sit here, at the family table, with all his brothers, passing bread and soup around, asking for the salt, pouring a glass of milk.

As if their family hadn't exploded ten years ago with an epic fight that sent the brothers in all directions. Colt and Dodge were even talking, laughing as Echo sat beside Dodge, handing him the butter.

And Noemi slurping soup beside him only added to the strangeness. As if she, too, always belonged.

Except she didn't, and she'd made that pretty clear when she'd outed him in front of his entire family. Not that he'd wanted to lie—at the time, on the plane, it seemed like the only way to convince Noemi to come to Alaska with him.

He hadn't meant for Dodge to overhear. He'd apparently let his emotions run that op because a clear-thinking man would have seen the problem with his deception. Namely, lying to his family.

So maybe she'd done the right thing.

So why did it sit inside him like a burr?

Colt was looking at Noemi, laughing. "You're just like Ranger when you eat. Loud."

"What?" She put down her spoon. "How will the cook know you like it if you don't make noises of appreciation?"

It was good soup. Savory chicken in garlic, with carrots, potatoes, and pieces of dumpling. Not one of his mother's recipes—he had her entire box memorized. "Yes. Really good, Flo."

She was pretty—blond hair pulled back in a messy bun, blue

eyes, about the same height as Echo. She wore an oversized flannel shirt and a pair of yoga pants, and it occurred to him that the shirt looked vaguely familiar.

As if she'd dug it out of the closet of clothing the brothers had left behind.

She sat beside Colt, quiet, glancing at him as he leaned on the table, still clearly sore as he brought the spoon to his mouth. But definitely better than the last time Ranger had laid eyes on him.

Weird that Flo didn't speak. Or know her name. But she watched them with eyes that said something was working in her head.

"What would you add?" his father asked Ranger now as he looked over at him. He tore off a piece of bread and dunked it into his soup. "I mean, it's delicious, but Ranger always liked to experiment with his mother's recipes."

"Remember the orange pancakes?" Colt said. He turned to Flo. "My mom had this family recipe for pancakes, and Ranger thought it might be easier to just add the orange juice to the batter, get the entire breakfast in one easy pancake."

"I still think it's a good idea." Ranger shrugged. "I'm not done perfecting it."

"Ranger cooks?" Noemi said. "No wonder you're such a foodie."

"What can I say? Food is life." He set down his spoon. "In this case, the soup is perfect. Thanks, Flo."

She smiled back.

He reached for his milk.

Missed.

Instead, he hit it with the back of his hand.

It started to topple—

"Whoa!" Noemi grabbed it before it went totally over, leaving just a puddle on the table.

"Sorry." He threw his napkin onto the mess as Noemi held up the glass.

She set it back down without a word, but he glanced at her. She smiled at him, winked.

And the world righted. So maybe she wasn't angry with him.

Maybe, in fact, she'd saved them from . . . well, he couldn't imagine that sleeping with her in Larke's room would lead to anything but trouble.

Trouble he was starting, very much, to want.

"Can you pass the bread, Echo?" Noemi said, and Echo picked up the basket.

"Too bad we don't have any fufu," Ranger said.

She laughed. "You'd have soup down your shirt."

"What's fufu?" Dodge asked.

Ranger coughed into his hand. "It's . . . um . . . I don't even know how to explain it. Playdough that you can eat?"

Noemi laughed. "It's a dough made of cassava that you use to scoop soup into your mouth."

"You don't chew it," he said and looked at her. She wore a sweatshirt she'd purchased in Virginia, and yoga pants, and her dark hair was pushed back with an orange headband.

Yes, she'd definitely saved them.

"We have flights piling up in the books, Dodge," his father said from the end of the table, changing the focus of conversation. "Remington Mines has a shipment of parts on the way that they need flown up to Nash's place. And Doc Everly wants to head out to Spike and Nola's place to check on the baby."

"I remember them." Ranger turned to Noemi. "He was a former paratrooper. Moved here with his wife and daughter before I left for boot camp. Has he struck gold yet?" he asked his brother.

"Some. Now he has a son, and his wife just had another baby." Dodge glanced at Echo. "Nearly on the deck of the Sky King chopper."

"Seriously?" Ranger asked.

"I had to set the bird down right in the parking lot of the

hospital and they wheeled her out—she had the baby in the elevator, I think."

"You have all the fun," Ranger said. This time his hand made it around his milk glass.

"Nash is probably building on to his place on Cache Mountain."

"I wonder if he's seen any more of that Russian guy who got away," Echo said.

"Got away from what?" Ranger asked.

Dodge reached for another piece of bread. "It's a long story. Involves a rogue bear and a couple of Russian poachers." He glanced at Echo. "I'll have to ask Deke next time we're in town."

"Deke Starr?" Ranger said. "Is he a ranger?"

"County Sheriff."

"No lie. Wow. That's a twist."

Dodge met his gaze, gave a slow nod, a half smile. "Shows you that even the worst troublemakers can turn their lives around."

"I heard that, big bro," Colt said. "Sometimes you need a troublemaker to get the job done."

The table went silent, the sudden rush of what they'd gone through a fine point on the conversation.

"Thank you for what you did, Colt," Noemi added quietly. "You probably saved us all."

"No. You did," Ranger said. "If you hadn't tried to escape, we would have never found a back way in."

Colt nodded. "I know you didn't want to leave, but you did it because you had to. To save us all. It wasn't just brave, it was our only hope."

She smiled at Colt, and Ranger stifled the terrible urge to put his hand on hers.

"I'm just grateful that God brought my boys back home," his dad said. "Now I just wish Larke was here."

"How is she feeling?" Dodge asked. "The baby okay?"

Baby?

Dodge laughed. "Oh, the look on your face, Ranger! The man without emotions has cracked. Yes, Larke is having a baby." His voice fell. "We hope. She already lost one a few months ago."

Oh—

"She's doing well," his father said. "She had an ultrasound a week ago and the baby is fine."

Ranger nodded, then turned back to Dodge. "I have emotions."

"Yeah you do. Hungry, cold, and tired."

Everyone laughed.

Even Noemi.

Huh. "I'm just . . . focused."

"We know, bro. This from the guy who streamlined his breakfast so he could get to his training regimen." Colt turned to Noemi. "He'd get up at five a.m. in the middle of winter, thirty below, and go for a run."

"He was a SEAL," she said.

"He was fourteen." Dodge raised an eyebrow.

"I got it done," Ranger said.

Dodge lifted his glass. "Yes, you did. The only easy day was yesterday, right bro?"

More laughter.

Colt set down his spoon. "How long do you have leave? You must have gotten an extension to spend this much time away."

He was silent as he ate his soup, trying not to swear. He knew it would come up. Just not on the first night—

"It's open-ended," Noemi said suddenly. "He's been given a change-of-duty opportunity, and he's still figuring it out."

"Really," Dodge said. "Are you thinking of leaving the teams?"

And now he felt it. Noemi's hand moving to his knee, under the table. Settling there.

"So, you're taking over Sky King Ranch's flight service for good?" Ranger said to Dodge.

Dodge's eyes narrowed, then slowly he nodded. "Actually, we're also Sky King Rescue. The northern affiliate of Air One out of Anchorage." He looked at Colt. "There's room for everyone."

Colt stilled, looked at him. "I'm just here until I'm back in working order."

"Right," Dodge said. "Well, I hope you'll stick around long enough for our wedding. We're getting married this fall."

Ranger had slipped his hand under the table, wove his fingers through Noemi's.

Okay, so she wasn't his wife.

Maybe, however, she was his friend.

That would have to be enough.

But he had another so-called emotion to add to Dodge's list . . . desire.

And that was probably the most dangerous one of all.

The man was confusing at best. First, he'd nearly knocked over his milk. And Noemi wasn't a fool—Ranger hadn't *seen* the milk. So, there was that.

And then he'd done a blatant end run around Dodge's pointed return-to-the-teams question.

She thought he'd tell them the truth, then, about being medically discharged, which was why she held his hand, trying to offer some moral support.

Because, with all they'd been through, at least she could be a friend.

Weirdly, he clung to her hand nearly the rest of the dinner. Like a lifeline.

Which couldn't be right for a man who didn't need anyone.

See, confusing.

And now he was helping Flo with the dishes, neatly ignoring her as Dodge and his father talked over tomorrow's flights in the office off the main room.

Echo came down the stairs, a stack of clothing in her arms. "I'll show you down to the cabin."

Noemi left the house without another look back.

The sun hung over the mountains to the north, glazing the open field with a soft, rosy glow. The scent of pine and a hint of chill hung in the breeze, remnants of a winter reluctantly vanquished. She got her first good look at the ranch—rolling fields to the north and west of the lodge that curled around a lake, with the remains of a timber house on one end and three cabins set along the shoreline. Near the lodge, a gravel runway cut through the field, secured on one end by a Quonset hut. The doors were closed, but an image of an orange fixed-wing plane was painted on the front, the words Sky King Ranch arched over the top. The doors of another barn, this one the standard gamble-roofed variety, hung open, a pickup truck parked outside it next to the one Dodge had driven them home in from Anchorage.

Echo walked her down the path to one of the cabins. "The Kingston family has owned this land for two generations. It suffered a massive forest fire a few years ago, but they saved the lodge and cabins."

"Where do you live?" Noemi asked as they reached the cabin.

"A few miles from here, on a homestead. I run sled dogs and help guide researchers into the bush. I always thought I wanted to see the world, but never could make myself leave." She stood at the door, looking out over the water, where the twilight reflected on the lake. "And why would I, really?"

She opened the door. A far cry from Uncle Efe's turret with its travertine floors and high, vaulted ceiling, the cabin had quaint and cozy embedded in its rough-hewn log walls and open beam rafters. The open living area included a small but equipped kitchen, a worn brown leather sofa, a metal stove—now unlit—and two rooms off a small hallway, separated by a bathroom.

Echo put the clothes on the table. Turned. "Are you sure you want to stay here instead of with, um, your husband? You two looked pretty cozy at dinner."

Oh. Noemi considered her, then, "We're not officially married, as in, well, the biblical sense, so . . ."

"Ah," Echo said, her hands folded into her sweatshirt. "I get that. I once spent the night with Dodge in a tiny cabin—him on the top bunk, me on the bottom—and I don't think I slept all night." She winked. Her smile faded. "Still, I'd like it if you were really married."

Her too.

Echo's eyes widened. "You're in love with him, aren't you?"

"I—we—"

"Give it up. I saw the way you looked at him. I tried to deny that I loved Dodge for years, but the minute he showed up in Copper Mountain, it was like I woke up from hibernation. You don't forget the one who walked away with your heart, no matter how long, right?"

Noemi found herself nodding.

"So, lucky you, you married him. So why aren't you sleeping in the big house?"

"It's complicated. We didn't—"

"I know—"

"No, I mean I sort of, well, lied about us being married to some locals, and he went through with the ceremony to save me."

"Yep, that sounds like Ranger."

"Exactly. He's all about the op. He's not in love with me." If he had been, he wouldn't have walked away from her on their wedding night.

Echo looked at her, let a beat go by. Then, "Listen. I know

Ranger. He *is* a good guy. And yes, he always does the right thing, no matter what it costs him. But it doesn't mean that he doesn't deserve a happy ending."

"I don't have dreams. I have duty." She wished his voice didn't keep walking around in her head.

"You grew up with him?" Noemi inspected the pile of clothing. A pair of jeans, yoga pants, a T-shirt, sweatshirt, socks, and one very interesting hockey jersey. She'd already picked up toiletries and underclothing at the airport in Virginia, along with a change of clothes and the sweatshirt she was wearing, so this would do.

"All three of them," Echo said softly. Her hand lifted to her cheek, then swiped it.

"Are you okay?"

She sighed, nodded. "Yeah. It's just—well, I never thought they'd be all back together again."

"Ranger said something about a fight?" Funny that she remembered that, but she must've tucked it away, and with Colt's exchange with Dodge, it had worked free.

"Yeah. A big fight. Fists. Blood. Broken relationships."

"Over what?"

She swallowed, made a face. "Well, me. Sort of. But really, it was over their mother, I think, and the wounds she left behind. They never got over losing her. Even Ranger, although he'd deny it." Echo met her eyes. "He's never even dated, Noemi, so whether you want to believe it or not, him bringing you home is a big deal. A very big deal." She reached out and put a hand on Noemi's arm. "He might not be able to say it, but Ranger doesn't give away his heart easily. So, my guess is that once he does, it's for keeps."

Yeah, but he hadn't given her his heart, had he?

Echo looked at her. "Please don't break it."

Oh.

"So, if there is any part of you that wants to run up to the lodge and claim the man who calls himself your husband, do it. Larke's room is at the top of the stairs on the right."

Noemi just stared at her, eyes wide.

Echo laughed. "Oh boy. You two were made for each other."

"What do you mean by that?"

Echo shook her head, turned to the window. "Can you believe that two weeks ago, this was all ice and snow?" She gestured to the lake. "And then one day, spring arrived. The winds shifted, the sun burst out of the clouds, and suddenly the world is all wildflowers." She looked at Noemi. "Stop standing in the shadows. What do you really want?"

Her heart thumped. "It doesn't matter what I want."

Echo looked at her. "Yes, it does. But until you believe that, you'll be stuck."

Noemi drew in a breath. Swallowed.

"Welcome to Alaska, Noemi." She gave her a smile as she opened the door. "I think Ranger needs you, so I hope you'll stay." Then she gave a wink. "Out here in the bush, no one locks their doors, so, you know . . . top of the stairs on the right." Then she closed the door.

Top of the stairs on the right. It might as well be across the ocean.

Because, it seemed, that's where she'd left her happy ending.

THIRTEEN

I'm going to need answers, bro."

Ranger turned from where he was rummaging through his duffel bag, the one he'd left here, on the floor of his old bedroom, a few weeks back when he arrived with the news of Colt's captivity.

He'd galvanized Dodge into the epic rescue and left everything else behind.

Like his dismal future.

Dodge leaned against the wall of their joint room—they'd all shared the upstairs loft for years until Dodge had gotten sick of Colt and Ranger's nightly chatter and cajoled their father into building him a wall. Now, he was apparently jammed back into his tiny room with his single bed on the other side of the wall.

Which was still as flimsily thin as it had been years ago. "Was I talking in my sleep last night?"

"Your bed still squeaks every time you roll over." Dodge had risen early, obviously, and was already showered and shaved. Now he folded his arms over his chest. Big brother wanting answers, as usual.

Ranger turned back to the chaos of his clothing, mostly shorts, a couple pairs of jeans, flip-flops, and T-shirts. His bag looked like a bomb had exploded in it.

No less chaotic than his restless, stupid night's sleep on the bottom bunk in his old bedroom.

Because, *no*, he wasn't sleeping in Larke's bed. Especially not alone. Not when he'd sort of gotten used to the sound of

Noemi's breathing, the warmth of her body on the other side of the sheets.

What was *married*, anyway? He'd remembered promises made, both to Uncle Efe and Noemi, to protect her. To stay with her. To want her.

"*Maybe it's time to let yourself dream.*"

"Silence is not an answer," Dodge said. "What's going on?"

Ranger stifled the urge to resurrect old habits and go out for a run. He had, however, taken a shower and wrapped a towel around his waist. Now he grabbed a clean T-shirt, stood and looked at Dodge. "What kind of answers are you looking for?"

"Like . . . are you two really married?"

Ranger pulled on the T-shirt. "Honestly, I don't know."

Dodge raised an eyebrow. They'd barely spoken, really, since big bro had helped pluck him from the sea. Sure, they'd hung around in the airport, but they both conked out on the plane, and after Noemi left the lodge, he practically fled to his room.

To, apparently, stare at the upper bunk all night long.

And once, yes, he got up and stared down at the cabins, nestled under the wan moonlight. "We got married in Nigeria," he said now to Dodge. "Is that a legal wedding? I don't know. If you're asking if we—"

"Take a breath," Dodge said. "No judgment here. I'm just wondering . . . well, do you *want* to be married?"

Ranger looked at himself in the mirror. He could use a shave, his beard was a thick dark brown on his chin. His bruises were fading, and his shoulder felt significantly better despite his dunk in the ocean.

But the black dots still marred his vision, and it seemed the one in his left eye had gotten larger. No wonder he missed the milk last night. Yeah, he was a real prize.

"No," he said quietly, despite the thrum in his heart. "I just said that to get her here. Safe." He looked at Dodge. "Didn't mean to mislead you."

Dodge considered him a moment. "Okay, then."

Ranger knelt again and began to fold his clothing. "So, you and Echo, finally. I'm happy for you."

"Thanks."

He glanced up. "Thanks for going with me to get Colt. You didn't even blink." He raised an eyebrow. "Wanna talk about that?"

That. The epic fight. The one that involved the police and a hospital stay for Colt. And, if Ranger remembered correctly, some county jail time for Dodge.

"What's to say? It was ten years ago. I was stupid. Colt was stupid—"

"I wasn't stupid," said a voice behind Dodge, and Ranger stilled. Oh no—

"I was a jerk." Colt stood in the doorway, wearing his sweatpants, bare chested. "No, amend that. I betrayed you, Dodge, and I hate myself for it."

Dodge nodded, a wary gaze on Colt.

Colt had improved considerably over the past couple weeks, but even now, the man walked gingerly, and the climb up the stairs must have winded him, because he walked over to a desk chair and sat down, straddling it. "Wow, I'm out of shape."

"That's what happens when you get your insides rearranged," Ranger said.

Colt's mouth tightened into a grim line. "It wasn't the first time. Probably won't be the last."

Ranger glanced at Dodge, but his oldest brother hadn't moved, hadn't blinked. Then, quietly, "I'm sorry, Colt. I—"

"Nope. I was the jerk, Dodge, and we all know it. I'm the one who is sorry."

A beat and then Dodge smiled. "Just keep your hands off my fiancée."

"Rules, rules," Colt said and smiled back.

Ranger hadn't recognized the fist gripping his chest until it loosened. "And here I was worried you'd changed."

"What? Me?" Colt got up, pushed the chair in. "No, the only one changing around here, big guy, is you. Mr. Navy SEAL. Have you thought about what your wife is going to do when you're spun up? Noemi isn't exactly the sit around and wait type."

The question hung there, but he shrugged it off. "So what's up with Flo?"

"Ask Colt," Dodge said. "He seems to have made a new and special friend."

Colt walked over to his closet and opened the door. "What can I say? I'm beautiful when I'm asleep." He closed the closet. "Shoot. I was hoping to find my Copper Mountain Grizzlies T-shirt."

Dodge and Ranger said nothing.

Colt opened a dresser drawer. "I don't know Flo's story. She was here when I arrived."

"Has she said anything?" Dodge asked.

"She makes noises when she sleeps."

Dodge raised an eyebrow.

"Calm down. She fell asleep in the recliner next to my bed a couple times. Woke up with nightmares, I think."

"So she can talk?" Ranger said.

Colt raised a shoulder. "How did you find her?"

"We were out looking for Peyton Samson, one of Echo's friends," Dodge answered.

"I remember Peyton. Didn't Nash Remington have a thing for her?" Ranger asked.

"Yep. She was injured and found her way to his cabin. But we didn't know that—so we went out looking for her and sort of stumbled on Jane—or Flo, as Colt calls her."

"Florence. As in Nightingale."

"Yeah, I put that together," Ranger said.

The room silenced and Colt looked from Dodge to Ranger. "Okay, Range, let's back up. That's twice you've dodged the question. What's the deal, bro? You AWOL?"

"What—? No. Of course not."

And . . . he was only making it worse. Shoot. He'd have to tell them someday. He just needed some time to figure it out. "I'm separated from the Navy," he finally said, and as usual, the words thickened his throat. "Medical."

Colt's mouth opened. "You hurt?"

He looked away, winced. "Um . . ."

"Wait. It's Ghost, right?"

Ranger frowned. "You know about Ghost?"

Colt shrugged. "Any time an operator gets killed, it makes its way around the Spec Op community. Ghost was a good guy. I met him in Syria, remember?"

"Yeah." Ranger glanced at Dodge. "Colt's Delta group intersected with our team. Just a couple times."

And of course, Ranger had also connected with Dodge once, when they were both in Afghanistan.

"The Navy sidelined you, huh? PTSD?" Colt said, still looking through his dresser drawers. "I could have sworn I left that shirt here."

PTSD. Yes, that felt close enough. Ranger nodded. Because he was certainly stressed out about the idea of his world closing in.

And sure, maybe he should come clean. But it just felt so stupidly ironic that the one guy who'd always had a plan found himself aimless, in his old bedroom, folding his mess of clothing.

"You talking to anyone about that?" Dodge said.

"What?"

"The anger. Frustration. Whatever." Dodge spoke like he got it. Met his gaze too.

Ranger looked away. "The VA assigned me someone in San Diego, but . . ."

"You were too angry to go," Dodge finished for him.

Something like that.

"No. It wasn't anger," Colt said. "It was the same thing that made him into a SEAL. That made him the number one sniper in his unit." Colt met Ranger's gaze. "Pride. Ranger solves problems. He doesn't have them."

Silence. "Well, Colt is still going in for the kill, I see," Dodge said.

Ranger's jaw hardened. "It's not pride. I have a wife who needs my protection."

"There you go again. Is she your wife or not?" Colt leaned against the desk.

"Yes. No—I don't know."

"Yeah, you do," Dodge said. "And that's the problem." He walked over to the bookcase filled with trophies, books, and pictures and picked up a frame. "You want the girl. You just don't want to admit it."

Ranger made a face. "Oh no, I admitted it. On our wedding night—which ended up with me sleeping on the floor."

"Oh, buddy, do you need the talk?" Colt said.

"Keep it up," Ranger growled.

Colt laughed.

"And?" Dodge said. "What happened?"

"She didn't take it seriously. She never takes anything seriously."

"And you're nothing but serious."

"That's not true."

Dodge handed Ranger the picture. In it, Ranger stood with his mother on a glacier, holding trekking poles, only his tiny five-year-old face showing. "I barely remember this picture," he said, "but I do remember sitting at home while Mom took you hiking. It was that last summer before she got sick and you two stayed out all night. I was so jealous."

"I remember being cold." But Ranger smiled. "No. Actually,

I have a pretty vivid memory of watching the aurora borealis. It was in May, and Dad had flown us into the Muldrow Glacier. We spent the night there."

Ranger handed him back the picture. "Mom always wanted to climb Denali. I think maybe it was her way of saying goodbye to the mountain."

"Or to you." Dodge put the picture back, ran his thumb over their mother's image. "She knew us, bro. Knew what we would become. Me, a pilot. You, the guy who wanted to save the world."

"What about me?" Colt said.

"Oh, she knew you were just trouble," Ranger said, but he grinned. "Naw. Mom knew you could make anyone smile."

Colt wore a strange expression.

Dodge spoke through the silence. "You have mom's patience, Range. Her ability to endure and focus. And her ability to die to her feelings and do what's best for everyone else. That's why I was so angry with her for so long."

Ranger frowned.

"She knew she was dying. And yet she came home to spend the summer with us. Away from medical help, pain meds, even shutting down her chemo."

"I don't think—" Colt started.

"She was terminal—yes. But she never told us. Never prepared us for the fact that she would die. Just . . . one day, collapsed."

Colt looked past them, out the window. Yeah, well, he'd been there, with her, when she'd started hemorrhaging. Their father had loaded him into the plane alongside their mom and taken off for Anchorage.

"I never said goodbye," Ranger said. "I was out with Grandpa."

"Me too," Dodge said. "The thing is, she didn't want to burden us with her grief. But that's not how family works. We're supposed to bear it together."

Colt raised an eyebrow. "Um. We're not exactly that family."

"Maybe we should be," Dodge said. "And that's my fault. I was angry, and I didn't make room for your grief. And Ranger—I get it. You put everything into your dream of being a SEAL. You're all work, no fun."

"And Noemi—she made you have fun," Colt said.

"Yes. And that's the point. She's fun, but guys, trust me . . . I'm no big deal to her."

Dodge stared at him. "Dude. She *married* you. You're a big deal."

"No, he's an idiot," Colt said.

Ranger looked at him.

"The only reason she said you weren't a big deal back then—and I remember this—is because she was afraid that she was *not a big deal to you*. C'mon, even I can figure that out. Women respond. You keep them at a distance, that's where they'll stay. You let them know you want them and—well, they'll want you back."

"Okay, we got the picture," Dodge said.

"I'm just saying. Read between the lines, bro."

"I'm with Colt," Dodge said. "Have you *seen* that hottie you dragged home? Why are you not on your knees, begging her to stick around?"

Ranger smiled. But yes, maybe he should be on his knees.

"I spent ten years away from Echo. Ten years I regret. If you want to be married to this girl, don't let her sleep in the flippin' guest cabin. I say Nigerian weddings count." Dodge held out his fist to Colt, his gaze on Ranger.

Colt met it, also looking at Range. "Boo-yah. And by the way, I called it four years ago." He grinned at Dodge.

Right.

"Everybody calm down. She's not going anywhere. At least not until I figure out why the Boko Haram is still after her."

"You hope she's not going anywhere, smart guy," Colt said.

"She's the daughter of Master Chief Sutton. She knows a few tricks. And remember, I've seen this girl in action. She regularly got in the face of Abu and made friends with the skinny kid who guarded us. I think she even stole Freddie's phone."

Freddie's *phone*.

Ranger wanted to give himself a face-palm. "That's *it*! Freddie's phone. I think we still have it. Do you think they could use it to track her?" He went over to his pack and opened it. Riffled through his belongings and . . . oh man. There it was. "But it's off."

"Has it been off the entire time?" Colt asked.

"No. Noemi tried to fire it up when we were at Uncle Efe's house. It didn't hold a charge."

"But it might have connected with a cell tower, at least briefly," Colt said. "And that's enough for someone who knows how to track the signal to find it."

"Abu Mussaf doesn't seem like a man with the technology to track a cell phone," Ranger said. He handed the phone to Colt who opened it and pulled out the sim card.

"And that, brother, is the answer to your question of why Abu wants her," Dodge said. "Someone else is behind this. Someone with technology. Someone who very much wants to keep what Noemi and Colt saw in Nigeria on the Q.T."

"Oh, you mean the dead bodies in the church? The ones with smallpox?" Colt said.

Ranger looked at him. Then at Dodge.

And then at Flo, who stood in the doorway, her face ashen.

"Hey," Colt said, turning to her. "You okay?"

She looked at him, then swallowed, and smiled. Held out a stack of clothing.

"She does your laundry?" Dodge said as he came over to retrieve the stack. "Thanks, Flo."

She smiled and shrugged, her gaze glancing off Colt before she left. So maybe Ranger had imagined it.

"Well, we can't solve it now." Dodge peeled a pair of jeans off the stack and tossed them to Ranger. "So put on your pants. I have a broken tractor that needs your golden touch."

It took a moment for Noemi to get her bearings. To recognize the sunrise filtering into the window, the honking of a goose, the rise of a chickadee's call, water lapping against a dock. The smell of eggs and bacon sliding under the door to her small room.

She wasn't in Nigeria anymore.

She opened her eyes, stared at the ceiling rafters.

"*You two were made for each other.*"

Yeah, thanks for that, Echo, because the man had tromped through her dreams all night long—rescuing her from rivers, hiding with her in an odorous market, dancing with her down the aisle. Eating unique foods.

In truth, there was probably no amount of miles she could put between her and Ranger Kingston to forget him.

She'd just have to learn to live without sleep.

She got up and riffled through the pile of clothing Echo had left and unearthed a long-sleeve thermal shirt and a pair of yoga pants. And then, call her sappy, she also grabbed the hockey jersey.

She headed to the shower.

Oh, her hair. Grimy from her dip in the water, the Nigerian sun hadn't done it any favors and it needed a hot oil treatment, and soon, to soothe all the brittle ends.

She didn't have a comb, so she towel-dried it, surrendering to the fact that it would have to do for now, then dressed herself and emerged from the bathroom.

Flo sat with a cup of coffee at the small table, looking out at the water. A few Canadian geese floated on the surface, which mirrored the Denali massif in the distance. Noemi glanced at the clock hanging on the wall. "Please tell me that doesn't say ten a.m."

Flo nodded. She also pointed to a stack of clothing on the chair. She must have gone to the house to fetch more clothes.

"More hand-me-downs? They're really cleaning out Larke's closet. You don't suppose there's a prom dress in there, do you?"

Flo smiled, shrugged.

Noemi came over to the table. "By the way, did you sleep okay? I thought I heard something in the night." Crying, actually, or maybe it had been her, somewhere in her dreams. She certainly had a bevy of shouting lodged in her memories.

Flo looked over and smiled, nodded, but her eyes were red.

Noemi had seen—and lived with—her share of terrorized, displaced, and traumatized refugees over the years, and frankly, Flo checked every box. From making dinner, trying to fit in, to cleaning up and then fading away before anyone could notice her, becoming invisible, Flo bore every mark of a woman who was just trying to survive.

Noemi poured herself a cup of coffee, noticed that bacon lay on a platter, and along with that, a bowl of scrambled eggs. She fixed a plate and brought it over to the table.

"Thanks for breakfast."

Flo nodded.

Noemi picked up the bacon. "So, here we are. A couple of homeless gals, hanging out in a resort. Not such a bad gig, right?"

Flo smiled at her.

"Or . . . sorry. You might not be homeless. I, however, am totally homeless. I mean, my grandparents still live in Maine, but I haven't seen them in a couple years. We email sometimes, but . . . anyway, yeah."

In the distance, the lush forest rose, and a hawk circled in the sky.

She finished the bacon and grabbed her fork. Dug into the eggs.

"Everything I own is in a storage container in San Diego, and I'm not exactly sure what I'm going to do next with my life. I mean, I can't hide here forever, right?"

Flo was watching her now, obviously curious. She shrugged.

"Yeah. Maybe we can." She finished off her eggs, picked up her coffee. "So, my plate is full today. A few hours of trying to figure out why a terrorist in Nigeria wants to kill me, and then a good long stretch of watching the man I love do mental gymnastics trying to figure out if the wedding I roped him into back in Nigeria means he needs to pledge me his undying love here." She took a sip of coffee and glanced at Flo. She now sat with her arms folded over her chest.

"I know. I sound a little cynical. It's just . . . well, Echo told me last night that I was living in the shadows. But I've been doing some thinking and it seems to me that when you're in the shadows, you never get burned. What fun is it to get your heart broken, right?"

Flo nodded slowly.

Noemi took another sip of coffee. "And then I guess I'll end the evening watching Ranger struggle as he tries not to tell his brothers that he's going blind and that his life is imploding. But no, he doesn't want me to be a part of that. Because I'll just, I don't know, get in the way of all that despair."

Flo cocked her head.

"I know. I shouldn't have said anything. It's his secret to tell. But I thought . . . let's just get it out there. Besides, I can count on you to keep it on the down low, right?"

She got another nod from Flo, another smile.

"See, we're cohorts already. The outsiders in the cabin by the lake. We should create a club. Maybe an official handshake."

Flo held out her hand.

Noemi took it. "Perfect. Stop by later and we can paint our nails and dance in our nighties under a pale moon."

Flo laughed.

Sound, coming out of her mouth. Noemi stilled. "So, you're not mute. You just . . . don't want to talk."

Flo's mouth shifted to a grim line.

"Okay, sister. Your secret is safe with me. Really. But if you ever want to talk, I'm just across the hall. Unless, you know, terrorists find me out here in the bush. Okay?"

Flo swallowed, her blue eyes on Noemi's. Then she nodded.

Noemi took her last sip of coffee. "Okay. Good talk. I'll do the dishes."

She cleared the table, ran water, and cleaned the dishes while Flo headed into her room.

She hadn't emerged by the time Noemi finished.

Huh. Whatever had happened this morning—either here, or maybe up at the big house—had done a number on her.

Maybe she should find Ranger. Make sure he hadn't decided to run back to Nigeria and track down Abu.

She pulled on a flannel shirt from the pile—she loved these things—added it to her layers under the jersey, stepped into some worn Uggs, and trekked up to the house.

Movement inside the open door of the barn caught her attention and she detoured over. The barn was the typical cows-and-horses variety, but as she drew near, she saw it was packed with old vehicles—minibikes, a motorcycle, snowmobiles, and a collection of old cars and trucks. The scent of hay mixed with oil and gasoline suggested they'd herded any livestock away in favor of the used car lot.

The three Kingston brothers, along with their father, were all huddled around an ancient red Massey Ferguson tractor. The engine panel was off, and Ranger was crouched next to it, his good arm wedged up inside.

Oh, he was handsome today, wearing a flannel shirt, his sleeves rolled up, a pair of jeans, and work boots. Was there nothing the guy couldn't kill it in?

"Hey there, kids," she said as she walked up. "Whatcha up to?"

"The starter solenoid linkage has come undone again," Ranger said, making a face. His arm was greasy to his elbow where he'd been clearly trying to operate on the inside of the engine. He closed his eyes, as if to concentrate.

"One more time, in English now."

He looked over at her, blinked, his gaze falling on her jersey.

Then he looked away, as if rattled. "The rod that pushes the starter button is out of place."

Interesting. "So . . . it won't start?" She held up her hand. "Wait. I can answer that for myself."

Colt was sitting on an overturned bucket. Dodge hovered over Ranger, as if he wanted to help. Barry stood, wiping his hands with a rag.

She walked over and looked at the engine. "This is old."

"1964 Fergie," said Barry. "Belonged to my father. He and Ranger spent hours and hours on this baby, keeping her running. It hasn't moved, really, since Range left. But we thought we'd try and seed the field, get some hay growing. We've sold our cattle, but Dodge has some crazy idea to bring back the horses, so . . ."

"I've got to put the rod back in place," Ranger said. "I'm trying to get my fingers around a little set screw. If I can find it, I can tighten it down and then we'll be able to start her up."

He made a face, grunted. "But I think the screw is missing. It must have vibrated loose and fallen out of the bell housing."

"Are you sure?" Dodge said.

Ranger pulled his arm out. "Yep. I've torn this engine apart with Pops so many times I could rebuild her blindfolded. Look around, see if you can spot it."

Dodge scoured the ground while Colt stepped over to a bench and flicked through a tin can full of screws.

"I think it would be easier just to buy one," Barry said.

Ranger grabbed the towel his father threw at him. "You're right. We'll take a trip into town, get a set screw."

He stood up and pulled down the engine cover.

"Perfect. Anyone up for a ride?" Dodge said. He glanced at his youngest brother, who nodded.

"I'll go to town," Noemi said.

She thought they meant by car.

But no, Dodge walked over to the Quonset and pressed the button to open the door. Inside sat a large helicopter, on skids, a smaller orange plane with oversized fat wheels, and a yellow-and-maroon high-propeller plane with floats.

"Where's Dad's Otter?" Ranger asked.

Dodge made a face. "That's a long story."

"I see you got a new plane." Ranger gestured to the plane. "Is that a de Havilland Beaver?"

"Yep." Dodge ran his hand along her body. He wore a flannel shirt too, clearly the uniform of the day, and a pair of jeans. Range had mentioned at some point that they were triplets, and he was right—they all filled out flannel shirts like some kind of Alaskan calendar models.

"It belonged to Nash, but it needed some serious repairs, so I bought it from him."

"Why?"

Dodge looked at him. "It's for the Sky King SAR service. We'll use the Super Cruiser for our bush service."

He indicated the orange plane, the one with the four seats in the back. He walked over to it and hooked a hydraulic lift to it, moving it out of the hut and toward the runway.

Wait. "We're *flying* to town?" Noemi said.

"Best way to get around." Dodge grinned at her. "Welcome to Alaska."

"Dodge is the best pilot in the state," Barry said, grinning at his son. "Flew Pave Hawk rescue choppers for the military. And he's a natural behind the stick. You're in for a treat."

She glanced at Ranger.

"Really," he said. "It'll be fun."

Fun. Except, as they rose above the ranch, and her heart settled back into her body, and she began to breathe again, yes, definitely.

Ranger sat in front, in the other cockpit seat—two big men jammed into a small space. But they seemed like they belonged there. And Dodge flew with a confidence, a muscle memory that made her settle back and enjoy the ride.

She wore headphones, listening to Dodge as he called his dad in the office at Sky King Ranch. Then, he toggled the mic. "Noemi, out the starboard window, you'll see the Cache Mountain range. It's just south of Denali but acts as a border to the valley. Most of our flights are past that range, although Remington Mines sits in a valley just south of there."

She sat behind Dodge and stared out the window. The mountains ran in layers—green, jagged hills in the lowlands; a darker, rugged ridgeline behind that; and rising up from the back, a white-peaked and lethal range of glorious peaks.

Below them, they were leaving behind the three tiny cabins seated on the lakeshore, as well as the red-tin-roofed lodge house. The Kingstons' land stretched out as far as she could see, awash with early blooming wildflowers in purple, yellow, and white.

"To the left, you can see the massive Copper River. It flows out of the park, all the way down to Anchorage. The city of Copper Mountain is to the east of that, in the shadow of, well, Copper Mountain."

It was like floating, flying in this little plane, despite the noise and the rattle. The aircraft just sort of scooted along in the air. She pressed her forehead to the window and stared down at the tiny houses, many of them with smoking chimneys. There were trucks and a few planes and larger lodges, which she guessed might be resorts.

"The Bowie brothers have added a bunch of cabins," Dodge said to Ranger, pointing out some small buildings next to the massive river. From here, it looked almost brown, and fast flowing, clogged with logs and other debris.

"How are Hud and Malachi?" Ranger asked.

"Oh, you know. The usual. Businessmen by day, troublemakers by night." He laughed. "Actually, they're opening up a remote, fly-in fishing and hiking lodge to go along with their resort on the Copper River. We'll probably do some flying for them."

"What about the Starrs?" Ranger asked.

"Winter's the only one still flying. Goodwin opened up a sport outfitters place. Shasta is still doing odd jobs around town, often working at Starlight Pizza." He glanced at him. "You're not going to believe it, but Levi Starr opened up a pizza joint. You should give him your salmon pizza recipe."

"Yum," Noemi said, reinserting herself in the conversation. "Really?"

"It's made with smoked salmon, capers, shallots, and cream cheese, and it'll blow your mind." Ranger wore a hint of a smile.

Something about him felt different today. As if he'd stepped into a different version of himself. One he'd left behind years ago.

She liked it.

"Getting the itch to fly, Range?" Dodge said.

Ranger looked at him. "I don't think—"

"C'mon bro. I know it's been a while, but it's like riding a bike. Just take the yoke."

Ranger reached out and gripped it. "I have the yoke."

"I'm hands off," Dodge said.

"You can fly a plane?" Noemi asked.

"I don't have my license, but Dad taught all of us."

They passed over the river, toward town, and below she spotted thicker, residential communities nestled in between great swaths of green. A school with a football field, or maybe a hockey rink, sat in an expansive cleared area, and beyond that, what looked like the downtown area.

"How big is Copper Mountain?"

"Depends on the time of year," Dodge said. "We're starting to get the Denali climbers and park hikers, as well as fishermen and hunters. Copper Mountain can really get rockin' at night. You should stop in at the Midnight Sun while you're in town, grab some lunch. There might even be a band playing—it is Saturday afternoon."

It was Saturday?

Dodge got on the radio and called into the small municipal airport in the distance. She couldn't see it.

The airport radioed back and gave them coordinates.

"Okay, Range, take her down."

Ranger looked over at Dodge. "No, sorry—"

"Dude, I'm right here. I'm not going to let you crash. Take her in."

"No! Take the yoke."

"Range—"

Ranger lifted his hands from the yoke.

"What are you doing?" Dodge grabbed it. "Sheesh—you know better than that."

Ranger's jaw hardened. "Sorry. I'm not . . . you're the pilot here, Dodge, not me."

Silence stretched between them.

Dodge said nothing as he lined up the plane for approach. Then he took them down and slid like a whisper onto the runway.

Ranger looked at him, nodded. "Beautiful."

It was an attempt, at least.

"Thanks," Dodge said. They taxied in and parked not far from a small hangar. "I need to check on some cargo and pick up groceries from Gigi's for Spike and Nola. How about I meet you back here in an hour?"

Ranger had climbed out and now came around and helped Noemi get down. "Does Dad skill keep a truck here?" he asked his brother.

"Yep," Dodge said as he walked around securing the plane.

"We'll drive home. Don't wait for us."

Dodge looked at him then, frowning.

Ranger reached out for Noemi's hand.

Huh. Okay. She slipped it into his.

"See you at home," Dodge said as Ranger pulled her away.

"Still think I'm going to run?" she said as he led her toward the hangar.

"I'm trying to keep myself from running," he said darkly.

Oh. So they were there.

He walked out past the hangar, past the office, and through the gate out into the street.

"Are we going to talk about it?"

"Eventually."

"Can we do it over a hamburger?"

He looked down at her, gave her a smile. "Probably."

"If there are fries involved, then I'm all ears, sailor. And you'll have the added bonus of saving my life."

"I'm all about saving lives." His hand squeezed hers.

Which was why, probably, he hadn't landed that plane. And with that thought, her heart gave a little spasm.

The sun was high, and with the summer-like temperatures, it seemed the town had indeed come to life. SUVs stuffed with camping equipment, children running in the main park and climbing on a massive copper moose statue, some hikers walking with backpacks while others sat at picnic tables outside of what looked like a barbecue restaurant. The smells emanating from the house-turned-restaurant made her want to moan.

"That's the Midnight Sun. We'll grab some lunch there in a bit."

He kept holding her hand as they passed the park office, a couple hikers sitting outside on the deck.

"Hey, Kit," Ranger said to a woman with long black hair.

She looked up at him. "Ranger Kingston?"

He smiled, nodded to her. "You still leading climbs?"

"Booked full," she said. "Come up with us sometime?"

"Maybe," he said, and kept walking, past an outfitters store and then into a hardware store located just beyond it. An old building, with creaky wooden floors and a long glass counter, and thousands of bins filled with screws, washers, and nuts that ran along one wall. A big man sat on a stool at the counter, red hair, and a barrel body. He rose as Ranger came in.

"Ranger Kingston. First your brother, and now you. Don't tell me that Colt is back too."

"Hey, Ace," he said and let go of Noemi's hand to shake the big man's. "Yes, actually he is, but I'm not sure if he's sticking around."

"Are you?"

Ranger laughed. "Dunno."

"I suppose you're still on the Teams. Hard gig to give up."

Ranger made a noise of agreement.

"Moose will be sad he missed you. He's down in Anchorage running Air One Rescue. Did you hear your brother joined up with him?"

"I did. Tell Moose hi for me. Say, we're looking for a set screw for a 1964 Ferguson tractor."

"That old Massey your dad has? I think I got something."

He led Ranger over to a bin and stirred his finger through the contents.

Meanwhile, Noemi wandered the store, her gaze on the array of hard candy in jars along the counter.

"For the kids," Ace said to her as he dropped the screw in a bag. He turned to Ranger. "I'll charge it to your dad's account."

"Thanks," Ranger said.

"Stay safe, son," Ace said.

Ranger nodded, grabbing Noemi's hand.

Funny that he hadn't introduced her. But what was he going to say . . . *This is my wife*?

"You okay?" she asked as they stepped outside.

He wore a strange look. "How am I supposed to come back to this town?" He shook his head. "I thought this would be easier."

"Calm down." She put her hand on his arm. "You don't owe anyone any explanations."

He paused to take a deep breath, then led her across the street to the barbecue place. A band had set up in the parking lot, playing country music, and a few couples were two-stepping, not well, in a cordoned-off area.

The smell of hickory lifted off a smoker that puffed gray into the sky. A woman with blond hair tied back into a small ponytail stood at a large grill.

"Midnight Sun Saloon," Ranger said as he led her to a picnic table. "Best burgers in town."

"You made promises," she said as she sat down.

That coaxed out a smile. "Be right back."

She watched as he went up to the grill, and the blond woman greeted him. Handed him a massive basket of fries. He chatted with her, nodded, and then looked back at Noemi.

She lifted her hand and smiled, and the blond lifted her chin in acknowledgment.

Oh, Noemi dearly wondered what he'd said.

Ranger returned with a tray of food—the fries and two burgers. "I had Vic add her special sauce."

"Vic, huh?"

He sat down, straddling the bench. "She used to be a cop in the Lower 48. Has a story, I'm sure, but nobody knows it. Your eyes are going to roll back in your head for these fries. She dips them in fish batter before deep-frying them in peanut oil."

"So, not exactly healthy," she said, but took a fry and stuck it in her mouth. "Oh my. My heart be still."

"Right?"

She dipped one into a puddle of barbecue sauce. "What were you two talking about?"

He also dipped a fry into the sauce. "Her sauce recipe. I worked for her one summer. Learned a few tricks." He popped the fry into his mouth. "She asked about the beautiful woman I was with."

She reached for her burger. "Are you flirting with me?"

"I'm just glad you're here with me."

Oh. Heat went through her, infusing every cell in her body.

He reached for his burger. "Bison burgers. They are amazing."

She took a bite, chewed. "Oh, they are different. More . . . robust." She reached for a napkin. "So, how bad is it getting? Your vision?"

He chewed his burger, then set it down and reached for a napkin. "It's slow. Bigger dots, larger shadows. But I . . . I'm starting not to trust myself. And I think that's the hardest part."

"Could you have landed that plane?"

"I don't know. Maybe. But . . ." He looked at her. "I didn't want to take any chances."

"Clearly Dodge doesn't know."

He shook his head, took another bite of his burger.

"You need to tell him. Your family. They're going to find out."

"I don't want their pity. I need to figure this out before I tell them."

"No one is going to pity you, Range." She set down her burger, took another fry.

"Please. You don't?"

She frowned at him. "Not even a little pity. I'm just trying to keep up."

He grinned at her. "Now you know how it feels."

She opened her mouth to reply, but a man came over. Brown hair, blue eyes. The guy had fitness written all over him—not just in his hiking pants and fleece but in the emblem of Denali Sports embroidered on the breast.

"Danger Ranger, is that you?" He held out his hand.

Ranger stood up from the table and shook it. "Goodie. Wow, look at this—you grew up and got a responsible job."

"Trying. And who is this?" Goodie asked, turning to Noemi.

"This is my friend, Noemi."

At least now he was speaking the truth. She held out her hand. "Hello."

"Noe, this is Goodwin Starr, old hockey pal and all-around troublemaker."

Goodwin took her hand. "I like your jersey."

She lifted a shoulder. "I found it in a pile of giveaways."

Goodwin smirked. "I'll bet." He winked. "Did he tell you that along with being a hockey star, Range is also the genius behind Sergeant Vic's super sauce?"

"Really? No. He left that out." She cocked her head at Ranger.

His jaw had tightened. "Goodie—"

"One night, he accidentally put hot sauce instead of chili oil in the sauce, and it was a hit. After Vic nearly killed him."

Noemi wiped her fingers on a napkin. "Why do you call him Danger Ranger?"

Goodie reached over and snagged a fry, glanced at Ranger. "Because he was the guy who stood at the edge of the lake while we were polar bear jumping, shouting, 'Hey, that's dangerous!'"

"It was! There were currents—"

"Listen. He's no coward. It's just he was always trying to keep Colt out of trouble. So we started calling him Danger. As in 'Danger, Danger, Will Robinson.' You know, *Lost in Space*?"

She grinned. "That explains a lot."

Ranger's mouth opened.

"Hey, there's Deke." Goodie raised a hand to someone behind Noemi. Then he lowered his voice and looked at Ranger. "Does he know you're back? *Are* you back?"

Ranger took a breath, but in that moment, Deke walked up.

Deke was the sheriff, by his uniform. He had dark hair and a wary confidence betrayed by the way he smiled, slowly, and reached out for Ranger's hand. "Danger."

"Madman. I like your duds."

"Comes with a car." He turned to Noemi. "This guy harassing you?"

"Completely," Noemi said. "Arrest him."

Deke laughed. "I like her."

Ranger looked at her. "Me too."

"So, giving Vic any more hot recipe tips?" Deke turned to Noemi again. "Have you heard the story?"

She nodded.

"Still saving the world?" Deke asked.

"Yes," she answered for Ranger.

"Hey," Deke said. "By the way, tell Dodge that we finally got a name on that Russian we arrested a few weeks ago. He matched an international database. Igor Petrov. Apparently, he's part of a big crime organization in Russia."

"And he was here, poaching?"

Deke lifted a shoulder. "That's what Idaho says he was hired for."

"Idaho?"

"Local guide—former guide," Goodie said. "He's warming a bench down at county lockup, waiting for his trial date."

"Anyway," Deke went on, "I thought your brother should know so if he runs across the other guy while he's out in the bush, he knows to stay clear."

"I'll tell him," Ranger said.

"I hope you're sticking around for the Memorial Weekend

Dance and fireworks tomorrow night." He glanced at Noemi. "By the way, did the man tell you he can dance?"

She smirked. "Oh, I've seen his moves."

"Then you've been warned. Hope to see you two around." Deke lifted a hand as he left.

"I'm getting a burger," Goodie said and headed to the grill.

Noemi turned to Ranger. "Now I get it."

He sat back down. "Get what?"

"Why you don't want to tell your brothers that you're going blind."

He drew in a breath.

"Sorry. But that's it. You've always been the one to keep your brother Colt—your fellow team members, me—out of trouble. That's the sniper's job. Danger Ranger. Except—how are you going to see trouble . . . if you can't see?"

He picked up a fry, dragged it around the sauce. From the stage, the band sang a cover from Brett Young, "In Case You Didn't Know."

"It's not about the seeing. It's about focus. It's about nothing on the horizon." He looked away. "It's about being truly blind."

A couple people got up and went to the grassy dance area.

"My mom died pretty suddenly. She seemed to be fine, and then one day she just collapsed. Dodge and I were out in the field with my grandfather. Dad put Colt in the plane, and he took off. She died on the way . . . we never said goodbye."

She pushed her food away.

"She's buried in a family plot on the far edge of our property. It was the fall, and I remember standing there, the wind blowing, snow in the air, and I kept thinking, *Now what?* I was scared and overwhelmed and after the funeral, I ran down to my grandfather's house. That old Massey Ferguson we were working on? It was constantly broken, and he was working on it. My grandfather was a tough old guy—served in Vietnam, on one of the original Underwater Demolition Teams, had massive, scarred hands, wore the same grimy gimme cap for thirty years . . . But he was solid, you know? Big and strong, and I thought I could just climb on his lap and cry. And I did, for a bit. And then, weirdly, he said . . . 'That's enough.' And he pushed me away and told me to stick my hand in that engine and connect the starter solenoid linkage."

"What you were doing today."

"Yeah. Same problem. His hands were too big to get in there, so he talked me through it, helped me focus on the job, and after a while, I had fixed it. And . . . I felt better. I know this is crazy but having something to focus on sort of took the panic away. It kept me from fixating on what I lost, kept all the emotions from catching up to me."

Yeah, that might be why, after her dad died, she'd spent the past few years doing everything but come home to stare at her belongings, packed together in a storage unit in San Diego.

"That did it for me. I decided pretty young I wanted to be a SEAL, like my grandfather. Mostly because I sort of had a light I could run toward. I stayed the course and I could outrun the grief."

"Except you have nothing to run toward now." Even as she said it, she heard Echo's words. "*Stop standing in the shadows . . .*"

His mouth made a grim line and he nodded. "Colt says that I like to solve problems."

She touched his hand.

"This is one problem I can't seem to solve."

She stood up. "I got a problem you can solve."

"Yeah?"

"I need someone to dance with."

He considered her, his eyes bright in the sunlight. Then he got up. "For a fake wife, you sure are a good friend."

She took his hand and walked toward the dance area.

There was nothing fake about it.

FOURTEEN

If this was what dreaming felt like, Ranger was all in.

It had started on the dance floor when, instead of dancing the two-step, Noemi put her arms around his neck and just held on.

And he didn't know why, but the grip of her on him, as if his life wasn't completely dismantling, had somehow eased away the sense of panic.

Stupid Dodge, suggesting Ranger land the plane. He'd nearly gotten them all killed. And sure, maybe they would have been just fine, especially with Dodge at the helm, too, but in Ranger's darkest nightmares, he missed something and flipped the plane. Killed his brother—or Noemi.

Nope. No one else died on his watch, period, full stop.

Sorry, Ghost.

Colt was right—Ranger was the problem solver, the one who saw danger and averted it. The sniper.

And he'd been proud of that.

Maybe too proud.

As he and Noemi swayed, listening to the band sing a country love song . . . *"Let me stay here longer"*. . . as Noemi's smell and the way she laid her head against his chest sank into him, he heard her words.

"Not even a little pity." And then, *"I'm just trying to keep up."*

He knew she was trying to make him laugh, but frankly, his silly heart took off at a gallop and hadn't slowed down since.

It didn't help that she suggested he make Vic's barbecue sauce recipe for dinner and put it on venison steaks.

She helped him pick out the ingredients at Gigi's Grocery, making no big deal out of it that he couldn't clearly read the labels. Then, she simply got in the driver's seat of the truck parked at their hangar at the airport, found the keys in the glove compartment, and drove them home.

Even fought him for control of the radio. As if that's just the way they did things, being the old married couple they were.

At home, he dug out a number of steaks from the deep well, and as they defrosted, he shooed Flo out of the kitchen and started chopping green onions.

This he could do with his eyes closed.

Meanwhile, Noemi had wrapped a flour cloth around her waist and went to work with him, handing him ingredients as he shouted them out, seasoning the steaks, and even chopping up the butternut squash for the squash with rosemary and coconut milk side dish. She tossed the salad. Shook up the homemade dressing.

And all the time, she sang along to KTNO, Copper Mountain's Good News Radio station's oldies hour.

"Highway run . . . ," she sang into a spoon, "into the midnight sun . . ."

He was whisking butter into the barbecue sauce, laughing as she danced around the kitchen. His heart was weirdly exploding. Sort of felt like when he evacked from a successful op.

No, better.

Because maybe this wasn't just an op anymore. It was something bigger. Better.

"Maybe it's time to let yourself dream."

"Sorry, Flo!" The words came from the kitchen table where Colt, Dodge, and Echo played a game of Sorry!

"Calm down, Colt," Dodge said. "Flo has three pieces in home."

"I'm comin' for you next, Dodger."

"You wish."

The fire crackled in the stone hearth, and his father sat in his recliner, his glasses on, reading on his tablet.

Yes, it all felt very, very close to something that might be lodged deep into the secret places of his heart.

"Is the oven hot?" he asked Noemi. He'd stuck a cast-iron pan into the preheating oven to heat it.

"Yeppers." She grabbed a couple hot pads to retrieve it.

"Put it on the stove." He reached to start the gas. It clicked on and she brought over the pan.

"This thing is massive," she said, carrying it with two hands. "It'll feed a small army."

"Or just me and my brothers." He winked and put the steaks into the pan, searing them on one side, then the other. "Okay, put it back in the oven and set a timer for two minutes."

She opened the oven and put it in.

Meanwhile, he stirred the squash, then ran his fingers down a sprig of rosemary to loosen the fronds.

"That's a trick."

"I watch way too much *Hell's Kitchen* in my free time," he said and sprinkled the herbs on.

"Smells amazing."

"The trick is the coconut milk. Stir this and I'll check on the steaks."

He didn't quite know how it happened, but as he turned, the shadows crossed his eyes and his vision turned black and just like that, he'd slammed right into her. She banged into the island, then went down with a loud cry.

"Noemi!"

She reached up for the counter, wincing. "Sorry, that was my fault—"

"No, it was mine. I didn't see—"

"It's okay." She pressed her hand on her hip, still wincing. "I need to learn to stay out of your way when you're manning the kitchen. It's like a tactical operation."

He didn't know why, but her words found his chest, burrowed in. He put his hands on her shoulders. "No. You're not in the way, Noemi."

She stilled, looked up at him, her beautiful golden-brown eyes on his.

Maybe the room had gone quiet at his words, he didn't know, but around him the world seemed to still.

Focus.

Noemi. She was the one thing that could make him stop thinking about what he'd lost. Keep the emotions from piling up, taking him under.

The one thing he could run toward.

Her chest rose and fell, and she caught her lower lip in her teeth. Oh, he wanted to kiss her—sometimes the taste of her could rise up in him, turn him hungry.

Right now, he was starving.

She put her hand on his chest. "Ranger—"

The oven timer went off, and he jerked away.

She did too. "I'll get it. Make a path to the stove."

"Copy."

She opened the oven and took out the pan, carrying it again with two hot pads to the stove. He drizzled the barbecue sauce on the steaks and let them simmer in the juices.

Noemi pulled plates from the cupboard, went to the table and shooed away the gamers.

Echo declared Flo the winner, then helped set the table, and suddenly, it was family dinner.

The miracle of it swept over him as they all sat down and even held hands as his father prayed. Weirdly, cotton filled his chest, his throat thickening.

He was turning into a sap.

Still, he just wanted to breathe it in. *"This is what happy feels like."*

And right then, shoot, Noemi's words from today filtered back. He had to tell his brothers—his family—the truth.

"I need to—"

"This is amazing sauce, son," his dad said after taking a bite of steak. "Is this the sauce you made for Vic?"

"Yeah. Except I added some chipotle peppers that Noemi found at the grocery store."

His dad forked a piece of squash. "Your mom cooked with her heart. And you seem to have the same knack."

"Can I just mention the orange pancakes again?" Colt said.

"Or how about the bacon and hot fudge ice cream?" Dodge looked up at him and grinned.

"What are you saying, Dodge? I loved that," Echo said. She looked at Ranger. "Anytime you want to put bacon on my ice cream, I'm in."

"Thanks, E."

"You ever leave the SEALs, son, you could make a living at being a chef."

"Um—"

"Did you get the tractor working?" His father looked at him.

Oh. "No. We got back too late. I'll fix it first thing in the morning."

"Perfect. Fussy machine. You and your grandfather were the only ones who could keep her running."

"Sometimes the Massey would quit on me, right in the middle of the field," Colt said, "and all Ranger had to do was drive by, give her a little pat, and she'd start right up and hum."

"It wasn't quite that easy," Ranger said. Yes, this steak was good. But he might consider marinating it more. Venison needed extra time in the vinegar-and-wine bath.

"It wasn't just the Massey either," Colt said. "Remember

that time Deke and Goodie drove over a boulder in the front yard with their dad's Ram pickup and popped a hole in the oil pan?"

"I remember Ranger bathed in grease for a week trying to take it off," Dodge said.

"I stole the replacement part from Dad's junker in the garage. I don't think their dad ever knew." Ranger grinned.

"Your dad never knew either, buck," his dad said.

Oh. "Oops."

From across the table, Flo smiled, ducked her head. He liked her, despite the mystery around her. It seemed strange, however, that no one else seemed to care that she didn't have a name, a past, a story she could tell.

Maybe someday.

"It's okay." His dad winked. "I've been stealing parts off those cars for years."

"By the way, I saw Deke in town today," Ranger said, turning to Dodge. The squash *was* good, maybe one of his best. And Noemi had added feta cheese and peaches to the spinach salad, under a balsamic dressing. Delicious.

She was sitting beside him, quiet, and glanced at him occasionally.

The dream team.

"Yeah?" Dodge said to his words about Deke.

"He said to tell you that they identified the Russian you captured—which, by the way, I still need to hear that story. Apparently, he's a part of some big Russian crime syndicate."

"Really," Colt said. "The *Bratva*, here, in Alaska?"

"Any sign of the one who got away?" Echo asked.

"He didn't say. But his last name was Petrov." Ranger reached for more salad.

"Petrov?" Colt said. He'd put down his fork. "As in General Arkady Petrov?"

The table went quiet.

"Russian general. Communist. Tried to get General Stanislov killed last year in an attempted coup?" Colt looked around the table. "Seriously? Nobody? Rumor is he wants to turn Russia back into a superpower. And his henchmen are the Bratva. They bombed a metro a few years ago, and some say they tried to kill President White during his inauguration."

"There was an assassination attempt on President White?" Ranger said.

Colt nodded. "Yes. A plot cooked up by VP Jackson. She didn't resign for health reasons—she's sitting in a federal prison! Some say she was doing the bidding of a Russian general—aka Arkady Petrov."

Everyone looked at him.

"Seriously. Don't you guys listen to podcasts?"

"Of the conspiracy theory variety?" Dodge said. "I like to keep my fiction in a book."

"You'll rethink that when General Petrov pushes the red button and turns DC into scorched earth."

"This isn't the Cold War," Echo said. "The Russians aren't trying to start World War III."

"There's a rumor that General Petrov has his own branch of the Bratva, the Petrov Bratva, and if these guys worked for the general, then they were here for a reason. And it wasn't poaching. They're dangerous. Very dangerous. Think elite Russian killers."

Next to Colt, Flo had put down her fork, pressed her hand to her mouth.

Colt looked at her. "Sorry."

But Ranger couldn't get past this particular spill of information. Especially from Colt, who still hadn't come clean on why *he'd* left Delta. "What exactly did you do after you left the military, again?"

Colt met his gaze, his eyes hooded. "I worked private security for Jones, Inc. Why? Are you looking for a job?"

"Why would Ranger need a job?" his father said.

Dodge looked at him, as did Colt.

Shoot. Not like this. But . . .

Noemi put her hand on his arm. Squeezed.

Great. Now everyone was watching.

Fine. "I'm out of the Navy."

Dodge put down his fork. "I thought you were on medical leave."

"No." He pushed his plate away. "Actually . . ." Wow. This was harder than telling his SEAL mates. "The truth is, I'm going blind. Macular degeneration."

And of course, the silence was a hand around his throat, choking him.

"So am I, son."

Ranger looked up at his father, who wiped at his mouth with a napkin. "I feared that one of you boys would get this. It's genetic—a terrible curse for a family of pilots."

Ranger wasn't exactly a pilot, but . . .

"How bad is it?" his dad asked.

"Dots. Shadows. I can't see well at night."

"Can't land a plane," Dodge said softly.

Ranger lifted a shoulder. "That's probably true without the blindness."

Dodge's mouth twitched up one side. "Sorry, Range."

Yeah. Not as much as he was.

"What are you doing about it?" Echo asked. She'd taken Dodge's hand.

"They've mentioned anti-VEGF injections, but . . ."

"I'm getting laser treatments in Anchorage. They seem to be helping." His father gave him a small smile. "I'll introduce you to my doc."

It did nothing for the giant, burning fire in Ranger's chest. He shouldn't have told them. Now he just wanted to push away from the table and, well, run.

So much for the dream.

And then from beside him, Noemi spoke up. "He's going to be fine. He has this ranch. An amazing family. And . . ." She looked at him, her beautiful eyes on him. "For Pete's sake, he is a Navy SEAL. If anyone can stay on their feet, it's Ranger. Trust me on this." She squeezed his arm again.

And suddenly, weirdly, he believed it.

"Yeah, what she said, Chef Ranger," Colt said. "I've never seen anyone with your taste buds. You're fearless."

Everyone laughed, and just like that, it was over.

And of course, not over, but the worst part was, maybe.

The part where he was no longer the family champion.

"Oh, you should have seen him eating my auntie Precious's goat meat soup. The look on his face when he saw the fish heads." Noemi shook her head, laughing. "How I wish I had my phone—" She blinked and looked at Ranger, eyes wide. "Oh my gosh! I think I know why Abu was after me." She put a hand to her forehead "Maybe. I don't know. But at the village, when we got there, I took pictures. Lots of them. And when I heard the commotion outside, I uploaded them to the cloud."

What? "You just now remembered this?"

"I . . . yes. I mean, they destroyed my phone the second they took it so I forgot, and then I didn't think anything about it, but what if . . . what if they were after me to delete it?"

Ranger drew in a breath. "I hardly think they'd be after you for some photos."

She shook her head slowly, glanced at Colt, and then back to him. "Wait until you see the pictures. Can I borrow a computer?"

"You can use mine," his father said and pushed up from the table.

And just like that, the dream blew apart.

Because he remembered, Noemi was only here until she was safe.

And then she was gone. And with her went the only world he wanted.

They were going to find her.

Tae sat, her entire body still as Colt's words about the Petrov Bratva clicked into place like the chambering of a bullet.

Sergei *Petrov.* He hadn't even tried to hide it.

Wow, she was stupid.

And worse . . . people were still dying while she hid out in the Alaskan bush.

Like a coward.

Tae's entire body went cold as she looked over Noemi's shoulder at the pictures pulled up on her cloud account on Barry's laptop.

Pictures of people whose bodies had been ravaged by small-pox.

They lay in a church, some of them piled on the altar in front, others in pews, more on the floor. Children, adults, the elderly.

They—she, Colt, Ranger, Dodge, Echo, and Barry—were standing around the kitchen island, behind Noemi as she scrolled through the shots of the small Nigerian village.

"Oh my—" Echo said and turned away, her hand over her mouth.

Yes, disgusting. Tragic. Horrifying. But a thousand questions filled Tae's mind, urging her to open her mouth. *Where were you when you took these shots? How long had these people been dead? What were their levels of decomposition? How did the open wounds present? And, most importantly, did you exhibit any symptoms after you left the church?*

Thankfully, behind her, Colt elaborated, having also seen the terror. "When we got to the village, it was eerily quiet, so we started looking around. We entered a few homes and found the bloody remains of deathbeds. It was weird."

"I took a few pictures of that too. I don't know why. Something inside me said it wasn't right." Noemi flipped to another picture of a bedroom, and indeed, someone had died here, the bedding splotched with old, dark blood. She flipped to another room with the same horror.

"We smelled the church from a ways away," Colt said. "Or at least I did, and so did Dr. Aaron. He told us to cover our faces, so we pulled up our shirts, and Selah and Noemi pulled up their headscarves."

Tae could still hear Colt's voice from this morning. *"Oh, you mean the dead bodies in the church? The ones with smallpox?"*

She nearly blew her cover then, nearly gasped, nearly walked into the room to grab Colt by the shoulders and interrogate him.

This couldn't be happening. Except, of course, it was.

She'd already seen it.

"You wore headscarves?" Ranger asked. He stood on the other side of Noemi. He'd been weirdly silent since dinner ended, and now he stood over her as they viewed her pictures on the cloud.

Tae wished he'd meant their travel snaps of Nigeria.

"Yes. We knew the village was right on the border of Fulani country, so we thought maybe we'd stay under the radar if we wore scarves," Noemi said.

"We walked into the church, then, and the smell . . . it was rough. And the flies." Colt shook his head. "I can't believe Noemi stayed in there, taking all these shots."

"I just started snapping pictures." She was scrolling now, again, through the snaps of the victims. Silence fell hard at a picture of a young mother dressed in a coral dress who lay with her toddler daughter on her chest. Then a father with two boys sprawled beside him.

"Who brought them into the church?" Dodge said. "It's weird—some of them are just sort of tossed in, others more deliberately posed."

"How long after this were you captured?" Ranger asked.

"We heard the truck while we were still in the church," Colt said. "I went out with Fraser and Moses, our interpreter, but the men jumped Fraser right off. Then they shot Dr. Aaron when he ran out, shouting."

"It happened so fast," Noemi said. "By the time Selah and I got outside, they'd grabbed Blessing. Fraser was in rough shape and Dr. Aaron was losing blood fast. They tied Colt up and threw us all in the truck."

At Noemi's words about Colt, Tae glanced over at him. His mouth formed a thin, grim line. Yes, no wonder he was beaten so badly. And he was probably still beating himself up on the inside.

"Then they burned the church and drove away," Noemi said.

She flipped to another picture. Three girls, maybe eight years old, lying on the altar.

"They piled the bodies there," Ranger said, "and then for whatever reason, drove away. You just showed up at the wrong place, wrong time."

Ranger reached over and closed the screen. "So, now we need to know why."

He pulled out a cell phone and put it on the island. Then he turned, folding his arms over his chest as he looked at Noemi. "We think maybe this is how Abu found us in the market. And then at your Uncle Efe's house."

Noemi picked up Freddie's phone, searching for the power button.

"It's off now," Ranger said. "And Colt took out the sim card, so they can't track us here, but . . ." He touched her shoulder. "Did you see anyone else in camp? Anyone who might have, well, better technology than Abu and his thugs?"

And maybe no one but Tae was thinking it but Russia had the technology, right?

Except, the Russians didn't support Islamic terrorists and

had pledged to fight the Boko Haram. At least that was their official stance. It didn't mean that the Petrov group wasn't into something sinister.

Unless Abu hadn't been with Boko Haram at all.

And the *Petrov* Bratva. Tae just couldn't escape the idea that she was the connective tissue.

Noemi shook her head to Ranger's question. "I was just trying to survive."

"Think, Noemi."

She blew out a breath and Tae felt for her. *"It's up to you or we all die."*

Shoot, not now. She turned, walked away, wishing she had someplace else to run.

She found herself heading through the entry, then outside where the sun had just barely set, the deep, purple sky dotted with light, a waxen moon hanging to the east. The breeze lifted—the temperatures were still in the forties at night. She rubbed her arms.

"You okay, Flo?"

She turned, and Colt stood behind her. She hadn't heard him come out. Those brown eyes were on her, and yes, the man could most definitely see right through her. See her lies, see her fears, see . . .

Well, see that she knew exactly what was going on.

And wanted to keep running.

She drew in a breath, the words gathering. *I'm scared, Colt. Because—*

"Don't worry. Whoever was after Noemi isn't going to find us here. You're safe."

Oh. He offered a smile, and it was so sweet her eyes burned.

And then a tear edged her eye. No—not now!

"Flo?"

She shook her head, wiped it away. She was tougher than this.

But shoot if she didn't let him put his arms around her and

pull her to himself. He smelled good—flannel and cotton from his T-shirt—and that thick beard scuffed against her neck. Inside his embrace, against his solid but still-broken chest, she felt what she'd been hoping for in her escape to Alaska.

Safety.

Noemi might be ill.

"Think, Noe," Ranger said. His voice was soft, but in it she only heard, *You idiot.*

She'd stolen a cell phone from a terrorist and hadn't given a second thought to the idea that they could use it to track her.

Track them. Into a market in Okwagbe, or even to bomb her uncle Efe's house.

"This is all my fault." She pushed away from the counter. "The attack on my uncle's place—" She put her hand over her mouth, looked at Ranger. Shook her head.

"Noemi—"

She put out a hand to stop him, then turned and headed for the nearest door, the front door to the massive wraparound porch. The moment she stepped outside, the brisk air hit her, swept out her breath, and slammed reality into her bones.

She'd nearly gotten her Nigerian family killed. Gotten Ranger killed. *Again.*

Only then did she realize that she still held Freddie's lethal cell phone in her hand. She dropped it onto the porch and, with a shout, sent her foot onto it.

The phone splintered and scattered into pieces across the dark floorboards.

"It's dead. They can't find you—"

"How do you know that?" She rounded on Ranger, who'd come out onto the porch. "Who knows that they haven't put a tracker on me and they'll show up with AK-47s at the ranch and take out your *entire family*!" Okay, she sounded hysterical, but seriously. *Seriously!* "Who are these people?"

"That's what we're trying to find out," Ranger the Calm and Serious said as he came toward her. "But they won't find us here." He put his hands on her arms. "I promise everything will be okay."

She stared at him a moment before she stepped away. "Do. Not. *Promise* me anything!" She whirled around and headed for the stairs.

"Noemi!" Footsteps followed her, but she hit the dirt path and kicked out into a run.

And no, she hadn't a clue why she was running, but it just felt—no, she *had* to run. Had to flee this terrible tearing inside her heart.

She'd wanted this too much. And now, as usual, life laughed at her.

She didn't know why she tried.

"Noemi!"

"Stay away from me, Range!" She threw the words over her shoulder, cut up as they were by the emotion choking her. "Just stay away!"

Of course he caught her. Somewhere between the house and the cabin, in the field of wildflowers now being trampled by her chaos. "Noemi!" He gripped her arm. "C'mon, give a guy a break. I'm still on the mend here."

She slowed, rounding, also breathing hard. Her eyes blurred, especially with the sight of him holding his arm close to his body, his chest rising and falling.

Great. Now she'd hurt him *again*. It just didn't stop.

"Let me go, Ranger. I'm . . . I'm no good for you. You were right all those years ago to push me away. I'm trouble, and I'm just going to get you hurt."

His eyes widened. "What? Wait—seriously? That's why you think I pushed you away in Key West?"

"Yes! Why *else*?"

"Because I was going to hurt *you*! Because I only had room for one wife, and that was the Team. Because your father spoke sense into me when I woke up from nearly drowning and told me that I could worry you into your grave!"

She stared at him. Then she shook her head and turned away. "Still my fault."

"How is that?" He kept up with her as she headed to the cabin.

Fine. She stopped. "If I hadn't flirted with you. Made you fall for me—"

"You've got to be kidding me. You didn't *make* me fall for you—"

"I tried to tell you, that this, we"—she gestured into the space between them—"we're no big deal. That you didn't need to take it seriously—"

"*Of course* I took it seriously. Have you met me? I take *everything* seriously. I didn't stop thinking about you for four years. I know I blew it at your dad's funeral, but . . . yes, you were, you *are* a very big deal."

Her breath hitched, her eyes glazing. "Then you're a fool." She walked past him.

"Wait one second, Princess." He stepped out and blocked her path. "I'm a pretty smart guy, but you're going to have to explain this to me." He didn't smile. He stood in front of her, his outline against the deep purple of the sky, the fading sunlight in his blue eyes.

Clearly planted, and not moving. "Why am I a fool?"

"Fine. Okay." She folded her hands over her chest, holding herself together. "People I love die. My mother. My father. And clearly fate—or let's put a fine point on it, God—has it out for me. And now you too, buckaroo, so you'd better brace yourself."

His eyes narrowed around the edges. "I'm sorry about your

parents, Noemi. But God doesn't have it out for me. Or you. Or your parents."

"*Really?* Wanna explain for me why every time I'm in your life, you're left in pain and gasping for air?"

"Noemi, that's not remotely true."

"It is true, Range. Everyone I love dies." She held up her hand. "Look how many times God tried to take you away from me in Nigeria."

"Or how many times he saved my life!"

She put her hands on his chest, keeping him from what seemed to roam in his eyes. "Listen. Tell yourself what you want, but . . . trust me. You don't know what it's like not to have anyone on your side."

"I'm on your side!"

"But you won't be." Her voice fell. "Someday I'll be too much for you. And then you'll walk away. Or better, send me away."

"You know me better than that."

She blinked at him. Yes. Yes she did.

Which meant she had to do the walking away. Her throat closed over her words, but she had to get them out. "Listen, here's the answer. You need to let me leave."

"What—no!"

"Yes! You need to take a lesson from my parents. I'm trouble, and the fewer attachments I make, the fewer people get hurt."

"That's crazy, Noemi. Your plan is to just keep moving?"

"No one gets hurt that way. And most of all, God doesn't notice me."

"I have news for you, honey. God very much notices you."

"Please, don't."

"What? He noticed you in Nigeria when you were among the hostages I came to rescue. He noticed you when I was dying and you bought a car with the money in my vest. He noticed you when the villagers wanted to kill us and your uncle the king showed up. He noticed you when Abu found us, but your uncle kept us safe. And he noticed us in the ocean when we were drowning and Dodge showed up like a giant eagle to pluck us out of the sea. He notices you!"

She stared at him hard. "No, he noticed *you*, Range. Don't you get it? I'm not one of the chosen ones! I'm the accident, the afterthought, the . . . well, like I said, I have to look out for myself because no one else will."

"I will—"

She gave him a look. "I don't expect you to see it."

He frowned at her.

"Range—God is on your side." She drew in a breath. "And he's not on mine. And don't preach at me because look at all God has given you—a family, this amazing place to grow up—and you *still* thought God abandoned you when your eyesight started failing."

"I was scared!"

She stilled. He kept his gaze on hers, just their breathing between them.

Then, softer, "I'm going blind, Noemi. You'd better believe I thought God abandoned me. The only thing I know—*knew*—was being a SEAL. It was the only thing I wanted. Or thought I wanted. And then suddenly . . ." He blew out a breath. "Suddenly I was waking up with you sitting at my bedside. I was bargaining for your hand in marriage and eating fish soup with my fingers. I was *dancing* down the aisle . . . I was living and breathing and discovering a life I thought I'd lost. And I realized that God *hadn't* abandoned me. I'd simply stopped trusting him. I thought my life had to be one way to be happy—but maybe . . ." He shook his head. "Maybe there is more for me. For us."

He lowered his voice. "Listen, I get it. But, Noemi, you are not too much trouble. Not for me. And especially not for God."

Her mouth tightened.

"Have you ever *tried* to trust God? Asked him for help? Talked to him?"

Once. Maybe twice. It hit her then that her requests had also involved Ranger, so there was that.

"Where is that bold, brave girl who stood up to terrorists? If you can stand up to them, then certainly you can ask God for help." He touched her cheek. "You don't have to always depend on yourself."

Her eyes filled.

"You are so beautiful, Storm."

Her breath caught at his touch. Oh . . . but the man had magnetic eyes and she couldn't move. *"Stop standing in the shadows . . ."*

"Storm?" she whispered.

"Jake nicknamed you that at the camp because he thought you were a force to be reckoned with." He stepped closer, his mouth near hers. "You are the only one who says that you're no big deal. Trust me—you are a very big deal."

Oh, *Ranger*.

And then he kissed her.

Everything exploded inside her.

This man. This amazing, frustrating, buttoned-up man—

His mouth was salty, savory, and as he kissed her, it was like tasting adventure, the vast wilderness and the dark sea. This was the man who'd cooked with her, sang "I Don't Want to Miss a Thing" by Aerosmith, and nearly kissed her in front of his family.

Yeah, she saw the desire in his eyes in the kitchen and tried to tell herself she'd been dreaming it.

Well, ahem. Apparently, she wasn't.

"Noemi," he whispered against her mouth, then dove back in and pulled her closer, molding her to him, his kiss slowing, deepening.

Focusing.

It was very, very heady being the object of this man's focus. And her entire body woke to a rush of lethal, desperate, terrifying emotions.

She loved him too much.

Too painfully much, and she hadn't a bone to resist him.

So she simply softened her mouth and let herself stop thinking. She wrapped her arms around him, letting her hunger for him take over.

She might even be crying. He was solid and strong and wrapped his other arm around her back, pulling her against the hard planes of his chest. The wind curled around her, chilly, but warmth radiated off him, into her, finding her bones.

This is where she belonged. Or at least *wanted* to belong. Right here, or there, or wherever Ranger was.

I will find you.

The words resonated inside her, but it didn't exactly sound like Ranger's voice. Deeper, maybe. She shivered with the power of it.

Ranger broke away. "You're cold."

No. "I . . ."

"C'mon." He took her hand and led her through the semidarkness down to the cabin.

"Don't you need a light?"

"I know this path."

She wove her fingers through his, held on as he led her to the lake. The setting sun traced a finger across it. He led her up the steps, then opened her door. Stood back.

"You're not coming inside?"

He stood in silence a moment, his chest rising and falling as if considering his words. "Noemi, of *course* I want to come inside. I want to be with you in the worst way." He swallowed, his eyes on her. "But, I need to know . . . do you want to be married to me?"

Echo's words sifted through her. *"He might not be able to say it, but Ranger doesn't give away his heart easily. So, my guess is that once he does, it's for keeps."*

She stared at him, the question aching inside her. *Do you love me?*

Because he hadn't said it, not really.

Still. *What do you really want?*

Ranger. She wanted this man who stood on the steps, his blue eyes on hers, her *husband*. "Yes."

He smiled then and stepped close, his forehead on hers. "Me too."

Her heart thumped with the thought of him, finally, in her arms. Where he belonged.

He sighed then and pulled away. "But not here, tonight, in a tiny single bed. And . . . I want my wedding to be more than an op."

He took her hands. "I want to do this right, Noemi. Because I'm only getting married once."

"If you ask the Ovie, he would say, twice."

The smile returned to his lips, and what had she been thinking, trying to run from this man?

He kissed her again, but she felt the control kick in, something holding him back.

She gripped the folds of his flannel shirt, savoring his touch, feeling his heartbeat, her entire body aching. *Stay.*

But he set her away from him and let out a long breath. "I'd better go before I decide to come inside."

Shoot. Ranger and his principles. But he was trying to be a hero.

Still, as he left, raising a hand to her in the moonlight; as she undressed and got into her lonely twin bed; and as she stared at the ceiling, listening to the wind against her dark window, she couldn't help but feel that it was too right.

She was too happy.

And that's what scared her the most.

FIFTEEN

"What problem are you working out now?"

The voice came from behind Ranger, from where he was standing by the engine compartment of the Massey. He'd replaced the set screw, but the tractor still sputtered. So he was replacing the spark plug wires to see if he couldn't get it to purr.

Now he looked to see his father approaching, holding a mug of coffee. He was freshly showered and wore a jacket against the nip in the air coming off the mountains.

Ranger took the mug. He was already buzzing with so much coffee inside him he practically vibrated.

"Trying to get the tractor to stop hiccupping. I opened the hood and got a good jolt. I realized there was a wire with a hairline crack, and it was arcing. So I'm replacing them one by one. Found some spark plug wires in your nest of extra parts."

"You know that's not what I mean." His father leaned against the workbench.

Ranger made a sound, deep inside. Yeah, he knew. "Crank the engine. I want to listen."

His father climbed into the seat and turned on the ignition. The tractor fired up with a cough, then settled into a hum. Ranger took a sip of his coffee, then suddenly spit it out on the wires and watched for sparks, a trick his grandfather had taught him.

The tractor hiccupped. Once, twice. "Turn it off. It's still missing."

His father turned it off and climbed down.

"So, is that your second or third pot of coffee?" He gestured to the thermos that sat on the bench.

"Lost count." Ranger unhooked the second wire from the tractor, running his fingers along it, feeling for the crack.

"When I went to bed last night, you were sitting on the stool, surfing the internet."

"Looking into that Petrov group." He picked up a new wire from the bench. "Colt was right—Arkady Petrov is rumored to be involved in all sorts of things—a metro explosion, an assassination attempt on one of his own generals. I didn't read anything about an attempt on the president, but that doesn't mean anything."

He walked back to the tractor and connected the wire to the distributor, then the spark plug. "Give 'er another go."

His father again turned the engine over. Ranger gave it another coffee shower. Again, it hiccupped. "Still not the right wire."

"Did you sleep at all?" his father asked as he turned off the tractor. He stayed in the seat.

"I got a few winks on the sofa." Ranger disconnected the next wire. "Dodge doesn't think he snores, but the man could mow down a forest."

He stood at the bench, taking a real sip of coffee. The early morning cascaded into the room, and outside, a scattering of lavender clouds crowned Denali and its massifs, the sky blue and bold.

The perfect day to ask Noemi to marry him. For real.

So why had he spent the night pacing, panic thick in his chest?

His eyes burned and he closed them, running his thumb and forefinger against them.

"Getting worse?" his dad asked.

"Sometimes."

"The drops help. I can still read." His tone softened. "It's going to be okay, son."

And maybe it was because he was tired, or just ornery, but he shook his head. "How can you *know* that?" He turned back to the tractor, reconnecting the wire. Noemi's voice from last night reverberated inside him. *"God is on your side. And he's not on mine."*

That had nearly broken his heart.

Now, it felt too terribly real. "I really got in over my head this time." He connected the wire to the plug. "Start her up."

His father turned it over. The tractor hummed. "Let it run for a bit."

Ranger stepped back. Sighed. "I think I want to marry Noemi."

"Aren't you already married?"

"We didn't, um . . . well . . ."

His father wasn't helping. Just staring at him, a half grin on his face. The tractor was churning diesel exhaust into the air, turning it acrid. He took a sip of coffee and again showered the wire.

Nothing. The machine settled down, impervious to the liquid.

"I think you got 'er done." His father turned off the engine. It died, leaving a quietness in the air.

Ranger closed the engine compartment. "I'm not sure if we're married or not. We went through the ceremony, but I always sort of considered it part of the mission objective—keep her safe."

"And that's changed?"

Ranger picked up a rag to clean his hands. "Maybe we're moving too fast. I sort of let my emotions get ahold of me last night and . . . maybe my focus needs to be on keeping her safe instead of . . ."

"Kissing her?"

He looked at his dad. "She is distracting."

His father laughed, and Ranger felt something ease in his chest.

Then he gave him a serious look. "Do you love her? Or do you just want to take her to bed?"

Ranger stared at him, speechless. Finally, "Dad. Really?"

"Well, I'm just putting a fine point on it. Because you haven't mentioned the real reason to marry—because you want someone to share your life with, forever, and create that sacred union before God. And hopefully, it's because you also love this woman."

He needed more coffee. "You know when horses run the Kentucky Derby, they have these little blinders on so they don't get distracted?"

"And they can only see forward, yes."

Ranger looked up. "When I'm with Noemi, it's like the little blinders are off and I see the whole world. I see possibilities and the world is in big, bright color and . . ."

"And even in the darkness, you see light."

He met his father's gaze and nodded.

"The aurora borealis."

Ranger frowned.

"Your mother was crazy about the northern lights. And so were you, when you were little."

"I remember."

"Did you know that the best time to see the northern lights is in winter? Not only does the light refract off the polar ice cap better, but the world is darker, son. The colors are more vivid against the darkness."

Ranger nodded. "Yeah. That's how it is. My world is always so black and white—and Noemi gives it color. She makes me laugh, and I feel like I can breathe. Like everything isn't life or death. Mostly, she makes me . . . feel."

"And I'll bet that scares you to death."

Ranger just looked at him. Slowly nodded.

"Son, you can't live without emotions." He held up his hand. "Don't get me wrong—a man in control of his emotions is a man who can make wise decisions. But it's not good to ignore them. Even God acted out of emotion—love—when he made his biggest decision ever. Sure, it was completely in accordance to his character, so in that way, it was logical. But to the human heart, nothing made sense of his decision to save us. To die for us. He did it because of love."

His father picked up the thermos. Tucked it under his arm. "The first time your mother was diagnosed with cancer was when she was pregnant with you three, did you know that?"

Ranger stilled. "No."

"Yes. And of course, you were triplets, so they thought you might not make it anyway, so they suggested she have an abortion."

"What?" Ranger picked up the debris of the old cables and dropped them into a bucket. Then he followed his father through the clutter of the barn toward the back door.

"Of course, Cee wouldn't think of having an abortion—and neither would I—but I have to tell you, I was terrified." He held open the door for Ranger, who ducked through it.

He blinked against the brightness of the sun.

His father closed the door. "I tried not to tell her, but of course she knew it. And that's when she made me start reciting the Twenty-Third Psalm every night before we went to sleep. 'The Lord is my Shepherd . . .'"

"'I shall not want.'" Easy to say when he was standing in the middle of his family's ranch, the world big and beautiful around him.

"Yep. You know it." His father started for the lodge. "And right now, you're walking through the valley of the shadow of death, son. But that's the thing . . . it's just a shadow. It's just the looming fear. And I get it—the death isn't only physical. It's the death of your dreams and your future and everything you ever wanted."

They reached the lodge and Ranger opened the door. "I used

to believe that God had a good plan for me. But this doesn't feel good."

"I know. But will we trust God only when things go the way we want? The verse says to fear no evil for God is with you. The evil is the lies Satan wants to tell you—that you'll never be anything. That you can't keep Noemi safe. That you'll be a burden." His father stepped inside.

Ranger followed him, unable to look at his father.

His father, however, didn't move. He kept standing in the entry, holding the thermos. "But that's why you have to keep reciting, Ranger. 'Your rod and your staff, they comfort me.' That's direction and protection. You don't need to know where you're going, just the one who is with you. And there is no one better to have on your side than the almighty God. He has a path, and it's good."

He clamped a hand on Ranger's shoulder. "You asked how I know everything is going to be okay. The answer is because every time my world gets darker, I see God more." He gave Ranger's shoulder a squeeze. Then he headed for the kitchen.

Ranger's own words to Noemi pinged back at him, a burst of light that made him blink. *"Have you ever* tried *to trust God? Asked him for help? Talked to him?"*

Maybe not.

Maybe Noemi wasn't the only one depending on herself to get out of trouble.

He blew out a breath and followed his father into the kitchen. The house smelled of burned coffee, and his father was dumping the sludge down the drain. Ranger slid onto a stool. "I got discharged two months ago." He didn't look at his father. "My spotter was killed because I couldn't see the shooter."

"Ranger—"

He held up his hand. "No, I really couldn't see him."

A pause, and then his father held the pot under the faucet, turned it on. "I understand, son."

"What you don't understand was that it wasn't the first time. And I didn't say anything." He watched the water rise in the pot. "I lied to the Navy because I didn't want to lose my job. And someone was killed. And I just don't . . . I don't want to do something that . . . well, that could get someone else I care about hurt."

His father turned off the water.

"So, I've been sitting in San Diego not sure what to do with the rest of my life. Rescuing Colt gave me something . . . but how can I ask Noemi to marry me if I have nothing for her?"

His father filled the coffee maker, set the pot on the burner, and switched it on. Then he turned to Ranger. "You've always spent your life looking forward, the destination in mind. But faith is stepping forward without knowing the destination. Your job, as a warrior of the Lord, is to listen. To walk in faith. You might not have anything for her, Range, but God does . . . and your job is to love her. Honor her. Protect her. Give her your life. That is your duty. God will provide the destination."

"I don't have dreams. I have duty."

The pot began to drip.

Huh. Maybe he could have both. "I love this girl. And yes, we're married, at least in Nigeria. But . . . it was part of the mission—"

"Did you make vows before God?"

"Yes."

"And did you mean those vows? With your whole heart?"

His father's questions stilled him. And for a second, Ranger saw himself in the bathroom of their room at Uncle Efe's, pushing in to kiss her. Yes, right then his emotions had been in charge—the emotions of a husband who wanted his wife.

It was the operator inside who'd pushed them away.

But maybe the operator didn't get to be the boss anymore.

"I guess I want her to know it's real. With me going all in, asking her to marry me. Saying vows I know I mean. I want to make it a big deal."

A smile slipped up his father's face. "Then I guess you'll need a ring."

His eyes widened.

"Your mother would want you to have her ring, Range."

"What about Dodge?"

"He wants his own ring for Echo—in fact, I think he's having one designed. But I think your mother's ring would be perfect for Noemi."

Ranger looked away, out the picture window, eyes burning.

"Go take a shower, son. You can't ask a woman to marry you, again, smelling like that."

He looked back to his father, now holding out a fresh cup of coffee, stolen from the early drips. "Love is the one thing that can change everything, Range. Don't be afraid of it."

He took the cup. "Thanks, Dad."

He went upstairs, showered and shaved, and was toweling off his head when he heard voices downstairs.

Dodge and Colt, now up, getting coffee. Colt's words hung in his head. *"Chef Ranger."*

He'd had a sort of idea somewhere around three a.m. about opening up the cabins, maybe turning the place into a real resort, with a working kitchen. Or maybe he'd just hang around and make sure everything stayed in working order.

He dug out a clean pair of jeans and a flannel shirt and was buttoning it as he came downstairs.

Flo was at the stove, cracking eggs into the cast-iron skillet. She wore her hair up, a sweatshirt and jeans.

"Hey, Flo. Is Noemi at the cabin?"

She turned and something on her face made him still.

And then a cold thread wrapped around him as she drew in a breath and shook her head.

Colt put down his coffee.

Dodge got up.

Ranger took a step toward her. "Um . . ." He looked at his brothers. "Is she here?"

"I haven't seen her," Colt said.

Ranger went to the entry and pulled on his boots.

"Range?" Dodge said. "You okay?"

Maybe he was panicking, his stupid emotions overrunning him—

He sprinted down to the cabin. Slammed open the door.

"Noemi!"

The doors to the bedrooms were open.

Empty.

What the—

He sprinted back out of the cabin, up the hill, slowing as his insides started to burn. Okay, calm down. Just *calm down.*

Maybe she went for a walk around the property.

He jogged over to the barn to grab a four-wheeler.

Stopped.

The Sky King truck—the one she'd driven home last night from Copper Mountain—was gone.

Because, of course, she'd walked out of his life again.

She knew it.

Absolutely knew it.

Noemi wiped the moisture from her cheek as she turned the Kingston's truck down the road toward town. It wasn't like Ranger's words were unexpected. *"Maybe we're moving too fast. I sort of let my emotions get ahold of me last night and . . . maybe my focus needs to be on keeping her safe instead of . . ."*

"Kissing her?"

She wanted to die on the spot.

Maybe it was her fault for walking up to the barn after hearing the tractor start up. Her fault for waking with the terrible, delicious hope that Ranger had meant his words—*"I want to do this right, Noemi. Because I'm only getting married once."*

But this. This was the truth. *"She is distracting."*

She'd turned around then, but not soon enough to miss his father's question. *"Do you love her? Or do you just want to take her to bed?"*

And then the silence that followed.

Run, just *run*.

The cabin had been empty, but she didn't expect a meaningful conversation with Flo as she packed.

Frankly, she felt for Flo. The woman had her own collection of nightmares and demons the way she was up, pacing the floor for the better part of the night while Noemi stared at the ceiling of her own bedroom.

They were a great pair of tattered souls.

At least she'd finally gotten the truth between her and Ranger. No games, no pretending.

She was a duty. A problem. A burden.

And so what if they had sparks? In the end, it wouldn't be enough.

She wouldn't be enough.

So she'd packed a bag with the meager clothing from Echo. She'd get to Copper Mountain and see if she could hitch a ride to Anchorage. It seemed yesterday that there were plenty of tourists there heading south.

And from there, she'd connect with her bank in San Diego, get some funds wired, and be, well, gone.

Vanish. And maybe this entire nightmare would vanish with it.

She headed south, along the highway, backward along the route she'd taken home yesterday. She'd leave the truck at the airport, hike back into town—no harm, no foul.

Overhead the sky arched a light, airy blue, the forest lush and deep green, the piney scent rich in the air.

Ranger's voice threaded into her thoughts. *"I'd better go before I decide to come inside."*

Good thing she hadn't woken up in his arms, because he was right.

She didn't want to wake up with regrets.

She turned east and crossed the river, then headed north again on the highway to Copper Mountain.

A girl could get lost up here, in the woods, and maybe Ranger was right about being safe. It wasn't like Abu or his men would follow her to America.

But his words about the Russian—Petrov—had stuck to her. Because it had irked her that Abu hadn't even tried to ransom them. Maybe he'd been waiting for them to show signs of infection, like Ranger had suggested.

Or sell them, like Colt had said.

But her thoughts returned to a conversation Fraser had with Moses, about the terrorist group moving them north.

How far north?

Siberia north? But she thought Russia was working with Nigeria to help fight the Boko Haram. Except what if they weren't . . . what if they were using the Boko Haram to test a virus that could kill the world?

Naw, it sounded like a Brad Thor novel, and now her imagination was getting ahead of her.

She passed a small float-plane hub, a number of tucked away neighborhoods, the lodge and cabins that Dodge had pointed out on their flight over. And finally the WELCOME TO COPPER MOUNTAIN sign, a piece of wood jutting from a pile of rocks. Someone with a sense of humor had added WELCOME TO YOUR LAST STOP above it.

She wished.

She bypassed Main Street, with the tug of the Tenderfoot Coffee and Bakery smells lifting into the air, and headed for the small airstrip just down the road.

She'd hike into town, like yesterday, maybe stop in at the bakery, or even the Midnight Sun Saloon, and see if she could find a ride south.

Her father would murder her, but she could take care of herself.

Really.

She pulled into the parking lot, debated parking the truck in the hangar, but the chain-link gate was locked on either side of the small reception building. Beyond it, the planes were lined up—red, yellow, green—and she spotted the Sky King Ranch hangar with its bold lettering.

Just yesterday, Range had taken her hand and held on like he might never let her go.

She hid the keys in the glove compartment where they'd been the day before. Then she retrieved her meager bag from the seat and shut the door.

A van had pulled up beside her.

Oh, she felt like a vagabond, in borrowed clothing, with nothing to her name.

Not unlike how she'd escaped the Boko Haram.

Weirdly, since then, she'd been rescued, fed, clothed, celebrated, married—elaborately, at that—then torn from her family, cast to sea, rescued again, relocated to Alaska, and again clothed. Given another taste of family.

She set out across the parking lot.

"God very much notices you."

Ranger's voice, unwelcome in her head. And then hers, in anger. *"I have to look out for myself because no one else will."*

Maybe—

The blow hit her on the back of her head, knocking her to her knees. She caught herself on her hands, but the second blow pushed her to the dirt.

The world turned to dots even as she screamed.

Then hands, yanking her up, around her waist as someone dragged her across the parking lot.

Her head—it spun, even as she thrashed, screaming. But her screams reverberated against her skull, her fighting futile.

She landed on the grimy, metal floor of the van. "No!" A knee slammed into her back and suddenly hands wrenched hers behind her back. She twisted, got an elbow out, a knee up.

Caught a glimpse of her attacker. A man, he wore a grimy brown jacket, a hat, a dark thick beard. He shouted at her. "Perestan!"

What—?

Then he hit her, a blow across her chin that turned her world to slurry.

She tried—and failed—to fight him as he zip-tied her hands behind her back.

He left her there, the side door shutting with a bone-jarring slam.

She faded in and out as the van jostled, driving her away, the road noise turning from highway to gravel. And then, the ping of dirt against the van windows.

It felt like her brains were banging to get out, and her wrists burned.

But her father was in her head.

"Survive. Move your hands to the front. Widen your shoulders, then your elbows." She climbed to her knees, ignoring the thunder in her head, and worked her arms down, desperation more than muscle memory. But that too kicked in and, in a moment, she sat on her backside and pulled her feet through.

"Now, break the zip tie."

She moved the locking bar of the zip tie to the top, between her wrists.

The van turned and she rolled onto her side, slamming against the side.

They'd gone off road.

"Ignore the pain. Focus."

Funny. Now Ranger was in her head.

She put her wrists together, then pushed herself up, back on her knees.

The van was slowing.

She had to be fast. With her teeth, Noemi pulled on the length of zip tie to tighten it down—the tighter it was, the easier to rip.

"Lift your arms up, pull down fast and hard, pulling your shoulder blades together, your hands apart."

Her father again. She took a breath as the van stopped.

Then she jerked down hard.

The zip tie held.

What—?

The front door opened, closed. Footsteps to the passenger side.

"God very much notices you."

She hoped he noticed her in the back of this van, somewhere in the bush, trying to stay alive.

Please!

She jerked hard, again, putting everything she had into the force.

The ties ripped.

The door opened. She rolled onto her back and sent her feet into the chest of her abductor.

He jerked backward. Tripped.

Went down, as if a hand had pushed him to the ground.

Noemi slid out of the van, her feet already moving.

A curse followed her, and the world threatened to tilt, but she refused to let it trip her.

Focus. A narrow, rutted path cut through the forest.

She veered off it, straight into the thick dark woods.

Now, *evade*.

SIXTEEN

Breathe. Just breathe. Drive faster!

Ranger wanted to shout the words at his brother, who was driving like a ninety-year-old granny.

No, a granny would be going faster.

He exhaled hard and long.

Dodge glanced over at him. "We'll find her, bro."

Ranger looked out the window.

See, this was what stupid emotions did. Got a guy all knotted up inside with the what-ifs.

Noemi was fine. Just. *Fine*.

Not kidnapped by terrorists, fighting for her life.

Not picked up by a couple rabble-rousing wannabe hikers who saw how beautiful she was and—

Stop.

She was probably just at the bank, trying to wire money to herself, and now he felt sick. He hadn't even thought about the fact that she was without cash, and how that might make her feel, and . . .

"Dude. You're going to feel like an idiot when she's at the grocery store, or buying herself some clothes."

"She *took* her clothes. Flo checked."

Flo had definitely looked rattled too, which hadn't helped. As if she knew something.

He'd figure that out later. Right now, he just wanted one answer.

Why?

Because he'd stood outside her cabin and practically ripped

his heart out of his body and handed it to her. *"But, I need to know . . . do you want to be married to me?"*

"*Yes.*" She'd said yes. And then he'd done the noble, right thing, the thing that took all the strength in his body, and he'd walked away from her.

He blew out another breath.

Dodge turned on the defroster. "The windows are starting to fog." They'd turned east, over the bridge, the river high and foamy and dark with the runoff of the mountains.

Ranger looked at his brother. "I can't figure it out, okay? Why she walked away. I told her that she was a big deal. That I got it that—"

"Did you tell her that you loved her?"

"Can't she figure that out?"

Dodge shook his head. "Maybe it's not a matter of her figuring it out as much as you confessing it."

Ranger's jaw tightened.

"Confessing it makes it real. And real means you have to reckon with it. Stop dodging around this marriage for duty's sake and get to the heart of the fact that you married her because you wanted to. And maybe your head didn't, but your heart did. And hello, maybe you're exactly where you are supposed to be, despite your hardheaded, super-duper focused self. Maybe God used your issues to give you exactly what you wanted."

Ranger frowned at him.

"Yes, I'm talking about myself. I came home, thinking I was getting Dad out of a jam, when really, what I wanted was to come home. To be with Echo. To reclaim the life I had run from. And God used my stupid pride to get me here.

"So get over yourself and tell the woman you love her, already."

"If she isn't already halfway to Anchorage."

"And so what if she is—find her."

"I will find you." His words to her, long ago, rattled through him.

Yes.

"So, why do you think she left?" Dodge jerked the wheel to avoid a rut in the road.

"I don't know. Maybe she got scared. The pictures online freaked us all out, and Colt's rundown of the Russian mafia didn't help."

"You think this Petrov group is really a threat?" Dodge asked.

"I think that after what Noemi went through, anything is a threat. I don't blame her. Like Colt said, she stood up to terrorists every day, and I haven't even thought about how triggered she might be. I should have never let her sleep alone."

Dodge raised an eyebrow.

Ranger let out another sigh. "I just mean that I shouldn't have left her alone."

Dodge nodded, his smile tight.

"Just drive faster."

They neared town, passing the school, and then Dodge took a right and pulled into the train station. "It's worth a check."

Probably.

They parked and went in, but the morning train to Anchorage hadn't yet left, and Noemi wasn't sitting on any of the benches on the platform, inside or out.

So, no train.

"Let's see if anyone in town has seen her before we assume she's hitchhiking."

Oh, if she had hitchhiked, hopefully the ghost of Master Chief Sutton would reach out of heaven to haunt her, long enough for Ranger to find her and wring her pretty neck.

Calm down. He glanced out the window. *Please, God.*

Dodge pulled up to the Midnight Sun Saloon. It was still closed, but a few cars were parked in front of the Tenderfoot bakery, and a small crowd of hikers stood outside Bowie Mountain Gear.

"Let's split up," said Dodge. "You head over to the outfitters, see if they saw anyone hitching this morning. I'll go into Tenderfoot."

Ranger headed over to Bowie Outfitters, the name on the door not bypassing him. So Mal and Hud were expanding. Well, good for them. They needed a break after the terrible deaths of their parents.

A number of hikers sat on benches, more leaned against the railing. "Hey," Ranger said. A woman with long blond hair stood next to a man with a familiar face. "Orion?"

"Ranger?" Orion Starr was a longtime local, former Para Jumper. Brown hair, solid build. He'd had his knee replaced after an injury in Afghanistan but before that had spent his summers climbing Denali, last Ranger knew. He lived not far from Sky King Ranch. He wore a light jacket, Gore-Tex pants, and hiking boots. "What are you doing in town? Escape from the Teams?"

Ranger shook his hand. "Something like that."

Orion laughed. "Don't let my buddy Ham hear that. He's constantly recruiting for his Jones, Inc. outfit. You'd be a great fit."

Range stared at him. "Hamilton Jones? I was just with him in Nigeria."

"Oh. Wow. I heard he'd just gotten back, but we haven't debriefed yet. Jenny and I are taking the long way around from our honeymoon." He gestured to the woman next to him. "Jenny, this is Ranger Kingston—we sort of grew up together. His family runs a bush service in the area."

"And an SAR service—Dodge joined up with Air One out of Anchorage."

"Cool."

"Hey—actually, I'm looking for someone." Ranger looked

around the group. "Her name is Noemi. She has dark skin, brown hair and eyes, about five three."

"Haven't seen her," Orion said. "She in trouble?"

"I don't know." He made a face. "I hope not."

Orion glanced at his wife. "Jenny and I are outfitting for a day trip down the river, but we're here if you need help."

"Ranger!" Dodge came running over, up to the deck. "I just saw Deke and he says he got a call from the airport—the Sky King truck is there. Hey . . . Orion?"

"Hey, Dodge," Orion said and held out his hand.

"Later," Ranger said, pulling Dodge away. They jogged to Dodge's truck and Ranger slid into the passenger seat.

Dodge pulled away from the curb.

Deke leaned against his cruiser, his hands in his pockets, waiting for them when they arrived at the airport, and Ranger's hope that Noemi might be with him died as Deke motioned them over to where he stood in the middle of the lot.

Ranger slid out, the truck still running. "What did you find?"

"The truck is fine, but when Sylvie came in, she found this pile of clothing in the lot. She thought it was weird, so she called us. But in the pile was this." He pulled out a Copper Mountain Grizzlies hockey jersey. "Isn't this your number, Range?"

A fist closed over his chest. "Yes."

"Your friend Noemi was wearing it yesterday, right?"

He nodded. Oh . . . he bent over, put his hands on his knees.

"You okay?"

He put his hand out. "Just . . . stay back." Shoot. And this is why he shouldn't let someone this far into his life.

Master Chief Sutton knew exactly what he was talking about.

Ranger stood up. Looked at Deke. "Does the airport have security footage?"

"Let's find out," Deke said.

Ten minutes later, they were huddled over a computer in

the back office, Sylvie at the helm, pulling up this morning's cameras.

"We have a shot of the gate, but it doesn't show the parking lot," she said. Indeed, the camera angle only caught the entrance, not the entire lot, but it did capture the Sky King Ranch truck as it pulled in, and then out of the frame to park in the lot.

Ranger wanted to back it up, see Noemi's face.

See if he could somehow read her mind.

"Look at this," Sylvie said.

On its heels a white van pulled in, turned to follow the truck into the lot.

Ranger's heart pounded. "Can you back it up?"

Sylvia, midthirties, her black hair in a ponytail, backed up the video.

"You recognize that guy at the wheel?" Deke asked.

Ranger peered at him. He wore a gimme cap, his face hooded, but something— "Is that a gold front tooth?"

"That's the Russian poacher who was with Idaho," Dodge said. "He got away when we were attacked by the grizzly."

Ranger shot him a look that said, *You were attacked by a grizzly?*

Deke leaned in. "Can you get a license plate on that, Sylvie?"

She zoomed in, and the capture was fuzzy, but enough to read the plate.

Deke stepped away to call in a record search.

"You think this Russian guy took Noemi? Why?" Ranger asked.

Dodge stepped back, ran a hand over his mouth, as if considering. "I don't know. But it's strange, right, that he'd be hanging around here? If that was even him."

Deke returned. "The van is registered to Rolly Brown. He's got a place off Montana Creek, south of here about forty miles."

Ranger glanced at Dodge. "You go home. Stay by the radio. I'm riding with Deke."

"We'll find her, bro," Dodge said.

Ranger nodded, hot on Deke's tail.

Thank heavens, Deke drove with a fire behind him. They took the highway south, turning east on Yoder while Dodge headed west, back over the river.

They passed a couple resort rentals, then a massive mining area—reminding Ranger of Remington Mines to the west—and then the forest closed in. Here, fewer homesteads carved out the wilderness, the mighty Montana River cutting southward. They crossed the river over an old bridge, and the wildness turned mountainous, with ridges and foothills thick with pine and birch and spruce.

"I haven't seen Rolly in town at all," Deke said, his hands white on the wheel. "I should have figured out something was wrong." He looked at Ranger. "He's a homesteader. A real sourdough, but I should have thought to check on him."

"You think this other guy did something to him?"

"He has his van."

Right.

The road turned from gravel to dirt, and dust and rocks flew up and pinged against the windows. It began to narrow, and even the dirt turned grassy as they turned off again and slowed, winding into the woods.

A darkness settled over the car as they crept deeper, the forest heavily shadowed.

Deke slowed as the house came into view.

And beside it, the white van.

At first glance the log cabin looked abandoned. The structure had settled into the ground, the thick logs off-kilter, the only window boarded up. Snowshoes leaned against the wall near the door. A muddy stoop, however, suggested recent habitancy, and the smell of smoke still hung in the air.

They pulled up.

"Stay here," Deke said.

Ranger just looked at him. "No. You stay here. Give me a gun."

"Can't do that."

"Fine. I don't need one." He got out, glanced around the area, but saw no one.

Still, he quick-walked to the van.

The door was open. He half crawled inside. A broken zip cuff lay on the floor. And in the shadows, something glistened. He touched his fingers to it.

Not grease. Blood. He smelled it. Still tinny. Fresh."There's a shallow grave over here," Deke said as he walked around the van. Ranger's heart nearly stopped. He turned, but Deke caught him. "It's not recent. It's packed down. It could be Rolly."

"There's blood in the van," Ranger said.

Deke headed for the cabin, Ranger behind him.

The place reeked of smoke, the rot of old food, and age. Deke cleared the room, then walked to the other side of the open space and lifted what looked like a backpack.

On the table was a sat phone. Ranger picked it up, turned it on. Static.

"Turn that off," Deke said. "Whoever is on the other end can track it."

"Perfect," Ranger said. He looked at Deke. "You might want to step outside." Because a quietness had settled inside him, the panic shoved into a dark, locked place.

Which only left a lethal stillness.

Deke considered him, and Ranger didn't care. He brought the sat phone to his mouth and toggled the switch. "*Prevyit Tovarish*. If you're listening to this, my suggestion is that you let her go. Because if I find you with her, then I promise you, you're dead."

Then he set down the sat phone and held his hand out. "Now I need your phone. I need to call my brothers."

"Range—my guys can handle this."

Ranger just gave him a look, something calm, serious, and focused.

Deke handed him the phone.

Dodge answered on the first ring. "Did you find her?"

"No." Ranger paced to the door, then stepped outside. "We're at Rolly's cabin. We found the van, but there's blood inside, so I think she's hurt. But she's not here and—" He saw it then—two sets of footprints in the mud. "I think she ran. But he's after her."

"She's in the wild?"

"If I were her, that's where I'd go. Lose myself in the bush. And she has her father's SERE training. She knows how to evade and hide."

"What do you need?"

His team. But maybe he had that. He kept walking down the drive, following the footprints. "You and Colt, here, now in the chopper. She can't have gone far—she's probably only been on the run for an hour, maybe two, but even at that, she can't cross the river, and—I found where she went into the forest." Broken branches, a deep footprint into the soil of the road.

"Chopper is fired up. What else do you need?"

"Bring a couple hunting rifles."

Silence. "Yep."

"And, Dodge, hurry."

"Already in the air, bro." He hung up.

Ranger stood at the edge of the forest, his gaze on the hole she'd made, the trampled loam. The urge to follow her nearly pushed him into the woods.

Breathe.

He had to wait for his brothers.

Or . . . He turned, saw Deke standing by his car, on the radio. "Stay here."

"Ranger—"

Ranger took off into the woods.

Noemi, stay alive. I'll find you.

Death was out there, Noemi knew it even as she squirreled herself under a decaying tree the girth of a bear that had crumpled to the forest floor. She'd dug a well into the mossy loam, a shadow melding with the forest.

Except she wasn't a shadow because she was breathing too hard, and probably she'd made a neon trail scrambling through the woods and into this hiding place.

She just needed a place to grab hold of her thoughts.

"Control the situation."

Yes, yes—thanks, Dad.

But maybe she needed the Master Chief in her head right now.

It was better than being alone.

She'd run a mile, at least, over the last hour, zigzagging through the forest, her line of travel dictated by the flow of land as she ran into gullies, followed deer paths and finally a tributary of water. Her entire body itched, thanks to the plunge through the icy river she'd crossed. Mud encased her Uggs, saturated her yoga pants, the heavy sweatshirt. She debated ditching it, but she might need it tonight when it got cold.

And wasn't that a lovely thought.

She ducked her head, the enormity of her situation casting over her.

Alone. In a massive forest rife with bears and wolves and one mad Russian man tracking her. And no one knew where she was. Because, *ahem*, she'd stolen a truck and run.

Because her stupid heart had gotten a little wounded.

She was smarter than this. This was exactly why she didn't let herself get involved. Care.

Fall in love.

"The problem is not going away. You're in shock, but you can't let panic control you. Evaluate the situation."

What, like her own stupidity in leaving Ranger? So what if she was a mission objective. Right now, she'd choose safety over love.

Ranger's duty over his heart.

A foot crunched in the woods beyond her enclave. She ducked again.

"I know you're out here," a voice said, thick with an accent. "I will find you."

She held her breath.

"Don't get up. Death comes from the inability to manage your fears."

Well, that was certainly true.

Her own voice burned through her. *"I'm trouble, and the fewer attachments I make, the fewer people get hurt."*

She'd certainly committed some self-sabotage there. The suicide of her heart.

She peeked up, over the log. Caught her breath.

The man stood just twenty feet away.

She eased back down, crouching.

"Understand your situation. Situational awareness can help you see answers that you might miss when you panic."

Like Ranger, his eyes on hers, thick with desire. *"I want to be with you in the worst way."*

"Situational awareness is understanding yourself in relationship to your environment. To see your threats and resources . . ."

Yes, this was her problem. She had no situational awareness when it came to Ranger Kingston.

She just had her rebellious heart.

Her pursuer was moving away, his feet crunching through the forest, fading.

Observe. Analyze. Decide.

"Execute."

She found her feet, crouched, then in a burst, took off in the opposite direction of the man. The trees slapped at her, their thick arms enclosing, then snapping as she ran through them. She trampled over mealy logs and thick pine needles, her breath harsh in her throat.

If she could get far enough away, she could hide for the night, then circle back to the van. If she could find it.

A bird startled, rushed through the canopy, scolding her, and she looked up—

Her foot landed in a well, her ankle twisting, and she crumpled, flying forward. She slammed into a tree, and pain exploded through her shoulder, down her entire body.

A scream ripped free before she could clamp it down.

No—*no!*

She lay there, breathing hard, listening.

No movement behind her, but who knew how far her scream had traveled.

Her ankle burned. She sat up, put her hands around it. It didn't feel broken—but when she tried to move it, she had to clamp down on another cry.

Perfect. Now she could just lay here like bait. She put her hands over her face, trying to hold back the rush of emotion.

Her father wouldn't be proud of her. Not when she'd let her fear win.

Fear had launched her out of her hiding place.

Fear ignited her run from Ranger, in Alaska. In Key West.

Fear had been at the helm nearly her entire life.

"Noemi, you are not too much trouble. Not for me. And especially not for God."

She closed her eyes against the voice, but it thundered through her.

"I will find you."

She opened her eyes, the voice like adrenaline inside her.

Ranger?

But the forest was silent.

"Hide. You are more at risk of detection during movement."

The Master Chief again.

She grabbed the tree and tried to pull herself up. Put weight on her ankle.

Okay, so maybe it wasn't broken.

But it still hurt.

She dropped to her hands and knees and started to crawl, hardly noticing the scrapes and cuts from the debris on the forest floor. Her surroundings were easier to see from here, below the tree limbs. She worked her way over a downed tree, sweating from the pain of her injured ankle, and in the distance heard water rushing.

Maybe she could find a cave near the edge, or a burrow. Something preferably uninhabited. Then she'd wait until night and find her way back to the van.

She dug in, found her feet, despite the pain, and limped toward the sound.

Behind her, the forest lit up with destruction, tree limbs breaking, the loam crunching and she turned, searching.

Froze.

"*Ya nashol tebe!*" The Russian man plowed through the forest straight for her.

She ignored the pain and took off running. She didn't care that she was screaming—let the world know she wasn't going down quietly.

Adrenaline brought her out into the light, to the edge of a brown, swollen river.

And that's where he brought her down. He tackled her, slamming her into the rocky shore. The river rushed in her ears, her head wound reopening, the world spinning.

"Resist."

She rolled, got a knee up between her and her attacker. "Get. Off. Me!" She brought her arms close and up between them, then exploded, kneeing the man in his soft parts, elbowing him across the chin.

He jerked away from her, cursing, stumbling away.

She scrambled to her knees.

His foot caught her in the stomach, and she flew across the beach.

She crumpled into a ball, her breath gone.

Help!

He pounced on her, grabbed her shirt, pulled her up.

His rank breath poured over her, his dark eyes raked her, and then he smiled.

Gold tooth.

She didn't know what it was about seeing that front gold tooth, but it simply stunned her, something so foreign and shocking and—

She slammed her fist right into it.

He jerked back, blood exploding on his face, his hand over his mouth.

Then his expression darkened.

His own fist came at her. She threw up her hands to protect herself, but the blow spun her. She landed in the rocks, the river just a few feet away, spitting at her.

"Escape!"

She hit her knees, scrambled for the river. "Help! Help!" She didn't know who she was asking—but maybe—*Please, God!*

He caught her hair, his fist tight in it, and she jerked back. Screamed again, her hand on his, holding her hair.

"Sooka!"

She jerked, kicked, slammed her elbows into him as he dragged her against himself. "Why? Why are you doing this?"

He laughed. *"Vas problema!"*

Yeah, well, she knew this. "Get used to it!" She brought her fist down, hard, between his legs. Target down.

He swore, jerked back, and she wrenched free.

And then, ankle fracture or no—she ran straight for the river.

SEVENTEEN

Ranger would recognize that scream anywhere.

He slowed from where he'd been following what he hoped were her tracks in the forest. He'd followed her at least a mile into the woods, pausing to search the river when he came to it. He'd found her footsteps—wide and flat from Larke's Uggs—and another set, deeper in the mud—on the other side, and right about then Dodge had called him on Deke's cell.

Dodge set down the Bell 429 chopper on a wide patch of shoreline—Colt sitting in the back, Echo in the side seat.

Colt opened the door of the chopper. He wore his warm clothes, boots, and a radio headphone earpiece secured behind his ear. And, he held a .300 Winchester Magnum across his knees, the scope on the top. He handed out another radio, with the earpiece, to Ranger, along with a .357 Taurus handgun.

A bear gun. Well, at least it was something.

Ranger stepped back, away from the rotors, and secured the earpiece.

Dodge's voice came through, and he confirmed.

Then, "A quick visual says you're in a canyon," Dodge said. "There's a ridgeline running northeast of here, and a bigger river—the north fork of the Montana River. It's pretty swollen right now, so it's a natural barrier. It heads southwest, so there's a corridor here, Range."

"Can you get Colt high enough to do some recon?"

Colt wore a dark cap and matching dark jacket. He was nodding. "I saw a pretty good ridge overlooking the river. You get me near that, and I'll have a good view to the river."

"I'm following a trail. She's headed north, but someone is after her. How's your aim, bro?" Ranger asked.

"I got ya," Colt said and shut the door. The chopper rose over the tree line.

He headed back into the woods, watching, listening.

He refused to ask why. Because the answer would only gnaw through him. *"Did you tell her that you loved her?"*

He took off in a run.

"You married her because you wanted to."

Yes, yes he did.

"Maybe you're exactly where you are supposed to be."

Ranger let that sink into his bones even as he found a nest where she'd taken cover, hidden. He pressed his hand against the scraped moss, the trampled loam.

"I will find you."

He stood up, toggled the radio. "You see anything, Colt?"

"Just getting into position."

He imagined that Dodge had hovered over the ridge to let Colt jump off.

But for the first time ever, he was glad he was boots on the ground, the tip of the sword.

He wanted his hands on this guy.

And, he wanted answers.

"I'll keep scanning the woods," Dodge said on top of Colt's words.

He confirmed, then set off, following the footprints—she'd taken off at a run. He picked up his pace—

The scream ripped through him, shredding the quiet of the forest.

Noemi!

It sounded like a scream of pain, shock maybe, rather than fear. It didn't matter. He started to run, pinpointing the sound.

Hang on. The trail was easy—so many broken limbs, crushed, mealy logs, disturbed forest.

"Get over yourself and tell the woman you love her, already."

Yes, fine, as soon as—

He stilled as he saw the scuffed tree, a swipe of blood against the trunk. His heart caught in his throat.

Another scream lifted. It galvanized him, pushed her name to his throat.

He bit it back even as he ran.

Noemi. Hang on—

"Help!"

The sound of it splintered through him.

"Help!"

He burst out of the forest onto a rocky shoreline. And up the river—oh no—a man was scrabbling after the woman he loved, who was making hard for the river.

The swollen, chaotic, lethal river.

"Stop!" But he was still fifty yards away when the man tackled her.

She rolled over, kicking at the man, but he was pushing her into the river, his hands on her throat.

She hit his back, kicking, her screams silenced.

They fell into the rapids together and just like that, the river took them.

"No!"

He arrowed for the river and charged in.

Ice. The glacial chill speared him, and it caught his breath. Focus.

He braced himself on a rock, and yes—there. Still fighting her assailant, her fists slamming against his face—way to go, Storm—

The two banged against rocks as they tumbled toward him and Ranger braced himself against a boulder.

He launched himself at her attacker. His arm caught the man

around the neck, his fist in his kidney. The man reeled back, and the shock of Ranger's attack released his hold on Noemi. She broke free.

Ranger lost her in the clutter of foam and spray and chaos.

Especially when the Russian slammed his elbow into Ranger's face. The world exploded into darkness, but he held on. The river took them, twisting them.

Ranger crashed into a boulder, the blow sending a shock up his spine. The man wrenched free but held his arm and turned.

A rock was fisted in his hand, and Ranger barely got an arm up to deflect it. Even so, the blow landed on his wound, still healing, and the pain slashed through him.

He grunted, holding in a howl. The man snarled—his lip broken, bleeding—and headbutted him.

Ranger's head snapped back, and it hit against the boulder.

The world spun.

Hands closed around his neck, pushing him down, into the water. He managed a breath, but the grip tightened.

Ranger punched up, connected with a gut. The man's hands refused to loosen.

C'mon!

He punched again, but it felt flimsy, and the river grabbed them up again.

They were spinning, slamming against more boulders, still the man's hands on him.

His lungs burned. Mind over matter. He had plenty of air in reserve.

Calm down.

Focus.

He worked his thumbs into the man's wrists, finding the pressure points. And squeezed.

The hold broke, and Ranger surged up, his open palm landing on the man's chin.

He broke the surface and gulped in air. Saw the man's fist barrelling toward his face and again threw up his arm.

But it wouldn't work. Slow, broken, his wound had turned his reactions slushy.

The blow rang his bell, turned him around.

The man leaped on him.

But Ranger's feet touched the bottom, and he scrambled for shore, his attacker on his back.

He shot up an elbow, but it missed.

Again, the grip on his neck, and now it pushed him down, into the water.

He couldn't get up. The man lay on him, refusing to dislodge.

He was going to die. Right here in a dirty river, in three feet of water—

The grip on his neck jerked, and in a second, he was freed. He pushed up, breathing hard, turned.

Noemi stood in the water, holding a branch like a bat. "Get up!"

Right.

But the sight of her standing over him, her shirt bloody, her golden-brown eyes on fire, her dark hair in a spiral halo around her head, looking at him with such ferocity—it simply blew up his heart.

Wow, he loved this woman.

"Now, Ranger!"

He scrabbled toward her, clutching his arm to his body. Shoot, he might have dislocated his shoulder. He'd just about reached her when she screamed.

He turned, but this time the Russian man ran past him and dove at Noemi.

Tackled her into the rocky shoreline.

"Oh no you don't!" He hit his feet, but not before the man grabbed her up and pulled her against himself. And from somewhere on his body, he'd pulled out a knife. Not a big one—

maybe a six-inch hunting knife—but one long enough to spear her carotid artery. He held it up to her neck, right below her ear.

Shoot—Ranger should have gotten his hands on that.

But it hit him then. This man wasn't just a poacher.

He knew how to kill.

"Stop! Or I cut her."

Noemi had her hand around his wrist, her jaw tight.

"Stop!" Ranger held up his hands. "Please."

The man stood there. "Kneel."

Ranger knelt. "Please don't hurt her—"

"We will do what we want with her."

We?

"Lie down."

Ranger didn't move. Around him, the river roared, the wind brushed through the trees.

"Down!" The man jerked Noemi, and she grunted, but her eyes were peeled on Ranger.

Obey everything. He willed the words to her in his stare.

She swallowed. Nodded.

The man took a step toward him, his grip firm on Noemi as he shifted her to his side. Ranger saw the kick coming.

Gut reaction. He ducked, let it pass over him, then rolled. "Now!"

His shoulder about exploded, but he ignored it, came up beside the man and sent his fist into the side of his head.

Noemi broke free.

The Russian took the blow, but held on to the knife, whirled, then swept Ranger's feet from under him.

He slammed into the ground.

The man landed on top of Ranger.

Ranger barely caught the blade before the knife tipped into his chest. The blade sliced into his hand, the blood turning his grip slick.

Noemi screamed, and dove onto the Russian's back.

He slammed his elbow into her face, coldcocking her.

She fell off and Ranger grabbed the man's wrist. The man bore all his weight down on the knife, the blade precariously near home.

Ranger had no arm strength.

No technique.

Just the very strong urge to survive.

No, to *live*.

He closed his eyes, putting everything he had into keeping the blade from finding his sternum.

"Duck."

The voice sounded in his ear.

He still had his earpiece.

"Hurry up!" he growled as he threw his head to the side.

The Russian's eyes widened.

And then, just like that, the shot blew the man away. An impossible shot, for anyone but Ranger.

Or Colt.

Maybe it ran in the genes.

The man jerked back, falling off Ranger, a head shot that made him wince with the gore of it.

But he ignored it and scrambled over to Noemi.

She lay still on the rock. He reached for her, then realized his hand dripped blood.

He squeezed it into a fist, then worked his hand under her neck. "Noemi, honey . . . wake up." He leaned close, to check her breathing.

Her arms came around him, suddenly, abruptly, and pulled him against her. "Range. Please tell me you're okay."

He nodded, pushed himself up.

Tears ran from her eyes. "I thought I'd lost you. I thought—"

"I told you, Princess, I'm not going anywhere." He scanned her face. "And I'd really appreciate it if you wouldn't either."

Her breath caught, and then her mouth opened.

And, shoot, he just couldn't take the chance that something other than what he wanted could issue from her so, "I love you. I've loved you since that day in Key West when you burst into my life and . . . just . . . stop freaking me out, okay?"

She just blinked at him. "I . . . I just keep getting you in trouble."

"Yeah well. I'm a SEAL. I live for trouble."

Then he bent down, and as the chopper hovered above them, thundering in its approach, he kissed her.

As the world shuddered around him, it sounded very much like the unleashing of his heart.

"I feel like we're right back where we started." Ranger sat on the ER table, his hand on a tray while a doc stitched up the terrible gash on his palm.

Noemi lay on the opposite bed, her newly shaved head propped up on her hands as another doctor tended to her wounds.

He grinned at her.

She couldn't smile. Not yet.

Not when she'd nearly cost him his life.

Wow.

She'd left him. Twice now, and yet, he'd still shown up. Still nearly died for her.

And . . . said he loved her.

Her eyes filled. "Why did you come after me? You nearly died, again!"

"Hey," he said, but he couldn't reach out to her. Not with his other shoulder in a sling. Because of course he'd dislocated it trying to keep her alive.

She closed her eyes.

"Look at me."

She opened them.

"I told you. Till death do us part."

Oh, *Ranger—*

People invaded the ER, first Dodge, then Colt and Echo, and finally Flo and Barry, who had probably driven to the Copper Mountain clinic after Dodge had picked the two up in the chopper.

"You okay?" Echo said and came over to Noemi. She wrapped her hand into hers. "We were so worried."

Shoot, and now her eyes really burned.

"Hey . . . what's going on?" Dodge said, following Echo into the room.

"She got hit in the head," Ranger said, "so now she's thinking that this is all her fault."

Noemi stared at him. "It is! If I hadn't left—"

"Yeah, well, if I hadn't *let* you leave—"

"You're not the boss of me."

"Everything. Obey *everything*. You agreed."

Her eyes widened. "Oh, you really think you're something, don't you, sailor."

He laughed. "There we go."

"All done," said the doc behind her. "Just a few stitches, but head wounds bleed like crazy." He snapped off his gloves and walked around the table. "I'd really like to get a CT."

"I'm fine," Noemi said and sat up. But whoops, the world shifted.

"Right. Okay," the doc said. "I'm ordering a CT and a night in the hospital for observation. And ice for that ankle. It's not broken, but it's swollen."

"C'mon, doc, give a girl a break."

Ranger's doctor also finished stitching him up. She wrapped a gauze bandage around his hand. "You could use an night of observation too. Maybe also a CT."

"I'm fine. Really."

She gave him a tight-lipped look. "You all are a stubborn

lot. Okay, let me know if you have any headaches, and I want to see you back here in a week to check on those stitches. And keep some ice on the shoulder."

He nodded as the doctor left the room, then turned to Noemi.

"I'm not going anywhere," he said, meeting her eyes.

"Please, just take me home," she said quietly.

He stood up, walked over to her. "Sorry, babe. If the doc says you're staying, you're staying."

She put her hands on his chest. "Listen. You can run a concussion protocol on me. Stay with me all night. Wake me up once an hour."

He glanced at her doc, who nodded.

Ranger put his forehead to hers. "Mission accepted."

Oh boy.

Three hours later, however, with her head pounding, she just wanted to sleep. Instead, she sat in the family room of Sky King Ranch, freshly showered, in new clothes, with a blanket around her, her foot elevated, a bag of peas draped over her ankle, and Ranger beside her. She kept trying to fit together the puzzle pieces of the Kingston brothers' conversation.

Not just that, but how, really, they had survived.

The last thing she saw, the Russian man had a knife to Ranger's chest. Her last memory was being elbowed in the face.

And then, darkness.

Except, even as she sat there, the sense of it returned to her.

Not darkness. Folds of something soft caught her, and in that moment, she had felt nothing. No panic. No fear.

Just . . . calm.

As if she might be floating.

And then, *I will find you*.

Yes, the voice. Deep, resonant, not from beyond, but *inside* her.

It covered her like a blanket. More than that. It was water, warm water, bathing her. Washing her.

And she had floated.

Ranger's voice had yanked her back, out of the water and into the light. He'd knelt over her, his arm behind her, searching her face, so much in his beautiful aqua-blue eyes, she didn't need the words.

Embraced them anyway.

The voice stayed with her, even now. *I will find you*. Colt was telling the room how he'd heard Ranger fighting, how he'd frantically searched for him as Dodge spotted him in the riverbed. Then, the moment when he told Ranger to duck.

In the kitchen, Barry and Echo were making frozen pizza. Flo stood with her arms around her, near the window where the sun hung low and cast long bruised shadows into the room.

"I can't believe you trusted him not to miss," Echo said as she opened the oven door.

"Yeah, well, with Colt you just have to trust your gut," Ranger said. "Even if it's screaming in terror."

"Funny, man. Don't worry. I just sort of closed my eyes and shot in your general direction." Colt winked.

Ranger grinned.

"What I don't understand," Dodge said from where he stood next to the hearth, "is why they took Noemi in the first place. If this guy was the Russian we saw in the woods a month ago, what was he still doing here, and why did he want Noemi?"

He folded his arms. "How did he even know that she was here?"

Silence, and a chill brushed through Noemi. "Maybe I—"

"Don't even think about suggesting you should leave," Ranger said.

Her mouth opened, and then closed. "He called me a problem."

"Yeah, well, you're not, so—"

"What if she is?"

Ranger looked at Dodge and Noemi put a hand on his arm.

Dodge held up a hand. "No, I mean—what if she's a problem

to the Russians? To Petrov? Why would he say that?" He looked at her. "Have you ever seen him before?"

"No. Trust me, I'd remember the gold tooth."

Dodge nodded.

"He said a lot of things in Russian, actually. I only caught a few of them."

"How did you learn Russian?" Colt asked.

"Oh, I don't know much. My dad had a friend from Russia. I only met him once—when we were overseas for a holiday. We were in Germany, and he came to meet my father. I remember him—Boris, I think. He was a nice man. Had a daughter a little older than me. I remember jumping on an in-ground trampoline together. She spoke Russian too, of course. Anyway, I picked up some words."

One that she wouldn't mention because he'd called her a name.

"You think he was this Petrov guy?" Ranger said

She looked at him. "A Russian gangster? I doubt it."

"Calm down. I'm not accusing your dad of anything. I'm just trying to figure out what they'd want with you. And I have a hard time believing it's because you took a few photos."

She stared at him. "Then why?" She leaned away from Ranger's warmth, rubbing her arms. "I wish he was here. He wasn't around much, but when he was, he always had the right words." She looked out the window, at the glaze of twilight across the vast plain. "He used to take me camping in Montana, at President White's ranch, if you can believe it. They were friends—"

"Your dad was friends with President White?" Colt said.

"Yeah. He even came to his funeral. It was before the election. I remember thinking how kind it was that he was there."

A beat passed. Then Colt said to Ranger, "How did you know we were taken?"

Ranger frowned. "Your buddy Ham called me. Said you guys hadn't checked in."

Colt shook his head. "We didn't have regular check-ins. There was no reason for Ham to expect—or not expect—our call."

"Then how did Ham find out?"

Colt slid off the stool and walked into the office.

The room turned quiet.

"Pizza anyone?" Echo took the pans out of the oven. Slid them onto a couple hot pads, then ran the cutter over them.

Dodge headed to the counter.

Ranger walked over to Noemi. He'd showered, too, and the smell of him swept over her. *"You can run a concussion protocol on me."*

"My dad was a good man. If it weren't for him teaching me survival skills . . ." She lifted her hand, wiped her cheek.

Ranger touched her face. "Of course he was. And he might have taught you skills, but it was you today, Storm."

She shook her head and put her hands on his chest. "No, Range. It was . . . it wasn't me. It was . . ." Her mouth tightened, and she swallowed. "Well, maybe I listened to you about asking for help."

He raised an eyebrow.

"Don't get excited. I'm just saying that maybe God noticed me."

Ranger ran a thumb down her cheek. "You're very hard to miss."

She smiled. "The thing is, when you showed up today, it was like . . . well, maybe I need to start noticing God too."

"Maybe you should also notice that you belong here if you want to. With this family. At Sky King Ranch. With me." He touched his forehead to hers.

She winced.

"Head still hurt?"

"A little."

"Maybe we should start that concussion protocol."

"I think that means sleep."

"And me, waking you up." His voice turned soft when he said it. Then he leaned down and kissed her neck.

"Hey!" Dodge said from across the room. "Nigerian weddings count!"

Ranger stood up, shot his brother a look, then back to her. "What he said." He put his good arm around her. "I'd sweep you in my arms and carry you up the stairs, but . . ." He nodded to his slung arm.

"Excuses, excuses. Well, don't get excited. Nothing is going to happen here, sailor."

"And see, it already starts. You have a *headache*."

She laughed, then winced. "Stop it."

He helped her up the stairs.

"You guys want pizza?" Echo shouted up after them.

"Leave them alone, E," Dodge said. "They're newlyweds."

Noemi smiled, fighting a laugh.

But Ranger didn't, and even followed her to Larke's room.

Oh.

He closed the door behind him.

She turned, and his gaze fell on her, thick with emotion—and something that she saw before, an ocean away.

"Range—"

"I have something for you. Stay here."

He slipped out of the room, and she stood there, unable to move.

And for a long moment, she was back on the beach, the soft wind raking the sand, the moon drawing a line through a platinum ocean.

"I used to imagine, after I got out of the military, that I might move back. Maybe help my father turn the FBO into a sort of resort where people could escape. We have horses and cabins and . . . it's a great place to raise a family."

The door opened. He held in his hands the coral necklace,

the one he'd given her at the wedding. "Where did you—how?"

"It was in my backpack when we got stateside." He held out the necklace, his gaze searching hers. "Still want to be my wife?"

"Are you brave enough to be my husband?"

"I'm a—"

"SEAL, I know."

"No. I'm a Nigerian prince. Or did you forget I'm married to a princess? Besides, I bought you for a price. You're mine, Emuvoke."

She laughed. "Please, stop. It hurts."

"Okay." He settled the necklace over her. "You're still so breathtaking."

"With my head shaved, and—"

"You're beautiful." His eyes held hers. "I love you, Noemi. I might not have realized it then, but I meant everything I pledged to you that day. But I need to know—do you still want to be my wife? My real, forever wife?"

As she watched, he knelt down in front of her. And pulled out a ring. It was a simple diamond in a square setting, two rectangular diamonds on either side.

Her eyes widened. "Wait, are you—"

"If you'd just stop talking for a second."

She closed her mouth.

"Noemi Emuvoke Sutton. You drive me crazy."

Her mouth tightened.

"And I can't live without you. You are light to my world. My best reason for coming home, my biggest emotion, and my best chance at living happily ever after. You are the dream and the duty, and if you'll let me, I will love you with everything inside me for the rest of my life. Please. Please stay married to me."

She touched his handsome face. "You do know that the only easy day was yesterday, right?"

"I have that sense, yes."

"And you won't decide, someday, that you're tired of me. Or that I'm not enough for you?"

She couldn't believe that she'd said that, but . . .

He looked at her, a softness in his gaze. "You are way more than enough for me, Storm. I'm just trying to keep up."

She smiled then. Drew in a breath. "Then, yes. Of course, sailor. I'll stay married to you." Then she leaned down and kissed him, slowly, beautifully.

He stood up and pulled her against himself—as close as he could get with his wrecked arm. Then, as he deepened his kiss and let out a sound of desire that felt like he'd been holding it in for a very long time, she knew.

There would be no annulment.

Because Nigerian weddings counted.

EPILOGUE

Tae was overreacting.

Really.

Maybe always had been. Her panic had driven her to run. Had landed her in an Alaskan blizzard.

Maybe this wasn't about her at all.

She slid onto the stool at the island, Noemi's words cycling through her. *"He called me a problem."*

Maybe because the man who'd taken Noemi hadn't been a Petrov, hadn't been camped out in Alaska looking for her.

She had simply let Roy sit in her head for too long. *"It's up to you or we all die."*

Who was she? Just a researcher, really. Someone who'd experienced too little sunshine for too many years researching the biggest biological threats to the world.

Dreaming up conspiracy theories during her off time.

No wonder the man's words had gone to her head, stirred up her panic.

She was really just a woman who'd fallen for the wrong man.

Except . . .

"Pizza, Flo. I doctored it with extra cheese," Echo said and pushed the board with the pizza toward her.

She took a piece and reached for the red pepper flakes. See—she could still play this game. In fact, she'd managed not to wake in a puddle of hot sweat last night.

She was safe.

"Okay, hand over the red peppers nice and easy, and no one gets hurt," Dodge said.

What—?

Oh. She'd mounded a nice pile of red pepper flakes onto her cheese pizza. She picked up the piece and knocked off the pepper flakes.

"Here," Echo said and handed her a glass of milk. "Just in case."

Thanks. She almost said it. Almost easily, casually gave away her entire cover.

Undone weeks of hiding with one slipup.

She closed her mouth, smiled at Echo.

Barry was taking another pizza out of the oven.

"Do you think we should take up pizza for Range and Noemi?" Echo asked.

"I think the last thing they're thinking about is pizza," Dodge said and leaned down to kiss Echo on the forehead. "I'm a little jealous."

"Calm down there, Dodger. Our big day will be here soon."

"I'm open to eloping."

"My mother would kill you with her bare hands."

"Have you found a place to have the wedding, yet?" Barry asked, cutting the pizza. "You know you can use the lodge, right?"

"My mother wants something in town, but we'd like to keep it small. Family only," Echo said. She looked at Tae. "Family and friends."

Oh. Tae's chest thickened.

"Hey. Save some for me," Colt said as he came out of the office. He walked over to the counter and picked up a plate, and the memory of being enclosed in his arms last night swept through her. In truth, she might have developed a crush on the man. He was unbreakable, in spirit and body, it seemed. Funny. Lethally handsome with that dark brown hair, delicious brown eyes.

And his voice . . . she'd let it sit inside her and hold her as she drifted off to sleep last night. *"Don't worry. Whoever was after Noemi isn't going to find us here. You're safe."*

Safe.

Yes, she should just calm down and get that through her head.

"So," Colt said as he lifted a piece of pizza to his mouth. "I talked with Ham about how he knew we were taken. Apparently, he got a call from one of his contacts, a guy named Roy. He didn't say how Roy knew, but he was the one who alerted him to me and the others being grabbed."

Tae coughed, her pizza lodged in her throat. *Roy?* She reached for her milk.

"You okay, Flo?" Colt said.

"She piled enough red pepper on her pizza to power a small city," Dodge said.

Yes, that was it. She swallowed the piece, forced a smile, but . . .

Roy?

It had to be a coincidence.

"He did suggest that Roy might work for a certain international three-letter agency, however," Colt went on, "so you have to ask . . . why would the CIA be interested in a small group of terrorists—really, Flo, you okay?"

She'd pressed her hand over her mouth without thinking. Now, she looked at Colt, nodded.

But even after she removed it and smiled at him, he stared at her, then frowned.

She dug into her pizza again, her mouth turning to fire.

"Call me Roy. I'm here to help—"

She slid off the stool. What was Roy, a man she'd met on a

cruise to Alaska, doing involved with a kidnapping in Nigeria? And how did it involve a Russian poacher in Alaska?

Probably, Noemi had just been in the wrong place at the wrong time. And Roy—it was a common enough name. And so, probably, was Petrov.

She headed for the door, however, her feet under their own power.

She hadn't a clue what she was doing, but instincts said she couldn't stay.

"Hey!"

She turned, and oh no.

Colt had come out of the house after her. He had recuperated enough—and probably his spectacular save of his brother earlier today had helped—for him to move like a warrior. He stalked toward her.

She stilled, the urge to bolt defeated by his brown eyes pinning her.

"What's going on?"

Nope. Not staying. She whirled, but he caught her arm, turned her back around. Held her with both hands, his dark gaze. "Flo . . . I know you're hiding. Running, even, and I'm getting the feeling it has something to do with what happened today." He cocked his head.

She stared at him, the immensity of it all rushing over her, but it congealed into one solid thought.

What if he believed her? What if she wasn't alone anymore?

And what if Roy was right—it *was* up to her?

Or, they all died.

If anyone could help her save the world, it was Colt Kingston.

She took a breath.

Behind them, a car rolled into the driveway. She glanced over Colt's shoulder even as he turned.

A sheriff's cruiser. As she watched, a man got out.

"Deke," Colt said. He hadn't let her go completely, but now slid his hand down to hers and grabbed hold.

A man who could multitask.

The sheriff met them at the back stoop. "Hey. We pulled a cell phone off the body, and our tech guy was able to access the calls and pictures. He's still working through it, but . . . I thought you should see something." He reached into his jacket and pulled out a piece of paper.

Unfolded it. "We printed this from his text messages." He glanced at Tae as he handed the paper to Colt.

Colt released her hand. "What?" Then he glanced at her.

Oh, she didn't want to look, but—

She froze.

The top picture was easy—Noemi. Probably taken at the terrorist camp, she wore an abaya and hijab, but her face was perfectly outlined.

So, she *had* been targeted.

But it was the second picture that had her turning cold.

A woman sitting in a restaurant, smiling, laughing, nursing a cup of coffee. The picture was taken over the shoulder of her companion-slash-date. A Russian man named Sergei Petrov.

A woman Tae might not recognize today for her easy trust and innocent heart.

Colt's stare bit into her. "Flo? Is that you?"

She swallowed.

And then she turned toward her cabin, her heart slamming against her rib cage.

Run— Just. Keep. *Running*.

"Flo!" Footsteps behind her, but she didn't slow until she got to the cabin. What was she thinking? That he couldn't just break down the door?

He was faster than her, even in his weakened state.

She hit the porch the same time he did.

He slammed his hand on the door as she tried to open it. "Not a chance!"

She whirled around and slammed her hand into his chest. "Get away!"

He caught her arm at her wrist, then the other one as she swung that too. Trapped her hands against his chest and stared at her as they both breathed hard.

Then, quietly, but not gently, "Enough games, sweetheart. Spill."

WHAT COMES NEXT . . .

Colt was in worse shape than he thought.

One good look at himself in the mirror would have said that he probably shouldn't be climbing at seven thousand feet, where the air turned into a whisper in his lungs, where his heart had to work double time, and where every movement turned his muscles into a fist.

But the view. Oh, the view from atop Avalanche Spire, just south of Denali National Park could just about stop his heart anyway.

Colt scanned the area with his binoculars.

From the north, the massive Denali range rose, snowcapped and magnificent, its hulking mass thundering across the horizon. A blue-gray shadow fell upon the mountains below, sweeping down to the rich greens of a pine and fir forest, the deep blues of valley lakes set in pockets inside the rising peaks of the foothills.

Snow and ice still capped a number of low-lying peaks, glaciers running off the edge like frosting to drop into crystal clear moraine lakes. The air smelled of summer—wildflowers, fresh lakes. The sunlight hung on long into the day.

"I see the plane," he said, his gaze dropping to a small white-and-red-striped crumple of metal caught in one of those glaciers, about a half mile down from the cliff where they stood. "Right where you left it, Tae."

He lowered his glasses and shot a glance at Taylor—Tae—Price. She wore her blond hair in a singular braid, had on a pair of black Gore-Tex hiking pants, a warm jacket, and a wool hat against the still-crisp Denali wind.

Her mouth tightened at the edges. "It wasn't there when I left it."

Colt's brother Dodge had walked over, and now gestured for the glasses. Colt handed them over.

"Looks like the plane slid," he said. "I can see the trail where the melt carried it."

"They must have landed in the valley above, and the glacier melt carried it down the slope," Echo, Dodge's fiancée, said. She had put down her backpack and was taking a drink of water. Echo, her own hair in two golden-brown braids that stuck out of her knit hat, glanced at Tae.

They stood on a ridge just above where they'd put down the Piper Super Cub, searching for the downed plane. Even the chopper wouldn't have been able to put down closer to the wreck, so taking the plane gave them more search area reach to confirm, well, that Tae hadn't been lying.

Not that Colt thought she was outright lying, per se, but with the position of the plane, it seemed a little far-fetched that the story went down the way she'd told it. The one that included a kidnapping, her attempts to crash the plane, surviving not only a late-season blizzard but also the crash that supposedly killed the pilot and her kidnapper.

"I can't believe I survived either," Tae said, maybe realizing that no, none of it really added up. Still, here she stood, daring him *not* to believe her words even as he stared at the crumpled evidence. Dodge and Echo had found her in a gully nearly ten miles away, so maybe . . .

"We need to get to the plane," Tae said. "My backpack is

inside. It has my research and . . ." She looked at Colt, her pale blue eyes on him, a small glare headed his direction.

Fine. Whatever. He'd sort of thought there might be a little something between them over the past few weeks. She had, after all, sat by his bedside during those early days after his extraction from an op-gone-south in Africa. Heard his nightmares. And he'd witnessed one of her own.

But after he'd cornered her and forced the truth out of her two weeks ago, something had changed between them. The big chill.

He should have expected that, maybe. No one liked being interrogated.

"We'll have to traverse the glacier," Dodge said. "It looks pretty precarious." He glanced at Colt. "You sure you're up for this?"

Colt didn't want to bristle at his brother's question, but still, it burned through him. "Of course."

If it hadn't been for the beating Colt had suffered while being captured by a group of terrorists in Nigeria, he would have been out here two weeks ago. Right after local sheriff Deke Starr had turned up with the proof that someone *was* after Tae—someone meaning some Russian mafia group.

And now he sounded crazy, even to himself.

Clearly, he was desperate to put a little hero back into his reflection in the mirror. The one that stared back at him with reddened eyes and fading bruises. He didn't go to sleep every night without replaying that moment when the truck of jihadists pulled up in a small village and forced him and his fellow security officer to their knees. When, for the first time in years, he prayed that God hadn't completely abandoned him. Maybe, maybe not, because somehow most of them survived, including Noemi, his brother Ranger's wife, who had been an aid in Nigeria.

It didn't mean that God was actually looking out for Colt.

He attributed God's favor to Noemi, and Selah, the other humanitarian aid worker, and maybe even the doctor Colt had been tasked to protect. In his dreams, Colt shot first or threw his body in front of the good doc, taking his bullet. Thankfully, the doc had survived, but no thanks to Colt.

Which meant, bottom line, he'd failed.

Sometimes, before Colt dropped off into his sweaty nightmares, he backed all the way up to the moment they'd found the dead bodies of the villagers in the church. In that moment, he listened to his gut instincts that said, *Run*.

Instincts he'd honed during his years as a Delta Force operator. Except he wasn't that guy anymore. Wasn't even a security pro for Jones, Inc., at least not until he healed up from his broken bones and bruised insides.

Which meant he had plenty of time to focus on Tae and her crazy story about being chased by international terrorists all the way to his backyard in Alaska.

"While you were learning to fly, I was climbing and rappelling," Colt said now to Dodge. "And don't forget that one year I actually worked at the Denali Base Camp, coordinating Sky King Ranch flights."

"I remember," Dodge said as he pulled out crampons from his pack and hooked them to a carabiner. "Dad was afraid you were going to actually attach to one of the climbing crews and head up the mountain."

Colt also dug out his crampons and hooked them to the outside of his pack. The snow was soft, but it didn't mean it wasn't lethal. "I was seventeen. I wasn't allowed up."

"Since when do you follow the rules?" Dodge handed Echo the rope, one end already affixed to his harness. She clipped in.

Colt hiked up his own harness. "When it matters." He turned to Tae, who was struggling with her rig. "You could wait here . . ."

"I know how to climb. I used to climb the wall back at my

gym in Seattle." She stepped away from him when he reached to help. "Besides, I want to be there when you see that I'm telling the truth."

"I never said you weren't telling the truth." He glanced at Dodge, whose eyebrow rose.

"Really?" She rounded on Colt. "When I told you my story, you stared at me so long I thought maybe you were suffering from a hit on the head."

Yeah, well he was, a little. "It's just . . . the whole thing sounds like something out of a Brad Thor novel. You being kidnapped off your cruise ship by your boyfriend—"

"A Russian spy!"

"Right." He held up a hand. "A Russian spy named Sergei. Who then forced you on a plane to hijack you to some secret lab in Russia."

"I never said that." Her mouth tightened. "I said that I thought he might be taking me to Russia. And that's why I freaked out. Why I opened the door to the plane—"

"Because you were *trying* to crash."

"Wouldn't you?" She was tightening her harness. "Isn't that part of your oath as a soldier? Escape, survive—or something like that?"

"But you're not a soldier."

"My father was. And . . . well, I wasn't going to . . ."

And then she stopped. Again. Right where she always stopped—before she told him the *why* behind everything.

Secrets. Tae was full of them, and he wasn't going to let them get him, or his family, killed.

"See, you don't believe me again."

"What?"

"It's your face." She moved her open palm in a circle before him. "You think I'm crazy." She turned to Dodge. "Do you think I'm crazy? That I dreamed all this up?"

Dodge held up his hand. "I think we're wasting time."

Probably. Because although the sun was still high, Colt's chest was really starting to ache from the lack of oxygen.

He took the rope from Echo, tied a figure eight knot, and attached a carabiner to it. Turned to Tae. "It's not that I don't believe you. It's that you're not telling me everything, and I know it."

Her mouth tightened again, and he had been an interrogator long enough to know he'd hit on truth. "Do you know how to—"

"Yes." She took the carabiner from him and attached it. Met his eyes. "You'll see. We'll get down to that plane and you'll find two dead bodies. And then I'll get my backpack and prove that it's all true. I'm not crazy."

"For the last time, I never called you crazy."

She hiked an eyebrow at him.

Okay, when he'd first heard her story, he might have paused for a long moment, let it sink into his head, let the what-ifs surface.

What if what she said was true—that she *had* been kidnapped by the Russian mob? Why? And sure, he'd tried to pry that bit of truth from her, but she'd clammed up.

Almost as if she didn't trust *him*.

So maybe their little trek out to the bush to confirm her story had as much to do with her trusting him as it did with him trusting her.

He clipped the tail end of the rope to his harness.

"Here's how this will work," Dodge, always the boss, said. He wore a Gore-Tex outfit and a wool hat. Frankly, the fact that Dodge had agreed to go along on this crazy search . . . well, maybe things were going to be okay between him and Colt, after all.

"The climb down isn't terrible, but once we reach the glacier, walk only in my steps. I'll test the snow, but this time of year, the ice can give and then—"

"You could fall a thousand feet to your death," Colt said.

Dodge gave him a look.

Well, maybe someone, and he wasn't saying who—ahem, *Tae*—should think about what she was getting into.

"If that happens," Echo said, rolling her eyes at Colt's words, "hit the ground with your ice axe and hold on. You're the only one stopping said person from, well"—she gestured at Colt—"what he said."

He shot Tae a final look.

"Please. I hiked through the wilderness, alone, for five days. Survived a blizzard—"

"Barely," Dodge said, probably remembering that day when they'd found her, nearly frozen, in the snow near a ranger cabin.

Tae gave Dodge the same look she'd given Colt. So, gone was the quiet, sweet girl who'd made them all soup.

Colt's fault, really, and for a moment he was back at the cabin two weeks ago, after he'd seen her picture taken from an assassin's phone, targeting her. He'd practically ran her down, shoved his hand over her shoulder, holding the door closed so she couldn't escape, and said, his tone tight and serious, "*Spill.*"

She'd morphed right in front of his eyes from quiet, hidden Flo, aka Florence Nightingale—his nickname for her—to Marie Curie, fierce, determined, and brave.

Even, maybe, a little bossy.

"You sure you want to know?" she'd asked.

Maybe he should have said no. Because now, as they prepared to climb down the mountainside, he sorta missed Florence.

"Let's go," Colt said.

Dodge was right. The boulders created a sort of stairway down the mountainside, into the valley where the glacier spilled over the side of the cliff.

Tae watched as Echo trekked in front of her. She had also grown up in Alaska and possessed the sure steps of a mountain goat.

But Tae handled herself just fine, holding on, checking her steps, careful.

Deliberate.

The sun, of course, still hovered high, although by Colt's guesstimation, it might be nearly eight in the evening. Maybe they should have camped on the ridge after their hike from the valley floor where Dodge put down, especially since dark clouds seemed on the distant horizon. But Colt was as eager to prove Tae right—or wrong—as she was.

Frankly, he was rooting for wrong. Because the idea of some Russian terrorist after her—and as a by-product, his family—had Colt's gut in all manner of knots.

Then again, if she'd made it up . . .

So maybe *right* wasn't such a bad option.

Dodge reached the edge of the glacier field. Maybe a thousand feet across, the glacier was a quietly moving river, with thousands of tributaries running through cracks in its gnarled, veiny blue surface. The frozen river fell from the top of the valley down to the edge of a cliff that dropped another thousand feet to a glacial lake below.

Working its way over the cliff, maybe forty feet from the edge, sat the mangled six-seater Beechcraft Bonanza, its wings shorn off, the fuselage twisted. It had cleanly landed, but dragged the tail, which broke off, spinning the aircraft so that it then cartwheeled, taking off the wings.

It had ended up on its back, a fallen albatross, wheels up.

A stiff wind caught Colt's jacket, slipped down his back. He sat on a boulder and attached his crampons, then unhooked his ice axe from the pack.

"Maybe just Colt and I should go," Dodge said.

Colt nodded, brutally aware of the way his heart had started to hammer. Sheesh. He wasn't scared, but the sweat down his back and his hard breathing had him thinking that if someone fell . . .

He might not be able to pull them back up.

Which meant that if Dodge went down, they both went down.

"No," Echo said, saving him. "We go together."

Dodge's mouth made a grim line, but he nodded.

"My steps, your steps," Dodge said and started out.

Echo followed, then Tae, and finally Colt.

Quiet. Footsteps crunched in the snow. Dodge pressed the handle of his ice axe into the surface, testing for strength, step-by-step.

They edged out—ten feet, twenty, thirty.

"Stop," Dodge said, and Colt froze. "There's a bridge here. We'll need to go around."

An ice bridge. The kind that spanned a crevasse. The kind that could disintegrate with weight and bring them all down.

Dodge backtracked while they stayed put and rerouted. He found where the crevasse ended, and they crossed over.

The pain in Colt's chest had started to ease. See, they'd be just fine.

"It looks like the door is missing," Dodge said as they drew closer. "Is that how you got out, Tae?"

"I don't know. I woke up outside the plane, strapped to my seat."

Dodge stepped up to the empty carcass, looking through the open tail of the plane.

"Any dead bodies?" Colt said, catching up. Dodge had left about twenty feet of rope between them. Echo caught up to him, then Tae.

"I think so," Dodge said.

Tae started inside.

"Wait," Dodge said. "This plane is sitting on ice. One wrong move and this whole thing could break free, go over the cliff."

"I need my pack," Tae said.

"I'll get it." Colt shot a look at Dodge. "Anchor in?"

Dodge nodded and pressed his ice axe into the glacier. Echo pressed hers in too, and then they both unclipped their carabiners and affixed them to the axes. The rope from their anchors stretched out to first Tae, then Colt. "I'm going with you," Tae said.

"Stay here." Colt glanced at her. "I promise to get your pack."

She opened her mouth, closed it. "Please don't die."

Huh. Well, well. He gave her a smile.

She drew in a breath. "You'll see I'm not lying."

Right. He turned to the wreckage.

The back seats had been ripped from the body, one of them gone—probably Tae's, given her story—the two middle seats lay mangled on the ceiling-now-floor of the plane. He eased up, through the wreckage, to the front. An odor of gas hinted the air.

Wind whistled through the cockpit window, but as he drew closer, he spotted a corpse, hanging from a seat in front. The pilot.

"I have a body!" he shouted. He came closer, pulling up his scarf. The man had frozen, clearly, but with the thaw, had started to decompose.

"What about Sergei?" Tae shouted to him.

He grabbed a dangling seat belt, listing in the wind. "Where was he sitting?"

"He wasn't—he was . . . "

The hiccup in her voice made him turn. She had turned a little wan. "He was trying to strangle me."

Oh. And the quietness, the horror of her words simply ripped through him.

"I had opened the door, was trying to wreck the plane." She offered a tiny smile, a hint of Florence. But he was starting to like Marie. She *was* brave.

"Maybe he was thrown out, like you," Echo said.

Tae nodded. "Do you see my pack? It's purple and has my name on it."

He searched the front compartment. "Not here."

"I shoved it under one of the seats," she said and stepped inside the plane.

And that's when it started to give.

"Tae, stop moving," he said, climbing back toward her.

"That pack has all my research in it." She fell to her knees, searching under the mangled seats.

The plane shifted . . .

"I see it!" She lay prone, reaching out under a seat. "It's wedged in here!"

He reached her, grabbed her harness. "Tae, we gotta get out of here!"

"Colt!" Dodge shouted.

And that's when the entire plane broke free.

"Tae!" Colt tugged at her.

"I can almost reach it . . ."

The plane began to slide. Slowly, but, "Tae, *c'mon!*"

"I'm stuck!"

The plane picked up speed. The rope that tethered them to Dodge's ice axe was uncoiling, twenty feet of it that would yank Tae first, then Colt.

And if she didn't get unstuck—

He yanked hard on her jacket. She shrieked and landed in his arms. They fell against the fuselage. The entire plane shuddered.

And that did it. The plane jerked, screaming toward the edge—

"Hold on!" He wrapped his arms around her.

The plane sailed over the edge into the bright blue of the Alaskan sky.

Susan May Warren is the *USA Today* bestselling author of more than 85 novels with more than 1.5 million books sold, including the Global Search and Rescue and the Montana Rescue series. Winner of a RITA Award and multiple Christy and Carol Awards, as well as the HOLT Medallion and numerous Readers' Choice Awards, Susan makes her home in Minnesota. Find her online at www.susanmaywarren.com, on Facebook @SusanMayWarrenFiction, and on Twitter @SusanMay Warren.

Connect with

Susan May Warren

Visit her website and sign up for her newsletter to get a free novella, hot news, contests, sales, and sneak peeks!

www.susanmaywarren.com

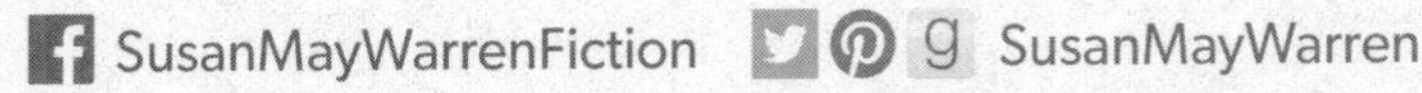

SusanMayWarrenFiction SusanMayWarren